We always lie to strangers

to strangers

TALL TALES FROM THE OZARKS

We always lie

TALL TALES
FROM THE OZARKS

ILLUSTRATED BY *Glen Rounds*

to strangers

by Vance Randolph

GREENWOOD PRESS, PUBLISHERS
WESTPORT, CONNECTICUT

Library of Congress Cataloging in Publication Data

Randolph, Vance, 1892-
    We always lie to strangers.

    Reprint of the ed. published by Columbia University
Press, New York.
    Bibliography: p.
    1.   Tales, American--Ozark Mountains.   2.   American
wit and humor.   I.   Title.
GR110.M77R295   1974   398.2'09767'1   74-12852
ISBN 0-8371-7765-0

16477

Originally published in 1951 by Columbia University Press,
New York

Reprinted with the permission of Columbia University Press

Reprinted in 1974 by Greenwood Press,
a division of Williamhouse-Regency Inc.

Library of Congress Catalog Card Number 74-12852

ISBN 0-8371-7765-0

Printed in the Untted States of America

TO FRANCES CHURCH

Preface

THE MATERIAL for this book was all gathered in the Ozark region, most of it since 1920. I am sorry that it is impracticable to credit each item to the individual from whom it was obtained, as I have done in *Ozark Folksongs* and some of my other publications. Several old friends and neighbors who helped me in this enterprise do not wish to be mentioned here, and there are other reasons for omitting many informants' names. Whenever it has seemed permissible to identify the teller of a particular story, I have done so in the text. In case such identification was not advisable, I have named the village or the county where I heard the tale and let it go at that.

For assistance of one kind and another, during the period in which this stuff was collected I am indebted to Mr. Arthur Aull, Lamar, Missouri; Mr. Lew Beardon, Branson, Missouri; Dr. Charles Hillman Brough, Little Rock, Arkansas; Mr. Mayhem Gleason, Anderson, Missouri; Mr. Frank Hembree, Galena, Missouri; Mr. Lewis Kelley, Cyclone, Missouri; Mr. Otto Ernest Rayburn, Eureka Springs, Arkansas; Mr. Will Rice, St. Joe, Arkansas; Mr. Emmett Rickman, Pineville, Missouri; Mr. Fred Starr, Fayetteville, Arkansas; Mr. Carl Withers, Wheatland, Missouri. Miss Georgia Clark, reference librarian at the University of Arkansas, and Mrs. Ann Todd Rubey, head of the reference department in the University of Missouri library, helped me check bibliographical references. Mr. Floyd C. Shoemaker, secretary of the State Historical Society of Missouri, supplied important items from the library of that society.

Several of these stories originally appeared in *Folk-Say,*

Esquire, the Kansas City *University Review,* and the *Arkansas Historical Quarterly.* Others were first printed in my book *Ozark Mountain Folks,* published by the Vanguard Press in 1932, and in *The Camp on Wildcat Creek,* issued by Alfred A. Knopf in 1934. Some of the tales were included in two pamphlets, *Funny Stories from Arkansas* and *Funny Stories About Hillbillies,* published and copyrighted by E. Haldeman-Julius, Girard, Kansas, in 1943 and 1944. I am grateful to the publishers of these books and periodicals for permission to reprint the material here.

V.R.

Eureka Springs, Arkansas
September 6, 1950

Contents

We always lie
to strangers

TALL TALES FROM THE OZARKS

1 Introduction

BACKWOODS HUMORISTS EVERYWHERE have a predilection for the tall tale, and the Ozark hillman is no exception. The pioneer hates a liar. In the early days there was little cash in the country, and there were few written contracts. People depended upon each other, and a man's word had to be good or the neighbors would have nothing to do with him. The hillfolk live close to the pioneer tradition, and liar is still a fightin' word in the Ozarks. But there's no harm in "stretchin' the blanket" or "lettin' out a whack" or "sawin' off a whopper" or "spinnin' a windy" when they involve no attempt to injure anybody. "A windy ain't a lie, nohow," said one of my neighbors, "unless you tell it for the truth." And even if you do tell it for the truth nobody is deceived, except maybe a few tourists.

The ignorance and credulity of city folks provide a constant temptation to the village cut-ups. In 1947 a fat man from Jasper County, Missouri, stopped at a hotel in Eureka Springs, Arkansas. He was alone, but the only available room had two beds in it, one double and one single bed. A tourist from Chicago noted this, and the Missourian remarked that such rooms were furnished especially for newlyweds. "It's one of our old Ozark customs," he said soberly. "The bride's mother always goes along on the honeymoon. Sleeps in the same room, too." The tourist had seen many strange sights in Eureka Springs, and was prepared to believe almost anything, but this story seemed so outlandish that she asked the manager of the hotel about it. The manager crossed his fingers and confirmed the fat man's tale. Perhaps the tradition is not always observed nowadays, he admitted. But no Arkansas hotel would offer a bridal suite which did not have a place for the mother-in-law in the bed-room. The hotel-keeper's serious manner convinced the tourist, so she told her friends about it, and soon all the "fur-rin" guests were giggling over the quaint marriage-customs of the hillfolk. They spread the hilarious news back in Chi-cago, too. And now, every so often, some visitor from Illinois stops a native and asks him about this mother-in-law business. Most of the local people have heard the tale by this time and are glad to give it a boost. That's the way a lot of odd stories about Arkansas get started.

A good story-teller is an asset to any group with sufficient intelligence to appreciate his wares. One of the best float-trip guides in Missouri is so old and feeble that he can scarcely handle a boat, but he entertains everybody with tall tales around the campfire at night. "Jeff ain't no good to work," I was told, "but when it comes to stretchin' blankets on a gravel bar, he's the best hand we've got." Jeff makes more money than boatmen half his age, and many anglers from Kansas City and St. Louis will not go fishing without him. I called at Jeff's cabin once, and his wife answered my knock. "Jeff ain't here," she said sourly. "He hangs round the boat-landin' all day, a-lyin' to them fool tourists." The woman did not realize that telling whacks is an essential part of Jeff's business, and in a large measure accounts for his popularity among sportsmen from the city.

The best windies in the Ozark country are told by men. Backwoods women don't care for such yarns. Much of the other folk-material that I have collected in this region—folksongs, riddles, proverbs, and superstitions—was obtained from women. But the grotesque hyperbole of the tall tale does not appeal to the feminine sense of humor. It seems to me that most country women fail to see the distinction between a whack and an outright falsehood. "Never trust a windy-spinner," said a pious lady in Noel, Missouri "Why, old Buck Turney will tell the truth an' then lie out of it, just to keep his hand in!" Buck certainly did saw off whoppers for the tourists. But I never knew him to spread slander, or lie about money, or betray the confidence of a friend. I would take Buck Turney's word against that of any preacher I ever met. It so happens that all of the real story-tellers whom I have known personally were honest men and good citizens.

Few of the old-timers ever heard of Rabelais or Baron Munchausen, but forty years ago they still referred to "Lyin' Johnny" Colter as the champion story-teller of all time. Colter visited what is now Yellowstone Park about 1807, and returned to Missouri three or four years later. His tales of geysers, fossil monsters, subterranean noises, and volcanic phenomena were regarded as droll inventions, and made his name a byword for a hundred years. Within my own memory a native of Benton County, Arkansas, somehow wandered into western Kansas. When he came back home and told his neighbors about the vast prairies they grinned delightedly, but didn't believe a word of it. "Percy is still talkin' about them big old fields," a farmer told me several years later. "Fifty mile o' pasture, with nary a rock nor a stump! We know it ain't true, of course, but I sure do love to hear him tell the tale!"

A kind of mock acceptance is necessary, however, and the effect of a tall tale is spoiled if the home folks appear openly incredulous. A boy near Thayer, Missouri, rushed into the cabin, shouting that he had seen a hundred possums in one pawpaw sapling. The father shook his head. "That ain't reasonable, son," he objected mildly, "they'd bust the tree plumb down." After some argument, the boy admitted that maybe there were only seventy-five possums in that particular pawpaw. The discussion continued, with the whole family joining in to discredit the story. Finally the youngster lost his temper. "God durn you all!" he cried. "I won't come down another God durn possum!"

It is a mistake to assume that backwoods humor is merely a matter of grotesque exaggeration. The Ozark story-teller appreciates understatement also, and knows more of irony than many sophisticated comedians. Our summer visitors are accustomed to people who appear more prosperous than they really are, but the rustic who makes light of his wealth is new to them. "Come out to my shack, an' stay all night," said a shabbily dressed cattleman. "The roof leaks a little, but we always let company sleep in the dry spot." The city feller accepted the invitation, and his eyes popped when he saw the "shack." It was a big stone ranch house of perhaps thirty rooms, with a swimming pool, golf course, and so forth. The roof was made of green tiles, and didn't leak ary drop.

An old gentleman from northwest Arkansas visited Kansas City in the 1930's, and one of my friends took him to dinner at a place where the waitresses were naked. The old man was a deacon in the church, and I thought he might be terribly shocked, but it appears that he showed no signs of perturbation. Several weeks later I was in his village, and asked what he thought of the nude waitresses in Kansas City. "Why," he answered, "I don't remember seein' no nude waitresses." I stared at the old codger for a long moment. "You mean to say you've forgotten the girls at the Chesterfield Club?" I demanded. "No, I ain't forgot 'em," he said, "but they wasn't nekkid." He gazed into the fire, and grinned a little. "They had shoes on," he added.

The old crack about the man who would rather lie on credit than tell the truth for cash is well known in the hill country. The Ozarker frequently does saw off a whopper in circumstances which seem futile and foolish to an outsider. A farmer in McDonald County, Missouri, brought me several nice bass, remarking that he had ketched 'em with his bare hands. The fish had been shot with a rifle, and I could see the bullet holes in their backs. There was no reason for such a falsehood, since noodling fish and shooting them are both illegal. This man and I were old friends and had been fishing together many times. He knew that I wouldn't believe his noodlin' story. But for some obscure psychological reason he had to tell it, anyhow.

The best story-tellers work in groups, and their smooth team-play is fascinating to witness. The chief narrator speaks slowly to a picked group of listeners, who know exactly when to put the proper questions and when to hold their peace. The whole thing seems delightfully casual, but every word is weighed, and the timing is perfect. Some of the finest windies are never told directly to the tourist; it is better to allow him to overhear them, as if by accident. Frank Payne and W. D. Mathes, of Galena, Missouri, used to make a specialty of this technique. They would talk together in low tones, very seriously, with their backs toward the "furriner" to whom the story was really addressed. These men were artists, and people came from miles around to see them do their stuff.

There are few stronger ties than those of some fantastic tradition held in common, and hillmen who appreciate the old-time humor are bound together in a sort of brotherhood. These fellows are not much inclined to formal organization, but it appears that several "windy circles" had regular meetings in the 1880's and early 1890's.

It has been said that the Missouri Foxhunters' Association began as "a kind of liars' syndicate, with headquarters at Rushville," but this is vigorously denied. Foxhunters' conventions used to be held at least once a year in every Ozark county, and that goes for Arkansas and Oklahoma as well as Missouri. Everybody knows that liars' contests were

sometimes featured in connection with these affairs. A typical convention lasted four or five days, with one evening devoted to the telling of windy stories. Foxhunters' meetings were generally well attended, but "Liars' Night" always brought out the biggest crowd from town. At Bartlesville, Oklahoma, the merchants used to donate valuable prizes for the champion story-teller, and doubtless the same custom was followed elsewhere.

Arthur Aull, editor of a newspaper at Lamar, Missouri, told me that there had once been a liars' lodge at Lamar, where men met to swap whoppers behind locked doors, but the old-timers were very reticent about it. Years ago I heard some racy anecdotes concerning the Boss Liars' Club, founded by the late Cal Hammontree at Springfield, Missouri, in 1888 or 1889. "It was actually taken as a compliment to be called a liar," marveled Robert L. Kennedy, veteran newspaperman. "Several local men had fine lithographed certificates of membership in the club. The B.L.C. was long a village joke around Springfield."

A group called the Mollyjoggers, organized by Cy H. Patterson in Greene County, Missouri, about 1895, was chiefly devoted to the telling of tall tales, though considerable time was wasted on stud poker and practical jokes. The members had a big iron bullfrog, painted in natural colors, which they set up on the river bank for strangers to shoot at; later they obtained several iron rabbits, and even a deer which looked like the real thing at a little distance. John F. Dunckel wrote a book [1] which included some of the yarns told around the campfire. Dunckel had to keep the club records, he said, because the duly elected secretary was illiterate. The Mollyjoggers are all gone now; the last member was Wilbert S. Headley, who died in 1935. But there are men still living who visited the camp, and some of

[1] *The Mollyjoggers* (n.d.), pp. 83.

the Mollyjogger stories have been told and retold all over the Ozark country. Many of the best items are credited to "Old Wid" Crumpley, a farmer who lived at Oto, Missouri, not far from the Mollyjogger campground at the mouth of Finley Creek.

A more colorful organization was the Post, which flourished in Howell County, Missouri, from 1900 to 1918. About fifty prominent citizens joined in a clandestine fraternity, with signs, grips, passwords, and an extraordinary ritual said to have been written by Senator John C. Harlan, of Gainesville. The Post was an elaborate imposture; its sole purpose was to play outrageous jokes on "furriners" and newcomers. "The folks in Gainesville ain't satisfied with lyin' to the tourists," an old man told me. "All them doctors an' lawyers an' merchants an' county officers have took a solemn oath, an' they'll drop their business any minute, just to make some city feller *believe* one o' them big windies!" The only description of the order that I have seen in print was written by Amos R. Harlan.[2] I have interviewed several men who knew all about the Post, and they say that Harlan's story is substantially correct, although he toned it down a bit and changed the names of the principal characters.

The most important windy circle in the Ozarks nowadays is the Polk County Possum Club. Founded at Mena, Arkansas, in 1912, this outfit still throws an annual banquet at the Mena Armory. The event takes place early in December, and the date is announced in newspapers all over Arkansas. Every guest gets a serving of possum if he wants it, but most of 'em eat roast turkey. Hillfolk in overalls and calico rub elbows with city people in evening dress. Funny stories and wisecracks have their place, but tall tales are always a feature of the meeting, and the chief reason for the Possum

[2] *For Here Is My Fortune,* pp. 61, 93–106.

Club's existence. Ed Watkins, aged ex-mayor of Mena, presided at the banquets for many years. The president's chief function is to stop any speaker who says anything that might conceivably be true "Alfalfa Bill" Murray, sometime governor of Oklahoma, was booed and hooted to his seat in 1938, when he attempted to make a serious political speech. Congressmen and other notables have been joyously howled down, while a ragged tie-hacker who can spin windies is received with honor and acclaim. In 1946 the Possum Club met with an attendance of more than five hundred, and John Ab Hughes, of Hatfield, Arkansas, was elected to the presidency. On this occasion the man who brought in the biggest possum was given a prize, and the club sent the possum to a Missourian named Harry S. Truman. The best published account of the Polk County Possum Club is in John Gould Fletcher's book,[3] but many of the finest Possum Club stories have never been printed.

There are numerous difficulties in the way of a man who tries to collect these Ozark stories for publication. Some of the best backwoods tales are too coarse for the literary market, and cannot be/cleaned up without eviscerating them. Others depend for their effect upon an intimate knowledge of Ozark life, a knowledge which few readers possess. Some folk humor is too subtle for print anyhow, just as certain types of folk-music cannot be compassed by the conventional notation. Songs may be recorded phonographically, but this doesn't work so well with folktales. Several of our best hillbilly yarns flopped when Bob Burns tried them on the air. Such stories are humorous, rather than comic or witty. They move slowly and aimlessly and are told with a kind of deadpan zest, just as the traditional ballads are sung.

[3] *Arkansas*, pp. 377–382.

One must see the story-teller, as well as hear his voice, in order fully to appreciate this kind of material.

Many of the windies in this collection were contributed by elderly folk in the more isolated sections of the Ozarks. The second-growth hillbillies in the towns often take a dim view of the traditional humor of their forefathers. Despite this prejudice, some Ozark stories have been printed in the country weeklies, and a few find their way into the metropolitan press. The latter are generally snapped up by the radio comedians and the gagmen of Broadway and Hollywood. I suppose some chips drift the other way also, in these degenerate days. Even the Pine Ridge boys come down to hear the radio occasionally, and doubtless the real hillman sometimes cribs a wisecrack from the synthetic hillbillies of radio-land.

Some of the wildest absurdities are exaggerated accounts of the narrator's own adventures, or the exploits of men whom he has known personally. Others are strangely garbled fragments of pioneer history and legend. Still others are British folktales, and specialists can doubtless trace them back to their dim beginnings over the water. The names of the characters change, and the scenes are shifted from one hilltop to another, but the basic plots remain. I believe that some tall tales have been kept alive by oral tradition, right here in the Ozarks, for more than a hundred years.

"Arkansas has no monopoly on tall stories," the official state guidebook [4] assures us.

Similar yarns are to be heard all through the Southern mountains and, for that matter, throughout the United States. Countless Arkansans, however, seem to have been blessed with an ability to concoct variations of the standard stories [and it cannot be denied that] these solemn fantasies occupy a prominent place in the State's folklore. More stories seem to have ripened

[4] *Arkansas*, p. 98.

in the hills than in the Delta, and nearly every upland county boasts of a citizen with a reputation for telling whoppers. Perhaps it was the isolation of the Ozarks and Ouachitas during the nineteenth century that nourished the imagination of mountaineers.

Scholars could probably write volumes about the derivation of these stories, but I know little of such matters and have no access to the literature. I am content to record the tales as they were told to me, and leave the consideration of provenience to the folklorists who spend their lives in libraries.

The making of books is mostly drudgery, but I had a wonderful time collecting the material for this one. There are certain affective ties between these items and me, because of intimate and remembered experience. One story recalls an uproarious party at the old House of Lords, in Joplin, Missouri. And there's another that I first heard near Hot Springs, Arkansas, from a boy who rode with the wild bunch and got his picture in all the postoffices. Sprinkled through the manuscript are the contributions of my wives and sweethearts, with their preposterous kinfolk at Fort Smith, Arkansas, and Pineville, Missouri, and Sallisaw, Oklahoma. I remember also the master possum hunters of Scott County, Arkansas, and an ordained preacher who could neither read nor write, and three sprightly Missouri schoolmarms, and two bankrobbers, and several families of horse traders and shell diggers and patch farmers. Fascinating people, all dear to me for one reason or another. Most of them are dead now, of course, but I have not forgotten. The enthusiasm for the Ozark hillfolk which inspired my youth has suffered no decline these thirty years. I should like to believe that a little of this personal warmth could somehow be passed on to those who read the printed pages.

2 Steep hills and razorbacks

SOME OF THE BACKWOODS FARMS in the Ozarks are pretty steep, and steep also are the stories that the natives tell about them. Many of the wildest of these tales are true, at that. The old gag about the farmer falling out of his cornfield sounds like a tall tale, but people who live in the Ozarks know that such accidents are not uncommon. A friend of mine in McDonald County, Missouri, fell out of his garden patch, taking a heavy wagon and two horses along with him.

The disadvantages of cultivating hillsides are played up by the story-tellers, but somebody always points out that there are two sides to every flapjack. A man once remarked to me that if we could only get Newton County, Arkansas, smoothed out, it would be bigger'n the whole state of Texas. Another loafer admitted that this might be true, but said that he liked Newton County just as it is. Hilly country is always better than level land, because you get more farm for your money. "Up where you come from," he told a visitor from Illinois, "a man just plows forty acres flat. But when a feller owns a forty in Newton County, he farms the top an' all four sides, too."

Jim West, a radio comedian from Springfield, Missouri, used to tell a long tale about a farmer plowing on a steep hillside. The plowshare caught under a big old root, the man began to holler, and the horses pulled harder than ever. I forget some of the details, but the result was that they turned the whole farm upside down, all in one piece. Yes, sir, an' found a coal mine underneath!

There are many ancient stories about the narrow, cramped valleys between precipitous cliffs. In some hollers, the traveler is told, the hounds have to foller a fox in single file, and learn to wag their tails up and down instead of sideways. Some canyons are so narrow that they are really one-way streets; even a deer cain't turn around, but has to run straight on through, or else walk back'ards to git out.

"Some of the roughest country I ever saw is right here in Missouri," writes Casper Kilroy.[1] "I know one especially hilly part of the state. It so happens that razorback hogs got their start in this section. If a hog got too fat he just naturally stuck between the walls of the valley, and had to thin down before he could amble along."

Driving on our fine new highways, a traveler often sees crops growing in places which appear quite inaccessible. "How did they ever get up there to plant the stuff?" is the first question that occurs to him. The truth is, of course, that many of these cultivated patches are not so steep as they appear from a distance. But the blanket-stretchers have other explanations for the tourist trade. A man near Lowgap, Arkansas, told me that he had often seen his neighbors plant corn with shotguns. They just put seed-corn into their guns instead of shot, he said. Then they wade out into the Buffalo River and fire at the bluffs over their heads.

Near Hollister, Missouri, a lady tried to buy a little packet of pumpkin seed, but the storekeeper didn't have any. "We don't plant no punkins here," she was told. "We raise these here big crookneck squashes instead. A punkin will bust loose an' roll plumb to the river, but a crookneck always hooks itself round a cornstalk."

A reporter asked a man near Fayetteville, Arkansas, how

[1] *Missouri College Farmer,* Jan., 1947, p. 22.

he ever managed to dig the potatoes in his almost perpendicular patch. "We don't have to dig 'taters in this country," was the answer. "We just cut off the end of the row, an' let 'em fall out."

There is another yarn about a poor chap who went out to grabble a handful of 'taters for breakfast, and the 'taters got out of control. Before he could git 'em stopped, his whole crop went a-bouncin' off down the mountain and was lost forever. I heard this one from a boy named Sharp, at Pack, Missouri, but it is known in many parts of Missouri and Arkansas.

One hears of an orchardist near Rogers, Arkansas, who never bothers to pick his apples at all. He selected the site for the house very carefully, and landscaped the hillsides a bit. So now, when the fruit is ripe, he just opens the cellar door. Then he goes out and shakes the trees, and the apples roll right down the hill into the cellar.

Several persons in Taney County, Missouri, have told me of a certain bootlegger who set up his bar in a berry shed on a steep hillside. The boozers who fell to the floor rolled out of the place at once, thus automatically making room for more customers.

An adaptation of this yarn applies it to a place of worship, a Pentecostal brush-arbor near Forsyth, Missouri. When one of the worshipers fell down and began rolling and kicking about, he was helped out of the tabernacle by the ever-present force of gravity. As the meeting ended, prostrate Holy Rollers were piled four deep in a gully, and the preachers still had plenty of floor space to do their stuff.

I have often been assured that some particular field is so steep that it is impossible to gather the crop in a wagon. The only way to utilize the corn is to feed it right in the field, just turn the hogs in and let 'em eat the stuff. And in very steep fields it is necessary to pole the hogs. This means that

the farmer fastens a pig to the end of a long pole, and holds the pole out in such a manner that the animal can reach the ears. When the corn crop fails, the hogs must be held up to the oak trees, where they feed on acorns.

A related story is told of sheep by Marion Hughes.[2] According to this account, the pastures are so rugged that the shepherd must hold his sheep by their tails while they feed along the ledges. "When the herder goes out of a morning," Hughes writes, "the sheep will bawl and run to him and turn around and back up. They all want him to take them by the tail first, and hold them out to pick."

When a man wants to clear a patch of ground for a cornfield, according to another variant of this ancient wheeze, he lies flat on his stomach with each hand grasping the tail of a goat. Creeping slowly along, he dangles the goats over the bluff while they chaw off the sprouts.

A St. Louis newspaperman once declared that he had visited a place in Baxter County, Arkansas, where the farmers put spiked boots on all their goats, as otherwise the critters couldn't git to the pasture.

In a particularly rugged part of Van Buren County, Arkansas, it is said that the hogs always travel in pairs. "Them hills is so damn' steep," I was told, "that one pig has to scotch whilst the other'n does the rootin'. They spell each other, o' course. You turn a razorback out by himself, in that country, an' he'll starve plumb to death." I have often seen hillmen scotch a wagon by putting a rock under the wheel, to keep it from rolling down hill. But just how one hog manages to scotch another is something else again.

It was a man in Fort Smith, Arkansas, who remarked that his pasture was a little steep. When he put the cattle out to feed they always worked in couples, two cows tied together by the tails. "Then you can hang 'em over a ridge," he said,

[2] *Three Years in Arkansaw*, p. 42.

"one on each side. Pullin' ag'in each other thataway, there won't neither one of 'em fall."

Eureka Springs, Arkansas, is probably the hilliest town in the Ozark region, and the folk who live there tell some pretty rugged stories. "The old-timers here are the windiest people I ever seen," said old man Dennis, standing beside the big spring in Basin Park. "Take three drinks of that water, an' you'll never speak the truth again." In Webb's restaurant on Spring Street they've got a mural painting by a local artist who signs his work "By Golly." Just below the picture is a large sign: ALL THE LIES YOU HEAR ABOUT THE OZARKS ARE TRUE. People in this community like to recall the man who could look up his big chimney and see the cattle feeding in a neighbor's pasture. The old residents still laugh about a citizen who was digging a well in his back yard, but suddenly busted through the bottom of it and fell right out into the big road.

When I was gathering supernatural tales some years ago, I asked an old gentleman at the Basin Park Hotel if he knew any local ghost stories. After some thought he replied in the negative. "There's ghosts in Texas, an' maybe in Oklahoma," he said soberly, "but not here." I waited for awhile, without any comment. "This country is just naturally too rough for ghosts," he added gently. And anybody who has visited Eureka Springs will understand exactly what the old gentleman meant.

This reminds me of the drunken farmer who got lost in the streets of Eureka Springs. The pavement is not level by any means, and the poor fellow was staggering along with one foot on the sidewalk and the other in a deep gutter. A woman came along, and the farmer called to her for help. "You're just drunk," she told him. "Is that it?" he said, much relieved. "By Gosh, I thought maybe I was crippled."

The country down around Oden, not far from Pine

Ridge, Arkansas, is a bit precipitous in places. "This part of Arkansas is so rough," writes N. L. Hopson (*Arkansas Gazette*, May 10, 1942), "that when lads around here go hunting they take a dog, a gun and a spade. They use the spade to shovel out a place in the mountains, so the dog can stand and bark at the squirrel."

Otto Ernest Rayburn [3] tells of a pioneer who cut a big hickory tree on a steep hillside. It rolled to the bottom of the hollow, and pretty well up on the opposite side. Then it came rolling back up toward the chopper, and like to a run over him. Down one side and up the other, it kept on rolling. The limbs were soon torn off and lost, and the bark was worn off the tree. After watching it roll about two hours, the woodcutter went home. Next day he was off to the War Between the States, and was gone for a year. Home on furlough, he went out to see what had happened to the hickory log. It was still rolling, but just about petered out. It was so worn down that the soldier picked it up, and used it as a ramrod for his musket until the end of the War.

I have heard variants of this tale in many parts of the Ozark country. Uncle Jim Harlan, of West Plains, Missouri, told a story in which the log kept on a-rollin' until it was reduced to the size of a toothpick, and was used as such by one of the Howell County pioneers. Harlan belonged to a prominent pioneer family, and was the central figure in many local tales. "Jim never done no braggin' himself," said an old resident, "but some of his boys might have stretched the blanket a little, when they got to talkin' about what a hell of a feller he was."

A Little Rock newspaperman said that a certain Arkansas county was so rough that when a cyclone went through the county seat it had to be provided with an escort of State Police. I interviewed a legislator from this district, and he

[3] *Ozark Country*, pp. 262–264.

denounced the cyclone story as a vile slander, disseminated by a few disgruntled Communists or Republicans. But he admitted that the sheriff back home always hired a body-guard during Court Week. I expressed a desire to visit this turbulent county at once, but the man said it was quite impossible. "The road's too damn' steep," he said. "Why, you couldn't get over Filthy Mountain if you was ridin' a turpentined wildcat!"

A friend of ours in Stone County, Missouri, lived alone on a high bluff, miles away from any road. As we floated down the river one day in a boat, my wife pointed out the old man's shanty far above our heads. "That feller must have a turrible time gettin' home," remarked a boatman named Frank Payne. After a moment of silence he returned to the subject. "I reckon he has to walk, an' drag a rope behind him." The whole party roared at this, and I laughed as loud as anybody. I have often chuckled since, remembering the incident. But even today I'm not sure just what Frank meant, or what was so damned funny about it.

Some Oklahoma humorists used to say that Arkansas farmers always have one leg shorter than the other, by way of adaptation to the rugged terrain. Because of this, it was alleged, one could recognize a hillbilly anywhere. I knew a bartender in Joplin, Missouri, who limped rather badly. He said that it was caused by a bullet wound he got a-fightin' for his country in the Spanish-American War. Nevertheless, this man's friends all called him "Arkie," pretending to believe that he must have come from Arkansas, since one of his legs was a little short.

An elderly man in Van Buren, Arkansas, told me with considerable indignation of a slanderous item published by a Chicago newspaper. Some foreign doctor had examined a lot of babies in North Arkansas and discovered that their legs were just like those of babies born in Illinois. The paper went on to say that adult Arkansawyers have one leg shorter than the other, and scientists had hitherto assumed that this disparity was congenital. "Them damn' fools better stay home an' kill their own snakes," the old man growled. "The funniest legs I ever seen was on them tourists that comes down from Chicago in the summer time." I tried to change the subject, but it was no use. "I reckon Bob Burns is about the sorriest-lookin' human that ever come out of this country," continued the old gentleman. "But even Bob—hell, his *legs* is all right!"

People in Arkansas tell the same stories, of course, but they always locate the limping hillmen on the north side of the Missouri line. Governor Charles Hillman Brough, of Little Rock, remarked to me that "in some parts of Missouri the men have one leg shorter than the other, a deformity caused by generations of plowing on steep hillsides." And another Arkansas politician spoke seriously of a "Missouri wagon" which had small wheels on one side and big wheels on the other, so that it could be used on the mountain trails of what he called the "Puke Territory."

Raymond Weeks, of Columbia, Missouri, in a story called "Arkansas" [4] says that "all Arkansas pigs, without exception, have their legs shorter on one side than on the other." They live on cone-shaped mountains, he explains, and each pig always walks around a hill in the same direction. "All Arkansas pigs are either lefters or righters," says Weeks. The pig in Weeks' story was carried up into Missouri and entered in a race; she won over all the fastest pigs of Missouri, and then took off toward the setting sun. This pig was a "lefter," and therefore on comparatively level ground she "described her inherited curve across the desolate plains of Kansas, down through the corner of the Indian Territory and into her native state of Arkansas."

[4] *The Hound-Tuner of Callaway,* pp. 139-155.

The short-leg theory applies primarily to human beings and swine, but sometimes it is extended to other animals, and has even been adapted to imaginary varmints such as the side-hill hoofer, which I have described elsewhere in this book. Several Arkansawyers have used it with reference to turkeys and other domestic fowls.

E. W. Alley, writing in the *Arkansas Gazette* (Oct. 5, 1947), recalls a peculiar breed of chickens raised by the White family, pioneers in the wilderness south of Mena, Arkansas. They were small, thin chickens called "Waterloo Plovers." Their eggs were golden brown "with a rainbow extending around the larger end." Men who ate the Plovers' flesh grew strong and wise; women who fed on Plovers' eggs became tall and beautiful. Some birds belonging to the White family ran off to Pigeon Roost Mountain, where they crossed with the wild pigeons. The result was a wild fowl which ran around the mountain, circling close to the summit. These hybrids were known as Waterloo Bonneys, and were plentiful for many years after the wild pigeons disappeared. "Instead of having two legs of equal length," wrote Mr. Alley, "these fowls had one leg shorter than the other by about two inches. They had fed around the mountain top so long that nature had at last fashioned one leg shorter than the other, so in feeding they might stand upright with no discomfort." Mr. Alley adds that many pioneers, including the Steel, Norwood, Gilliams, and Collins families, ate these birds. He attributes the good looks and intelligence so prevalent in Polk County to the fact that the people were nourished upon fowls descended from the Waterloo Plover strain.

Related to the yarns about the steepness of Ozark farms is a whole cycle of tales about rocks and hard times. One often hears the remark that a certain piece of land is so rocky you cain't raise a fuss on it. Richard Pilant, of Granby,

Missouri, once told me about a farm so infertile that "two red-headed women couldn't raise a ruckus there." I have heard many similar expressions. "Bob calls that there place a cornfield," said one of my neighbors, "but the soil is so thin you couldn't raise hell on it with a barrel of whiskey!"

"The land is so God-awful pore down our way," remarked a man from Dallas County, Missouri, "that everything grows kind of weak an' spindlin'. My coon dogs are so triflin' they have to lean ag'in a stump before they can bark treed." Another fellow nodded soberly. "It's too dry mostly, an' even when we do git water it ain't no good. Down in the draw below my house, it takes three bullfrogs to live a month!" And Mirandy Bauersfeld, radio artist who used to live in Joplin, Missouri, wrote me: "We owned our own farm down yander in the Ozark hills, but the land was so pore and wore out you couldn't hardly raise a umbrella on it. I recollect in one drought year our corn was mighty pore. Paw used to go out with a peck measure, walkin' up and down the rows. Sometimes he'd have to cover two or three acres to git nubbins enough for a mess of roastin' ears."

These tales often arise through somebody's desire to "run down" another man's community. A resident of Protem, Missouri, admitted that times were pretty hard in his section of the country. "But I reckon it's lots worse up around Springfield, where *you* come from," he said. "They tell me the land's so pore up there that they can't have no camp-meetin's. Even a singin'-teacher has to swaller a shovel full of horse fertilizer before he can raise a tune."

Some stories featuring the traditional antagonism between Missouri and Arkansas are still common along the border. In a Missouri village I sat with a bunch of loafers, and there was one Arkansawyer in the crowd, so the boys began to make dirty cracks about Arkansas. Finally one fellow said that he spent seven weeks in Harrison, Arkansas, with nothing to eat but hemlock bark. Upon this the Arkansas man stated, very positively, that he had lived near Harrison for twenty years, and that there wasn't a hemlock tree within a hundred miles of the place. "Of course there ain't," said the Missouri boy smoothly, "on account of the soil's too thin. We trucked our hemlock bark all the way from St. Louis." The poor chap from Harrison had nothing more to say, but he looked sort of dazed all evening.

Speaking of a certain bleak section near the Arkansas-Oklahoma border, old Pawpaw Johnson, of Hollister, Missouri, once remarked: "I walked for three days through that country. Except for ticks and chiggers, the only living thing I saw was a poor skinny chipmunk. He was gnawin' on a flint-rock, with big tears a-runnin' down his face."

Colonel A. L. Prather, who lived at Kirbyville, Missouri, used to tell of a newcomer who bought a tract of rocky land. The poor fellow worked himself almost to death, without any results to show for it. One Sunday he sat down on a rock near his cabin. A groundhog peeped out of a hole, and showed its teeth at him. The animal looked fat and well fed. Suddenly the landowner took the deed out of his wallet, and thrust it down into the groundhog's den. "Feller," said he, "if you can make a livin' on this here farm, you're the one that ought to have the papers."

In McDonald County, Missouri, my neighbor's little boy recounted a long series of misfortunes. "The fruit all froze in April," said he, "an' the corn burnt up in August. An' now the colt done *come a mule!*" A city feller was delighted with this naïve remark, and tried to lead the boy on to further revelations. Noticing a long row of beehives, he said that there would surely be sweetenin' enough to keep the family all winter. "Hell no," cried the little chap. "Paw says the queen has been layin' up with a tumblebug, an' the honey all tastes like cow-chips!"

One of the famous Weaver brothers, who owned a farm in Greene County, Missouri, was quoted as saying that his land was so pore and dry in 1936 that the rabbits had to carry basket lunches whenever they ran across it. And a man near Fayetteville, Arkansas, told me of a desolate region where "the trees are so far apart that the woodpeckers have to carry their own lunches."

A citizen of Flippin, Arkansas, discovered that the rabbits had just about ruined his kitchen garden, and the old woman urged him to put a tight wire fence around it. He made a careful inspection of the patch, then refused to build the fence, saying that it would be cruelty to animals. "Why," said he, "all them rabbits that lives in our garden would starve plumb to death, if they couldn't go out an' git somethin' to eat once in a while."

Casper Kilroy [5] repeats an old story about the rocky ground in southern Missouri.

I was visiting in an especially hilly part of the state [he writes] and was talking to one of the natives. Zip! A cat ran past. I watched it in surprise. *Zip! Zip!* Two more cats ran past. Within fifteen minutes thirty-four cats ran past, all going in the same direction. "Where are all those cats going?" I asked the native. "Aw, don't pay no attention to that," he replied. "It's fourteen miles down to the junction, and that's the only place around here where they can find any dirt."

A real-estate man in southwest Missouri had a stock answer for all "furriners" who opined that the land he showed them was too rocky. "Oh," he would say blithely, "all the rocks you see are on the surface." Just what he meant by this I don't know, but it seemed to reassure some prospective customers. The expression is often used figuratively, to minimize obvious flaws or defects. I once heard it employed by a man who was trying to sell a secondhand piano.

[5] *Missouri College Farmer*, Jan., 1947, p. 22.

When the customer remarked that the instrument was pretty badly battered up, he said: "All them rocks you see are on the surface, ma'am. If that pianner was brand new, I couldn't sell it to ye for twenty-two dollars." And the woman bought the piano.

Jesse Lewis Russell [6] tells a good story about a village realtor who was trying to sell a rocky little farm. He explained to the sucker that flint-rocks are necessary to productivity, and that land is no good without 'em. Stones retain moisture, prevent erosion, keep vegetables from getting dirty, and so on. Just then a man began loading some rocks into a wagon, to haul them off the field. "Let's get out of here," said the land agent. "We might get tied up as witnesses in court. That fellow is *stealing* those rocks!"

There is another ancient tale about an old hillman who was delighted when somebody gave him a watermelon. He put the melon in one end of a gunny sack and a rock in the other end, and threw the sack across the saddle in front of him. A tourist noticed the melon hanging on one side and the rock on the other. "Wouldn't it be more economical," he asked, "to carry another melon instead of that stone?" The mountaineer eyed him coldly. "Yes, I reckon it would be a savin'," he answered. "But I'm eighty year old now, an' I don't figger on livin' till the rocks give out."

The old-timers say that Stone County, Missouri, was named for a pioneer family, but there's no denying that it is pretty rocky. People who live in less rugged parts of Missouri all pretend to look down on Stone County. A lawyer in Springfield, less than fifty miles north, told me solemnly that Stone County was not only the most poverty-ridden county in the state, but "headquarters for the biggest liars in America." I objected mildly, remarking that I had "heard different." The man shook his head. "You can hear

[6] *Behind These Ozark Hills*, p. 69.

anything in Stone County," said he, "except the truth, an' bacon a-fryin'."

There are many old japes about the small corn which is grown on the rocky hillsides. In Searcy County, Arkansas, a boy told me that his neighbors raised corn which never grew more than fifteen inches high. "It's what they call goober corn," he said. "Goober corn? What's that?" I asked. "Well," came the measured answer, "I didn't see no ears, so I figger the corn must grow underground, like peanuts."

One sees humorous references to small corn in the newspapers sometimes. Spider Rowland [7] tells of corn down in Sharp County, Arkansas, so puny that "the crows had to wear knee-pads" to pull it up.

A boy near Jasper, Arkansas, told me that a certain piece of land was so poor it would grow nothing but bumblebee corn. When I asked what sort of corn this could be, he answered that the stalks are so short that "a full-grown bumblebee can set on the ground an' suck the tassel." Lew Beardon, of Branson, Missouri, said that "some of the old-time corn was pollenated by bumblebees standing flat-footed." It seems that this term is applied also to the poor "shoe-mouth" cotton of the mountain districts. John Gould Fletcher [8] refers to "bumblebee cotton, so small that a bumblebee, by stretching its legs, could reach from the bolls to the ground."

At the old Nash farm on Bear Creek, in Taney County, Missouri, Aunt Sarah Wilson saved her seed, and planted a little patch of this old-time corn every season for fifty years. I saw her crop there in 1940, the only real bumblebee corn in the whole region, so far as I know. The stuff only grows about three feet high, and then tassels. The ears are small, never more than five inches long. The grains are deep blue

[7] *Arkansas Gazette*, July 14, 1948.
[8] *Arkansas*, 1947, p. 226.

in color, instead of white or yellow. It looked to me like very inferior popcorn. The old residents on Bear Creek tell me that in the early days everybody raised blue corn like Aunt Sarah's and that there was no other kind of corn in the Ozarks. It is said that the first white settlers got the seed from the Indians. The Chickasaws used to plant it on gravel bars, with a dead fish in every hill by way of fertilizer, and never cultivated it at all.

Corn of this sort, or even modern corn, sometimes flourishes in very rocky places. That is what Marion Hughes [9] had in mind when he wrote: "It takes two men to plant corn in Arkansas; one pries the rocks apart with a crowbar, and the other shoots the seed down the crack with a syringe." When I first came to the Ozarks I saw a man plowing in a field full of rocks; the whole farm seemed to consist of rocks and gravel, without a particle of dirt in sight. I watched the plowman for awhile, and concluded that he must be crazy. I had seen the lush cornfields of Iowa and Illinois, and it did not seem possible that corn could grow in a rock pile. But when I came back later in the season, that corn was eight or nine feet tall.

The civic boosters in the towns often assert that wild hogs or razorbacks are extinct in the Ozarks, but everybody knows that it isn't true. The *Missouri Conservationist* [10] mentions four wild hogs killed in Oregon County, Missouri, and one of the boars had "tusks that measured seven and one-half inches in length." The old-timers say that razorbacks never get fat and that there are seldom more than three pigs to a litter, usually only two. The wild hogs I have seen were comparatively small and thin, with large heads. They run like deer and fight savagely when cornered. They kill and eat small dogs sometimes, and farmers say that they devour

[9] *Three Years in Arkansaw*, p. 10.
[10] April, 1948, p. 10.

lambs and young goats. I believe it is true that these hogs
gobble up rattlers and copperheads, and seem unaffected by
snake venom.

Under certain conditions, wild razorbacks will attack
human beings. Bert W. Brown [11] declares that the onslaught
of a wild sow in Stone County, Arkansas, forced him to
climb a tree and remain treed for several hours, despite the
fact that he fired twice at the animal with a pistol. And the
redoubtable Spider Rowland [12] says that once in Sharp
County, Arkansas, "wild hogs kept me up a tree all afternoon." Marion Hughes [13] told a similar tale of a man treed
by a wild sow, but almost everybody in Arkansas said that
he was a liar.

Though stoutly contending that the razorback does not
exist "outside the imagination" and that Ozark hogs are just
like hogs in any other part of the United States, the guidebook *Arkansas* [14] comments on the razorback anecdotes:

Like all true folk-myths, the razorback stories have an unknown
origin. Assume that someone commented on a temporary scarcity of acorns and the consequent thinness of his hogs. A second
man would agree, saying that his sows were able for the first
time to squeeze through the garden gate. A third would testify
that he could now hang his hat on the hips of his hogs. The next
would aver that his swine had to stand up twice in order to cast
a shadow. One man was almost bound to swear that *his* hogs
were so desperately starved he could clasp one like a straight
razor and shave with the bony ridge of its back.

What the scientific folklorists would think of this theory I
don't know, but it's in the official guidebook of the State of
Arkansas, and I quote it here for the sake of the record.

It is a strange thing that the backwoods farmers, the boys

[11] Kansas City *Journal-Post*, April 17, 1932.
[12] *Arkansas Gazette*, Sept. 15, 1948.
[13] *Three Years in Arkansaw*, pp. 107–109.
[14] Page 99.

who actually raise hogs, should delight in telling windy stories about how small and thin and puny their animals are. While the Chamber-of-Commerce people, who live in town and do not raise hogs at all, should be in such a perspiration to deny these tales. But that is the situation, as any traveler can tell you.

Sometimes a small-hog story is slipped into a droning narrative on a totally unrelated subject. A man in Boone County, Arkansas, was in the midst of a long tale about a local bank robbery. "Just about five minutes before old man Myers shot Henry Starr," he told a gaping tourist, "here come young Jim Blevins a-ridin' up on a mule, with four dressed hogs in his saddlebags." The tourist's mind was so occupied with the killing of Henry Starr that the absurdity of the hog story passed unnoticed. Perhaps twenty local men heard this crack and laughed about it later. That casual reference to the Blevins hogs was the purpose and climax of the whole story, from the hillman's point of view. Henry Starr and the bank robbery were just used as window trimming.

One night I sat with two hunters beside a campfire on a White River gravel bar. We had found a piece of heavy iron wire, and were using it to broil bits of deer liver, with alternate strips of bacon from the store at Mincy, Missouri. "I git mighty tired of this store-bought bacon sometimes," one fellow said. "I killed one of my prize hogs t'other day, aimin' to git a little fresh meat. But the cat run off with the carcass, whilst I was a-bilin' the water to scald it." The fact that the speaker was an outlaw from Oklahoma, who had probably never owned a hog in his life, somehow added punch to the tale.

A related yarn is credited to a physician in Barry County, Missouri. It seems that one of the doctor's neighbors had seven hogs, and decided to butcher them all the same day.

He used an old washtub for a scalding barrel, and hung the animals up on the clothesline as fast as he got 'em scraped. Suddenly the fellow noticed that there were only six on the line. "Good Lord, we're a hog shy!" he cried. The old woman came out of the cabin, stirred around in the dirty water with a stick, and finally located the seventh hog away down in the bottom of the tub. Much relieved, they fished the lost hog out and hung it on the clothesline with the others.

Down near Mountain Home, Arkansas, they tell of a farmer who owned a big boar. One day a chicken-hawk flew away with it, and the man figgered that his boar was gone forever. About a month later he heard the animal squealing out in the woods, and finally located it in the top of a tall pine tree. There seemed no way to get the boar down alive, so he shot it through the head with his rifle. The poor creature was very thin, and its stomach was full of pine cones. When the farmer's wife tried to cook it, the whole hog boiled down to four pounds of lard and a short quart of turpentine.

"The razorbacks down in Arkansas," said a Missouri cattleman, "are so all-fired thin they can run through a stove-pipe." And this brings us to another old tale, about a sow with several little pigs. She started to run through a joint of stove-pipe at the town dump one day, but the pipe was smaller than the standard size, so the old sow got wedged into it. It was a short length, so she could run around with it all right, since all four legs were free. But her tits were inside the pipe, and the little pigs couldn't suck, so they all starved to death.

Marion Hughes [15] repeats many ancient razorback stories. Most Arkansas hogs are very small, he says, and some varieties roost in trees, but they do not lay eggs. Hughes saw

[15] *Three Years in Arkansaw*, pp. 18–29.

one very large hazel-splitter "that dressed fourteen pounds with its head on, and six and a half with its head cut off." In judging a hog they catch it and hold it up by the ears; if the head goes down and the tail flies up, they turn it loose to fatten another year. Some of these hogs have such large heads that the owners tie stones to their tails, to keep them from pitching forward on their snouts. The smaller fish-hogs, says Hughes, are usually shot and dressed like bullfrogs; the Arkansawyers just eat the hind legs and throw the rest away. The so-called tryo hog, which is no bigger than a cat, lives mostly on bugs and flies. It requires a whole hog to season an ordinary pot of beans. At butchering time the boys bring in hogs by the sackful, and the women just gut 'em like rabbits and scrape 'em in a pan of hot water. These little hogs are generally salted down for the winter in cracker boxes; just put in a good layer of salt, then about six hogs, then another layer of salt, then more hogs, and so on until the box is full.

Most of the ten "breeds" of Arkansas hog described by Marion Hughes exist only in the blanket-stretcher's imagination, but the mule-footed hog is something else again. Uncle Jack Short, of Galena, Missouri, told me seriously that he had seen hogs with solid hooves, in Stone County, Missouri. And the *Christian County Republican*, a weekly published at Ozark, Missouri, carried the following advertisement on Dec. 30, 1943.

INFORMATION WANTED concerning what used to be known in this locality as "mule-footed" hogs. Anyone still having this strain or any information pertaining is asked to communicate with me. Floyd C. Goddard, Box 234, Olds, Alberta, Canada.

I always intended to write Mr. Goddard and try to find out just what he learned on this subject, but never got around to it, somehow.

The old folks say that a farmer near Clinton, Arkansas, had a lot of hogs that were so puny and lean the wolves and wildcats wouldn't touch them. Finally a black bear carried several of these skinny hogs off alive and penned 'em up in a rock shelter under the bluff. For weeks on end that bear stole corn every day and carried it to the cave, in order to fatten the hogs up so they'd be big enough to eat. But after months of hard work, according to the story, the bear seen it warn't no use, so he turned the critters out to pasture.

"These hogs o' mine is so thin, it takes two of 'em to throw a shadder," said a backwoods humorist near Mena, Arkansas. "They ain't got no stren'th, neither. Why, I seen four of 'em workin' tandem, tryin' to pull up a turnip." Another man in the same neighborhood told me that his yearling pigs were so small and lean that they could slip through a chicken-tight fence, to steal kafir-corn from the poultry.

Rome Nelson, a veteran of the War between the States who lived near Crane, Missouri, was credited with developing a variety of razorbacks called the second-row strain. The idea is that any wild hog can reach through a rail fence and pull off ears of corn from the nearest stalks. But the Nelson hogs had such slender heads and long snouts that they could reach the second row of corn, according to the local storytellers.

I have heard also of razorback hogs with such long noses that they can drink buttermilk out of a jug. In dry times, the old folks say, a wild hog need not come to the creek for water. When he wants a drink, he just sticks his snout down a crawdad hole. These burrows are common in many places, and the hillfolk believe that a crawdad always digs till he strikes water, no matter how deep it may be. According to one old tale, a certain long-snouted sow always drank out of crawdad holes, even when plenty of surface-water was available. Not only this, but she pumped water from the crawdad hole through her own body and out on the ground, so that all the other pigs could satisfy their thirst. In some versions of this yarn, the sow's owner trained her to pump enough water to irrigate his garden-patch in dry weather.

One hears many stories of the razorback's ability to get food under difficult conditions. "One of them wild shotes," a hunter told me, "can hear an acorn drap a mile off, an' run fast enough to ketch it on the second bounce."

In Polk County, Arkansas, they told me of a man who found two or three wild hogs in his garden patch every morning, though it was fenced with wire and apparently hog-tight. He had to open the gate and drive 'em out. One morning very early he hid in the brush and watched, to see how the razorbacks were getting past the fence. The pigs climbed up on a hillside, swung far out on a trailing grape-vine, and let loose when they were directly over the garden. This was told me for the truth, but I'm afraid it's only a tall tale like the rest of 'em.

A very old and widely known hog story, sometimes credited to Rome Nelson of second-row fame, concerns some Missouri farmers who shipped their finest boars down to a state fair in Little Rock. They figured these males would sell for big money, since the Arkansawyers must surely be anxious to improve the razorback breed. The backwoods hog raisers looked at the great boars with interest. "They sure are big an' fat," a hillman admitted, "but they wouldn't be no good in this country." When the Missouri breeders profanely demanded to know why this fine stock would not do for Arkansas, the hillman answered: "Unless a hog can whip a bear an' outrun a panther, he'd never live till the first frost!"

It is said that one Arkansas farmer did import some fat northern hogs, just for experimental purposes. But it was no use. The animals would disappear, one after another, and be gone about ten days. Then they would stagger home very thin, hardly to be distinguished from the native swine. Finally it was learned that the fat hog would try to crawl through a holler log into a goober patch, and get stuck. He couldn't get out until he had lost a lot of weight, enough to reduce him to the size of an ordinary razorback.

Wild hogs are sometimes seen with what appears to be a big ball of dried mud on their tails. There is an ancient wheeze to the effect that this weight causes a razorback to "sleep himself to death." As the ball grows large and heavy, according to the tale, it pulls the hog's skin back so tight that the animal can't get its eyes open. Being blinded, it cannot find food enough to keep alive. Another version of this story, which I heard in Taney County, Missouri, is that the skin is drawn back so that the hog can't *shut* its eyes. In this case, the pore critter dies from lack of sleep.

Some hillmen claim that the average razorback is so thin that he needs a ball of mud on his tail to preserve a proper balance, otherwise he'll pitch forward and stick his bill into the ground. The head is the heaviest part of an old-time hazel-splitter anyhow, and that's why he can't root down hill.

One of Lowell Thomas's tales [16] relates the tribulations of an Arkansas farmer who owned a breachy razorback. To prevent the animal from digging under his fence, the man drove stakes deep into the ground. Unable to root its way out, the hog rolled its tail in the dirt until a large heavy ball of dried mud was finally attached. Then "in the manner of a college athlete making a hammer throw" the creature swung the tail round and round. Finally the great ball of mud flew right over the fence, pulling the hog along with it.

[16] *Tall Stories*, p. 17.

Louis Hanecke, who used to run the Allred Hotel in Eureka Springs, Arkansas, is credited with a yarn about wild hogs that broke into a still-house and got gugglin' drunk; then they ran through the woods in packs, killing deer, cattle and even bears. Some hillfolk near Hot Springs, Arkansas, declare that these whiskey-maddened razorbacks climbed trees to pull down coons and bobcats. Even the official state guidebook [17] refers to a hog that "knocked over somebody's barrel of mash, and subsequently went off down the valley, hunting wolves."

Bob Burns and other radio comedians have repeated different versions of an old story about a hog that rooted out some dynamite from under a ledge, where it had been hidden by boys who were interested in dynamiting fish. Having eaten several sticks of dynamite, the hog wandered up to the back door of a farmhouse. An ill-tempered farmhand drew back his foot and delivered a tremendous kick. There was a terrific explosion, which killed the hired man, tore the roof off the cabin, and damaged almost everything in the neighborhood. "For three or four days," said the farmer, "we had a mi-i-ighty sick hog on our hands."

Not far from Eureka Springs, Arkansas, there are several round pot-holes in the bed of a little creek. It is said that the pioneers threw heated stones into these pits, and scalded hogs there. The place is known as Hog Scald to this day. An old-timer told me that he had lived near Hog Scald in the early 1880's. There used to be a bramble-thicket near the pot-holes, he said, about where the road is now. "We used to git the water good an' hot," he explained, "an' throw the hogs in alive. They'd jump out a-squealin', an' run right through them bramble-bushes. The thorns would take the bristles off slicker'n a whistle, so we didn't have to scrape 'em at all."

At Newport, Arkansas, some jokers were talking about

[17] *Arkansas*, p. 100.

the strange customs of the people in a nearby settlement called Oil Trough. The folks up that way, I was told, "never cut up their hogs at butcherin' time, and don't even bother to gut 'em. They just feed nothing but salt and spices for a week, then shoot the critter an' smoke the whole hog!"

Another odd story, which the newspapers sometimes credit to a man named Lemley, of Thayer, Missouri, is that when the farmers in that neighborhood butcher a hog they find that the meat is already smoked. This is due, it is said, to the brush fires which are so common there. The whole region is smoky from September to Christmas, and the local pork is literally smoked on the hoof.

There are no medium-sized hogs in the Ozarks, if one believes the story-tellers. Most of the swine in the backwoods tales are very small, but there are a few really gigantic razorbacks among them. Ben Edmonson, of Springfield, Missouri, told reporters [18] that he once raised "a hog big as a cow."

Nancy Clemens, who used to do feature stories for the Kansas City *Star*, had a good one about a Missourian trying to sell his farm to a man from Arkansas. "Does the river ever flood this here pasture?" asked the hillbilly. "Hell no," replied the farmer, "we ain't had no high water in forty years." The hillman noticed a ring of mud on every tree trunk, about six feet above the ground. "Then how did that mud git away up thar?" he asked. "Oh, it's them damn' hogs of mine," said the Missourian, "they're allus a-rubbin' ag'in the trees." The hillman said no more, but prepared to take his departure. "Well, do you aim to buy the farm?" the Missourian asked. "Naw, I don't want the farm," said the Arkansawyer, "but I shore would like to git a start o' them hogs."

In describing an unusually large hog, the hillman generally

[18] Springfield *News and Leader*, Feb. 28, 1934.

says that it's as big as a plow horse. Don West [19] has one of his characters trying to sell a sow. The creature was so big, he said, that "I could work her to the plow, if I could guide her!"

Here's one that a friend of mine heard near Gravette, Arkansas. A farmer was bragging about his boar, which was so all-fired big that he used it to pull the plow. Another farmer listened to this whopper, then declared that he too broke ground with a razorback, but dispensed with the plow altogether. The first thing, he said, is to tie a heavy rock on the hog's head, to keep its nose down. Then you just grab the animal by the hind legs and trundle him wheelbarrow-fashion across the field, tearing up the turf with his snout. A different and less decorous version of this yarn used to be told up around Southwest City, Missouri.

I have heard several stories about how the old-time razorbacks used to root up the rocky ground, to an extent unknown among modern swine. It is even asserted that Kemp Morgan, who was a kind of Paul Bunyan of the Oklahoma oil fields, used a gang of giant razorbacks in laying his great pipe lines. He just drove the hogs tandem ahead of the crews, and they rooted out a big ditch faster than Morgan's trucks could bring up the pipe.

One seldom sees this sort of thing in print nowadays. But as recently as March 22, 1948, according to the Associated Press, an Arkansas congressman named Brooks Hays stood up in the House and shouted: "If all the hogs in Arkansas were one hog, he could stand with his front feet in the Gulf of Mexico, his hind feet in the Atlantic Ocean and with his tremendous snout, dig another Panama Canal!"

For the logical ending of all big-hog stories we cite a tale attributed to Bob Burns of Van Buren, Arkansas, although the old-timers say the yarn was old before Burns

[19] *Broadside to the Sun*, p. 153.

was born. Anyhow, Bob repeated what he called a "legend" that the Ozark Mountains owe their very existence to the activities of great prehistoric razorbacks. In ages past, according to this theory, the Ozark country was flat, covered with giant oaks. The acorns were much bigger than they are now, and the hogs which fed upon the acorns grew to gigantic size. When the mast failed one season, these colossal beasts became desperate with hunger, and went raging up and down the land in search of food. They rooted deep in the ground, scattering rocks and trees and gravel every which way. This "tearin' up the earth" produced the deep hollers and high ridges that we call the Ozark hills today.

3 Fabulous monsters

THERE ARE MANY LEGENDS of gigantic beasts and fabulous varmints in the Ozark country. It may be that credulous backwoodsmen believe some of them even today, but I wouldn't know about that. At any rate, the stories are still in circulation. Hillfolk tell them to their children, just as parents elsewhere used to entertain their offspring with yarns about dragons, centaurs, griffins, mermaids, and the like. Perhaps the children don't really believe all this, but it sometimes amuses them to pretend that they do, and thus the tales are preserved and transmitted from one generation to the next. Some of these items seem to be local, confined to certain clans or family groups. Others are much more widely known, and have even been published in the newspapers.

One of the latter is concerned with an extraordinary reptile called the gowrow which terrorized rural Arkansas in the 1880's. Several stories about the gowrow were attributed to Fred W. Allsopp, sometime editor of the *Arkansas Gazette*, but I have been unable to find them in his published works. I asked Mr. Allsopp about this once, but he just laughed and said that all he knew of the gowrow was what he read in the Missouri papers. According to the legends, the gowrow was a lizard-like animal about twenty feet long, with enormous tusks. There is a persistent report that gowrows hatched from eggs, soft-shelled eggs as big as beer kegs. Some say that the female carried its newly hatched young in a pouch like a possum, but the old-timers do not

agree about this. The gowrow spent most of its time in caverns and under rock ledges. It was carnivorous, and devoured great numbers of deer, calves, sheep, and goats. Perhaps the creature ate human beings, too.

A traveling salesman named William Miller was credited with killing a gowrow somewhere near Marshall, Arkansas, in 1897, and many wild stories were told about this exploit. There is no record that Miller ever showed the carcass of the animal to any local people. Miller once declared that he shipped the gowrow's skin and skeleton to the Smithsonian Museum in Washington, D.C. But a newspaperman who interviewed the officials at the Smithsonian was unable to confirm Miller's claim.

Otto Ernest Rayburn [1] reprints an unidentified newspaper account of Miller's encounter with "a gowrow of the goofus family" in Searcy County, Arkansas. Miller had been unable to overtake the gowrow, but lay in wait for it at the entrance of a cavern.

This cave was evidently the home of the animal [the newspaper story continues] as here were found many skeletons, skulls and bones, as well as parts of human flesh of recent victims; but the monster had not returned to its lair. Miller and his posse laid in wait, trembling in their shoes. Presently the earth swayed as if another earthquake were taking place. The waters of the lake began to splash and roar like the movement of the ocean waves, and they realized that the monster was approaching. As it came within range, all hands fired, and after several volleys were discharged, succeeded in killing it. But it died hard. A couple of huge trees on the bank were lashed down, and one of the assailants was killed by it before it breathed its last. The gowrow was twenty feet in length, and had a ponderous head with two enormous tusks. Its legs were short, terminating in webbed feet similar to but much larger than those of a duck, and each toe had a vicious claw. The body was covered with green scales, and its back bristled with short horns. Its tail was

[1] *Arcadian Life*, June, 1935, pp. 18–19.

thin and long, and was provided with sharp, blade-like forma-
tions at the end, which it used as a sickle. The animal was a
pachyderm, with long incisors and canine teeth, which apparently showed its relationship to the ceratorhinus genus, supposed long since to have disappeared from the earth.

In the same magazine story Rayburn repeats a tale which
he had from Clio Harper, of Little Rock. It seems that there
is a very deep fissure called the Devil's Hole, near the Self
postoffice in Boone County, Arkansas, on land owned by
E. J. Rhodes. In trying to explore this cave Rhodes descended by means of a rope, landing on a ledge some 200
feet below the surface, but could go no farther. Later several
men went to the Devil's Hole with 1,000 feet of clothesline.
They fastened a heavy old-fashioned flatiron to the end of
the line, and let it down into the hole. When the weight
reached a depth of about 200 feet it struck something,
probably the ledge discovered earlier by Rhodes.

It was at this point [according to Harper's story, that] things
began to happen. The men heard a vicious hissing sound as if it
were some angry animal whose den had been rudely intruded.
The rope was pulled up and it was found that the handle of the
iron was bent. Jim, the guide, swore he could see the marks of
teeth upon it. A large stone was then attached as a weight and
thrown in. Again the sibilant sound when it struck the ledge,
and when the rope was drawn up the stone was gone. The rope
had been bitten in two as clean as though it had been cut with a
knife. Fastening another stone to the line, we cast again. Again
it ran out to the 200-foot ledge, again the hissing sound was
heard and when the rope was drawn up the stone was gone and
the rope was found to have been cut in two as clean as by a
knife. The marks of sharp teeth were clearly discernible. For the
third time the cast was made, and the third time the rope was
bitten in two.

Disregarding a local theory that the mysterious phenomena
of the cave were caused by the spirit of a dead Indian, at

least one member of the party, according to Rayburn's account, contended that a gowrow must be responsible. It might well be, he argued, that Miller's posse had not killed the gowrow. Maybe the great beast had "played possum" and fooled 'em. Perhaps, after Miller's departure, the gowrow migrated to Boone County and settled down in the Devil's Hole, where it may be living to this day.

I have met elderly men in Missouri and Arkansas who publicly declared their belief that a few specimens of the gowrow may have survived into the 1920's. But whether these fellows were in earnest, I do not pretend to say.

My old friend Pete Woolsey, who used to run a restaurant in Bentonville, Arkansas, was a little offended when I grinned at his version of the gowrow story.

"I don't see nothin' so unreasonable about it," said he. "Them scientists over at the State University are tellin' people that there used to be elephants right here in Arkansas. *Elephants,* mind you, with red wool on 'em two foot long!"

"That's different," I answered. "That was thousands of years ago."

"Would you rather believe them professors, talkin' about red elephants in Arkansas before America was *discovered* even, than my Grandpaw's story of what happened in his own life-time?"

"Listen, Pete, did your grandfather ever see a gowrow?" I asked.

"No, he didn't. I never seen a painter, neither. But lots of old-timers did see painters, an' killed 'em too, right here in this county. I've listened at them hunters a-talkin', an' there ain't no doubt in my mind that there was plenty of painters here in the early days. My Grandpaw heerd about the gowrow, just like I've heerd about painters."

Pete began to look kind of indignant, as if somebody had intimated that maybe his grandfather was a liar. Pete

Woolsey was not a man to be pushed too far. So I suggested that we take a drink, which we did, and said no more about gowrows.

A gentleman at Mena, Arkansas, told me a long story of a Missourian who claimed to have captured a gowrow alive. This fellow had somehow induced the animal to eat a wagon-load of dried apples, which had swelled its body to such a degree that the beast could not get back into its burrow. He was exhibiting it in a tent, charging twenty-five cents admission. There was a horrible painting of the monster out front, showing it in the act of devouring an entire family of cotton farmers. When a good crowd was seated, there came a terrible roaring noise backstage, with several shots and a loud clanking of chains. Then the show-man staggered out in full view of the audience, his clothes torn to shreds and blood running down his face. "Run for your lives!" he yelled, "the gowrow has broke loose!" Just then the back part of the tent collapsed, with more thunderous roars and chains rattling and women screaming. The spectators rushed away in a panic, without stopping to get their money back.

Eleanor Risley, author of *The Road to Wildcat,* was present when I heard this tale. She remembered that a similar yarn had been popular years before in Alabama. The name gowrow was not used in the Alabama version, though; it was some other sort of wild animal that the fellow pretended to have in the tent.

Down near Argenta, Arkansas, the old-timers used to speak jokingly of a mythical anachronism known as the jimplicute. This was a kind of ghostly dinosaur, an incredible dragon or lizard supposed to walk the roads at night, grab travelers by the throat and suck their blood. It is said that the jimplicute was invented by white people shortly after the War between the States, to frighten superstitious Negroes. Oddly enough, the name of this bloodthirsty beast seems to have struck the fancy of newspapermen. Walt Whitman, writing in the *North American Review* [2] mentioned a Texas newspaper called *The Jimplicute*, and it is said that a *Weekly Jimplicute* was published at Illmo, Missouri, as recently as 1940.

Another apochryphal varmint was the famous high-behind, a lizard as big as a bull, whose hind legs were ten times longer than its forelegs. This creature, according to some children I met near Big Flat, Arkansas, lies in wait for human beings on the trails at night and "laps 'em up like a toad-frog ketchin' flies." Some people call it the "hide-behind," because it always hides behind some object so that nobody ever gets a really good look at it. Woodsmen say that the beast can "suck in its guts" so that it is slender enough to stand up behind a tree and be almost concealed. A man named Burke, in Joplin, Missouri, told me that the correct name of the creature is "*nigh*-behind," but the significance of this was not explained to me. Under whatever name, the high-behind is dangerous and an enemy to all humanity. In Taney County, Missouri, one of my friends learned that the sheriff had a warrant for his arrest, so he ran off to California and has never been heard from since. Some of this man's kinfolk said later that the poor fellow "un-thoughtedly" walked up the Bear Creek road at midnight and failed to return. They found a few drops of blood and some mighty peculiar "sign" in the trail next day, so they "figgered the high-behind must have got pore Sam." Or at least that's what they told the authorities, and never cracked a smile in the telling.

The kingdoodle or whangdoodle is another big lizard, doubtless related to the gowrow, the jimplicute, and the high-behind. One night near Waco, Missouri, a drunken

[2] Nov., 1885, p. 435.

possum-hunter and I heard a strange booming sound in the woods along Spring River. "What's that noise?" I asked. The possum-hunter listened for awhile. "I don't know," said he, "but it sounds like a whangdoodle a-mournin' for its dead." One of my neighbors in McDonald County, Missouri, told his children that the kingdoodle looks very much like an ordinary mountain boomer, except for its great size. The mountain boomer, or collared lizard, seldom attains a length of more than ten inches, while the kingdoodle is "longer'n a well-rope, an' fourteen hands high." It is strong enough to tear down rail fences and pull up saplings, but is not bloodthirsty, and I never heard of its killing livestock or attacking human beings. Not far from Jane, Missouri, my wife and I stopped to look at a small building which had fallen off its stone foundation and rolled into a ditch. Probably a high wind was responsible, but a little boy who lived nearby didn't think so. "I reckon the old kingdoodle must have throwed it down, in the night," he said soberly.

The gollywog, as described to me by White River guides who claim to have seen it, is a giant mudpuppy or water-dog, which means salamander in the Ozarks. But a full grown gollywog is often eight or ten feet long, as big as an alligator. It spends most of its time in the water and moves about only at night, which explains why it is seldom seen except by illegal giggers and commercial fishermen. The gollywogs upsets boats sometimes, but its main business seems to be the destruction of fishing-tackle, particularly trammel-nets and trotlines.

Looking through a collection of old letters and newspaper clippings in Greene County, Missouri, one finds occasional cryptic references to the willipus-wallipus. Asked where he was bound, a celebrated Missourian replied that he was going out to fight the willipus-wallipus, meaning that it was none of the questioner's damned business. I thought at first that the willipus-wallipus must be another legendary animal, but learned that it was a large road-building machine, a sort of roller propelled by a powerful steam engine. When a big stone statue was sent on a flatcar to Springfield, Missouri, to be set up in the graveyard, it was so heavy that several teams of horses failed to move it. But the old willipus-wallipus dragged the thing from the freight depot right through the town to the cemetery. An old resident of Springfield assured me that the machine was always known as the willipus-wallipus, and said that he had never heard it called by any other name. I queried May Kennedy McCord about this, and she commented upon the question in the KWTO *Dial*.[3] "Whenever there's something you have no name for," she writes, "you just call it a willipus-wallipus. It is on record that a long time ago in Springfield they had a road-making machine listed in official documents as a willipus-walli-pus."

The snawfus, according to some backwoods folk, is just an albino deer with certain supernatural powers, puzzling to human beings, but not dangerous. Some hillmen in Arkansas say that it can make tremendous leaps into the treetops; one man told me that a snawfus was a big white buck which could "fly through the timber, quiet as a God damn' hoot-owl." A woman near Protem, Missouri, said that as a girl she heard the snawfus described as a deer-like creature "that hollers *hallyloo* in the pineries of a night" and is never seen by ordinary human beings at all. If a man should see a snawfus, it's a sign that he ain't long for this world. "Most of the stories you hear about the snawfus is lies," she added, "like these here fairy-tales that folks tell their children."

Miss Leila A. Wade, who lives on a farm near Republic, Missouri, once published an account of a walking tour through the Ozarks under the title "On the Trail of the

[3] Springfield, Mo., Oct., 1946, p. 3.

Snawfus." [4] After reading all twelve installments I went to see the author, and she told me that the snawfus has been known in the Wade family for a long time. "As far back as my recollection goes," she said, "any mystery, such as an unexplained sound in the night, a strange bird flying too fast for identification, anything in short that we did not understand, brought the conclusion that it must have been a snawfus." None of Miss Wade's people ever actually saw the snawfus, unless it was her cousin John, who once glimpsed a strange animal on the banks of War Eagle Creek in Madison County, Arkansas. "But secretly," she told me, "I always thought of it as a snow-white creature, larger than a deer, with an antlered head and wings like sprays of dogwood blossoms. I always hoped I'd see it sometime." Miss Wade added her impression that the animal "emitted spirals of blue smoke, which drifted away in delicate rings, and covered the hills." As a child she had never doubted that the glamorous blue haze which hangs over the Ozarks in the autumn was due to smoke exhaled by the snawfus.

A miner named Burke, who used to live in Joplin, Missouri, always contended that the snawfus was an albino deer of enormous size. So big, indeed, that few hunters had ever seen more than one of its legs at a time, and its broad flowering antlers were often hidden in the clouds. "They tell me," he said, "that it takes a jaybird twenty minutes to fly from horn to horn!" But Burke was a joker, and his account of the snawfus was never intended to be taken seriously.

I have heard several related tales of white deer with flowering boughs in the place of antlers. In Jasper County, Missouri, they used to tell of a pioneer orchardist who caught an albino fawn, and reared it as a pet for his children. It grew into a fine big buck, with "horns like a rockin' cheer." One day the man tied the deer up, and grafted some fine

[4] *Arcadian Life*, Oct., 1936—Mar., 1938.

Arkansas Black scions on its antlers. The deer's horns leaved out every spring thereafter, and growed the finest big red apples you ever seen! The reader may doubt the story, because he has heard that a deer's antlers fall off every year, but the old-time deer hunters [5] never accepted this, and many hillfolk do not believe it today.

In connection with the snawfus legend, J. H. Storey, of Pineville, Missouri, said that his father "used to spin an old windy" about an Arkansawyer who ran out of bullets, so he loaded a musket with plum seeds and sallied forth to kill a deer. He fired at a white buck, and hit it in the head; the animal dropped in its tracks, but sprang up and ran off as he approached. The hunter never did get his white buck, but several years later he began to hear tales of an albino deer with a plum tree in full bloom growing out of its head, instead of ordinary antlers. The people I knew in Pineville had never heard of the snawfus, but when I told Mr. Storey about it he nodded understandingly. "Ain't it funny how people try to make everything bigger'n it really is?" he said. "Somebody must have seen that white deer with the bloomin' tree on its head. Then they just made up the part about wings, an' flyin' through the treetops, an' all the rest of it! I reckon that's how most of them big windies get started."

The bingbuffer has no part in our oral tradition nowadays, so far as I know, but one still finds references to it in old newspapers. The *Missouri Historical Review* [6] reprints a piece from the Jefferson City *Daily Tribune*,[7] where the following description is credited to Colonel W. J. Zevely.

The hinge-tailed bingbuffer is nearly, if not quite, extinct at this time [said the Colonel]. I think the last one was killed in Osage County about 1881 or the spring of 1882. The animal is shaped something like a hippopotamus, only considerably larger

[5] *Ozark Superstitions*, p. 241.   [6] April, 1944, p. 367.   [7] July 23, 1891.

and has a flat tapering tail which sometimes reaches the length of forty feet. Its legs are short and owing to the great weight of its body locomotion is necessarily slow. But nature supplies the hinge-tailed bingbuffer with the means of obtaining food. Underneath the jaws is a pouch that will hold at least a bushel. When in quest of food the animal fills its pouch with stones weighing from two to three pounds each. Where the tail joins the body there is a hinge, and when the animal desires to kill anything it takes a stone from the pouch with its tail, and hurls it with wonderful accuracy and force to a distance of several hundred yards. Talk about the accuracy and execution of a rifle-ball! You just ought to see a hinged-tail bingbuffer throw a stone. . . . As I said before, I believe the last one was killed some years ago.

Robert L. Kennedy, old-time newspaperman of Springfield, Missouri, used to tell the story of the orance, which he said was brought into prominence by Lee Holland and John G. Newbill. "These two wags of half a century ago," said Kennedy, "would be talking quietly about the orance, which would be mumbled so as to catch the attention of someone who was trying to overhear the conversation. Then when one or the other moved away he would be told in a louder voice 'They have taken it over to Joplin.' Most people thought it was an animal that was referred to, while others figured it must be some sort of projected factory that Springfield was trying to get, and had lost it to Joplin. Sometimes a man with a good ear would catch the word 'orance' clearly, and would want to know the details. He would be asked if he were not informed on the subject, and would reply that he was not. Then he would be told that the matter was of such grave importance that it should not be discussed in public. This would be kept up until the victim discovered that he was being played with. Some fellows would get furiously mad, and walk off mumbling words which did not sound like 'orance' at all." The whole thing was only a rib, probably limited to a few business men in Springfield, and never had any wide circulation. Oddly enough, the name orance is still known to some old settlers in southwest Missouri, but nowadays it means only a peculiar sort of legendary wildcat, more commonly called the wampus.

The most dangerous wild animal that ever really lived in the Ozarks was the panther or painter. The pioneers feared these beasts, and apparently with good reason. No less an authority than Wayman Hogue [8] says that when he was a boy in Van Buren County, Arkansas, painters used to kill children occasionally, and would even climb down the chimney after a newborn babe. Because of their genuine fear of painters, the pioneers were frightened by any noise which suggested the screams of these animals. There are several stories of backwoodsmen who, when they heard the whistle of a steamboat or a locomotive for the first time, thought it must be some enormous wild beast. Doubtless some of these tales are based upon real incidents.

Jean Graham [9] tells of the *Flora Jones*, the first steamboat that came up the Osage River to Harmony Mission, in Bates County, Missouri. It was in the spring of 1844. An old settler plowing in his clearing heard "a long wailing cry, followed by an angry roar," and figgered it must be some kind of super-painter. Stopping only to get his rifle, he rode madly into Papinsville. The people there had heard the terrible screams, and all able-bodied men gathered with dogs and guns.

They pictured a varmint of gigantic size, to match the volume of its howling voice [writes Graham]. They figured it must be an unheard of species from the Rocky Mountains or some other remote region. The daughter of the house where they had congregated had just gone down to the river three or four hundred yards away for water. While the men made ready the unearthly sound came to them again from the direction of the

[8] *Back Yonder*, 1932, pp. 170–181.
[9] *Tales of the Osage River Country*, pp. 18–22.

river. The devoted father and others of the men mounted their horses and dashed after the girl, to rescue her from the beast. She met them half way, her eyes wild with terror and her hair streaming behind her as she ran. They saw her safely home, and her father bade her stay inside the cabin while they were away.

The dogs apparently failed to pick up any odor, but the varmint was certainly approaching. The hunters cocked their rifles and "made ready for the monster which they could hear puffing, blowing and roaring as he floundered along," evidently following the river. When the *Flora* finally steamed into view the backwoodsmen were so astonished that no word was spoken for a long time. Some of the settlers may have heard rumors of steamboats back East, but the *Flora Jones* was the first that any of them had ever seen. There were many such boats on Missouri rivers after that, for the Osage was navigable as far up as Oceola in those days.

Masterson [10] quotes a story from the New York *Spirit of the Times* [11] about an Arkansas planter who moved across the border into the wilderness of the Indian Territory. One evening he heard several very loud, shrill screams. The noise frightened the cattle, set the dogs to barking, and scared the womenfolk into fits. Everybody said it must be a painter, and a tremendous big painter at that. The planter took six Indians, four Negro men, and nine hound-dogs; they hunted through the whole country from Grand River to the Verdigris, but found no painter sign. Later it was learned that the mysterious sound was the fog whistle of a steamboat, the first steamboat that ever came up Grand River.

Panthers were common in the 1850's and 1860's, perhaps even later. But they were very rare in the Ozark country by 1900. The last Missouri panther was killed in 1927, according to the Missouri Conservation Commission. As for Arkansas,

.[10] *Tall Tales of Arkansaw*, pp. 61–62.   [11] Nov. 22, 1845, p. 458.

the official guidebook published in 1941 says that "only a few remain, and these in the most remote sections" (*Arkansas*, 1941, p.15). For all practical purposes panthers are extinct, but the hillfolk are still afraid of them. Hardly a month goes by without a panther being reported in some part of the Ozark country, and people always get pretty much excited.

I have seen two of these panther panics myself. Early in January, 1938, farmers near Lamar, Missouri, were frightened by noises which they thought sounded like a painter a-hollerin'. Arthur Aull, editor of the Lamar *Democrat*, told 'em it was all damned foolishness, since not even a wildcat had been killed in the neighborhood for nearly a quarter of a century. The last "cat-varmint" to show up in Barton County was a bobcat shot in 1913, and its stuffed skin may still be seen in Selvey's store on the Lamar public square. But the men who heard the screeches in the woods at night were not convinced. Elmer Curtis, who lived at a nearby settlement called Milo, said that the painter had eaten one of his hound-dogs. Ralph Pitts found some round cat tracks in the dirt, and these tracks measured nearly four inches in diameter. Pete Garrett and a fellow named Mann actually saw the animal at a distance, and described it as "bigger than a dog, with a long tail." Even the people in town began to get a little nervous, and women and children didn't go out much at night. Arthur Aull told me that a certain merchant who lived right in the middle of Lamar would not step outside of his house after dark without a six-shooter *in his hand!* Many respectable citizens in the Ozarks carry revolvers, but they generally keep 'em in their pockets. One day more than 150 men gathered with dogs and guns at a point east of Milo, and searched the whole countryside. They flushed three or four coyotes, but couldn't even find the track of a bobcat, let alone a painter.

When I lived in Galena, Missouri, there was a good deal of talk about the "Stone County Monster," which many thought must be a panther. In June, 1945, a woman and her babe were alone in a backwoods shanty near Abesville, Missouri. It was just getting dark. The woman heard a scratching at the door, and opened it to see a gigantic beast standing upright like a man. It was tan-colored, she said, with a long tail, staring eyes, and big teeth. She slammed the door, and the varmint nearly tore the cabin down trying to get in. Next night the thing returned, and the story spread far and wide. Some animal trying to get the baby, people said, reviving old tales of panthers that used to climb down chimneys, attracted by the odor of the mother's milk. Neighbors came by the dozen, and armed men patrolled the holler all night. Several hunters glimpsed the creature; one fired at it and claimed to have found blood on the grass. The story grew, and frightened farmers for miles around. G. H. Pipes, who was running a café in Reeds Spring, Missouri, told me that people there talked about nothing else for weeks. A man named Warren, of Reeds Spring, swore that some large animal sprang at his truck as he was going to church one night, and leaped up several times in an effort to get into the vehicle. Some yokels said that the Weaver Brothers had a circus somewhere near, and that a great panther had escaped from a cage. The tales grew wilder and wilder. Local men made their families stay in the house after dark, and carried weapons for their own protection. Finally the whole excitement died down gradually, after four weeks of hell-raising. Some people maintained that the monster was nothing but a big collie dog, deserted by its owner who had been drafted into the army. The dog was hungry, and probably did go scratching at the doors of houses at night. When armed men were marching about, the animal kept out of sight. But there are men and women in Stone County today who profess to believe that there really was a panther there in 1945, prowling about in search of a young infant to devour.

Similar "painter scares" have occurred in many other Ozark communities. Sometimes the varmint has supernatural qualities, as in the "Panther Curse" story reported by Collins.[12] Naturally, the widespread fear of panthers has had an influence upon the incredible monsters of the fireside legends. Near Sallisaw, Oklahoma, one hears old stories of the wowzer or woozer. This beast is a kind of super-painter, five or six times the size of an ordinary mountain lion. The wowzer kills cattle and horses by biting their heads off, just as a polecat kills chickens. One of these great cats is said to have destroyed a wagon-train in pioneer days, killing upwards of thirty oxen in a few minutes. The freighters fired their guns at him, but to no effect. No human beings were hurt, save a woman who was inside one of the covered wagons. In killing the oxen the wowzer upset the wagon, and the woman suffered a broken leg. An old man told me that the Indians claimed wowzers never killed a human being except by accident, and were never known to eat human flesh. The wowzer disliked the smell of human habitations, and never came near houses except when driven by hunger.

People who live in Arkansas generally attribute the big-cat stories to Missourians, or Oklahomans, or Texans. There is a general feeling that Texans in particular are inclined to exaggerate everything, at least everything in Texas. One finds many allusions to this tendency in print. The *Arkansas Gazette* [13] commented editorially: "Two lions that escaped in Texas nearly got away, and no wonder. Texans who saw them probably thought they were house cats."

In central Missouri there are tales of the great gally-

[12] *Folk Tales of Missouri*, pp. 121–123.　　[13] Jan. 2, 1948.

wampus, described as a kind of amphibious panther, which leaps into the water and swims like a colossal mink. These creatures are supposed to kill livestock sometimes, but a gally-wampus never attacks human beings unless he is cornered or "some damn fool gits to crowdin' him." One man told me that his grandfather's corn patch near Jefferson City, Missouri, was ruined by a gally-wampus, which "come down the creek so fast that he couldn't stop at the Big Bend, an' skidded right on down the valley through the cornfields." The old man went on to explain: "Of course it was high water, or maybe a big wind, that flattened the corn thataway. But Grandpap always said it was the gally-wampus done it. The gally-wampus was kind of a joke, in them days."

G. H. Pipes, of Reeds Spring, Missouri, tells me that the old-timers up on Roark Creek say the valley is full of wampus-cats. There really are some bobcats in that region. I saw a big one that Del Taylor killed near James River in 1945. The Ozark bobcat, also known as the bay lynx, seldom weighs more than thirty pounds, and never more than forty. Even where they are abundant, bobcats are rarely seen by human beings and are certainly not dangerous to human life. But Pipes says that the wampus-cat is something else again, much larger and of most uncertain temper. In his book *Strange Customs of the Ozark Hillbilly*,[14] Pipes mentions the wampus, but says merely that it is "a bloodthirsty animal of some kind, found only in the wildest sections of the Ozarks."

A man who worked in the timber near Waldron, Arkansas, told me that the lumbermen down that way were always joking about the whistling wampus, also known as the whistler. This was supposed to be an immense black cat with supernatural intelligence, which lured woodsmen to

[14] Pages 3–4.

their doom by whistling at them from dark cedar thickets. When a timber worker was asked where he had been or required to account for an unexplained absence, he answered that he'd been out hunting the whistler. Another fellow in the same vicinity said that lumbermen all over the country belong to a secret society called Hoo-Hoo and that the name represents the beguiling cry of the whistling wampus. According to the guidebook *Arkansas* (1941, p. 214) the "Concatinated Order of Hoo-Hoo" was organized at Gurdon, Arkansas, in 1892. Old newspaper files tell of a national convention held by the Order of Hoo-Hoo in Pine Bluff, Arkansas, January 29, 1906. A street parade was followed by a banquet at the Hotel Truelock, where "twenty-three Kittens were initiated and the degree of Black Cat was bestowed upon them."

When I heard a man near Southwest City, Missouri, telling some children about the whistling whoo-hoo, I supposed it was identical with the whistling wampus that hollers hoo-hoo at lumbermen in Arkansas, but this is not the case. The whistling whoo-hoo is not a cat-varmint at all, but some kind of supernatural cyclone. It looks like an ordinary tornado, but is really a vast gaseous demon which enjoys destroying people in wholesale lots. The old folks allege that the whoo-hoo story is of Indian origin, but the Indians whom I interviewed say that they never heard of any such nonsense.

It is said that the hickelsnoopus and the ring-tailed tooter are members of the wampus or hoo-hoo family, enormous cats which go screaming through the forests at night. But I have been unable to get any definite information about these creatures.

In Johnny Kling's place in Kansas City they used to tell big stories about the cross-eyed crud, which was some kind of monster found in the Missouri River. Years later, according to the Kansas City *Star* [15] the name was applied to a comic fish-bait fabricated by L. J. Townsley and Frank DeCou. About 1900 the miners around Joplin spun tales about darby-hicks and moogies, but these were supposedly nocturnal varmints, and I have not been able to get any light on them. May Kennedy McCord [16] says that people at Granby, Missouri, used some strange words in the old days. Ask a hunter if he'd killed anything, and he might answer: "Oh, three mogies an' a geek-squaw."

Another mythical varmint often included in an unsuccessful hunter's bag is the chaw-green; it resembles a bear, they say, but has a long tail striped like a barber-pole. The chaw-green is alleged to steal tobacco, which it chews and spits like a man. Also known as a tobacco thief is the bear-behind, which has hindquarters like a bear, but a head which resembles that of a certain Missouri congressman; the name of this creature is a kind of pun on bare-behind, and there are several allegedly funny stories about it.

At Forsyth, Missouri, I heard some old-timers joking about a fish hound, but I paid little attention. In other sections of the country a fish hound means a very ardent fisherman, or sometimes a fish warden who goes snooping about checking licenses and creel limits. Also, I have heard stories of dogs trained to plunge into the water and catch suckers in the shoaling season, and these dogs might well be called fish hounds. The boys at Forsyth, however, were speaking of a mythical varmint usually mentioned by anglers who come home without any fish. "There ain't no bass *here* nowadays," said one man peevishly. "The fish hound must have cleaned 'em out." A fish hound is neither human nor canine, but a hybrid creature with feathers on its back and fur underneath. Some say it's a cross between an otter and

[15] March 22, 1936.
[16] Springfield, Missouri, *Leader and Press,* June 4, 1942.

some large fish-eating bird, others that it is sired by a mink and dammed by a di-dapper. A di-dapper is a common diving bird, a kind of grebe.

My old friend John Wickware, of Pittsburg, Kansas, was talking with a guide identified only as "Snazzy" on one of the James River floats. Snazzy was describing a peculiar fish that some tourist had caught. Nobody on the river had ever seen anything quite like it. It weighed about three pounds and was taken on a plug. The funny thing about this fish was that there were scales on one side of the body, rather like those of carp, but the other side was covered with smooth skin like that of a catfish. "I reckon it was what you'd call a bastard cat," said Snazzy. Whatever the name, the creature is probably related to the fish hound of Forsyth.

Most of the backwoods yarn-spinners have something to say about the side-hill hoofer. According to one common version of the tale, the hoofer is similar to a beaver in appearance, but very much larger, about the size of a yearling calf. It lives in a burrow on some steep hillside. This animal always runs around the hill in the same direction, since the legs on one side of its body are much longer than those on the other side. If by any accident the hoofer falls down into the flat country it is easily captured, since on level ground it cannot walk or run at all. The female lays eggs as big as water buckets, and one egg will furnish breakfast for twenty-five men. "But they taste kind of strong," an old man said soberly. Oscar Ward, a deer-hunter from Kansas, told me privately that the real Ozark hoofer has two big grabhook claws on its tail, so it can hang to the crest of a ridge and rest its legs.

Hawk Gentry, of Galena, Missouri, remarked that the side-hill hoofer is "kind of like a kangaroo, only built sideways." Gentry says that some of them run around the hill

clockwise, the others anti-clockwise, and there's an awful
fight when the two varieties meet; they can't easily dodge
one another, for the hoofer can only move *around* the hill,
and goes up or down by means of long gradual curves. In
other words, a hoofer can run rapidly on one level, but it's
difficult for him to gain or lose altitude. These creatures
sometimes attack men, just as a bull does, although they
feed only upon vegetable matter. It is easy for a man to
avoid the hoofer's attack, since he need only walk straight
uphill or straight downhill for a few steps. They say that
when a hoofer falls over on its side it is unable to get up,
and just lies there and screams until it starves to death.
Many are killed by falling off hillsides, and I have heard of
one particular hollow in Marion County, Arkansas, which
is half full of hoofer bones.

There are old tales also of the side-hill slicker and the
side-hill walloper, but I have been unable to learn much
about these animals. It may be that they are identical with
the side-hill hoofer.

Another of these side-hill stories concerns the baldknob
buzzard, an enormous vulture which they say was formerly
common in White County, Arkansas. The man who told
me this one is a resident of St. Louis, but he had the tale
from his grandfather who lived near Bald Knob, Arkansas.
The bird was much larger than the turkey-buzzard or the
black vulture, and must have been something like the condor
of the California mountains. But the outstanding feature of
the baldknob buzzard is that it had only one functioning
wing, the other being rudimentary. Because of this disability,
the bird was always a little out of balance and could fly
in one direction only. It always circled the hilltops from
left to right. "Do you suppose your grandfather really believed all that about the baldknob buzzard?" I asked. My
informant looked a bit shocked. "Believe that stuff? Of

course not. It was just one of those old stories. But he always *acted* as if he believed it. That was part of the joke, you see."

A half-witted boy near Rolla, Missouri, rushed into the crossroads store to report a wild turkey "big as a cow," that ate up ten acres of corn in one evening. The village loafers were delighted, and began to elaborate upon the boy's story. A few days later, it was said that the big turkey was finally caught in a bear-trap baited with two bushels of popcorn. The great bird uprooted the post to which the trap was attached, but the woods were full of hunters by this time, and the turkey was riddled with bullets before it could get under way. Butchered like a steer, it weighed 150 pounds to the quarter, 600 pounds altogether. The women who picked it got feathers enough to fill seven bedticks, and old man Suggs used the quills to pipe water from the spring to his new barn. Two of the local strong men ruptured themselves trying to pull the wishbone, but they never even cracked it. An old settler kept that pulley-bone for many years, and it is said that he used it as a yoke for breachy steers, to keep them from busting through the fence. This is the story as I heard it in 1934. God only knows how the Phelps County whackers have dressed it up nowadays.

Over at West Plains, Missouri, there used to be a story about a very large bird, known as the giasticutus. Some of the old settlers said that it was the invention of a bunch of jokers in St. Louis; others thought that Mark Twain had something to do with it. One man told me that it all began in an anecdote related by Eugene Field when he was very drunk one night in the Planters' Hotel. Whatever its origin, there is no doubt that some country folk believed the tale. Only a few years ago there were men and women still alive who claimed to have seen the monster, which had a wingspread of about fifty feet. It was a bird of prey, like a prodigious chicken-hawk, with a great boat-like beak and a habit of carrying off full-grown cattle. But all this happened so long ago, I was told, that one cannot obtain any definite facts about the giasticutus today.

A man in Chicago wrote me at length about his experience with the giasticutus in Christian County, Missouri, many years ago. He says he used to be a college professor in Missouri, and repeats the story of a man named Moorhouse who lived at a place called Windy City, somewhere near Sparta, Missouri. Walking in his pasture one Sunday, Moorhouse found a black feather fourteen feet long, with a quill as thick as a man's leg. The professor declares that he has "seen and hefted" this feather, which is now fastened with baling-wire to the rafters of a certain hay-barn near Highlandville, Missouri. I used to know some people in that neighborhood, and I queried them very cautiously on this subject. But not one of them had ever heard of the giasticutus, or the man named Moorhouse, or the fourteen-foot feather.

A few giasticuti have been reported from Greene County, Missouri, but they were comparatively small. Floyd A. Yates, in a pamphlet called *Chimney Corner Chats* [17] tells of a hawk twenty-four feet from tip to tip, which carried off a yearling calf. A pretty big bird, all right, but less than half the size of the giasticutus of Howell County. A yearling calf is quite a load, but a 1,600-pound Harlan bull is something else again.

I have not heard the giasticutus story from the windy-spinners in Carroll County, Arkansas, but have reason to believe that such tales are still current here. In 1946 a newspaperman from New Jersey came to see me in Eureka Springs, and asked if it were true that some chicken-hawks in this region have a wingspread of sixteen feet. He said

[17] Springfield, Missouri, 1944, p. 4.

he had heard some farmers discussing such a bird at a wagon yard near his hotel. I suggested that the story was probably told for his benefit, but the poor fellow did not think so. "Those chaps never even glanced at me," he said earnestly. "They were talking among themselves, all about crops and the like." Finally I said flatly that there are no sixteen-foot hawks anywhere in the world, and let it go at that. The man thanked me and went his way, but I'm afraid he was still inclined to believe the whopper he had "overheard" in the wagon yard.

As recently as April 25, 1948, according to a United Press dispatch, an enormous bird was sighted at Alton, Illinois, just across the river from St. Louis. Walter F. Siegmund, a retired Air Force colonel, told reporters that it looked about the size of a small pursuit plane. E. M. Coleman said it was flying at about 500 feet, and was so big that it cast a shadow over his house and that of a neighbor at the same time. "I thought at first it was a glider," said Coleman. "Then I saw it flap its wings. It would soar for a time and then flap. It appeared to be gray and black in color, and was much larger than any bird I've ever seen." Several other persons near Alton saw the big bird, but their descriptions did not differ essentially from that given by Siegmund and Coleman. The United Press story did not mention the giasticutus, and it may be that the people in Alton never even heard the name. But the item was carried by many Missouri and Arkansas papers, and I imagine that many a second-growth hillbilly thought of the old giasticutus legend when he read his paper that morning.

Every country boy knows that even the timid little screech-owl will attack human beings under certain conditions. To one who has seen this little bird tearing at a man's face, the idea of a great horned owl following its example is alarming. Tales of giant man-eating owls have been associated with Hemmed-In Holler, an almost inaccessible valley near Compton, Arkansas. A farmer named Henderson, who lives near the head of the Holler, discounted these yarns. He once killed a horned owl which measured six feet from tip to tip, and doesn't believe they grow any bigger. But in many wild, isolated places one hears of enormous booger-owls with a wingspread of ten or twelve feet, so bold as to carry off lambs, calves, dogs or even children. When Don West [18] moved his family into a desolate hollow near Winslow, Arkansas, the natives tried to discourage him. "Certainly I knew," he writes a bit uneasily, "that owls do not eat children as some wags would have me believe." The old-timers are not so sure about this. Eagles and owls do kill turkeys and even lambs, so perhaps a big owl *could* carry off a baby.

Frank Payne, an old-time guide at Galena, Missouri, had several good stories about the galoopus, a big black eagle which nested in the bluffs over the James River. This bird lays square eggs, since ordinary eggs would roll to destruction before they could be incubated. Frank told me that in the early days he and W. D. Mathes used to gather galoopus eggs by the dozen, boil them very hard, and paste playing-cards neatly on the sides. Mathes operated the float-trip company in those days, and Frank sold the eggs to the tourists for poker-dice. One of Frank's cronies said the galoopus was so big that its shadow wore a trail in the stony soil of Barry County, Missouri, almost paralleling the gravel road now called Highway 44. Payne himself would not vouch for this. "The trail's there, all right," said he, "but I ain't sure the galoopus is responsible. Maybe the Injuns done it, for all I know."

In one of the gaudy rooming houses on Central Avenue, in Hot Springs, Arkansas, I met an old gentleman named

[18] *Broadside to the Sun*, p. 32.

Barnes, who spoke of the legendary whiffle-bird, which always flies backward in order to keep the dust out of its eyes. Some damn' fools call it the guffel-bird, the old man added, but that is provincial or dialectic. May Kennedy McCord [19] writes: "Down in my neck of the woods they are always talking about the whiffle-bird, the bird that flies backwards because he doesn't give a whoop where he lights."

Leather Standridge, veteran river-guide who lives in Stone County, Missouri, used to tell tourists about the ponjureen, a kind of brant which feeds on wild pepper-berries in Mexico and Central America. This fowl returns to Canada in the spring, and always flies backward as it passes over the Ozarks. If anybody asks why it flies back-ward, Leather explains with a great show of reluctance that the ponjureen must fly that way in order to cool its posterior, burnt up on them damn' pepper-berries.

In some sections a mythical goose or swan which flies backward is known as the bogie-bird or booger-bird. The idea is that the bogie-bird doesn't care where it is going, but wants to see where it has been. Mary Elizabeth Mahnkey, of Mincy, Missouri, wrote me (April 4, 1945) that "a boy near Mincy is nicknamed Bogie, and his brother said he was named after the bogie bird."

Related to the ponjureen and the bogie-bird is the fillyloo crane, which not only flies backward but upside down to boot. A schoolmaster at Cotter, Arkansas, told me that the fillyloo's nest is built upside down, too; the eggs are lighter than air, he said, and if one is pushed out of the nest it rises like a balloon and is soon lost to view. Some old settlers talk of the gillygoo bird which flies upside down for one reason or another, but I believe it is identical with the fillyloo crane. A lady in Fayetteville, Arkansas, remarked to me that

[19] *KWTO Dial,* Springfield, Missouri, Oct., 1946, p. 3.

some water-birds really do fly upside down, and when I doubted this she showed me an article by Edwin Tearle in the *Ladies' Home Journal* [20] which states that in Florida "the great wood ibis, America's only stork, has been observed to go sailing along for hundreds of yards upside down." Well, it may be so. A strange wader appeared at Roaring River Park near Cassville, Missouri, in September, 1936, and the local bird-watchers identified it as a wood ibis. I asked them about this, and they described the bird in great detail. But nobody said anything about its flying upside down.

The fishermen in Taney County, Missouri, still tell tourists about the clew-bird, that sticks its bill in a gravel bar and whistles loudly through its rectum. "It looks like a crane, only bigger," one old settler remarked. "Mostly it sets its bill solid in them gravels, an' then spins round like a top, so fast you cain't tell what color it is." My friend Allen Rose, of Springfield, Missouri, who used to direct float trips on the James and White rivers, says that his guides called this creature the milermore bird, because its whistle can be heard for a mile or more.

Along the western border of Arkansas the milermore bird is apparently unknown, but many old-timers remember the noon-bird, said to inhabit the Kiamichi Mountains of Oklahoma. It whistles like a fire engine exactly at noon, hence the name. Some enthusiasts claim that it blows a reveille at 5 A.M., and even a curfew at 9 P.M., but these additions to the tale are frowned upon by the best story-tellers.

I have heard some mention also of the waw-waw bird, the thunder-bird, the yow-ho bird, and the toodalong buzzard, but they are only names to me. I have been unable to find anybody who can describe their characteristics or way of life.

[20] Feb., 1947, p. 152.

Some of the tales about aquatic monsters are more alarming than any of the bird stories. At a certain fish-camp near Branson, Missouri, the guides used to talk about an island that suddenly appeared in Lake Taneycomo, just after a great storm. At the same time a strange rhythmic rise and fall of the waters occurred. Every two or three minutes the water level would suddenly rise about four feet, then recede slowly. Some boatmen who investigated the matter discovered that the new island was really a gigantic turtle. Every time the monster breathed, the waters rose and fell. This story came to me at Columbia, Missouri, and I drove down to the lake to see about it, but the turtle was gone when I arrived. George Hall told me privately that Captain Bill Roberts, of Rockaway Beach, had killed the great reptile with a harpoon, and was serving the meat to his guests, who thought it was bootleg venison. But George Hall was a great joker, and I don't believe that Captain Bill had anything to do with the disappearance of the Taneycomo turtle.

Will Rice [21] recalls a turtle killed in the Buffalo River near his home at St. Joe, Arkansas, which "made a meal for forty families, with two barrels of soup left over." An even larger turtle in the same vicinity swallowed a mule that was swimming the river; when this monster was shot four years later, the mule shoes were found in its stomach. Really warmed up by this time, Rice goes on to tell of a big turtle that got under a thirty-ton power crane used in building a bridge and carried the whole business upstream on its back. The man who was operating the crane saved his life by jumping onto a gravel bar.

Stories of big turtles are not new in the Ozark country. The Reverend D. A. Quinn, a Catholic missionary who worked in Arkansas in the 1870's [22] is quoted as saying that

[21] *Arkansas Democrat*, April 11, 1948.
[22] *Heroes and Heroines of Memphis*, p. 265.

along the railroad between Memphis and Little Rock he saw "mud turtles, some *as long and wide as an ordinary door,* wallowing in the mire." According to *Ozark Life* [23] a man named Messinger caught a turtle in the Black River, in Arkansas, that weighed 186 pounds; it was taken alive, and shipped to a zoo in Indianapolis. The biggest turtle I ever saw in this region was a snapper killed by Jess Lewellan and Wilfred Berry, in White River, near Hollister, Missouri, in 1936. It was nearly four feet long, and they said it weighed 70 pounds. Jim Owen, of Branson, Missouri, exhibited the shell of this turtle in his store for several years.

From the earliest times there have been tales of big bullfrogs in the Ozarks. Captain Jean François Dumont de Montigny [24] records that in what is now Arkansas he captured a frog two feet long and 18 inches thick, weighing 36 pounds. It bellowed like a calf, he says, but could not jump at all because of its great weight. De Montigny reports another frog, even larger, but did not set down its exact weight and measurements.

More than a hundred years after Captain de Montigny's time, hardy Arkansawyers were telling of a pioneer whose oxen were killed by the Indians. Desperate because the plowing must be done without delay, this man yoked up a team of big bullfrogs. They worked pretty well, although they would jump and miss a thirty-foot span sometimes, while the plow and the cursing plowman were lifted clear off the ground. But by plowing the field both ways, most of the unbroken spots were caught the second time around. Plowing was no job for an old man, in them days.

A boatman on White River once sold me a mess of very large frog-legs. I remarked upon their phenomenal size, but the man replied that the really big frogs had been killed off

[23] Nov., 1927, p. 7.
[24] *Mémoires historiques sur la Louisiane,* II, 264–268.

years ago. "When I was a young-un," said he, "the croakers in these here bottoms was big as full-grown steers. We used to butcher 'em just like hogs, an' salt 'em down for winter. They was so God-awful big we had to slice up their legs like a quarter of beef, an' cut through the bone with a bucksaw. When they got to bellerin' of a night, they'd rattle the winder-glass ten mile off. Them big 'uns could jump two hundred yards, easy. I've saw 'em jump one hundred yards, straight up in the air, to ketch a chicken-hawk."

I asked a storekeeper near Calico Rock, Arkansas, if he had ever seen frogs as big as oxen. "Well," he said slowly, "I reckon they was as *heavy* as steers, but not so tall. They was built kind of chunky an' low to the ground. I recollect Pappy killed one once. We just chopped off one hind leg an' drug it home, an' let the carcass lay there for the buzzards."

Will Rice [25] tells of a man on Buffalo River who "grabbed a big frog by the leg. It jumped clear across the river with him hanging on, so that he had to walk a half-mile upstream to a shoal where he could wade back." Marion Hughes [26] was inclined to minimize everything in the state, but even he admits that near Horatio, Arkansas, "there was bull frogs that you could hear crocking for three miles." *Crocking* is the way he spelled it, too. As recently as 1949 [27] game-warden Rayburn Brooks of Maries County, Missouri, investigated a report that a local fisherman had killed a bull-frog weighing 21 pounds. He learned that the frog had been caught in 1948 instead of 1949. Also, he writes, it turned out to be "twenty pounds of bull and one pound of frog."

Many fantastic stories have been told about the Lake-of-the-Ozarks country, but one of the wildest broke in June,

[25] Kansas City *Weekly Star*, Sept. 11, 1946.
[26] *Three Years in Arkansaw*, p. 16.
[27] *Missouri Conservationist*, April, 1949, p. 15.

1935. Five men in two motorboats came tearing into port, white-faced and trembling. They had seen a gigantic animal, with one great eye like a punchbowl of green fire, a snake-like neck that rose twenty feet above the surface of the water, and a long red tongue that crackled like sassafras wood a-burnin'. One fellow was close enough to note the thick greenish scales on the creature's head and swore that its horny neck was studded with knobs the size and color of new basket balls. Charles Love, a deputy circuit clerk at the courthouse in Kansas City, took a party of armed men out in his launch. They searched the lake for miles, firing with rifles and revolvers at suspicious-looking objects in the water. But they didn't find the "Camden county sea-serpent." Love finally expressed the opinion that the monster was nothing more than a huge log, with one projecting branch which turned upward as the log rolled over in the current. But men who had seen the thing scoffed at this rational explanation. There are sober men in Missouri today who affirm that they encountered the varmint at close range, and others who saw it at a distance, "a-churnin' up the water like a God damn' steamboat," as one bug-eyed fisherman told me. I once thought I saw something like a young submarine myself, near Warsaw, Missouri, in the summer of 1936. But I could never be quite sure of it. The thing was quite a distance off, and we were all a little drunk that day, anyhow.

The Arkansas newspapers gave a great play to the "behemoth" which appeared in White River, early in June, 1937. A farmer named Bramlett Bateman rushed into the town of Newport, Arkansas, crying that there was a whale in the river "as big as a boxcar, like a slimy elephant without any legs." A lot of people hurried out to look, and several reputable citizens declared that they saw the creature. Newspaper reporters described the beast at great length, but the press photographers drew a blank. I drove down there myself and stared into the river for hours, but saw nothing but a lot of muddy water. The Newport Chamber of Commerce combined with Bateman to fence in the place, and then charged twenty-five cents admission. Signs were put up along the roads for miles around, THIS WAY TO THE WHITE RIVER MONSTER.

Groups of local sportsmen, armed with rifles, patrolled the banks day and night. These fellows wanted to kill the monster with dynamite, but the gamewardens wouldn't allow it, saying that the Arkansas law permits explosives to be used only to recover a human body. After a week of wrangling, Charles B. Brown, a professional diver, was employed to "beard the behemoth in its lair." This enterprise was sponsored by the Chamber of Commerce. They built a dance platform on the bank, with fiddlers and banjo-pickers from all over Jackson County. Local people sold soft drinks, sandwiches, and fruit. A public address system was set up, so that the crowd could hear a round-by-round account of the battle between the diver and the monster at the bottom of the river.

Finally Brown, wearing his diver's helmet and carrying an eight-foot harpoon, descended into the water. "There are some fish down there," said he, "also a lot of weeds, sunken logs, big rocks and pieces of old boats, but no sign of a monster." Later in the day he made another descent, which was equally fruitless. The crowd still watched the river and danced and drank far into the night. Brown dived again on the following day, but the crowd was pretty thin, and the refreshment concessions did very little business. About noon the Chamber of Commerce gave up the battle, and Bram Bateman went back to farming.

An Associated Press dispatch from Little Rock, dated Feb. 23, 1940, quotes Secretary D. N. Graves of the Arkansas Game and Fish Commission, who now believes that the "monster" was an overturned scow. It appears that a certain local shell-digger found a valuable bed of mussels at that point, very large shells used for making knife-handles and the like. Fearing that other diggers would muscle in on his discovery, this man sank the old scow and hitched it to a complicated set of wires. At one end the wires were fastened to the submerged roots of a tree; at the other end they led to a hiding-place behind some bushes on the south bank of the river.

The story goes that the old man started the tale of a monster in the river himself [said Graves]. When one or two persons would come down there, he would hide in the bushes and pull the "monster" up for a few minutes. But if a crowd was on hand, the monster didn't appear, because the shell-digger was afraid of being discovered. All this time the old man was working at night, digging the shells. Due to the crowds, the situation got clear out of hand, so one night he slipped in and cut the wires, letting the monster ramble on down the river. By that time—about two weeks—he had the shells all dug, anyhow.

The few persons who actually saw the monster noted that it had "hide like a wet elephant," and Secretary Graves says that the moss-covered bottom of a scow would have this appearance. Graves told reporters that he got this explanation from a filling-station attendant in Newport, who had it from the old shell-digger himself. "The story has the ring of truth," said Graves, "and I am convinced that it is true."

The filling-station story which convinced Mr. Graves does not altogether satisfy me. Awaiting further light, I am content to string along with the agnostics for the present. Let the White River monster join the distinguished company of the jimplicute, the gowrow, the snawfus, the kingdoodle, the giasticutus, the whistling wampus, and other fabulous critters that live only in the tales that are told around campfires in the big timber.

4 Rich soil and big vegetables

THE OZARK STORY-TELLER is always an extremist, and he will not walk in the middle of the road. The same man who delights in telling strangers how steep and rocky and altogether worthless his farm is, will be found the very next day boasting of its astounding fertility and describing the incredible crops that he has produced. Stories of the first type are the despair of realtors and Chamber-of-Commerce boosters, because nobody would buy such poor land. And the other tales are almost as bad, since outsiders regard them as a kind of caricature of the claims made by the land-office men, who expect their own whoppers to be taken seriously.

In contrast to the accounts of bumblebee corn that one hears in some parts of the Ozark country, there are extravagant tales of cornstalks as big as trees, with ears and grains in proportion. A character known as Billy Mansfield used to brag about the astounding productivity of his rocky little corn patch, vaguely located somewhere south of Pineville, Missouri. "Why, gentlemen," he cried, "I've growed cornstalks thirty foot high, with seven or eight big ears on every stalk. Instead of a tassel there was a round dingus like a gourd, an' when I busted one open there was about a quart of shelled corn in it, for seed. It run seven hundred an' fifty bushels to the acre, an' maybe twenty bushel of seed-corn in the gourds." Mansfield attributed all this to the fact that his land was fertilized by the dung of the mythical galoopus bird. "That ridge just below my house," said he, "was the biggest galoopus-roost in this whole country, 'cordin' to the old-timers."

My old neighbor Frank Hembree, sometime mayor of Galena, Missouri, once remarked that in the Horse Creek valley the corn grew so tall that the dogs treed coons right in the field, and the hunters would climb up a cornstalk just as if it was a white oak tree. And a few miles east of Hembree's bailliwick, a loafer was arrested for stealing an extension-ladder forty feet long from the village fire department. This man told the authorities that he just borrowed the ladder, so as to pick a mess of roastin' ears for his family.

"Mirandy" Bauersfeld, who used to live in Jasper County, Missouri, wrote me (Oct. 18, 1946) that her uncle Leander owned some of the finest farm land in the Ozarks. He raised some awful good stands of corn, she said. "One year the corn growed so high that it shut off the sun entirely, so the house was plumb dark twenty-four hours a day." And Ad Kirkendall, of Stone County, Missouri, claimed his corn grew so tall it was like a dense pine forest, only darker; you could see lightnin'-bugs in there at high noon, and the big owls hooted all day. Bob Burns once declared [1] that corn near Van Buren, Arkansas, "grows so high, year after year, that the moon has to go around by way of Missouri."

Nancy Clemens tells one she learned from her grandfather in Cedar County, Missouri, about the fabulous crop of 1887. The corn grew so big that farmers used lineman's climbers to get up on the stalks, and they cut off the ears with handsaws. One young fellow climbed all day, but darkness overtook him before he reached the first ear. During the night there came a heavy frost, and the poor chap nearly froze to death. The frost weakened the stalk somehow, and just before daylight it crashed down like a falling tree. The boy wasn't hurt much, but he lit away over in

[1] *Liberty*, April 11, 1942, p. 21.

the Creek Nation, about where the city of Tulsa is today. The folks had to send him fourteen dollars to pay his fare back home.

In some Oklahoma versions of this yarn the boy is marooned on the tall cornstalk for two or three weeks. "Herby would have starved," an old man in Tahlequah told me, "only we sent him up a mess of goober-peas every evenin'." When I asked how they managed this, the old fellow grinned wolfishly. "We loaded 'em into a goose-gun," said he, "an' shot 'em up to Herby."

Another variant has it that the boy climbed up the stalk in dry weather, but was unable to return because a sudden shower made the corn grow faster than he could descend. The boy's father tried to fell the stalk with an axe, but the damned thing was growin' so fast that he couldn't hit it twice in the same place. Two men came running with a crosscut saw, but they only pulled it once through the rind when the saw was wrenched from their hands and disappeared into the darkness overhead. When I heard this story in Russellville, Arkansas, in August, 1934, the boy was still aloft. He was living on green corn without salt, and had thrown down more than four bushels of cobs already. "If Tommy can just hold out till frost," a neighbor told me, "the damn' thing is bound to stop growin', an' we'll surely be able to git him down somehow."

In Gastley County, Missouri [writes John Langdon Heaton] [2] I once saw the corn growing to such an unprecedented height, and the stalks so exceedingly vigorous, that nearly every farmer stacked up, for winter firewood, great heaps of cornstalks, cut into cordwood length by power saws run by the threshing engines. One man, Barney Gregory, took advantage of the season to win a fortune by preparing cornstalks for use as telegraph poles.

[2] Botkin, *Treasury of American Folklore*, p. 599.

This is a good story in the real Ozark tradition, and the fact that there is no Gastley County in Missouri is quite beside the point.

Near Carthage, Missouri, it is said that the corn grows so big that the farmers shuck it right in the field and load it without any box on the wagon. They just roll the ears up on the running gears with canthooks. Some fellows claim that one ear of corn will last two horses a month. Whole crews of men go out with crosscut saws and axes to cut up fodder. The smaller cobs are soaked in creosote and used for fence posts. As for the big ones, they notch 'em at the ends like pine logs, and build cabins for the tourist-camps. The lumber company cut up some cornstalks and tried to sell 'em for telephone poles, but they wouldn't do; after they stood in the weather for a few months, the rind got so hard that the linemen couldn't stick the spurs of their climbers into it.

"The corn grows so God-awful big in Benton County," said W. Y. Shackleford, of Fayetteville, Arkansas, "that we don't use the cobs for cookwood, on account nobody cain't git 'em in the stove. We do burn 'em in the fireplace sometimes, by sawin' each cob in two, an' then splittin' the pieces into four-foot sticks with the choppin' axe."

Will Rice, of St. Joe, Arkansas, once reported [3] that "two tall cornstalks were blown across a neighbor's barn, smashing it in and killing three cows during a high wind last week." Rice told this as a tall tale, of course. But some things that really happen in his neck of the woods are almost as hard to swallow.

The owner of a roadside tavern in McDonald County, Missouri, used to do a little farming on the side. "One year the corn growed so damn' big," said he, "that I couldn't git

[3] Kansas City *Star*, Sept. 4, 1940.

even a nubbin through the corncrib door, an' the stock couldn't do nothin' with it. We had to shell it for the critters; just prized the grains apart with a crowbar, an' knocked 'em off the cob with a sledge-hammer. One night a feller drove in after dark, and told me to give his horses five ears of corn apiece. I tried to tell him it'd be too much, but he says nobody can tell him how to feed his own animals, and he had plenty of money to pay for it. So I got out my team, an' drug ten ears up to the barnlot with a log-chain. Took us three hours to do the job. Next mornin' one of them fine big horses was dead. 'Good Godamighty!' the feller hollered, 'you've done foundered my mare!' But she warn't foundered, 'cause she hadn't et nothin'. The first grain of corn she tackled had stuck in her throat, an' the poor critter had choked to death."

Not only does the corn in these fireside tales attain gigantic size, but there is often a phenomenal rapidity of growth. Gerstäcker [4] mentions his meeting with a settler in Arkansas who was known as "Lying" Bahrens. This fellow told Gerstäcker that "he had but a small tract of land, but it was the best and most fertile in the whole world; that he could grow everything on it except common garden beans, because the corn grows so fast that it drags the beans out of the earth!"

Gerstäcker heard that story in 1842, but the same corn-and-bean yarn was told in Carroll County, Arkansas, as recently as 1931. A few years ago, near Bentonville, Arkansas, I heard men speak soberly of corn which grew so fast that the roots were pulled right out of the ground, so that the stalk blew away or the plant perished for lack of moisture. One fellow said that he and his son worked twelve hours a day all through the growin' season, trying to pull the roots

[4] *Wild Sports in the Far West*, p. 154.

down and stick the ends back into crevices between the rocks. By this means they managed to save about one-fourth of the crop, he told me.

At Lanagan, Missouri, an honest husbandman declared that the soil in his backyard was so God damn' rich that when his woman "throwed shelled corn to the chickens they had to ketch it in the air, or go hungry. Whenever a grain touched the ground, it sprouted so fast that the stalk was a foot high before the chicken could git to it."

A county officer in Barry County, Missouri, owned a farm in the Flat Creek bottoms near Jenkins, which he declared was the richest land in the whole country. This man told me that he planted forty acres of corn in one day, and the stuff grew so fast that some of the stalks were higher than his head before dinner time. On the way back to the house, just at dusk, he picked an armful of prime roastin'-ears.

Colonel T. B. Thorpe [5] was telling some Yankees about the enormous corn which grew on his Arkansas farm.

The crop was overgrown and useless [he said] because the soil is too rich, and *planting in Arkansas is dangerous*. I had a good-sized sow killed in that same bottom-land. The old thief stole an ear of corn, and took it down where she slept at night to eat it. Well, she left a grain or two on the ground, and lay down on them; before morning the corn shot up, and the percussion killed her dead. I don't plant corn any more. Nature intended Arkansas for a hunting ground, and I go according to nature.

It is true that Colonel Thorpe was an extravagant story-teller who lived in the wilds of Arkansas more than a century ago. But similar tales are told today in the Ozark country, and not by backwoodsmen either. Casper Kilroy, writing in a journal published by the Department of Agriculture at the University of Missouri [6] tells the citizens that

[5] *Spirit of the Times*, March 27, 1841, pp. 43-44.
[6] *College Farmer*, April, 1947, p. 22.

about ten years ago the Agricultural Experiment Station sent a
new kind of fertilizer to a county agent in the Ozark country.
It was supposed to grow corn on a rock pile, and they wanted
him to try it out . . . This farmer took his hoe, filled his pockets
with seed corn, and took the sack of fertilizer to the field with
him. He dug a hole with the hoe, threw in a grain of corn, and
then a double handful of fertilizer. Things started happening.
That corn plant sprouted and was ten feet high before the
farmer could get out of the way . . . He ran for his axe to
chop the cornstalk down. By the time he got back the stalk was
six feet across at the base, and he couldn't chop fast enough to
keep up with it . . . The farmer made another trip home, got
his log chain, snared the chain around the cornstalk, and it
pinched itself to death.

When the big stalk fell, according to Kilroy's story, one
of the ears struck end-on and made a hole in the ground
thirty feet deep. They say that hole is used as a cistern to
this day.

There is a pleasant rural atmosphere about Springfield,
Missouri, perhaps because so many of the citizens are trans-
planted hillbillies. But it is the biggest town in southern
Missouri, with a population of some sixty thousand. The
loafers in Springfield used to regard themselves as very
metropolitan, and visitors from smaller communities, particularly those south of the Arkansas border, were designated
as "apple-knockers" who had "come in on a load of pumpkins." It ain't true, ordinarily. Arkansawyers eat a few
pumpkins themselves, and feed the rest of 'em to the cattle.
But in 1932 there was an odd scarcity of pumpkins in south
Missouri. Pumpkins were selling for two cents a pound
wholesale, which was five times the price of corn. In November, 1932, farmers from Arkansas really did come a-ridin'
into Springfield on loads of pumpkins. I would never have
believed this, if I hadn't seen it myself.

Many pumpkin stories circulated around Springfield in
connection with the "famine" of 1932, but the only one I

remember now was credited to a fellow named Mansfield, who came from McDonald County, Missouri. "There's just one crop that you cain't raise on my land," he told the boys in the wagonyard, "an' that's punkins. I planted a little patch of punkins one year, an' the vines growed up an' filled the whole damn' valley level full, plumb to the tops of the ridges. It looked just like a high flat prairie, an' so thick the cattle couldn't find the creek. But there wasn't no punkins at all. The vines growed so dang fast they just wore the punkins out, a-draggin' 'em over the rocks."

Related to this is the story of the seed salesman, who claimed great things for a new variety of pumpkin he was pushing. "Plant them seeds in good rich dirt," said he, "an' you'll git the biggest punkins in the world! Yes, an' the fast-growin'est punkins, too!" Somebody objected mildly, saying that really big pumpkins always mature slowly and that pumpkins which grow rapidly never get very large. The salesman denounced this notion, saying that *his* pumpkins were both big and fast-growing. Developing this thesis, he declared that these new pumpkins were *all* big, not one runt in a patchful. "The vines grow so all-fired fast," said he, "that the little-uns is all knocked off!"

In W. R. Draper's *Arkansas the Wonder State* (p. 16) is a news item credited to Will Rice, of St. Joe, Arkansas.

John Byrd, whose migrating pumpkins caused some neighborhood disputes a few years ago when the vines wandered into neighboring fields, breaking down rail fences by growing big pumpkins on top of them and even blocking the water courses, now says his pumpkins will be used this year to move some heavy log graneries and barns, and the seed is now being planted around these buildings. As the pumpkins grow they will lift the buildings off the foundations and then the buildings can be rolled along as on ball-bearings.

At a party in Rolla, Missouri, an old friend was telling me about one Buck Hodge, who raised the liveliest crop of cucumbers ever seen in Phelps County. It seems that Buck planted five or six hills, then shouldered his hoe and started for the house. He heard a noise like thunder, gradually growing louder, although the sun was shining and the sky was clear. Suddenly he perceived that the trouble was in the cucumber patch behind him. Dirt and gravel flew high in the air, cucumber vines burst out of the ground and writhed about in all directions. Buck dropped the hoe and ran for his life, but the vines caught up with him before he could climb the fence. They sprang up all about him, and grew so high that he lost all sense of direction. Buck struggled and yelled for help, but the twisting tendrils held him fast. Desperate, he reached for his jack-knife, but a big cucumber was wedged into his pocket, so he could not get hold of the weapon. At this point the story-teller was called away by another guest, and I never did find out what happened to Buck Hodge.

Stories about gigantic potatoes are common, ever since the days of Colonel Thorpe,[7] who said that the potato hills on his Arkansas farm were so big that travelers mistook them for Indian mounds. Of the modern yarns, one of the best is attributed to Pogey Mahone, who lived not far from Little Rock. According to this tale, a potato grew so big it couldn't be dug nohow, so they built a new cabin over it, and cut a trapdoor in the kitchen floor. Whenever the kids began hollerin' for victuals, Pogey just climbed down through the trap and shoveled up a big chunk of 'tater. Mostly the family ate the stuff boiled or fried; it was only when they hankered for 'taters baked in the jackets that it became necessary to swap provender with the neighbors. The jacket on Pogey's 'tater was three feet thick, with bark on it like a hackberry tree, not suitable for cooking. That one potato lasted the Mahone family for fourteen years,

[7] Masterson, *Tall Tales of Arkansaw*, p. 58.

and when it was all gone the hole under the house made a fine big cellar.

Bob Burns [8] dressed up a tale that has been told in the Ozark country for more than half a century.

When I went out to the California Fair [says Bob], I saw the little puny Irish potatoes they had on exhibit. I called up an uncle of mine down home, and asked him to send out some Irish potatoes so I could exhibit 'em at the Fair. My uncle says, "How many potatoes you want?" I says, "Well, they only allow you to enter a hundred pounds of any one thing." My uncle said, "I wouldn't cut one of my potatoes in two for anybody." I asked him if he had any big sweet potatoes, and he said, "Yes, I've got one sweet potato here that's thirty-five feet long." And he said, "It woulda been longer, but one end of it growed over into the pigpen, and thirty-seven hogs have been livin' off of it all summer."

There is a story also of the Missouri farmer who grew a sweet potato so outrageous big that no attempt was made to dig it in the ordinary fashion. They had to grabble it out piecemeal, in fifty-pound chunks. The hole where they got out the first couple of tons looked as big as a stone quarry. One night the cow fell in, and by mornin' she had trompled up an' ruined more'n five hundred pounds of good sweet potater. The boys finally got a rope round her neck, an' drug her out with a wire-stretcher. Next day they built a five-rail fence round the 'tater, and three or four families was still usin' out of it, the last I heard. This tale was often credited to Will H. Green, a lawyer who lived in West Plains, Missouri, but I don't think Judge Green ever admitted that he was responsible for it.

Not far from Cape Fair, Missouri, a man told me that Bud Spurlock went up to Gentry Cave, where some "furriners" were digging bat-manure out of the cavern and selling it by the carload to florists in St. Louis. Bud carried

[8] *Liberty*, April 11, 1942, p. 21.

a pocketful of this magic fertilizer home. His woman had a sweet potater growing in a bottle of water, hung up in the kitchen. Just to see how the bat-manure worked, Bud put a little into the water with the sweet potater. That was just before bedtime. The 'tater growed so fast it busted the bottle in less than thirty minutes, and by morning the whole cabin was packed with a solid mass of vines. It was impossible for the Spurlocks to reach either door, but Bud kicked off a couple of boards at the back of the house and dragged his wife and kids to safety. He said later that it was only by God's own luck that they were able to get the children out alive.

Stories about sweet potatoes talking underground are well known in the Ozarks. One spectacled folklorist has suggested that they derive from European legends of vampires and the like. But I reckon they're just tall tales. Sallie Walker Stockard [9] announced her conviction that the soil of a certain potato patch in Jackson County, Arkansas, is the richest in the whole country. People passing this place heard a noise like distant thunder, or "like the grunting of well-fed swine," but which seemed to come from under the earth. One fellow finally lay down and put his ear to the ground. He could hear the sweet potatoes saying to each other: "Lay further, lay further, it's getting too *scrouged* in here." And Miss Stockard adds "That's the way potatoes grow in Arkansas."

Variants of this tale are applied to many valleys in Missouri as well as Arkansas. May Kennedy McCord, of Springfield, Missouri, used to tell about a farm where the ground was so hard that "you could hear the 'taters gruntin' half a mile off, a-tryin' to sprout." I heard another such story from Doc Keithley, in Taney County, Missouri. "Just put

[9] *History of Lawrence, Jackson, Independence and Stone Counties, Arkansas*, p. 190.

your ear to the ground, any good hot day," said Keithley. "You can just hear them 'taters a-grumblin' 'Git over! Make room!' "

A man near Pineville, Missouri, once declared that the sweet potatoes planted in his rocky little garden actually groan as they sprout. And another member of his family told me that the vegetables in a patch near the house made so much racket at night that the children couldn't hardly get a wink of sleep. Crossing this patch one night on an unrelated errand, I happened to think of the "talkin' 'tater" story. It was a warm night, right in the middle of the growin' season. So I lay down on the ground and listened for perhaps ten minutes. I did hear a sort of gentle rumbling in the ground, and two sharp little squeaks. But it must have been some animal, perhaps a mole or a shrew, or maybe some small rodent. I do not believe that the sweet potatoes had anything to do with it.

Some of the best windies are told for the truth by honest men, who have been "had on" by the old-timers. Karr Shannon [10] repeats the story that wild strawberries used to be so abundant along Strawberry River that "one could ride horseback only a short distance through the thick vines and the horse's legs would be bathed red with the juice from the berries." Shannon sets this down, not as a tall tale, but as a fact. To anybody who has gathered wild strawberries, however, it seems about as fantastic a story as any recorded by Colonel Thorpe, Marion Hughes, or even Bob Burns of Van Buren.

Our local tales of big watermelons always make the tourists laugh, but melons do grow pretty large in Arkansas. I have seen growing melons that looked as big as barrels, and was told that one of them would weigh about 150 pounds. A man near Hope, Arkansas, according to *Time* (June 22,

[10] *History of Izard County, Arkansas,* 1947, p. 3.

1936), raised a watermelon that weighed 195 pounds, and there are stories of much larger melons.

These big melons are grown for advertising purposes, to be exhibited at county fairs and watermelon festivals. The man who wants to raise a record melon leaves only one vine in the center of a large cleared space. He sets up brush arbors and slatted shelters to provide the proper amount of shade, and enriches the soil with special fertilizers. When the little melons appear he cuts them off the vine, all save one. This melon is force-fed through woolen wicks stuck into slits cut in the stem. The other end of each wick lies in a bowl containing a sugar solution or other liquid made up according to some secret formula. Sometimes growers inject fluids into the stem by means of syringes. Melons grown by such methods don't taste as good as an ordinary 25-pound watermelon, and there's no market for such monsters, anyhow. But they certainly astonish the tourists, and furnish splendid material for the story-tellers.

Avantus Green, of Little Rock, in a pamphlet boosting Arkansas and denouncing her detractors [11] says flatly that many melon-growers in Arkansas "feed all melons under 100 pounds to their swine." One prize watermelon was abandoned in the field, because the railroad did not furnish sufficient flatcars to ship it. "Left on the vine," writes Green, "it soured and burst, killing vegetation and animal life over a seven square mile area." The man who showed me this passage in Green's book adds the detail that a farmer, his commonlaw wife, and three small children were killed in the explosion, to say nothing of a herd of dairy cattle and other livestock. But maybe this is an exaggeration; Green himself just says "animal life" and lets it go at that.

The story of the exploding melon is not original with Green. I heard it near Noel, Missouri, about 1907 or 1908.

[11] *With This We Challenge*, p. 26.

A man named Groot, at Aurora, Missouri, told a similar tale
in 1940. "It got so all-fired hot one summer," said he, "that
our watermelons just swole up an' busted in the fields. Some
of them biggest ones roared like a cannon when they went
off. Killed buzzards away up in the air, the seeds just riddled 'em like swan-shot! People comin' along the road two
hundred yards away was wet to the skin, just plumb soaked
like they had been out in a hard rain!"

In the hills near Galena, Missouri, according to Frank
Payne, a ridge-runner grew a watermelon so big that it could
not be loaded on any wagon. Payne described the exact
method by which this monstrous fruit was fertilized and
cultivated, but his description would not pass the censors.
Finally, with the aid of his neighbors, the farmer hoisted the
great melon onto a platform made of logs. Then with two
sticks of dynamite he blasted a hole in the rear of the
melon, whereupon a great stream of water poured out and
flooded the whole place. Thus he was able to float the melon
down to Galena in its own juice, and anchored the raft
near the railroad bridge, just below where Jack Short's
house is now. He sawed the melon up into 100-pound chunks
and sold most of it to the tourists, but the whole village was
wet and sticky and full of flies all the rest of the summer.
The seeds of that big melon are still seen in old houses
around Carico and Blue Eye and Lampe and Oto and East
Elsey. The folks cover 'em with rag carpet and use them
for footstools and door-stops.

An old story went the rounds in Taney County, Missouri,
some years ago, about a farmer who raised a prize watermelon. Its weight was estimated at 800 pounds, but nobody
ever got a chance to weigh it. The farmer and his four
stalwart sons tried to roll it up to the highway, but their
combined strength couldn't budge it. Finally they got their
axes and cut it open right there in the patch. A great tor-

rent of water washed all five of 'em off their feet. The water flooded the whole valley, and some say it busted the dam near Forsyth, and drowned two of the Quackenbush boys. But serious-minded citizens of Forsyth have assured me that this is not true.

The radio comedians have not overlooked the big melon stories.

During the recent housing shortage [says Bob Burns] [12] it was nothing unusual to see families keeping house in half a canteloup. And down at Hope, Arkansas, I remember they had a bad drought one year and the water supply dried up. The Water & Power Company ran almost all summer on two leaky watermelons.

Tom Whittaker growed the biggest watermelon ever seen in Arkansas, according to the boys at a crossroads store near Mena. It was too big to be weighed, and the neighbors finally persuaded Tom that he ought to take it down to the State Fair. He started out with four yoke of oxen, and had a lot of trouble on the road, but finally got to Little Rock. When the judging began, Tom Whittaker's melon was nearly five feet long, bigger than any other melon on the ground. But the judges refused to give Tom first prize, because the big melon was too dark. "Too dark!" yelled Tom, who was in a bad humor anyway. "Hell, you damn' fools, that ain't no melon. We busted the melon when the wagon went off the road, just west of Owensville. That's just one of the seeds!"

A retired miner not far from Joplin, Missouri, raised such a big crop of melons that his hillside farm caved in, opening up two large limestone caverns. Perhaps it was just a landslide, or a cave-in due to old leadmines in the neighborhood, but the people who tell the tale insist that "it was them big watermelons done it." Some say that a level field sank two

[12] *Ford Times*, April, 1948, p. 18.

feet, from the sheer weight of melons. The owner of this melon patch was accustomed to raise canteloups for the local market, and often peddled them through the streets of a nearby town. Asked if he had made a good crop in 1942, he answered: "Vance, it took me two months just to count the money!"

There are many tales about fast-growing melon vines. I have heard one about a farmer who placed each growing melon in a little red wagon which he bought from Montgomery Ward & Company. This way, he figured, the melons could keep up with the rapidly spreading vines, and not be dashed to pieces on the rocky ground. The scheme worked pretty well, I was told, but the farmer had to spend all his profits for wagon repairs, new tires and axle grease.

The old folks tell several windies about monstrous turnips. In one harrowing tale a farmer put two big turnips into the cellar under his house. It was a mighty tight fit, but all would have gone well except that one of the turnips was not quite mature. During the night this turnip grew several feet thicker, so that the house was thrown off its foundation and rolled down the hill into the big road. The farmer escaped with a few fractures and abrasions, but his wife was killed. A man who visited the scene told me that a Ford car, parked in the front yard, was "mashed flat as a cow-chip" when the house rolled over on it.

A similar item is credited to Will Rice, of St. Joe, Ark. It appears that a farmer stored some turnips in a shed on the hillside above his house. In the night the turnips must have sprouted, because "the shed bursted and the turnips rolled down, knocked his chickens out of the roost, killed several, also one or two cows." Several other cows died shortly afterward, according to Rice's story, from eating too many of the turnips which were scattered all over the place.

A hillman told me about a gigantic turnip which he

grew near Fort Smith, Arkansas, in 1892. Something went wrong with the turnip patch that year, and only one plant matured. It was an unusually big one, but the man just let it alone, regarding the turnip crop as a total failure. Just before the first snowfall seven fine steers disappeared, and the farmer thought they had been stolen. Late in February he discovered that they had spent the winter inside that big turnip. "The damn' thing just growed till it filled the whole half-acre patch," said he, "an' them critters had et into it, just like it was a haystack!"

Some tale-tellers provide a kind of sequel to this big-turnip story. A blacksmith who has listened to the farmer's tale is reminded of the time he built a kettle for some Fort Smith Indians. It was so large that when he and his helper riveted the handle, working on opposite sides of the kettle, they were so widely separated that neither could hear the other's hammering. "For God's sake," cried the farmer, "what did them Injuns *want* with such a big kettle?" The blacksmith smiled. "Why, to cook them big turnips in," he answered smoothly.

A man who lived in the Big Red Apple belt near Rogers, Arkansas, was telling of a great crop he had once produced. "Them apples growed so big," said he, "that it only took four of 'em to make a dozen. We tried to turn 'em into cider, but the juice was so sweet it wouldn't ferment. Finally we just b'iled it down to syrup, an' sold it for long sweetenin'." Everything about this man's orchard was of enormous size, to hear him tell it. Even the wooly caterpillars, he declared, grew so ungodly big that the boys used to run 'em down with bear-dogs, an' killed 'em for the fur! Folks stretched the hides on the walls of their cabins, an' tanned 'em for laprobes. They was better than buffalo hides, he said, because the fur was so much longer an' thicker.

Melvin E. West, of Golden City, Missouri, told me a

good one about the big apples in the southern part of the state. It seems that West saw a CIDER FOR SALE sign, and stopped to buy some for the local FFA. They were going to serve it at a barn-warming and hayride. "Well," said the cider-mill man, "I sold all my cider last week, an' stored all the apples. But I reckon I can oblige you. How much cider do you want?" West replied that he needed about fifty gallons. "Young man," said the cider maker, "I don't mind hitchin' up the team an' wagon to bring apples up here to the press. I don't mind gettin' the press dirty, so I have to clean it again. But I'll be darned if I'm goin' to ruin a whole apple, just to get you fifty gallons of cider."

There are many tales of enormous trees and super-lumbermen. A fellow near Waldron, Arkansas, always maintained that he and his brother, back in the 1880's, had felled the biggest sycamore ever seen in Arkansas. "Me an' Jim chopped an' sawed from sun-up till dark, Sundays an' all, for three weeks before we cut through the trunk," he said. "An' when we finally got it cut, an' the damn' thing started to fall, it was about five o'clock in the evenin'. We run back four miles to git out of the way, an' then waited till it was plumb dark, but the top of that there tree hadn't hit the ground yet."

An aged foxhunter in Taney County, Missouri, once told me that there was a sycamore in the Bull Creek bottoms so unbelievable tall that no man in the world could see it all at once. It required four keen-eyed woodsmen, each looking as hard as he could, to discern the top of that tree in clear weather. Everybody laughed loudly at this, and the boys around the campfire seemed to feel that the old codger had "made it up" himself. But the yarn was well known in Arkansas more than a hundred years ago. The *Arkansas Gazette* (June 26, 1947) reprints the following from a Little Rock newspaper dated June 25, 1847: "It is said that the trees are so tall in Missouri that it takes two men and a boy to see the top of them. One looks till he is tired, and the other commences where he left off."

Another ancient wheeze, often paraphrased by the radio hillbillies [13] tells of a man who was driving a herd of cattle through Arkansas. They came to a stream which was too swift for swimming and too deep to ford. The herder picked out the biggest hollow sycamore he could find and felled it in such a way that the trunk spanned the river. Then he drove his herd straight through the tree, just like drivin' 'em through a covered bridge or a tunnel. Asked later on if they all got through safely, he admitted that they did not. "We're about fifty head short," said he. "They must have strayed off into one of them big holler limbs, an' got lost."

When a farmer brags too much about his land and his crops, his associates often try to surpass him, without appearing to doubt the original tale. In McDonald County, Missouri, a drunken old sang-digger was telling some tourists about his big farm in the Sugar Creek valley. "Lord God," he cried, "I've raised alfalfy ten foot high, and twelve cuttin's a year! I've growed cowpeas so all-fired big the cows cain't git 'em in their mouth!" Another old man nodded gravely, as if to acknowledge the truth of these statements. "I never had no luck with alfalfy, nor cowpeas neither," said he. "We done pretty good with our oats, though. The fact is, we raised so damn' many oats that we couldn't stack 'em on the farm where they growed! I had to go an' rent old man Price's pasture, just to stack them oats on!" The gaping strangers probably realized that both of these boasters were lying. But the strangers didn't know, as we did, that neither one of 'em owned a foot of land or had ever done any farming.

[13] See Bob Burns, *Liberty*, April 11, 1942, p. 21.

5 Hunting yarns

MANY OF THE WILDEST HUNTING STORIES begin with an old-timer exaggerating the abundance of game in the early days. It is not easy to tell just where the truth leaves off and the exaggeration begins. The old hunters all say that in the 1870's wild pigeons came to the Ozarks in vast flocks that actually darkened the sky, almost like an eclipse of the sun. There were so many birds that they sounded like a cyclone a-coming. They alighted in such numbers that they broke big branches off the hardwood trees. Ike Workman, of Taney County, Missouri,[1] said "I have seen trees a foot and a half through broken all to pieces by the weight of the pigeons." I have met men and women who claim to have witnessed these things, and I believe they were telling the truth.

When a man says that he often killed forty or fifty pigeons at one shot, my credulity begins to waver a little. Still, the pioneers used mighty big shotguns, some so big that they were not fired from the shoulder, but mounted on swivels like those used by market-hunters to slaughter wild-fowl in comparatively recent years. Jesse Lewis Russell [2] says that one of his neighbors in Carroll County, Arkansas, brought down ninety-nine pigeons at one discharge of his gun. And John Gould Fletcher [3] tells us that two hunters near Little Rock killed nine hundred pigeons in less than an hour. I have heard also of women burning sulphur beneath the pigeon-roosts at night; the fumes so affected the birds that hundreds fell to the ground and were killed with clubs. This may be true, too. At any rate, I am not prepared to deny it.

[1] Hoenshel, *Stories of the Pioneers*, p. 13.
[2] *Behind These Ozark Hills*, p. 63.   [3] *Arkansas*, p. 111.

In Christian County, Missouri, an old man told me that it was no use to fire into a flock of flying pigeons with a rifle. The single ball usually killed four or five birds, he said, but the hunter came home empty-handed just the same. When I asked for further light, the fellow explained that the flocks were so compact that the dead birds couldn't fall, but were carried along with the others by sheer momentum. The man who told me this was a solemn-looking chap, who had for many years been a minister of the gospel. Nevertheless, I record it as a tall tale, rather than the literal truth.

Many other tall stories have grown up about these big flocks of pigeons. Panthers, bears, wildcats, wolves, and smaller varmints were always skulking around pigeon-roosts in order to pick up cripples. According to one tale, a hunter rode up beneath a roost near West Plains, Missouri, tied his horse to an overhanging limb, and went in pursuit of a wildcat. The shot that he fired at this animal frightened a great many pigeons away. Relieved of their weight, the tree sprang upright, jerking the hunter's horse high into the air. The poor beast hung there until the man could get an axe and cut the tree down.

The old-timers say that the pigeons were never known to nest in the Ozarks, but just came here in the winter to feed on the acorns. No big flocks were seen later than 1882 or 1883, but the *Arkansas Gazette* of Nov. 22, 1890, carried the following item: "For the first time in many years wild pigeons were offered yesterday at the West Fifth Street market, but they were snapped up in a jiffy. The price was $1 per dozen." Paul R. Litzke, of Little Rock, Arkansas, recalls [4] that he flushed seven pigeons near Sweet Home, Arkansas, in January, 1894. It is said that the last wild pigeon ever seen alive was a male in the zoo at Cincinnati, Ohio, where it died in 1912. There are mounted specimens

[4] *Arkansas Gazette*, Jan. 16, 1949.

in the Ozark country yet; I saw one in the Elks' Club at Springfield, Missouri, a few years ago.

One hears occasionally of people in Missouri and Arkansas who have sighted wild pigeons in recent years, but the ornithologists say that the bird is extinct. The hillfolk who saw the great flocks never believed that the pigeons were exterminated by hunters, like the buffalo. "It cain't be," one old fellow told me, "there was too many of 'em. If every man, woman, an' child in this country had et pigeons every day, an' nothin' but pigeons, it wouldn't have made a dent in them big flocks." I have met a few Ozarkers who think that the birds must have been wiped out by some kind of food poisoning or some mysterious plague. But most of the old-timers are somehow persuaded that they all perished in the ocean. Not only this, but the hillfolk believe that many ships lost at sea in the 1880's and 1890's were really destroyed by pigeons. The story is that the pigeons tried to cross the ocean, but became exhausted. Whenever they saw a ship the weary birds alighted on it in such numbers that their weight actually sank the vessel. If the crew took to the boats, the pigeons sank them, too. I heard an old man at Fort Smith, Arkansas, describe such a shipwreck in a way to make one's blood run cold. Several hours later it occurred to me that the old man had never seen the sea or any boat bigger than an Arkansas river-packet. But he had seen the pigeons, and he was a natural born story-teller.

The pioneer tales about great hordes of timber wolves roving through the Ozark country have been mostly discredited by the scientists. But some of them are amusing, anyhow. Witness the following wolf-and-turkey yarn, given circulation by as honest a man as ever lived in this region. J. A. Sturges [5] sets down as sober fact the story told by N. C. Stafford and J. H. Cowan, "both respectable citi-

[5] *History of McDonald County, Missouri*, pp. 195–196.

zens of Cyclone township." These fellows said that there were lots of wild turkeys along Big Sugar Creek, but it was no use to hunt them, because the wolves were so abundant and ravenous. Whenever a hunter shot a turkey, a wolf would gobble it up before the hunter could retrieve it. Stafford and Cowen had started up the creek one night to shoot turkeys off their roosts, as was the custom in those days. "Plenty of roosts were found, and many shots were fired," writes Sturges, "but in every instance where the turkey fell more than a few yards from the hunters, it was grabbed by a wolf and carried away before they could get to it. The hunters only got three turkeys during the night out of perhaps as many dozen, the wolves getting the balance." I knew old Judge Sturges well, and one day I asked him about this story in his book. Sturges answered that he remembered the tale, adding that he had never been a hunter himself, but that he had seen plenty of wolves and turkeys in the woods near Cyclone, and thought there was nothing unreasonable in the story as told by Stafford and Cowan.

Turkeys were very plentiful in the early days, and there are quite a few in the backwoods even now. When I lived in Taney County, Missouri, in the early 1940's, we used to see wild turkeys occasionally; I helped to eat several which were probably trapped by my backwoods neighbors. The birds I saw were rather small and lean, but hunters say that there were enormous wild gobblers in pioneer days. Masterson [6] quotes Thorpe's old tale of the man who shot a turkey weighing forty pounds. "The thing was so fat it couldn't fly far," the story goes. "On striking the ground it bust open behind, and the way the pound gobs of tallow rolled out of the opening was perfectly beautiful!"

At the O-Joe clubhouse in Noel, Missouri, they used to

[6] *Tall Tales of Arkansaw*, p. 57.

tell of the boy who shot a big gobbler right through the middle with a 45-90 Winchester, which tears quite a big hole. The bird flew away as if unhurt, but the hunter saw something fall to the ground. It was a turkey's heart, still warm an' still a-beatin'. "It kept right on beatin' for awhile, but purty soon the beats came slower an' slower, till finally the damn' thing died right thar in my hand." The boy's parents laughed at the story, of course. But the next year another member of the family killed a big turkey with scars fore and aft, showing that it had been shot before. When the folks cut this gobbler open, they didn't find no heart.

I have heard another tale, of the hunter who shot a turkey's head off with a large caliber rifle. The head fell at the hunter's feet, still gobbling. The body of the bird flew round and round in the treetops, and finally disappeared over the crest of Gander Mountain. The man picked up the head, and stuck it in his pocket. Then he walked on toward home, and the turkey's head gobbled loudly all the way. There are people still living in southwest Missouri who believe that this actually happened and are convinced that it was a "token," a supernatural warning of some kind.

One remembers also the woodsman who saw a wild gobbler flying directly toward the cabin, so he rushed out and fired his big muzzle-loader. The gun went off with a loud roar, and when the smoke cleared the turkey's entrails were seen draped across the doorstep. Thinking that he must have blown the bird all to pieces, the man sat down on a stump and reloaded his gun. Half an hour later an odd fragrance drew him into the cabin, where he found a nicely roasted turkey hanging on the potrack. The shot had gutted the bird, which had fallen down the chimney in such a way that one leg caught on a hook over the fire. Hanging by one leg the turkey naturally turned around a few times while the feathers burned off. Then it just hung there, and roasted to a nice golden brown. And if you doubt this story, the man will show you the pulley-bone of that very same gobbler, hanging over the cabin door.

It was my impression that the scarcity of wild turkeys is due to the native practice of shooting them in season and out, particularly the killing of fryin'-size poults. But a man named Cummins, who lived on Bear Creek near Walnut Shade, Missouri, set me right about this. He said it was the illegal use of gobble-weed which had well-nigh exterminated the turkeys in his neighborhood. Gobble-weed is obtained from the Cherokees, he said, and consists of dried leaves and berries to be scattered on the ground. As soon as a turkey eats a bit of this stuff, it shuts its eyes and begins to gobble. All the hunter has to do is walk up and wring the gobbler's neck. "If a man had a ten-pound poke of gobble-weed," said Cummins, "he could ketch every dad-blamed turkey in Taney County!"

As recently as 1938 a fellow at Stuttgart, Arkansas, was talking about the great flocks of ducks that come to the rice fields down there. There are so many of 'em, he said, that the sky is literally covered with wings for days and weeks at a time. The air is so full of ducks, that millions of 'em have to march on the ground for the last fifty miles, or they would never be able to reach Stuttgart at all.

I have often heard coon-hunters tell of killing seven or eight coons in one tree, on the same night. These tales may be true, for all I know, since I never did much coon-hunting. But the yarn which follows is a typical backwoods windy. An old hunter near Hiwasse, Arkansas, told me that the best coon-dogs in Benton County treed one night at a big hickory, with a large cavity just above the first crotch. When the hunters came up, they were astonished to see the trunk of the tree swell to several times its proper size, and then gradually return to normal, while a great cloud of steam poured out of the hole above the crotch. This performance was repeated at regular intervals. When the tree was cut down the hunters killed thirty-seven coons, and many more escaped in the confusion. "They was packed in that holler like sardines in a can," the old man explained. "We figgered out that them coons all got to breathin' together, just like a lot of soldiers a-marchin' in step. Every time they'd breathe in, the trunk of the tree would swell up. Every time they'd breathe *out*, the tree would shrink up ag'in, an' we'd see the steam a-comin' out of the holler."

This "pooched-out tree" story is known all over the Ozark country and has been several times in print. I told it myself in *The Camp on Wildcat Creek*.[7] Hal Norwood included it in *Just a Book*,[8] remarking that the whole tree would "contract and expand like a horse breathing." Norwood credits his version to George Nall, a blacksmith of Lockesburg, Arkansas, and says the truth of the story was vouched for by A. D. Hawkins, a lawyer who lived in Little River County, Arkansas.

Squirrels have always been abundant in the Ozarks, and there are several tall tales about this. Tom Waring, of Kansas City, Missouri, told reporters that when the acorn crop failed in 1935 the whole southern half of Missouri swarmed with hungry fox-squirrels. Hordes of these creatures, he said, patrolled the banks of White River, looking so fierce that the float-trippers were afraid to land on the gravel bars. Hawk Gentry, veteran riverman of Galena, Missouri, confirmed Waring's tale, adding that he had seen hundreds of squirrels migrating downstream on clapboard shingles, with their tails stuck up to catch the wind.

There is a familiar story about a dog that treed a great number of squirrels in a big white oak. He just kept on chasing 'em to that particular tree until they hung in great

[7] Pages 99–103.   [8] Page 14.

clusters like bees or bats, so that they finally broke the tree down. I remember also a farmer south of Aurora, Missouri, who invited me to come out to his place for the squirrel-shooting. "Squirrels is so thick out my way," he said, "that some of the little ones have to sleep on the ground!"

People on White River still remember the two Purdy brothers, who were always playing jokes on the summer visitors. A sportsman from Kansas City met them in the woods. The bigger boy carried a muzzle-loading shotgun, and the little one had a claw-hammer stuck in his belt. After some idle talk, the city feller asked why they carried the hammer. This was what the Purdy boys were waiting for, and the younger one burst into tears. The tourist was profoundly shocked, but he persisted in his questioning. Finally the boy told him that the Purdys lived mostly on squirrels. There was no money to buy shot, so they loaded the old gun with rusty nails. "Every squirrel we kill nowadays is nailed fast to the tree," sobbed the boy. "An' that big so-and-so," pointing to his brother, "makes me climb up an' pry 'em loose with this here nail-puller!"

In January, 1940, it was reported that rabbits in Henry County, Missouri, suddenly became abundant and ravenous beyond all belief. When the farmers called their hogs at feeding time, great herds of cottontails came rushing into the barnyards. They pushed the hogs aside, overturned the feeding troughs and even upset several farmhands who were a bit slow in getting out of the way.

Here is an old story which has been credited to J. O. Cox, of Stafford, Missouri. According to the tale that was told to me, Cox was hunting in a snowstorm and chased a rabbit into a hole at the bottom of a hollow sycamore. What was his surprise to see another rabbit shoot out at the top of the tree, high above his head, and fall to its death on the rocks below. This happened three times, then Cox plugged the lower opening and felled the tree. There were twenty-nine cottontails in that sycamore. It was so full of rabbits that every time one ran in at the bottom, another was forced out at the top, like a pea out of a popgun.

Down around Eureka Springs, Arkansas, the boys make use of an ingenious trick to catch rabbits, according to a gentleman I met in the Basin Park Hotel. The boys paint round black spots, about six inches in diameter, upon the ends of saw-logs lying upon the ground. Then they send their dogs into the brush, to stir up the rabbits. When a rabbit sees one of these round black spots in the end of a log he thinks it's a hole, and when he tries to run into it he knocks himself unconscious. All the boys have to do is pick 'em up and put 'em in a sack.

Black bears were still common in some parts of the Ozark country in the 1890's, but only a few lived on past the turn of the century. The *Arkansas Gazette* of Feb. 8, 1899, carried a news item about two Fayetteville men who were attacked by a bear in the wilds of Washington County, Arkansas. I saw a freshly killed bear hanging in front of a store in Noel, Missouri, near the Arkansas line, in the autumn of 1900. The official state guidebook *Arkansas* [9] says that a 700-pound bear was killed near Mena in 1936, and intimates that bear-sign may still be seen in the Ouachita Forest. Similar tales are heard in Missouri occasionally; the *Missouri Conservationist* [10] printed a story about E. L. Mahan, who said he found bear-tracks on his farm near West Plains, Missouri, in the spring of 1948.

There is a man in New York today who goes about telling people that the Ozark country is full of bears. But pin him down, and he admits that he didn't see any bears, but only some bear-tracks in a cave. Well, it is surprising how long tracks will last in a dry cavern. As recently as the late

[9] Pages 15, 319.   [10] May, 1948, p. 10.

1930's there were guides who could take tourists into a cave and show them great piles of bark and leaves where bears used to sleep, and bones which bears had gnawed, with tracks and claw-marks all over the place. Sam Leath, of Eureka Springs, Arkansas, says that he visited such dens at Hemmed-In Holler, in Newton County, Arkansas, twenty years after the last bear in the vicinity had been killed. Rufe Scott, of Galena, Missouri, told me of a cave where "you can see big bear-tracks in the dirt, as plain as if they were made yesterday," although no live bears have been reported near Galena for at least forty years.

Tall tales about bear hunting are legion in the Ozark country, and are so ingeniously mingled with true stories and serious talk that it is hard to separate them sometimes. Right in the middle of an earnest discussion of big-game rifles an old hunter in Fort Smith, Arkansas, told me that the main consideration in hunting bear is not to chase the animal too far before making the kill. "If you run a b'ar too much," said he, "it'll spile the meat every time. A fat old sow b'ar will run till she plumb cooks herself, if you don't watch out. I shot a b'ar once, down on the Ouachita, after she'd run about four mile. Yes, sir, an' the steam squirted out of the bullet-hole twenty foot high, a-spittin' an' a-hissin', an' misted up the whole valley like a July fog."

A certain fleet-footed Arkansawyer, according to the fireside legends, always shot his bear in such a way as to injure but not seriously cripple it. Then he would run for home, with the enraged animal in close pursuit. When he reached the cabin, he would turn and shoot the bear dead. He figured it was easier than skinning and cutting up the critter out in the woods somewhere, and then packing the meat and skin home on his back. This way, the old woman and the kids could do most of the work.

There is an ancient story of the hunter who caught bears

alive and always tried to catch two of 'em at once. Then he tied their tails together and set them to fighting in such a way that each bear skinned and gutted the other. Bearskins weren't very valuable in those days, and this method saved the hunter the work of skinning and drawing the animals himself. Some hillfolk credit this windy to a legendary hunter called "The Big Bear of Arkansas" celebrated by Thorpe [11] who says that the fellow "received his nickname from a bear story which he never tired of repeating." Others say that the story referred to Jack Thomas, who founded the town of Thomasville, Oregon County, Missouri, in the early days. Jack Thomas was said to have killed more bears than anybody else in Missouri, and the stream known as Jack's Fork was named for him.

Fred Blair [12] repeats an old tale about bears which used to raid the cornfields. When the farmer came out with his shotgun, the bears fled, walking on their hind legs, with armloads of green corn, and big pumpkins balanced on their heads. Joe McGill, who used to live in Branson, Missouri,[13] says that he saw "a big black bear walking on his hind legs, carrying a pig in his arms. The pig weighed seventy-five or a hundred pounds." Hal Norwood [14] tells of a pioneer named Kinsworthy, who had forty acres in corn near Ben Lomond, Arkansas.

When corn began to get ripe the bears began to eat it. He could kill one every morning, but they did not stop destroying his corn. He conceived the idea of getting them drunk and taking the Negroes down early some morning and killing a lot of them with axes. He had the Negroes to hew a large trough and fill it with honey and brandy and put it in the corn field. He said that the next morning when he got in sight of his field he saw something throwing and something dodging. Upon approaching

[11] Masterson, *Tall Tales of Arkansaw*, p. 56.
[12] Clugston, *Facts You Should Know about Arkansas*, pp. 47–48.
[13] Hoenshel, *Stories of the Pioneers*, pp. 45–46.   [14] *Just a Book*, pp. 12–13.

closer he discovered that the bears had just drunk enough to make them funny and were throwing pumpkins at each other. He said they had ten acres of land as slick as a baseball ground.

Jim West, radio entertainer of Springfield, Missouri, used to tell one about a hunter who somehow fell into a big hole. The hole was thirty feet deep, and there was a bear at the bottom of it. The startled bear climbed out at once, and the hunter held fast to the animal's tail and was thus dragged up into the open air. Otherwise he could never have escaped from so deep a pit, and would probably have stayed there till he starved plumb to death.

Masterson [15] quotes a yarn from Porter's *Spirit of the Times* [16] about a bear hunter and his wife.

On one memorable occasion [the story goes] a bear had chased the trapper around a small tree at least forty times, striking at him with his paw. Bets seized a bowie knife and came to the rescue. Removing her petticoat she wrapped her arm in it, wedged it between the bear's jaws, and stabbed him with her toothpick.

The bowie knife was familiarly known as an "Arkansas toothpick" in the early days.

This tale is evidently related to the buffalo story which Featherstonhaugh [17] heard from John Percival, at Hot Springs, Arkansas, in 1834. Percival had wounded a buffalo bull, which chased him round and round an oak tree. He grasped the tree with his arms, and kept swinging ahead of the animal for more than four hours. Finally the buffalo became dizzy, and died from loss of blood. Percival's hands were mangled, and he was exhausted to the point of collapse, but soon recovered. Years later he revisited the spot, where he found "bones and abraded bark" to mark the scene of the struggle.

[15] *Tall Tales of Arkansaw*, p. 84.   [16] May 16, 1857, pp. 163–164.
[17] *Excursion through the Slave States*, pp. 112–113.

A very old story, said to have been printed in newspapers before the War between the States, concerns two men who were suddenly charged by a vicious bull. One shinned up a tree, the other plunged into a big hole in the ground. The man in the tree was puzzled by the antics of his friend, who kept jumping out of the hole, only to dive in again as the bull rushed at him. Finally he made a desperate sally, dodged the bull for the moment, and sprang into the tree beside his companion. "You damn' fool," cried the latter, "why the hell didn't you stay in the hole?" The other chap eyed him without enthusiasm. "There's a bear in that there hole," he said shortly.

One of the most widely distributed hunting yarns concerns a man who met a panther on a narrow ledge, to which he had fled when pursued by a she-bear with cubs. He couldn't go forward because of the panther, he couldn't turn back because of the bear. Resolutely he drew his knife, but the panther knocked it out of his hand. The great cat opened wide its mouth, when the intrepid hunter had a sudden inspiration. Springing forward, he reached down the varmint's throat, caught hold of the root of its tail, and with one swift pull he turned the critter inside out! Leaping over the body of the ruined panther, he left it lying there to distract the attention of the bear, which was still following close on his trail.

Collins [18] tells a story of "Bear Hollow, located three miles north and east of Jane, Missouri." In the early days, he says, Bear Hollow was so full of ferocious bears that settlers kept away. But finally a man named Brown followed three bears into a cave and killed them all. Also, says Collins, Brown had three daughters, and

one at a time they passed away and were buried in the cave where Brown had killed the bears. Each time a daughter was

[18] *Folk Tales of Missouri*, pp. 56–58.

buried, Brown planted a cedar tree to mark the grave. Today as tourists visit Bear Hollow Cave they may see three cedar trees which are cared for as in a park. Upon inquiry they are likely to hear the story. The three cedar trees mark historical grounds.

This tale is strange, because it is not at all in character for an Ozarker to plant cedar trees or to bury his dead in a cave. I lived near Bear Hollow for about ten years, and visited it many times, for good and sufficient reasons. I saw numerous caves there, and many cedar trees, and heard many tall tales. But I never happened to hear the story of the three bears, the three daughters, and the three cedar trees.

Many pioneer hunters were said to crawl into caves, armed only with knives or axes, and kill hibernating bears. This may be true, but it is hard for me to believe. Old man Shell, founder of the settlement known as Shell Knob, in Barry County, Missouri, was a famous bear hunter. Leila A. Wade [19] says that one winter Shell discovered a den near his home, with several bears in it.

Instead of killing the bears all at one time as a less experienced hunter might have done, he waited until they were sunk in the brumal sleep. Then entering the den, he selected a bear, cut its throat with a hunting knife, dragged the animal from the cave and dressed it without disturbing its fellows. Throughout the winter, when he desired fresh meat, he repeated the performance.

Ike Moore, of Moore's Ferry, Missouri, is quoted [20] as saying that he once followed a bear seventy-five yards into a cavern, but finally gave up the hunt and retreated when his pine-torch went out. A friend of mine asked Ike about this. "Well, it was a long time ago," he said by way of explanation. "I was young an' foolish in them days."

In 1932, at Otto Ernest Rayburn's camp near Galena,

[19] *Arcadian Life*, July, 1937, p. 13.
[20] Hoenshel, *Stories of the Pioneers*, p. 79.

Missouri, I met Raymond H. Gardner, a long-haired fellow who called himself "Arizona Bill" and represented himself as a cousin of Belle Starr, famous Missouri-born outlaw. Gardner told me that in northwest Arkansas he had "more than once" seen mountain boys creep into caves and kill bears with their six-shooters. "I never done it myself," Gardner said, "it always looked kind of dangerous to me." It looks dangerous to me, too. The story of Jim Harp and others as related by Cora Pinkley Call [21] confirms me in the opinion that experienced hunters in this region did not make a practice of crawling into bears' dens.

Years ago at Batesville, Arkansas, I heard the story of a gambler who took refuge in a small cave to escape a wounded she-bear. When the animal followed, he killed her with a lucky shot from his revolver. But the bear's body blocked the entrance, since it was too heavy for him to move, and he had no knife with which to cut his way through. The poor chap stayed there for two days and nights, then got so cold and hungry that he was desperate. Finally, as the tale was told to me, "he et that b'ar raw," and was thus able to get out of the cavern.

There used to be a character in southwest Missouri whose sole ambition, so he said, was to kill a bear with his teeth. This feat had never been accomplished, he declared, in the whole history of civilization, and the man who succeeded in doing it would be rich and famous forever. He had made three unsuccessful attempts, according to the tale. "Just to be safe, an' not run no risk of gettin' hurt," he carried a six-shooter, to be used only as a last resort, if the bear was getting the best of him. Each time he had been forced to use the gun, killing the bear in order to save his own life. After the third failure he gave up. "A full-grown wild b'ar cain't *be* killed by bitin' him," was his final conclusion.

[21] *Pioneer Tales*, pp. 25–26.

Some friends introduced me to this fellow, in the House of Lords bar at Joplin, Missouri. "Ain't he scratched up somethin' wonderful?" cried one of them delightedly. The man certainly was scratched and scarred, and one of his legs was permanently injured. But it may be that he was hurt in the jackmines somehow, instead of fightin' bears with his teeth.

In several backwoods settlements I have heard of great bears which caused the death of a hunter in some fantastic manner. One story has it that the man thrust a big homemade bowie knife through the animal's neck from the rear; the bear held the hunter close and swung its head from side to side, so that the poor fellow was decapitated by the point of the knife which protruded from the bear's throat. The hunter's body was found where it fell, with the carcass of the big bear only a few feet away.

According to another tale of this type the hunter fires with a high-power rifle, one of these modern weapons which will shoot clear through a bear and maybe a mile or so beyond. The instant the bullet strikes the bear's body the animal turns around, so that when the ball emerges from the other side it flies straight at the hunter and kills him deader than a door-nail. In this case also the bodies of the hunter and his quarry were found close together, and the men who found them reconstructed the action by a careful study of the "sign."

Near Cyclone, Missouri, I heard an oft-repeated yarn about a man attacked by a bear in broad daylight, right in the public road. He was unarmed, but snatched up a good throwin' rock and cast it with great force into the bear's open mouth, and thence down the creature's throat. The bear swung round and fled, but the hillman was fully aroused now, so he grabbed another flint-rock and dashed in pursuit. When he threw the second stone it entered the animal's rectum with such force that it met the first missile somewhere in the middle of the bear's body. As the two flints struck together, they produced sparks. The bear was fat, and its body took fire instantly and burned up like a barrel of oil. Nothing was left but a wide circle of scorched earth and a pile of blackened bones. "That'll learn bears not to monkey with me," said the hillman.

Tales of men and boys who kill game by throwing stones are common. It is true that almost any man in the Ozarks can throw with a force and accuracy astounding to one who was brought up in a city, or in a prairie state where boys have no rocks with which to practice. I have seen young men knock birds and squirrels out of trees with throwin' rocks. In one instance I remember that a boy killed a squirrel in this manner after I had fired twice at it with a target pistol. The Ozarker's expertness in this business has given rise to some tall stories, of course.

Fred Starr [22] tells of an Ozark boy who was knocking squirrels out of the tall trees with rocks, always throwing with his left hand. A pop-eyed city feller remarked upon the astounding accuracy of southpaws. "I ain't left-handed," the boy said. "But if I was to throw right-handed, it'd tear the squirrels up too bad."

Another old story, often repeated by Bob Burns and other radio hillbillies, concerns a boy sent out with a shotgun to get a mess of squirrels for the family. He put half a dozen carefully selected rocks in his pocket. "Some of them trees is so tall," he explained, "that a shotgun won't fetch a squirrel out of 'em. We ain't got no rifle, so I have to use these here throwin' rocks."

Lew Beardon, of Branson, Missouri, once remarked to me that when he was a boy on Bear Creek the whole family was pretty good at throwing stones. "The squirrels up that

[22] *Pebbles from the Ozarks,* 1942, pp. 20–21.

way," said he, "didn't dast come within fifty foot of the ground!"

Many people near Poplar Bluff, Missouri, will remember Charley Wolpers, a stone-throwin' wizard who lived there in the 1930's. The newspapers of Oct. 16, 1936, told how Wolpers went hunting with only five shells, but came home with seven rabbits. "After I shot five," he explained, "I run down two more an' killed 'em with rocks."

There are boys in the Ozarks who insist that they can catch rabbits without the use of guns, dogs, traps, snares, or throwin' rocks. "I just go out in the brush," said a boy at Caverna, Missouri, "an' slip along easy-like, an' pick them rabbits up." I have heard this tale so often that I am almost persuaded that there must be something in it. Perhaps some boy somewhere did catch a rabbit that way. But I will never believe that anybody can do the trick consistently until I see it for myself.

I was told at Southwest City, Missouri, that quail are so abundant in that vicinity that people just go out with torches at night and gather up as many as they want. There is one local character who makes a business of this kind of hunting. He always feels the birds carefully when he picks them up. The fat ones he keeps, while the skinny quail are released to grow another year.

Rufe Scott, Galena, Missouri, tells an old story about a feebleminded boy who lay down beside a log in the woods and fell asleep. When he awoke there were two wild turkeys on the log; he grabbed one of them and wrung its neck. Such a thing would not happen again in a thousand years, but the halfwit took it as a matter of course. On the way home he stopped at a neighbor's and gave them the turkey. "Don't you want to take it home to your folks?" the man asked. "Aw, they're easy ketched," the boy replied. "I can git plenty more."

I have always wanted to go over to Oklahoma City and meet Jack Abernathy, the preacher who chases wolves on horseback and claims he has caught more than a thousand of them with his hands.[23] S. E. Simonson [24] read Abernathy's book, and did the trick at least once, near Eudora, Arkansas. His pony outran the hounds, and the wolf was very tired. Simonson leaped off the horse and tackled the wolf barehanded. "I grabbed him by the neck, slipped my hands down to his muzzle and clamped his mouth shut," writes Simonson. "I was sitting on him when the dogs arrived. The other hunters soon rode up. We muzzled the wolf and I tied him behind my saddle, and returned triumphantly to Eudora."

A boy in Taney County, Missouri, told me that he had once sneaked into the Skaggs game preserve, a very large enclosure stocked with deer, and killed a fat young doe with his pocket knife. He went in after dark, he said, and blinded the deer with a flashlight. Then he "rassled her down" and cut the critter's throat.

This tale of killing deer with a pocket knife may or may not be true. But a close friend of mine did kill a four-point buck with a tiny vest-pocket pistol. He was standing beside a woodland trail when the deer appeared, and on a sudden impulse he snatched out the weapon and fired. The gun was a Remington .41 derringer, with barrels only three inches long. Such pistols were carried by the old-time gamblers, who generally shot from the pocket at a maximum range of three or four feet, just the breadth of a card table. A derringer is the last gun in the world that a man would choose as a hunting arm, yet here was a running deer killed instantly at a distance of about forty yards. The shooter was aghast, for he had always been a stanch defender of the game laws.

[23] *In Camp with Theodore Roosevelt*, p. 65.
[24] *Arkansas Historical Quarterly*, Winter, 1947, p. 420.

And now he had killed a deer out of season, on posted land, without any hunting license. Two of his grinning neighbors brought the deer into town under cover of darkness, so that the venison was not wasted. They cut off the antlers, too, and nailed them up in the deer-slayer's office. It may be that my friend is the only man in the world who ever killed a running deer with a derringer, but he is in no position to do any bragging about his marksmanship. And if he did tell the story, who would believe it?

I have been told of a physician from Kansas City who drove down to Taney County, Missouri, for the three-day deer season. He tramped the hills for two days, but failed to get a deer. On the afternoon of the third day he gave up and started back to Kansas City. Somewhere near Kirbyville, Missouri, in a dark holler, a big buck crashed out of the bushes and collided with the car. When the driver sprang out the deer lay kicking in the road and was finished off with a rabbit rifle. A few minutes later the deer, with the green tag properly tied to an antler, was wired to the front fender, and the doctor went happily on his way to Kansas City. Several years passed before he told the truth about how that buck met its death.

Several times I have heard about an old codger in northwest Arkansas who owned a large farm. There were many deer on his place, but he would not allow anybody to shoot there, and went to a great deal of trouble and expense to keep hunters away. This fellow was somehow persuaded to go deer-hunting on a neighbor's land, and in the closed season, at that. Down in his section of the country the boys do their hunting at night with a jack-light, and locate deer by "shining their eyes." Somehow the jokers fixed things so that the old man carried the gun himself, while somebody else manipulated the light. They led him by a roundabout way back to his own farm, and were delighted when the old scoundrel fired a load of buckshot which killed his prize Jersey calf.

Another old story concerns two town fellers who got permission to hunt deer on a farm in southwest Missouri. The farmer called one of these men aside, and asked him to shoot an old gray mare in the lower pasture. The mare had been a pet for many years, but was now hopelessly crippled, and no member of the family had the heart to kill her. When the two hunters came to the pasture, they saw the old horse in a fence corner. "I've got to try my new rifle, Steve," said the first hunter. "Watch me kill that old horse down yonder." The second hunter was horrified, and tried to stop his friend from shooting, but it was too late. The big rifle roared, and the mare fell dead. "Good God, you've played hell now!" cried Steve. "After this fellow lets us hunt on his place, and treats us so well, you have to kill his horse!" The first hunter just laughed. "I believe you've gone crazy," said Steve. The other man pretended to sober up a bit. "It won't do to go back by the house," he said, "we'd better sneak off through the woods and keep out of that farmer's way for awhile." Steve was still uneasy when they got home. Whenever the farmer came into town, for weeks afterward, Steve would leave his office and keep out of sight. The hunter who shot the horse told the farmer about the joke, and the farmer carried on by scowling ferociously every time he saw Steve. When somebody finally told Steve, months later, that half the people in town were laughing at him, he was mad enough to kill both the farmer and his hunting companion. But the folks down that way still think it was a plumb good joke, and they still laugh about it behind Steve's back.

In the woods around Galena, Missouri, the old folks remember a joke Frank Hembree played on Ad Kirkendall. These two had hunted and fished together for many years.

One day Frank remarked that some wild animal was killing stock in the neighborhood and that his dogs had trailed it several times. "It must be a painter, Ad," said he. "The damn' thing whips my dogs regular." Ad replied profanely that there hadn't been a painter in Stone County since Heck was a pup, and that no varmint in Missouri could whip *his* dogs. A few nights later he came over to Frank's place, with half a dozen of his best hounds. Frank got into bed and pretended to be sick. He persuaded his father, Uncle Sol Hembree, to go along with Ad after the varmint. A few minutes later, as soon as the hunters were out of sight, Frank got up and raced across the ridge ahead of the hounds. He concealed himself in a rocky ravine, and when the dogs came along he collared the two best ones and tied them up in a little cave. Then he yowled and screamed and spit like a panther, and lashed the other dogs till they ran away howling. Poor Ad was thrashing around in the brush on the hillside, with no light but a smoky lantern, yelling at his dogs, calling particularly for the two prize hounds that were tied up in the cave. Frank cut back to the house and returned to his bed. Ad came in briar-scratched and bruised and frightened, not far from tears. "Godamighty, Frank, it *was* a painter," he cried. "I seen him plain, an' he was ten foot long, anyhow. He killed my two best dogs, Frank. Just scratched their guts out, an' tore 'em all to ribbons!" Ad finally went to bed at Frank's house, after describing the chase in great detail. Next morning, after breakfast, Frank went out and brought in the two hounds, the dogs that Ad said he had seen torn to bits by the varmint. Ad's jaw dropped, then he flew into a passion. He went so far as to threaten Frank's life, and strode off raging and cursing. Twenty years later Ad Kirkendall was still sore about that joke, and would not suffer it to be mentioned in his presence. But everybody in the neighborhood knew the story by heart, and they still laugh in Stone County whenever the great panther hunt is mentioned.

Many stories about guns and shooting which seem very funny to the hillfolk are wasted upon readers who are unfamiliar with firearms. Every backwoods child has heard of the hunter who chased a giant buck, which always dodged around a knoll before he could fire. One day this man had the blacksmith bend his rifle barrel, so as to shoot around the mountain. Just after the big deer disappeared he pulled the trigger, and the animal ran completely around the hill four times, with the rifle-ball in hot pursuit. Finally the deer slowed up a bit by reason of exhaustion, and was killed by the bullet. It fell dead almost at the hunter's feet.

One day the body of young Jim Spelvin, who had a weakness for other men's wives, was found riddled with buckshot beside the new State Highway. Everybody knew who was responsible, but none of us cared to talk about it. The officers were questioning an old farmer who lived nearby. "I seen Jim go past my place," the old man said. "He was a-runnin' mighty fast, an' it looked to me like there was a swarm of bees after him. But if they was buckshot, I reckon they must have ketched up with Jim when he slowed down for the crossroad."

Long ago I heard the story of some country boys in Lonoke County, Arkansas, who built a very large muzzle-loading shotgun, the barrel made of water-pipe taken from an abandoned hotel. The thing was mounted on a wagon, to be fired at wild geese feeding in the fields. At the first discharge the gun busted and tore the wagon all to hell, but didn't hurt the hunters, since the trigger was pulled by means of a long cord. The explosion killed seventy-five geese and crippled many more. Most of the geese were not struck by shot, but by fragments of the water-pipe barrel. "It made a noise like thunder, only louder," I was told.

"The cows for miles around gave sour milk for the rest of the week!"

A politician near Mena, Arkansas, was mighty proud of his new shotgun. It was a ten-bore, which is two sizes larger than most of the guns used in the Ozarks nowadays. One day he was bragging about the piece in a tavern west of Mauldin, when a villager brought out an eight-gauge goose gun, a really gigantic thing. The politician had never seen such a gun before; it made his own pride and joy look like a child's pea-shooter. After awhile an old hunter remarked that he had a much larger shotgun at home. "Bigger'n that eight-bore?" cried the office-seeker. "For God's sake, how big is it?" The old man hesitated. "Well, I cain't exactly call the number of it," he said, "but it's a pretty big gun. Whenever it needs cleanin', we just grease a ground-hog an' run him through the barr'l."

Akin to this is the tale of an ancient Spanish cannon dug up in a field near Little Rock. "It was so God damn' big," an old gentleman told me, "that we burnt three tons of powder every time we fired the God damn' thing off! Why, it took two yoke of oxens to drag the God damn' powder into the God damn barr'l!" I pondered this story for awhile. "How did you get the oxen out, after the gun was loaded?" I asked. The old gentleman regarded me thoughtfully. "We tuck the God damn' yokes off," he said after a long pause, "an' driv the critters out single file, right through the God damn' touch-hole!"

When I first knew Frank Hembree he lived on a windy hilltop just west of Galena, Missouri, and was always bragging about his goose gun. An eight bore, full choke, with forty-four inch barrels. It really did kill game at phenomenal distances, the neighbors said. The story goes that one afternoon a flock of wild geese came over very high, and Frank fired both barrels. Then he did his chores, went to bed, and enjoyed a good night's sleep. Next morning he came out into the back yard just as two fine geese came crashing down into his little garden-patch. "That just goes to show," said Frank, "how high them geese was a-flyin'!"

A loafer whom I met in Pineville, Missouri, does not want his name mentioned in any "hillbilly" book, but he told me that he had known men who shot geese so high in the air that when the birds fell they buried themselves in the ground. The hunters had to carry shovels and mattocks to dig 'em up. If the ground was frozen, he said, these boys didn't go hunting at all. When a goose falls from a great height on frozen ground, it just explodes like a bottle of Choctaw beer, and you can't gather up enough pieces for stew, even.

Clarence Sharp, of Pittsburg, Kansas, is one of the best rifle shots in the Southwest, and I once saw him kill a flying mallard at an incredible distance with a 30–30 Winchester. When I expressed my astonishment at this feat, Clarence said that it was nothing out of the ordinary. "When I was a boy, near Dutch Mills, Arkansas, everybody shot geese with rifles," he told me. "I used to kill 'em so high in the air that we had to put salt on the bullets, in order to keep the birds from spoiling before they hit the ground."

Thomas Daniel, of Pea Ridge, Arkansas, in an old newspaper story reprinted by F. W. McCullough [25] refers to a character called Happy Bill, who declared that once in a fit of anger he fired his deer rifle at the moon and hit it. "I split the moon in two," said he, "an' one slab fell towards the ground like a big chunk of silver!" Another of Daniel's stories concerns Harry Madden, who shot the bill off a woodpecker so neatly that the bird went on pecking for a

[25] *Living Authors of the Ozarks*, p. 83.

full minute before discovering the loss. There was also Cal Jones, who killed six crows with one shot from a muzzle-loading rifle.

Sam McDaniels, who lives near Jane, Missouri, almost on the Missouri-Arkansas line, told me that one of his great-uncles had killed twenty-one deer with a single bullet. Probably I looked a bit incredulous, for Sam smiled and assured me that the deer were not killed by a single discharge of the gun. Not by any means. There were twenty-one shots, but only one bullet. The old hunter used a smoothbore of large caliber and low velocity, so that the ball remained in the body of the deer. He butchered the animals on the spot, and recovered the slug each time. Then he pounded it into shape again with the handle of his hunting knife, and loaded it into his gun. Sometimes, added McDaniels with a twinkle, the ball was so battered that it had to be melted and recast in the bullet-mold.

A half-legendary figure known in southwest Missouri as Abner Yancey is celebrated as the one-shot wonder of all time. Armed with a single-shot rifle, he was trying to get two squirrels lined up, so as to kill both of them with one bullet. The squirrels fell when Ab fired, and just then he "heerd turkeys a-yoikin' " in a nearby tree. Seven hens and a gobbler were sitting on a branch, and Ab's bullet had sped on to split the limb and catch their feet in the crack. Ab climbed the tree and wrung the turkeys' necks, but coming down he fell into a brush-pile, killing two big rabbits and a covey of quail. Wading into the creek, where one of the squirrels had fallen, he got his pockets and boot-tops full of fish, mostly peerch an' goggle-eye. While stringing the fish, Ab reached back to scratch a chigger-bite, and one of the buttons popped off his shirt into a bunch of hazel-brush. A moment later he heard "a lot of gaspin' an' gurglin' " in the thicket, and found a big buck rolling on the ground.

Ab cut the animal's throat with his hunting-knife, and found the lost button stuck in the deer's windpipe.

When Ab got home he had one deer, eight turkeys, two squirrels, two brush-rabbits, twenty-one quail and about fifty pounds of fish. "Pappy shore was proud when he seen me a-draggin' it all home," he said years later. "It was a sad day at our house, though, on account of Uncle Hen actin' up. Uncle Hen was a purty good feller, but he called me a liar when I was a-tellin' how I got that buck. Liar was allus a fightin' word in the Yancey family, so I just naturally had to kill him. I done it with my old huntin' knife, gentlemen, the same knife you-uns see a-stickin' out of my boot-top right now." The old-timers tell me that the story of Ab Yancey's great hunt was believed by everybody in those days. "Anyhow," as one old fellow added with a grin, "I don't recollect hearin' it conterdicted none, so long as Ab was alive."

Some windy-spinners add the detail that after Ab's bullet split the limb and caught the turkeys it went on to penetrate a bee-tree, and Ab carried off a piggin of honey along with his other loot. A piggin is a homemade wooden bucket, and the story offers no explanation of how Ab got the piggin.

I have heard a modified version of the old Ab Yancey tale in which the mixed bag is reduced to four turkeys, and the yarn appears somewhat less fantastic. According to this text the hunter sees the turkeys sitting on a limb, and fires at them. When the smoke clears the birds are still sitting in a row, flapping their wings and making a great noise, but not leaving the tree. The hunter thinks he has missed, but can't understand why the birds don't fly away. Approaching cautiously, his rifle at the ready, he sees that the bullet has split the branch in such a manner as to hold the birds' feet. An old scoundrel at Hollister, Missouri, told my wife this tale as the truth, claiming it as his own experience. Our city clothes and the fact that we were staying at the hotel fooled him. He couldn't have known that Sally was a country girl, raised in the wilds of McDonald County.

In some sections of Arkansas the old folks tell of a hunter who is far from home at nightfall and climbs a tree to avoid being eaten by bears. The moon comes up, and he sees a flock of turkeys sitting on a nearby limb. Taking his hatchet from his belt, he splits the limb, thus catching all the turkeys by their feet. Then he cuts the limb loose, and the turkeys fly away with him. When they get near his home, the hunter begins to kill turkeys by wringing their necks. The death of each bird slows the flight somewhat, and he keeps on killing 'em until only two gobblers are left alive. These flop their wings strongly, but the man's weight and that of the dead turkeys is too much. So the hunter descends gradually and safely, and gets home early after all, with a nice bunch of turkeys for his family.

The business of the turkeys carrying a man through the air is not uncommon in tales of this kind. "When I was a little chap," said old man Linkletter of Little Rock, Arkansas, "I was a great hand to sneak up on birds an' rabbits, an' ketch 'em with my hands. One time I seen some wild turkeys eatin' corn out of the chinks in our corncrib. I snuck up easy-like, an' grabbed two big gobblers by their legs. But they was too big for me, an' the next thing I knowed we was way up in the air, lookin' down on the trees. I was a great hand to figger things out in them days. I knowed that if I turned loose I'd be killed sure, an' every second I held on they was takin' me higher up an' further off from home. But then I figgered if I was to let *one* of 'em loose, the other'n might take me down safe. So I turned the biggest one loose. The other gobbler he flopped his best, but I was a little too heavy for him. So down we come, easy like one of these here parachutes. I was aimin' to wring his neck when we got down, but he flopped his wings an' drug me around in the briars till I finally give up an' turned him loose. I had to walk six miles to git home, an' Paw give me a lickin'. But I reckon I was pretty lucky, at that. If I hadn't figgered out what to do, I might have got hurt some way."

In several different neighborhoods, widely separated, I have heard the story of a man who fell down an old shaft or a dry well and couldn't get out. When the buzzards came for him he played possum, grabbed 'em by the legs, and tied them together with his leather shoelaces. Finally he caught so many buzzards that, by their combined strength, they lifted him out of the well. Some of the story-tellers say that he did not stop at the surface, but rose high in the air. When he was carried over a settlement, he cut loose the buzzards, one at a time, and was thus able to descend in safety.

Every Ozark yarn-spinner knows at least one version of the ramrod story. It usually begins with a duck-hunter sitting in a blind, loading his shotgun. He has loaded one barrel, and is just tamping the powder into the other when a flight of ducks appears. The hunter fires instantly, and when the powder smoke clears he sees something odd lying on a gravel-bar. It is about four feet long, and there seems to be ducks on both ends of it. "There was twelve big mallards," the man said later, "all skewered together on a hickory stick. I pulled 'em off, one at a time, an' washed the blood off'n the hickory. Damned if it warn't the ramrod out of my old shotgun. I'd pulled the wrong trigger an' fired off the left barrel, that didn't have no shot in it, but just the old ramrod a-settin' on top of the powder! It ain't everybody," he added complacently, "that has killed twelve mallards at a crack thataway, without no shot in his gun."

It seems that variants of this tale are known more or less

all over the country. Collins [26] tells the story of a certain old man Orton who saw a great flock of prairie chickens jammed up against a rail fence. Loading his gun, he fired so hastily that he forgot to take the ramrod out of the barrel. Sixteen prairie chickens were spitted right through their necks. Old man Orton just picked up the ramrod and carried 'em all home.

One hears also of the hunter who fell asleep in a bunch of cattails and awoke to find himself right in the middle of a big flock of wildfowl. With a shout he snatched up his gun and fired, but the barrels were full of mud and water, so that both of them burst. When the fellow recovered consciousness he held the shattered stock in his hand, but the barrels of his gun were gone. Twelve ducks, four Canada geese, and a stray pelican lay dead on the water, killed by fragments of the missing gun-barrels. This is supposed to have happened in 1932, on Lake Taneycomo near Branson, Missouri. Lowell Thomas [27] tells a more extravagant version of this yarn, which he got from a hunter on the Canadian River in Oklahoma.

The Ozark foxhunters tell a lot of fascinating windies, but they are all stories about dogs, and most of them are based upon an intimate knowledge of the various noises produced by foxhounds. They are told in a jargon scarcely intelligible to the uninitiated. The noun mouth, in foxhunters' parlance, doesn't mean mouth at all, but a dog's voice. The sound that the tourist would call a short bark is a *chop-mouth* in the Ozarks. A short treble bark is a *fine chop-mouth*, a short bass bark is a *coarse chop-mouth*. A series of staccato yelps in the middle register is a *calk-mouth*. A long tenor bay is a *bugle-mouth*, a similar but deeper tone is a *horn-mouth*. So it goes with *long-mouth, turkey-mouth, squealin'-mouth, goose-mouth, babble-mouth*

[26] *Folk Tales of Missouri*, pp. 39–40.   [27] *Tall Stories*, p. 79.

and many others. Every one of these terms has a definite meaning, and refers to sounds easily identified by a trained ear, but difficult of description. Such words as yelp, whine, bark, howl, and bay seem specific enough to the city feller, but they are too vague and general for a foxhunter. The terminology of foxhunting abounds in strange words and phrases, so that a casual conversation on the subject sounds like double-talk to the ordinary tourist. Most "furriners" are dumfounded when they learn that no fox is ever caught or killed by the Ozark foxhunters, save by some unfortunate accident. The hunters do not want to catch the fox, but only to hear the music of the dogs in pursuit of the animal. The pleasures of a fox-chase are dependent upon acute hearing, the perception of slight variations in pitch and tempo. The whole matter of foxhunting, including the tall tales about foxhounds, is a bit on the esoteric side, anyhow.

Several wild tales about foxhounds are concerned with the dogs' ability to find their way home under difficult conditions. It is said that C. F. Huff, of Hot Springs, Arkansas, took his best foxhound by rail to Crab Orchard, Kentucky, where he somehow lost her. This was in December, 1912. Two months later the dog limped into Huff's yard at Hot Springs. She had traveled at least 600 miles through strange territory, crossing the Mississippi, the Arkansas, and the White rivers in the dead of winter. This story was printed in newspapers in many parts of the country and discussed in several magazines.[28] Many readers regarded the newspaper account as a tall tale, but I have never met a foxhunter who saw any reason to doubt it.

"The smartest dog I ever saw," wrote O. O. McIntyre in his syndicated column (Oct. 20, 1933) "was an old pot-hound in the Ozarks." McIntyre lived in New York and

[28] Cf. an unsigned article "The Homing Instinct of the Hound," *Saturday Evening Post*, May 17, 1919, p. 80.

conducted one of the early rube-on-Broadway columns, but he spent much of his boyhood in Missouri and Arkansas. He was well known in Bentonville, Arkansas, which is still the source of some mighty fine pot-hound stories. It was only a few miles from Bentonville, according to one ancient tale, that George Spellman raised a mongrel foxhound named Booger. George declared that Booger was a perfect blend of many famous strains—Walker, Trigg, July, Birdsong, Bluetick, Goodman, Redbone, and Trumbo. The local fox-hunters laughed at these claims, but did not deny Booger's value as a general purpose potlicker. When George carried his big Winchester, Booger chased deer and ignored all other game. If the weapon was a squirrel rifle, the dog treed squirrels exclusively. When George brought out a shotgun, Booger would point quail like a bird dog. If he started out at night with a lantern, old Booger rushed on ahead to trail coons and possums as well as any tree dog in Arkansas. One day, so the story goes, George appeared at the gate with a cane fishpole over his shoulder. Booger hesitated only a moment, then snatched up a tin bucket and started a-digging for worms.

Sam Garroute, who lives not far from Aurora, Missouri, always claimed to have the best tree dog in the country. Smartest dog that ever lived, said Sam. Always knew just what sort of varmints were to be pursued. Ozark hunters "case" all skins nowadays, stretching them on boards made for the purpose. A skunk requires a board of a particular size and shape, a coon another, a mink still another. When Saw wanted to hunt coons, he just set a coon-board outside the door; if he wanted possums, he set out a possum-board, and so forth. The dog always located the proper varmint and ignored all other species. One day Sam's wife was red-ding up the house, and happened to set her ironing board outside for a few moments, just to get it out of the way.

The dog gazed at it open mouthed; there is no wild animal in the Ozarks whose skin could cover such a big stretchin'-board as that. The brag dog howled dismally and slunk off into the woods. That was seven years ago, and the dog has never been seen since. "I reckon he's still a-huntin'," Sam told the boys in a barbershop at Aurora. This ironing-board story is known in Arkansas, as well as in Missouri. Compare the text published in the *Arkansas Gazette* (Dec. 18, 1947) as part of a letter from J. C. McRaven, of Jacksonville, Arkansas.

Near Rolla, Missouri, I heard about a very intelligent night-dog owned by Buck Hodge. One night he treed a possum in a persimmon thicket, and when Buck knocked the possum out of the tree a lot of ripe fruit fell also. The dog paid no attention to the possum, but gobbled up the persimmons with every sign of satisfaction. The next night Buck heard him bark "treed" again, and found him standing at the foot of another persimmon tree. There was no possum in the tree at all. The dog was just calling Buck to come and shake him down some more persimmons.

The boys in Phelps County, Missouri, told me about a loud-mouthed fellow named Taylor, who was always bragging up his mongrel tree-dog. "Just last night," said he, "that there pup killed the biggest coon I ever seen. God-amighty, boys, that coon was four foot long, an' must have weighed a hundred pounds! He'll meat the whole family a month easy, an' we're goin' to use the hide for a wagon-cover!" A few days later a game warden arrested Taylor for killing fur-bearing animals out of season. "They fined me ten dollars, boys," the old man complained loudly. "Ten dollars, just for havin' one measly little coonskin, not much bigger'n a chipmunk!"

In Stone County, Missouri, I overheard several references to the "wheelbarrow" dog owned by Frank Hembree. I

supposed that Wheelbarrow was the animal's name, but Frank soon set me right. He said that Bulger was the best coon dog in Missouri, but since all four legs were frozen off, it was necessary to trundle him around in a wheelbarrow. "He just points his head the way he wants to go," said Frank, "an' I push him. It's kind of slow in a rough country like this, but we get a lot of coons thataway." Frank says that he and Bulger have caught as many as twenty coons in a single night, and he wears out two or three wheelbarrows every season.

Here's one that was told on Liars' Night at a foxhunters' convention near Guthrie, Oklahoma. There was a field contest between a valuable pedigreed coon hound owned by a Tulsa sportsman and a mongrel belonging to a local boy. The pedigreed dog passed a certain big oak without a sound, but the mongrel stopped and barked "treed." The hunters saw no trace of a coon, and couldn't even find any hole in the tree. But the mongrel refused to leave, so the judges finally ordered the tree cut down, to satisfy the dog's owner. The trunk was split open, and showed a small cavity that had grown over twenty-five years ago, according to a count of the annual rings. In the hollow was the skeleton of a coon, dead for at least a quarter of a century! "A coon hound," said the owner of the mongrel, "has got to foller a cold trail, or else he ain't no good. That there dog of mine," he added, "is a real coon-ketcher."

From Farmington, Arkansas, comes the story of a hunter who owned the best coon dog in all northwest Arkansas. When this superdog died, the owner was heartbroken. He could not bear to lose sight of the dog entirely, so he skinned the animal and made a fine vest out of the pelt. One moonlight night, walking alone in the big timber, he removed the vest and lay down to rest a little. The hunter fell asleep, and suddenly awoke to hear a great hullabaloo on a wooded hillside nearby. Hurrying over there, he found that his dogskin vest had treed three coons in one white oak and two more in another tree only a few yards away.

In the summer of 1947 somebody brought a monstrous dog to the Basin Park Hotel in Eureka Springs, Arkansas. A Great Dane, they called it, and the biggest dog I ever saw in my life. In a little park near the hotel some local men were discussing this great beast. One old gentleman remarked that when he was a young man he had imported two similar dogs to use in hunting panthers. "My hounds could trail the varmints all right," said he, "but a painter will back up ag'in a bluff an' kill hound-dogs till hell cain't rest. We figgered a couple of these here big dogs could kind of foller 'long with the pack, an' do most of the fightin'." Urged on by my questions, he told how one of the big dogs slipped his leash as the hunt started and killed four cows before he was shot by an irate farmer. The other big dog followed the pack until they cornered a large male panther in the hills near White River. The panther killed two hounds and severely wounded a third before the big dog reached the scene. "It was all over in a minute," said the old man. Then he puffed his pipe, and apparently regarded the story as ended. "But what happened?" I cried. "Did the panther kill the big dog, too?" The old hunter looked surprised. "Why, no," he answered. "That there big dog grabbed up the painter an' run off with it. The last I seen of him, he was just a-toppin' the crest of Leatherwood Mountain."

I thought about this for awhile, staring at the old gentleman's impassive face. Then I bade him goodnight, and tottered feebly back to the hotel.

6 Snakes and other varmints

SOME OF OUR MOST STRIKING STORIES about serpents, lizards, turtles, arachnids, and insects are folk beliefs rather than tall tales, and I have listed many of them in a previous book.[1] But there is often an intimate relation between the superstition and the windy story. Consider the case of the joint snake, by way of an example.

The common glass snake, or joint snake, is a legless lizard with a long brittle tail. When the creature is attacked, the tail snaps into several segments which wriggle about and attract attention while the reptile creeps away unseen, to grow a new tail several months later. This much is true, as any scientific snake man will testify.

Many hillfolk have seen joint snakes break apart, and most of them believe that the pieces join together again as soon as the danger is past, so that the joint snake goes on its way as good as ever. This is pure superstition.

A boy who lived up on Bear Creek, in Taney County, Missouri, told me about the time he struck a joint snake with a switch. It flew into several pieces, and he picked up one of these, about five inches long, and put it in his pocket. Several days later the boy saw the snake again. He knew it was the same snake, because it was using a corncob in place of the missing segment. This is a tall tale, of course, but a comparatively modest one.

An old joker in Benton County, Arkansas, showed me how a simple folk belief grows into a really extravagant

[1] *Ozark Superstitions*, pp. 240–263.

story. "Speakin' of joint snakes," he said, "did you ever hear about Jim Henderson's run-in with the granddaddy of 'em all?" I disclaimed all knowledge of this affair. "Well, Jim found some big logs a-layin' in the road one day, all sawed up into four-foot len'ths, just right for his fireplace. Jim hauled this here wood home, an' there was four loads of it. He ricked up three loads an' was just startin' on the fourth, when here come somethin' down the road. He thought at first it was a automobile, but it warn't. It was a joint snake's head. An' all that stuff Jim had ricked up, thinkin' it was wood, was pieces of that there snake. Jim he just stood an' watched them pieces unrick theirself, an' join up like a string of cars on the railroad. An' purty soon the whole business went a-crawlin' off down the road. Jim swears that there joint snake was four hundred foot long, if it was a inch."

The legend of the hoop snake is common in the Ozark country. Nearly all old-timers believe that a certain kind of snake puts its tail in its mouth and rolls hoop fashion through the hills. They also believe that the hoop snake has a deadly sting in its tail. It is true that there are snakes with horny appendages on their tails, but scientists say that these snakes are not poisonous, nor do they roll about like hoops. I have met honest farmers who swear that they have seen hoop snakes rolling through the tall grass, and there is no doubt in my mind that they are telling what they believe to be the truth. But the herpetologists are all agreed that the hoop snake is a myth.

The power of the hoop snake's venom can hardly be exaggerated, according to the old folktales. Otto Ernest Rayburn [2] reports the story of a woman who was attacked by a hoop snake, but the sting in the snake's tail barely touched her skirt. She washed the dress next day, and the

[2] *Ozark Country*, p. 267.

poison "turned three tubs of wash water plumb green!" But I have never heard of a hoop snake stinging a human being. When the hoop snake pursues a hillman, the fellow always dodges, so that the snake misses him. Usually the sting strikes a growing tree. The tree generally dies in a few days, and sometimes the leaves wither and fall within the hour.

Miss Rubey Poynor, Cassville, Missouri, tells of a certain Granny Skaggs who saw a hoop snake roll down a hill and wrap itself around a sassafras tree. This happened one Sunday morning as the old woman was going to church. When she came back, shortly after noon, every leaf on that sassafras tree was wilted.

Some people say that when the reptile's horn sticks into a tree, he cannot get it out and must stay right there until he dies. Another story is that a hoop snake can sting but once, like a honeybee; when he tries to pull the stinger out, the snake's entrails are damaged so that he lives only a few hours.

Carl Withers tells me that he was discussing snakes with an old man in Hickory County, Missouri, about 1940. "Some say there *is* hoopsnakes," the hillman told him. "I never seen one myself, but I think that any snake, if he'd take his tail in his mouth and practice, could learn to roll. But whether he'd have enough poison in that horn of his'n to deaden a tree, when he got there, I don't know." After a moment of thoughtful silence, Withers added: "I like to think of the snake practicing!"

The familiar story of the hoop snake which missed a man, but killed a white oak tree is related in the state guidebook *Arkansas.*[3] But this version of the tale goes on to say that fifteen years later the same man came back, cut down the tree for firewood, and absentmindedly used a splinter as a toothpick. "The hoop snake's poison, which had long since

[3] Page 97.

penetrated every fiber of the tree, had never lost its strength. The woodcutter died before sundown."

Whatever the truth may be, many old settlers tell of a man driving an oxcart through the hills, when a hoop snake came rolling down the trail and plunged its deadly stinger into the wagon-tongue. The driver killed the snake with his revolver, but the poison remained in the wood. A short time later the oxen seemed to be pulling very hard, but making little progress. The wagon-tongue had swollen till it was as big as a barrel, and the swelling had spread to the axle, which was so distended that the wheels could not turn. Lowell Thomas [4] says that this incident "occurred shortly after the Civil War, in the Ozark Mountains near Springfield, Missouri," and credits it to Jackson Jones, who later moved up into Illinois and became sheriff of Lewis County. I once heard a country doctor tell the Thomas version of this tale near Ozark, Missouri, some fifteen miles south of Springfield. The natives all pretended to take it seriously, and nobody cracked a smile. "Yes, sir," said one old codger solemnly, "them hoop snakes sure are pizen."

According to another variant, the wagon-tongue swelled so big that it had to be trimmed down with choppin'-axes. When the boys finally got it back to normal size, they had seven ricks of cordwood left over an' a pile of chips as big as a haystack.

Frank Payne used to tell of the hoop snake he encountered on the Bill Mathes farm, just south of Galena, Missouri. It bit the handle of his hoe when he struck at it, Frank said. In less than an hour the handle swelled up so big that they split it into four pieces, each as big as an ordinary fence rail. This story about the snake that bit the hoe-handle, causing it to swell up an' bust, is found in one version of the "Arkansas Traveler" dialogue reported by Masterson.[5]

[4] *Tall Stories*, p. 128.   [5] *Tall Tales of Arkansaw*, pp. 207, 347.

It was a rattlesnake, though, instead of the usual hoop snake.

During the First World War, when black walnut was very valuable and men came through the Ozarks buying every good walnut tree they could find, the boys in Howell County, Missouri, conceived a great idea. All they had to do, according to these enthusiasts, was to capture a couple of hoop snakes and train them to bite walnut logs. Thus, a small sapling could be turned into a great log five or six feet in diameter, worth a lot of money.

Coy Logan, a schoolteacher of Berryville, Arkansas,[6] repeats the old story of the hoop snake that struck a small sprout, which rapidly swelled into an enormous tree. The tree was sawed up into boards and used to build a chicken house. The tale is all orthodox so far, but Logan adds that when they painted the building, it shrunk until it was no bigger than a bird box. "The turpentine in the paint," he explains, "had taken the swelling out of the lumber."

G. H. Pipes [7] tells of a hoop snake which struck at a man, but missed, and the stinger broke off in a flint boulder. The rock popped and cracked and swelled, and in two days it developed into the rugged knob that is now called Hoopsnake Mountain. Another of Pipes' heroes thrust his rifle forward just as a hoop snake struck, and the deadly sting stuck fast in the muzzle. In ten minutes the gun became so heavy that the hillman had to drop it. Lying on the ground, it kept on swelling till the barrel was fifty feet long and big around as a washtub. This happened somewhere on Roark Creek in southern Missouri, not far from Reeds Spring. Unfortunately the rifle was buried in one of the landslides incidental to the formation of Hoopsnake Mountain.

Perhaps many of the hoop snake stories were told to

[6] *Ozark Guide*, Spring, 1946, p. 344.
[7] *Strange Customs of the Ozark Hillbilly*, pp. 28–29.

children in order to keep them out of the high grass. Or maybe some hillfolk really believed that hoop snakes were somehow connected with the powers of evil. People in Taney County, Missouri, still tell a tale about William Henry Lynch, the man who owned and developed Devil's Den, now known as Marvel Cave. Lynch was a Canadian and wore a pointed beard of a type not often seen in the Ozarks. It made him look a bit like the pictures of Satan in certain old books. One day old man Lynch came riding down from Springfield on a high-wheel bicycle, the first ever seen in these parts. "Here comes the Devil, a-ridin' a hoop snake!" a little boy screamed. "Yes," cried another, who noticed the little wheel behind the big one, "an' there's a young hoop snake a-follerin' like a colt!"

There really were some gigantic snakes hereabouts in the early days. The snakes run smaller nowadays, but we still have the big stories. Colonel A. S. Prather, of Kirbyville, Missouri, used to tell of the big rattler he killed with his revolver about 1880. The critter was coiled, he said, and the bulk of its body was as big as an ordinary washtub. And Mrs. C. P. Mahnkey, of Mincy, Missouri, told me that she saw a very large rattlesnake that a neighbor killed in 1885. An amateur taxidermist tried to preserve this reptile, and it required seven bushels of bran to stuff the skin.

Only a few miles from Mrs. Mahnkey's home town a boy swore that he had killed a rattlesnake so big he couldn't carry it home. The varmint was two foot thick an' longer'n a well-rope! He took his axe and chopped off the head and the tip of the tail, knowing that the folks would never believe his story without some objective evidence. The snake had only seven rattles, but they were as big as coffee cups, and the head was about the size of a water bucket.

An old-time railroader told me that when they were

building the road through Harrison, Arkansas, some of the section-men killed a rattlesnake so big that his rattles looked like a string of milk cans.

I have heard eye-witness accounts of very large serpents, some of them thirty feet long, in both Missouri and Arkansas. If these big snakes exist, they are not native to the Ozarks, but pythons escaped from some traveling circus. Charley Webb of Sayre, Oklahoma, really did find a fifteen-foot python in his barn, according to a United Press story of October 26, 1948. It was dead, however, having swallowed one of Webb's pigs which was evidently too big for it. A carnival outfit had offered $150 for the return of the reptile, but Webb had only the skin to show that he had captured it, and the carnies wouldn't pay off.

Then there is the story of the Arkansas farmer who met a monstrous bullsnake coming down the road. About thirty feet long, he said it was. What really worried him was the fact that it was coming tail first. He ran around behind the snake and chopped its head off with his axe, but the critter kept right on down the road. Looking closer, he saw a row of little black feet sticking out underneath the big snake's body. That bullsnake had swallowed a whole litter of pigs, one after another, and a snake always swallows its prey head first. So when the sharp little hooves had cut through the monster's belly, and the pigs started to run, the snake had to travel backward.

An old soldier in Cedar County, Missouri, used to tell about his two big mules, one of which wore a bell. They failed to show up one morning, and the owner supposed somebody had stolen them. Several months later he heard old Pete's bell, but it sounded strangely muffled. He and the boys went out to hunt for it, and finally found a tremendous bullsnake in the pasture. The snake was between forty and fifty feet long. Pete's bell was inside the snake, and it appears

that the bell rang only when the reptile moved about, pre-
sumably in search of more mules.

In Galena, Missouri, one may still hear the story of Frank
Hembree's big snake, a practical joke which has grown into
a legend in Hembree's own lifetime. Frank was a great
joker, and for a long time he went about talking of the great
serpent that he had captured. Thirty feet long, it was, an'
about as thick as Charley Craig. Frank kept it in his smokehouse, and warned everybody to stay away from the building, as there was no tellin' what a snake that big might do.

Finally a villager—some say it was old Sigel Galloway,
who was near-sighted anyhow—went up to Frank's place
and peered into the darkened smokehouse. Down to the
square he came at a full gallop, and there was no doubt of his
sincerity. "Godamighty, fellers, he's got it! He's got the
biggest damn' snake ever saw in these parts! Big enough to
eat pigs an' hound dogs, an' children even! There ought to
be a law ag'in people keepin' such critters!" Many citizens
were really convinced now, and some even complained to
Dr. J. H. Young, mayor of Galena. Dr. Young knew that
there was nothing in Frank's smokehouse but a few lengths
of stovepipe, with gunnysacks draped over them, but he
made no comment.

Hembree now circulated among the farmers who came in
to the village and offered to buy any sick calves, geese, or
turkeys that they might have. The big snake had to be fed
only twice a year, he said, but it ate enormously when it did
eat. The varmint would take a whole calf at a gulp, said
Frank, with five or six turkeys for a chaser.

I believe it is a fact that people drove to Galena from
several nearby towns, and some even came from Springfield,
nearly fifty miles away, to see Frank Hembree's big snake.
What's more I have heard solid citizens of Kansas City and
St. Louis declare that they actually saw it, through a crack or

knothole in the smokehouse door. But most of these people were discouraged by Frank himself, who told them that the great serpent was "on a rampage the last few days," and so dangerous that he wouldn't allow anybody to go near the smokehouse. Several persons assured me that "Cotton" Rogers of Galena took his wife and kids up there one Sunday to see the snake, but Frank said it had crawled down a deep hole because of the hot weather, and he refused to stir it up. "Cotton" and his family were a little indignant about this, but apparently they never doubted that Frank had the snake.

At this period Frank talked a good deal of taking the big snake on the road and exhibiting it at carnivals and street fairs. He said he could charge fifty cents for the privilege of peeking at the great reptile through a hole in the canvas, and make a lot of money. He and Tom McCord often discussed the project, in such a way as to be overheard by some credulous "furriners." With gaping tourists listening, Tom would say that he had a good truck, but couldn't get a cage strong enough to keep the snake safely. "If we'd have a wreck and the serpent was to get away," said he, "it might eat a child or maybe kill a lot of people, and we'd have a law-suit on our hands." And Frank would nod his head solemnly.

In 1937 or 1938 a sales-tax auditor came to Galena, and "Shike" Stewart set him on Frank Hembree. This man collected the tax that Frank really owed, as he was running a little café at the time. Then the tax man said: "Mr. Hembree, our records show that you have never paid any tax from your snake show." Frank laughed. "Oh, that's just a joke," he said, "I ain't got any big snake." The sales tax man replied seriously that he had heard different; that people all the way from Joplin to Kansas City had told him about the snake, and that he knew Frank had been charging a fifty-cent admission fee. Frank admitted later that he had a hard time convincing the tax collector that there was no big snake, and was "sweatin' blood" before he finally got rid of the fellow. Nothing more was heard of Hembree's big snake for some time. A local business man told me that Frank actually had to pay $3.10, but the general impression is that he didn't really pay anything. The boys certainly had him worried for awhile, though.

It is commonly believed, in the Ozarks, that snakes like milk and will suck a cow's tits to get it. I have known sober, serious-minded adults to declare that they have actually seen big snakes milking cows in the pasture. One fellow told me that he had twelve fine cows, but they gave practically no milk, because "dozens an' dozens of milk snakes was a-strippin' 'em." Referring to this matter, L. W. Shelton wrote in the Springfield, Missouri, *News and Leader:* [8] "That has happened with a cow now and then, but not with a herd. Some cows won't stand with a snake winding round her legs. Some will." My old friend Sam Leath, of Eureka Springs, Arkansas, not only believes that snakes milk cows but also that milk snakes sometimes slip into houses and suck women's breasts while the women are asleep and know nothing about it. Leath doesn't claim that he ever saw anything like this, but he heard the story told by someone whom he regards as trustworthy. He repeated the tale to Otto Ernest Rayburn and to me, and evidently regards it as the truth. It seems to me that a snake's mouth, full of needle-like teeth pointing backward, would make milking difficult. I am not prepared to say that the story is not true, but I should like to examine a cow or a woman that had been milked by a snake.

Many people in Taney County, Missouri, say that they have killed big timber rattlers with hair on them. "Like coarse bristles, black, about three inches long," the story

[8] April 29, 1945.

goes. "Mostly there's a thin scatterin' of bristles just back of the snake's head, an' maybe a few shorter ones about eight or ten inches from the tip of his tail." So many honest men told this story that I was almost persuaded that they had seen rattlesnakes with something like bristles on them. It occurred to me that some kind of parasites might have a hair-like appearance, but the experts at the American Museum of Natural History tell me that nothing remotely resembling bristles has ever been found on snakes anywhere; Dr. Charles M. Bogert, of the Department of Herpetology, suggests that the "hairs" might be cactus-spines, but this does not impress me, since the only cactus in this region is the prickly pear, which has short spines very different from the three-inch bristles which my neighbors insist they have seen on these Taney County rattlesnakes. So perhaps it's only a tall tale, after all.

There is a very general belief that the kingsnake, which has no poison fangs, can kill any copperhead or rattler. And there are people who say that the kingsnake is not affected by the venom of a rattlesnake, because it eats rattlesnake weed as an antidote. The story goes that every time a rattler bites the kingsnake, the latter hurries to a nearby snake-weed and nibbles off a leaf or two before returning to the fight. It is said that the kingsnake always makes sure that this particular weed is growing within easy reach; if the rattlesnake weed isn't there, the kingsnake will not fight the rattler.

A farmer near Hot Springs, Arkansas, told me that he once saw a blacksnake and a rattlesnake fighting. Every time the blacksnake was bitten it rushed to a snakeweed a few feet away, pulled off a leaf, and returned to the battle. By way of experiment the man uprooted the plant and moved it about ten yards away. A moment later the black-snake hurried over to get a dose of snakeweed. Finding the plant gone, the blacksnake fell into convulsions and died before the hillman could fetch the weed back. This whole thing doubtless began as a tall tale, but there are people in Missouri and Arkansas today who apparently accept it as a fact.

Thomas Hart Benton [9] repeats a curious old yarn about the rattler's fangs which stuck in a leather boot, and killed several persons who wore the boot, before anybody knew where the venom was coming from. Masterson [10] prints a version of this story from Polk County, Arkansas, adding that he found the same item in a manuscript dated 1714 in the British Museum. Scientists dismiss this tale as nonsense, but it still persists. I have heard it at least a dozen times myself, in widely separated sections of the Ozark country.

There is a story of a drunken cattleman, on a fishing trip in northwest Arkansas, who had a terrible diarrhea of the sort the old-timers call flux. He walked out into the woods to ease himself, but came back holding up his pants and yelling that he had been bitten by a rattlesnake. The marks of the snake's fangs showed on his buttocks, which soon turned red with some swelling. His friends dosed him with whiskey and sent for a doctor, but privately they thought he was doomed. Nevertheless, he still had the flux, and pretty soon he staggered out into the woods again, on the opposite side of the camp from the scene of his snake bite. This time the poor fellow came running back, yelling louder than before, shouting that he had been snake-bit again! His friends doubted this, but sure enough he showed the marks of the reptile's fangs on the opposite side of his posterior. Finally it was discovered that he had injured himself by sitting on his own spurs, and had never been snake-bitten at all. As soon as his friends took his boots off,

[9] *An Artist in America*, pp. 210–211.
[10] *Tall Tales of Arkansaw*, pp. 390–393.

the poor fellow was able to defecate in reasonable comfort.

Some of the best whoppers about an incredible abundance of serpents contain cryptic references to witchcraft and the like; I have discussed these supernatural snake-showers in *Ozark Superstitions.*[11] A man near Day, Missouri, told me seriously that a certain hollow was so full of snakes that they had regular runways through the weeds, "big as stove-pipes and slick as glass." I went to see this place, and the paths were there, all right. But I think it must have been groundhogs that made them, rather than serpents. Another fellow, referring to the same locality, said that the country is so rough and the hollers so steep that the serpents cain't climb out. They just go on a-breedin' an' gettin' thicker every year. "Why," said he, "there's snakes piled up three foot deep in some of them hollers!"

Yarns about very large turtles are not uncommon, and I have recorded two or three of them on pages 69–70. Nancy Clemens of Springfield, Missouri, reports another sort of turtle story that she got from a country boy near Zinc, Arkansas. A fisherman, according to this tale, found a very large nest of turtle eggs. He hatched them under hens, and when the turtles were yearlings he started to drive the herd overland to the Little Rock market. The animals traveled on the rocky roads until they all got sore feet and were forced to rest for days at a time. Finally the driver had every turtle shod with iron by a crossroads blacksmith. Everything was fine now, but when the turtles came to White River and missed the ford they all drowned, because the shoes were so heavy that they couldn't swim a stroke. Nothing daunted, the turtle-herder bought thousands of tin cans from a nearby tomato cannery. Then he heated some big rocks, and threw 'em into the river. After the water had simmered for awhile, he filled all the cans and sold 'em to

[11] Pages 159–160.

the big hotels in Little Rock and Hot Springs. Everybody said it was the finest turtle soup they ever tasted.

Another turtle story begins when a cowpuncher from Oklahoma, visiting an Arkansas hillman, was shown some very large potatoes. "Purty good," he said, "but nothin' like what we raise in Oklahomy." The hillbilly obtained some large yellow squashes and tied them to the branches of a pear-tree in the back yard. The cowpuncher stared at them with bulging eyes. "Them's mighty big pears," he admitted, "but I've saw bigger in Oklahomy." That night the hillman went down to the creek and caught an enormous snapping turtle, nearly three feet long. He put it in the Oklahoman's bed. The cowpoke saw the turtle when he pulled down the blankets, and called his host from the other end of the cabin. "For God's sake," he cried, "what's this in my bed?" The hillman glanced at the reptile, and replied that it was an Arkansas bedbug. The cowboy looked a bit pale, but he stuck to his guns. "Cute little feller, ain't he?" quavered the man from Oklahoma.

The way Isabel France [12] tells the tale, it was a Texan who was doing the bragging. The Texan claimed that everything was bigger down in his state, and the Arkansawyer replied reasonably that there might be some truth in this, but it surely didn't apply to cutworms. Whereupon the Texan told how many hundred acres of tomatoes, peppers, and so forth were mowed down every spring by the colossal cutworms of the Lone Star state. "Mister," said the hillman, "you don't know anything about cutworms. Why, the cutworms are so big *here* that the woman and I have to dip strings in coal oil and tie round our young-uns' ankles, to keep the cutworms from cutting off their feet!"

The cutworms really do get pretty bad in the Ozarks sometimes. As recently as 1948 they cut down most of the

[12] *Arkansas Gazette*, July 20, 1947.

early tomato-plants, and tomatoes are the hillman's chief money crop. Ralph C. Bates, who lives on Elbow Creek near Kissee Mills, Missouri, told me of a city feller who asked why gardeners always hang their hoes up in trees. "So the cutworms cain't reach 'em," replied one of Bates' neighbors. "The cutworms in this country don't approve of hoes, an' they'll snip off a hoe-handle every time they get a chance." It was in 1948, too, that I heard Joe Beaver, of Eureka Springs, Arkansas, tell one about a farmer who was trying to drag his new harrow out of the garden patch. "Why don't you just leave it lay, Paw?" asked the farmer's daughter. "That's a plumb good harrow," was the answer. "You think I'm goin' to leave it out there for the cutworms to chaw up?"

It is hardly possible to exaggerate the abundance of wood-ticks, but there are many tall stories about the size and ferocity of these pests. In Taney County, Missouri, I slept in a lean-to kitchen and awoke to find the whole place full of smoke and a great hullabaloo, with women and children crying all about. The pipe of the cookstove had fallen down, but we put out the fire without much difficulty, and there was no serious damage. Discussing the incident later, a neighbor suggested that "one of them big ticks must have fell down the chimney an' plugged up the stovepipe."

A doctor in Pineville, Missouri, said publicly that it is necessary to drink whiskey in the summer time in order to ward off the woodticks, which never attack a man who is thoroughly saturated with moonshine. "It ain't safe for a teetotaler to walk through the timber," he said. "Them ticks will be onto him in droves, like ants after a caterpillar!" It is a fact that total abstainers are mighty scarce in Mc-Donald County, but I'm not sure that the woodticks have anything to do with it.

They used to tell a strange story about the Harrycane

Bottoms, on Little Sugar Creek, near Jane, Missouri. It seems that the Rickman boys heard somebody down in the Bottoms hollering "Murder! Murder!" They all ran down there, but when they arrived breathless, it was nothin' but a big old woodtick that had got a tenpenny nail stuck in his foot.

The realtors assure strangers that there are no mosquitoes in the Ozarks, but we who live in these here hills know better. We have plenty of mosquitoes, and big ones, too. In pioneer days these pests were even more abundant than they are now. The Reverend Robert R. Witten [13] recalls his experience as a preacher at Poplar Bluff, Missouri, in the 1870's. "But oh, the mosquitoes!" he writes. "I have seen the air fairly darkened with them, and they would roar like a swarm of bees."

An old hunter told me seriously that if it were not for the mosquitoes, there would be no squirrels in the Ozark country. This seemed very odd to me, but he said the skeeters bite so savagely in mulberry time, that a man can't stand still long enough to draw a bead on anything. If it were not so, he said, the hunters would have killed all the squirrels long ago.

In some parts of Arkansas, if one believes the old-timers, it required two men to shoot a squirrel in the summer time. The first man fired a charge of small shot, to clean out the mosquitoes between the hunter and his quarry. With the insects out of the way, the second man could shoot the squirrel with his rifle.

Remarking upon the size of mosquitoes in the hill country, Thomas Bangs Thorpe [14] admitted that the insects are "rather enormous. But Arkansas is large, her rivers are large, her varmints are large. A small mosquito would be of

[13] *Pioneer Methodism in Missouri*, p. 34.
[14] *Spirit of the Times*, March 27, 1841, pp. 43–44.

no more use in Arkansas than preaching in a cane-brake."
And a hundred years after Thorpe's time, Bob Burns of
Van Buren was describing a certain variety or strain of the
Arkansas mosquito. They looked pretty much like ordinary
mosquitoes, he said, except that every one of 'em had a
two-inch white spot between the eyes.

Not far from Mena, Arkansas, they say that the skeeters
grow so big that hunters from up North have shot them
when they flushed, mistaking them for woodcock. Some
very large ones have been brought down by riflemen who
thought they were chicken hawks. Trappers tell of catching
them in steel traps set for wolves or bobcats. Some of 'em
are so big they can stand flat-footed on the ground and
drink out of a rain barrel. Two or three big ones make such
a racket that you can't hear it thunder. In wet weather a
lot of young mosquitoes got together in the bottoms east of
Mena and sang so loud that everybody thought there must
be a camp-meeting at Pine Ridge.

In southwest Missouri it is said that mosquitoes often kill
foxhounds; three or four of 'em will rassle a dog down and
then suck his blood until he's dead. In eastern Oklahoma the
boys frequently see jackrabbits running with mosquitoes
on their backs, mostly ridin' astride like a jockey on a race
horse. When the blood is all sucked out of the rabbit, the
mosquito dismounts and hides in the brush until another
rabbit comes along.

Dr. Oakley St. John, of Pineville, Missouri, used to tell
about the time mosquitoes raided his place on the Cowskin,
which is called Elk River nowadays. "I got into my tent,"
said he, "and tied the flaps shut. But the damn' things kept
bitin' me right through the tent. Some of 'em had bills two
feet long. Finally I took the hammer and began clinchin'
their bills. Just as soon as one stuck his snoot through the
canvas I'd bend it over and brad it with the hammer. There

he'd be, fast to the tent and flappin' like a turkey with its head cut off. This worked fine for awhile, till I had ten or twelve of 'em clinched. Then they all got together and flapped their wings at the same time. It was too much strain on the tent-pegs. They just pulled up the whole damn' camp and flew away with it."

Near Gaineville, Missouri, I heard the story of a pioneer who stepped out of his cabin at dusk and was surrounded by giant skeeters before he could get back into the house. He killed three or four with his revolver, and then crawled under a big brass wash-kettle in the back yard. The mosquitoes tried to pull the kettle off'n him, but he held it down. Then several of the biggest ones, striking with all their force, drove their bills right through the sides of the kettle. With the butt of his pistol the man clinched the end of every beak that penetrated. After five or six mosquitoes were thus riveted to the kettle, their frenzied struggles lifted the vessel clear of the ground. In the resulting confusion the hillman beat off his assailants and escaped. The big kettle rose slowly into the air and sailed away above the treetops. Several months later some boys, digging in a great pile of mosquito-bones on a gravel-bar near Cotter, Arkansas, found the kettle and sold it to a local junkman. It wasn't any good, except for the weight of metal in it, because there were six round two-inch holes right through the sides of the vessel.

There are other stories of mortal combat and even formal duels between mosquitoes and human beings. A horse-player in Hot Springs, Arkansas, declared that the big skeeters from Oklahoma wear blue Levi-Strauss pants and carry whet-stones in the pockets to sharpen their bills on. A professional wrestler in Joplin, Missouri, claimed he had killed four adult mosquitoes with his bare hands and had four notches on his forearms to show for it. But this fellow was given to boasting, and his associates did not believe the story.

When window screens were first introduced into the Ozarks, about the turn of the century, the big mosquitoes were baffled for awhile. But they soon learned to carry very small mosquitoes to a screened cottage and push them through the mesh. Feeding upon the occupants of the house, the little fellows grew very rapidly. As soon as they were big enough, they unhooked the screen doors and let the adult mosquitoes in.

Years ago the newspapers carried the story of a man in northwest Arkansas who was awakened by two mosquitoes beside his bed. They were about the size of ostriches, he said, but much more muscular. "Let's take this feller out in the woods an' eat him," said one mosquito. The other shook its head. "No, we better eat him right here. If we drag him out in the woods, the *big* mosquitoes might take him away from us."

Some scoundrels near Bella Vista, Arkansas, not far from the Missouri line, were trying to sell a tourist some fake Indian relics. One fellow claimed to have found the hulk of Noah's Ark half buried in a gravel-bar near Pineville, Missouri. There was much talk of the old battlefields, village sites, and so forth, with some reference to alleged evidence of Spanish exploration. Finally a farmer said that near his home was an old field where there must have been a terrible battle between the mosquitoes and the gallynippers. There were big bones lying all about, he said, some with dried flesh and tendons still adherent. In one place they had found the mummified body of a half-grown gallynipper, about the size of a man. It was wearing a chain-mail shirt, apparently of Spanish origin. A big skeeter's bill was stuck right through the mummy's chest, chain-mail and all.

Another Ozark windy is a tale of the lumber camps near Waldron, Arkansas, and concerns a yoke of oxen called Tom and Jerry. Both animals showed up missin' one morning, and several men set out to search for them. Jerry was soon located, but Tom was nowhere to be found. Tom always wore a bell, and presently the bell was heard on a distant ridge. When the loggers reached the spot, they were dumfounded to hear the tinkling of the bell directly over their heads. On looking up they saw a turrible big skeeter, almost as big as an airplane, settin' on top of a tall pine. Looking closer, they saw that he was picking his teeth with one of Tom's horns. "He'd et pore Tom plumb up," said the story-teller. "An' thar he set, a-ringin' the bell for Jerry!"

The guidebook *Arkansas*,[15] sponsored by the Secretary of State in Little Rock, tells of a hunter who caught a big mosquito in a bear trap. Figuring that maybe he could train it to drill wells, he buckled a mule's harness onto the beast. But the creature broke loose, seized a cow, and flapped away with it through the treetops. "That, of course, is an exaggeration," the book assures us. "Generally, it takes two swampland mosquitoes to fly off with a cow."

According to a yarn current in Fort Smith, Arkansas, somebody sent to Texas for a few pairs of giant wasps, the kind they call turkey hawks down there. The turkey hawk is like our common tarantula hawk, but a good deal bigger. It was hoped that the turkey hawks would kill off the big mosquitoes. But the turkey hawks and the mosquitoes mated, producing a dwarf hybrid no bigger than a goose, but with stingers at both ends. This nameless pest caused untold misery in the hill country for many years. And even today, it is said, elderly people around Fort Smith look with suspicion at anything with a Texas brand on it.

One good thing about them big mosquitoes, said a native of Blue Eye, Missouri, is that they enrich the ground somethin' wonderful. Skeeter dung is the best fertilizer in the

[15] Page 98.

world. So much better than cow chips or horse manure that there ain't no comparison at all. The only thing that approaches it is bat-droppin's, like the boys dig out of them big caves up on James River.

There is another ancient tale, purporting to explain the comparative scarcity of mosquitoes in some sections of the Ozarks. In the early days, according to the legend, skeeters were very large and troublesome everywhere. It was in the winter of 1859 that a hunter named Zack Benton crawled into a large cavern. The cave was warm because of a hot spring somewhere in its depths, and the walls and ceiling were covered with giant mosquitoes, hanging head downward like sleeping bats. Zack was a clever and public-spirited citizen, so he hastened to the settlement and told some influential men of his discovery. Realizing that here was an opportunity to rid the whole region of mosquitoes at one swoop, they hurried to the cavern with two wagonloads of home grown tobacco, which was piled up just inside the entrance. Having set this stuff afire, they plugged all openings with rocks, using moss and mud for chinking. Then the whole party camped nearby and spent the night in drinking whiskey and singing in celebration of their enterprise. Next morning the cave was opened, and the floor was found to be covered five feet deep with dead mosquitoes, some of them as big as turkeys. One of the largest hung for several days in front of Ed Jefferson's livery stable. The reek of the decaying insects annoyed the whole countryside for two or three summers. But there have been no mosquitoes in Poot Holler since then, except for a few little fellows which "follered the furriners" into the neighborhood in recent years.

Most of the grasshopper stories in the Ozarks stem from the great invasion of the 1870's, when it is said that grasshoppers devoured every green plant in the Middle West,

from North Dakota to Texas. There have been lesser plagues
since that time, but none to compare with the grasshopper
wars of 1874–1876. Men who saw the insects feeding in the
cornfields say that they made more noise than a herd of
cattle. People still living near Independence, Missouri, swear
that grasshoppers piled up in deep drifts like snow and actually stopped the Missouri Pacific passenger train. The city
employees swept up more than 3,500 pounds of grasshoppers
off the sidewalks of the public square.

Will Peacock, a city official at Independence, was quoted
in the Kansas City *Star* as saying that "there was a two-foot
stone fence around the courthouse lawn. The grass was nice
and green, and the hoppers crawled against the fence and
banked up against it until they climbed over each other
into the grass. They cleaned it off as smooth as a bone."
Mr. Peacock added that the chickens ate millions of the
smaller grasshoppers, while the big hoppers chased the
chickens. The dogfennel and Jimson weed were eaten clear
down to the ground, and Mr. Peacock says that he has
"seen very little of these two weeds in Jackson County
since."

Ben Yankee, another old Missourian, said that the cattle
mostly starved to death during the grasshopper season and
the hogs lived on slippery-elm roots. Another man, who
must be nameless here, swears that some of the hoppers were
ten inches through the thorax and had big front teeth like
beavers. They all chewed tobacco and spit on the sidewalks,
while some of them could whistle "Marching through
Georgia" through their teeth. "Every time we killed one
of the critters," a farmer said, "two more come to bury him."
Another remark, widely quoted at the time, was that it required two companies of militia to keep the hoppers from
moving the courthouse off the public square.

"Them grasshoppers would gobble up a rail fence like

tourists eatin' sparrowgrass," one early settler declared, an' sometimes they et big holes in stone walls. Our old sheep-dog tackled one of the biggest grasshoppers, an' throwed him down right in front of the corncrib. But the hopper just stuck up his hind legs, with two rows of big thorns on 'em, an' gutted pore old Towser slick as a whistle."

A farmer near Lamar, Missouri, reported that he heard a great uproar in his barnyard at high noon, and rushed out to find a giant grasshopper strangling his Shanghai rooster. The hopper was killed with a choppin'-axe, but the rooster was so shaken that he was never much good after that. The poor creature hid under a corncrib most of the time, neglecting his social duties altogether, and came out for food only at dusk.

The loafers at Southwest City, Missouri, tell of a man who left his team in the field while he went to a nearby still-house for a jug of whiskey. When he returned an hour later, four big hoppers had devoured a horse, and were pitchin' horse-shoes for the other one. In another version, the insects had eaten both horses, and were pitchin' to see who would get the harness for dessert.

The grasshoppers came to Bates County, Missouri, in 1875. As soon as the green stuff was all gone, they ate the putty off every window sash and gnawed the shingles till most of the roofs leaked. Some of them even chewed on an old sow until her back was raw and bleeding. The old-timers swear that this is the truth, and maybe it is. An old woman who lived south of Rolla, Missouri, in the late 1870's declared that the adult grasshoppers ate her turnips as far down into the ground as they could reach, and then let the young-uns down on ropes to devour the taproots.

Down near Cotter, Arkansas, they say that the hoppers began catching and eating fish after the vegetation was cleaned up. Great swarms of grasshoppers milled around on

the river banks, and some learned to dive after minnows just as kingfishers do. Others banded together and beached big hogmollies, catching so many that the gravel bars were white with fish bones. The larger hoppers lay in wait for ospreys and herons and minks and otters, often devouring the fisher as well as his finny prey. They robbed human anglers, too. It is said that a platoon of big hoppers captured three boatmen on White River and made them run trotlines for more than a week, devouring the fish as fast as they were taken off the hooks.

The old-timers at Forsyth, Missouri, tell of a farmer who narrowly escaped decapitation, when two hoppers flew past carrying a fence rail between them. They were taking the rail down to the village of Protem, to batter in the door of a locked corncrib.

An old soldier testified that he had seen grasshoppers overrun an army camp in the 1880's. They even attacked mounted officers, and some of these fellows were forced to use their sidearms in self-defense. On one moonlight night several hundred big hoppers were seen on the parade ground, drilling with the Springfield rifles they had carried out of the barracks.

Only one hillman, so far as I have heard, was ever benefited by the visitation of grasshoppers. This man, in northeastern Oklahoma, was about to lose his onion crop by reason of the dry weather. But when the insects swarmed into the onion patch, they began to weep copiously. The tears flowed so freely that they moistened the ground, and finally flooded the whole field, drowning many of the smaller grasshoppers. The farmer made an unusually fine crop that season, and the bodies of the drowned hoppers furnished excellent fertilizer for the next year's planting.

The old-timers allege that Professor C. V. Riley, state entomologist of Missouri, seriously advised the farmers to use grasshoppers for food. "Pull off their legs and wings and fry 'em in deep grease," said he. The hillfolk in southern Missouri were mighty indignant about this. "We're payin' that feller a big salary," shouted a local politician, "to show us how to combat these here insects that's a-devourin' our crops. An' what does he tell us? Why, to go out an' eat grasshoppers! Well, we may come to it, at that, if we git hungry enough. But we sure don't need no high-collared bug-hunter to rub our noses in it!"

Most of the Ozark stories about cockroaches and tumble-bugs are unprintable, but some of the lightning-bug yarns are innocent enough. In Argenta, Arkansas, there was a tale about an old fellow who drove a rattletrap Ford. Both head-lights had long been out of commission, but the man just caught a handful of lightnin'-bugs and put them behind the lenses. The glow which resulted was not too bright, but it was a lot better than no light at all.

Here is one which Lowell Thomas [16] credits to H. A. Hunt, of Little Rock. It seems that Sandy MacShan, hotel keeper at Collins, Arkansas, illuminated the village with his troupe of trained lightnin' bugs. These insects would swarm about the railroad station when the night train came through, and if any passenger got off, they would fly just above his head, thus lighting the traveler's way to the hotel. Some of the lightnin' bugs would hurry on ahead and line up so as to form the words "Hotel de MacShan" over the tavern door.

We were swapping whoppers one day in the Veterans Hospital at Fayetteville, Arkansas, in the spring of 1944, I think it was. When my turn came I repeated this Sandy MacShan story and asked the boys if they thought there could be any factual basis for such a yarn. An old infantry-man from St. Paul, Arkansas, said it all sounded reasonable

[16] *Tall Stories*, p. 25.

enough to him, except the part about the lightnin' bugs spelling out the sign. "That feller must have painted a pattern for 'em to foller, or else figgered out some kind of signals," he said thoughtfully. "It don't seem likely them bugs could learn to spell it *by heart* thataway."

7 Backwoods
supermen

TELLERS OF TALL TALES require heroes of superhuman strength and colorful accomplishment. "It has been said," writes John Gould Fletcher [1] "that in a society which is not industrial, the usual folk tale is one of physical prowess, and it is true that such are extremely common in the Ozarks." Apparently many of the backwoods demigods are somehow evolved from historical characters. Sometimes the story-tellers just borrow a great man's name, but often they make free use of his outstanding peculiarities as well. Some of the wildest windies ever heard in the Ozark country are based on the adventures of Colonel Davy Crockett, the bear-hunting Congressman from Tennessee.

Whether or not Crockett ever spent much time in the Ozarks I do not know, although he certainly stopped in Little Rock on his way to join the Texians in 1835. No matter, for it was not the historical Crockett who came to the country "a-ridin' a catamount, with a b'ar under each arm"; who always killed buffalo with his bowie knife, to save ammunition; who ate a bear-skin for breakfast, and rode a wild razorback from Fayetteville to New Orleans; who made a fire by whacking one of his important members against a flint-rock and catching the sparks in a piggin of elbow grease.

Even today many Arkansas notables speak of Davy Crockett with a kind of wondering affection, almost as if he were a native Arkansawyer. They feel that a man who

[1] *Arkansas*, p. 323.

could twist the tail off a comet, and do the other stunts credited to Colonel Crockett, must have grown up in the Bear State. The old-timers still call Arkansas by the old name, although the panty-waist legislature of 1923 changed the official title to the Wonder State. Some writers point out, however, that Arkansas was quite a place, even before Colonel Davy came to the territory. Avantus Green [2] repeats an old tale that when Crockett visited a Little Rock saloon he asked: "What are those slippery things all over the floor?" The bartender answered: "Oh, them's nothin' but eyes. The boys had a little fun gougin' last night, an' I ain't swept up yet."

When somebody offered Colonel Davy a flask of Ozark corn, in a Little Rock hotel, he tossed off the whole thing at a single drink. He did not change expression at the time, but later on he admitted that the stuff had burnt him plumb to a frazzle. "Gentlemen," said Crockett, "I et my victuals raw for two months afterwards. My gizzard stayed so all-fired hot, that the grub was cooked afore it got settled in my innards."

There are many stories about Crockett's snaggle-tooth grin, which so frightened wild animals that they fell to the ground unconscious. Even the *Arkansas Gazette* [3] which was violently pro-Jackson and therefore opposed to Crockett politically, mentions "the wonderful man who, it is said, can whip his weight in wildcats or *grin the largest panther out of the highest tree.*" According to one ancient tale, Colonel Davy saw a coon high up in a blackjack, and grinned at it repeatedly. But the animal did not fall. Enraged at this, Crockett took his axe and cut the tree down. What he had mistaken for a coon was only a big knot, which was marked somewhat like a coon because his deadly grin had stripped some of the bark off'n it.

[2] *With This We Challenge*, p. 61.   [3] Nov. 17, 1835.

Sometimes the following tale is related as Crockett's own experience, but it is really only a story that Colonel Davy used to tell about some unidentified backwoodsman. This hunter, weary of the chase, lay down at dusk under a big cedar on the crest of Whangdoodle Knob. Dozing a bit, he rolled over and came near busting his powder horn. This roused him a little, so he took the powder horn off and hung it on a yaller stob, supposedly a branch of the cedar tree above his head. When he awoke at dawn the powder horn was gone, and he couldn't even find the stob he had hung it on. He studied the matter all day, and the next night he climbed the Knob again, and sat down under the same cedar tree. Pretty soon the moon came up, a-ridin' mighty low. Seemed like the dang thing was going to light down like a turkey buzzard. The poor fellow was so frightened he forgot all about the lost powder horn. But just as he was starting down the mountain, he saw something mighty funny. So he just hunkered down right there, and the moon came a-slippin' by, so close it purty nigh blinded him. And there was his powder horn, a-hangin' on one end of the moon! He was shakin' like a leaf, but he reached up and unhooked the powder horn, and the old moon just silvered on past as though nothin' had happened. The folks at home like to died a-laughin' when he told 'em about it.

One afternoon, when Crockett was out hunting, he strayed so far that he had to sleep in the woods. Next morning he took a long running jump and landed on top of the rising sun, being wishful to ride home. But poor Davy was west of the cabin, not east as he had thought, and the sun was so high now that he dassent jump off. So there he set, and rode the sun for twenty-four hours, after which he dropped off within a hundred yards of his own doorstep. Variants of this yarn are still told by facetious hillmen, when questioned in regard to long or unexplained absences.

Another story has it that Crockett once dropped his powder horn into a deep pool, while crossing the creek on a log. A trapper named Hawley offered to dive down and recover it. Crockett waited for awhile, but Hawley did not come up. Finally Colonel Davy took off his clothes and dived into the pool, to see what was detaining Hawley. He found the trapper sitting on the creek-bottom, under twelve feet of water, calmly pouring powder out of Crockett's horn into his own. Stealing ammunition was a serious matter in those days, comparable to the crime of horse stealing on the western plains. When Colonel Davy returned to the settlement he carried two rifles and two powder horns. Hawley was never seen again.

Another historical character who became a kind of Ozark superman was Mike Fink, king of the keelboatman. He was never famous like Colonel Crockett, and the younger generation of hillfolk know little about him. Price Paine, a guide who lived on the Cowskin River, near Noel, Missouri, used to tell several good Mike Fink stories. According to one of these big tales Mike did not die at all, but disguised himself as a big catfish which stirs up storms by lashing the water with its tail. As late as 1920, according to Paine, there were still old-timers who said that floods which destroy lives and property are really caused by Mike Fink, the immortal water demon who hates all humanity.

The oil fields of Arkansas and Oklahoma are full of tall stories about a driller named Morgan. Newspapermen and magazine writers often call him *Gid* Morgan [4] or *Gib* Morgan,[5] but the old-timers say that his given name was Kemp. I have interviewed several men who insist that they knew Kemp Morgan in the early days, but their accounts vary widely. Perhaps several pioneer rope-chokers used the fa-

[4] Harry Botsford, *Saturday Evening Post*, Oct. 3, 1942, pp. 11, 71–72.
[5] Don Morris, *Life*, Mar. 17, 1947, p. 8.

mous name at different times and in different places. Some people think that there never was a flesh-and-blood Kemp Morgan, and they may be right.

James E. Duffey, an old-time driller who spent his declining years in Tulsa, Oklahoma, told me that he had heard hundreds of Kemp Morgan stories. He repeated several, but the only one I remember is about the time Kemp lost his drill in soft sand. The great driller couldn't figure out what was wrong, but it was learned later that he had busted into a prehistoric alum mine. What he thought was salt water was a strong solution of aluminum chloride, which made the hole shrink so fast that the drill could not be removed.

No exact figures are available, but the old-timers all agree that Kemp's first pipe line was the biggest ever laid anywhere. After the wells in that field went dry, the cattlemen used the pipe line as a highway. They drove herds of cattle through it on their way to the market in Kansas City. This avoided the hazards of bad weather, and prevented cattle rustlers from cutting into the herds. The only trouble was that some steers got to wandering around in the threads at the end of each mile-long pipe, and a few of the critters starved before they could be located.

Kemp Morgan was only one of several men who used to buy up dusters, which were cut up and sold to the settlers for use as water wells. These were not very satisfactory, because they warped badly if exposed to the weather. Some became so twisted that you couldn't get a bucket down to the water level. Many a dry well was pulled up, sawed into three-foot lengths, and ricked along the roads like cordwood. This salvaged material made very fine post holes. These portable post holes were a godsend to the hill-country farmers. There are places in the Ozarks where the ground is so rocky that it is almost impossible to dig a hole for a fence post.

There are stories in both Missouri and Arkansas of a very tall hillman, the tallest man ever seen in the Ozarks. Some call him Tree-Top Johnson, but the old-timers refer to him as Blinky Bluejohn, which means sour skim milk. One tale has it that Blinky was so tall he could not tell whether his feet were frozen or he had stepped into a forest fire. Neighbors always hired him to pick wild grapes, and stack hay in barn lofts, and build high chimneys, and rob chickenhawks' nests. Working in the woods, he hung his dinner bucket so high in a tree that nobody could even see it from the ground. When he wanted a drink of water, he just reached up and "squoze out" a cloud, so that the rain fell into his mouth. Backwoods folk still laugh about the time Blinky was converted, and several preachers got together to baptize him. The preachers belonged to a sect called Campbellites, and insisted on total immersion. They tried three or four rivers, but the bends in all these streams came too close together. Finally they agreed that Blinky could not be properly immersed in any body of water this side of the Gulf of Mexico. When Blinky heard this decision he cursed aloud, saying that the gulf was too damn' far away. After some wrangling, he gave up the whole idea, and never joined any church at all.

Not far from Sulphur Springs, Arkansas, a man told me that Blinky chewed enormous quantities of home-grown tobacco and that he had been known to extinguish a forest fire by spitting on it. The tobacco was so strong that it killed all vegetation, while chipmunks, lizards and other small creatures died in convulsions all over the place. On one occasion Blinky spat out a cud which happened to light on the top rail of a stake-an'-rider fence. The sun's heat caused the tobacco to expand a bit, and the frost that night covered it with a gray fuzz. Just after daybreak a man named Huggins came along, mistook the chaw for a coon, and put a rifle-bullet through the front end of it. One of the neighbors happened to see this performance, and old man Huggins could not deny the story.

My friend Tom Shiras, of Mountain Home, Arkansas, told me in 1944 that somebody had gathered up a lot of the Bluejohn stories and published them in a book for children. Something like *Mother Goose*, he said, with fine colored pictures. I have sought in vain for such a book, and so far as I can remember have never seen Blinky Bluejohn's name in print.

An old man at Sallisaw, Oklahoma, said that Blinky's real name was Toller and that originally he came from Fort Smith, Arkansas. The stories about Blinky's height, according to this informant, are mostly exaggerations. "But he was plenty big," the old man added, "about the size of two log barns." They say that Blinky used to hide in the pineries with a bundle of saplings in his right hand. When the wild geese came over he'd rise up all of a sudden an' knock down dozens of 'em, just like a boy fightin' bumblebees with a paddle. Once he stood flat-footed to look into a big nest on a mountain side; he reached up one great hand and slapped down an eagle that flew round his head, just as you or I would brush aside a mosquito.

There used to be a miner in Joplin, Missouri, who claimed to be Blinky Bluejohn's father. "Blinky is just a nickname," he explained to a crowd in Two Bills saloon. "The boy's real name is Maypole Boone Tooley, Jr. But his mother an' me ain't seen Maypole in forty years. He don't have no use for common folks, since he got so God damn' famous." The elder Tooley claimed to be nearly a hundred years old, although he didn't look a day over thirty. When pressed about this, he said he had four birthdays every year, and reckoned that might have something to do with it. I shall never forget his ninety-seventh birthday, which he celebrated by getting drunk and making a great uproar in a bawdy-house.

The crack about the age of Blinky's father recalls a guide who used to show tourists through the caves at Hahatonka, on the Niangua River, in Camden County, Missouri. His name was Charley Heimbaugh, and he must have been about forty years old when I saw him. But he always told the tourists he was seventy-five, and attributed his youthful appearance to drinking water from a spring in River Cave. It is said that some of the fat middle-aged women who visited the place drank so much water that they made themselves sick, and many carried large bottles of it back to Kansas City.

Another Niangua River guide had a long story of a man named Ticher, who said that he was present when his grandfather was born, and described the occasion in great detail. Ticher's brother thought this over for awhile, then he said: "Hell, I'm four years older'n you, an' *I* don't remember nothin' about it!"

Fred Starr, of Fayetteville, Arkansas, told me about Clyde Mitchell's encounter with a nameless "big feller" from the Tarpin Creek neighborhood. Mitchell raises the best dogs in the whole country, and he sold his finest coon-hound to this backwoods giant on a money-back guarantee. The big fellow returned the next morning, declaring that Old Blue was no good. He said the dog treed five times in one night, but each time he cut the tree down, and there wasn't no coon in it. Clyde couldn't figger that one out. Old Blue had never drawed no blanks before, and he had raised the dog from a pup. Finally Clyde decided to go along with this Tarpin Creek fellow, and they went a-huntin' the next night. It didn't take long to find out where the trouble was. Old Blue treed a coon every time, but this big fellow was so dadburn tall, he'd been cuttin' the tree off *above the coon.*

When they were putting an electric line through the wilds of southwest Missouri, in the early 1940's, crews came as soon as the area had been surveyed and cleared a right-of-way about fifty feet wide, cutting down trees and burning brush. This wide path running for miles up hill and down looked mighty odd at first. A stranger at a moonshiner's place on a hilltop gazed at it in astonishment and asked for an explanation. "Well," a loafer said solemnly, "one of them big fellers from Arkansas took a drink of Tom's whiskey here, an' that's where he tore down the brush, a-runnin' to the creek for water!" Another man confirmed this tale, adding that Tom's whiskey "stunk so bad that buzzards in the sky got loop-legged just from smellin' it." Tom just stood there, listening to this talk, not saying a word. But he looked mighty indignant.

In some settlements one hears half-serious tales of a giant blacksmith known as Bib Tarkey, who made enormous tools and household utensils, including a bullet mold to cast 600-pound cannon balls. There was a bumper crop of hay one year, and a shortage of mowers. Bib tore a piece of metal from a railroad bridge, and hammered out a scythe twenty-four feet long. With a crooked oak-tree for a handle, it is said that Tarkey cut eighty acres of grass in about thirty minutes, without any whet-rock. The implication is that he could have cut a great deal more, if he *had* found some way to sharpen his blade.

The old folks say that a big tavern-keeper at Indian Springs, Missouri, could lift more dead weight than any other man in the country. Nearly seven feet tall, this fellow weighed three hundred pounds, and not an ounce of fat in sight. He often toted two sacks of corn to McNatt's mill and carried the meal home under his arm. One day the boys decided to test him, just to see how much weight he could carry. They built a sort of platform, and set it on his great shoulders like a hod. Then they began to pile big rocks and pieces of old iron on the platform. They kept this up until he sank clear to his knees, right in the hard road beside the blacksmith shop.

According to another version of this story, the hero is Mike Allison, a gigantic private in the Confederate artillery. Bertha Job Hayes (*Arcadian Magazine*, April, 1931, p. 30) says that during the battle of Oak Hill somebody saw Mike carrying a "featherbed tick full of grapeshot, a prodigious burden" upon his back. He was "staggering in a zigzag fashion, sinking to his knees at every step, through the crust of the sun-dried earth made hard by a long continued drouth."

The boys south of Joplin, Missouri, used to tell one about a local "big feller" coming home from town, so drunk he could hardly sit his horse. About six miles out some fool in a fur coat suddenly appeared in the road. The startled horse jumped and threw the strong man to the ground. "God damn it!" he yelled. "Look what you've done now!" And with that he rushed at the fur-coated stranger and kicked him savagely in the groin. Then came a terrible fight, but the stranger was finally knocked senseless. The big feller was badly bruised and skinned up, but practically sober. He struck a match and was astounded to find that he had knocked out a full-grown bear.

An old-timer in Eureka Springs, Arkansas, told me a similar strong-man story. It seems that Louis Hanecke, who lived out on Leatherwood Creek, heard that a city fellow had lost a bird dog and was offering a substantial cash reward for the animal's recovery. One moonlight night Louis was walking along the ridge road, when he heard a rustling in the bushes and saw something that looked like the missing bird dog. He sprang forward and grabbed the creature, which fought like a wild beast. But the boy held on, and the two scrambled up hills and down hollers and across creeks and through briar-patches. When daylight came Louis's clothes were in rags and he was bleeding from head to foot, but the big animal seemed completely cowed and exhausted. When he dragged the creature out into the big road, young Hanecke saw that it was not a bird dog, but a rather shopworn panther.

There's another old yarn about a giant lumberman from Waldron, Arkansas, who used to pull up ten-inch white oaks with his hands, like a boy pullin' weeds in the corn patch. He could stand up and spit tobacco-juice "thirty foot from stand" against a strong wind. He belched after supper, and it blowed out two kerosene lamps in a house across the road, then he spit once and quenched a roaring fire of logs in the big fireplace. It was this same man, according to the legend, who drove his double-bitted axe so deep into a tree that the whole head went out of sight, and the green wood closed up tight around the handle.

Occasionally a hillman refers to Stacker Lee, a Negro gambler from Missouri, who gave his name to a Mississippi River steamboat and sold his soul to the Devil. He was seen to turn himself into a horse, and was suspected of many other transformations. It was old Stacker who went West and caused the earthquake at San Francisco in April, 1906. After an argument with a bartender, he stamped his big feet, and that caused the first shock. Still angry, he pulled up the bar by the roots; the water-pipes connected with that bar ran all over town, and Stacker kept a-pullin' till buildings were thrown down everywhere. The water all ran out, and that is why they couldn't put out the fires which destroyed the city. Stacker did not mean to do all this damage; he just intended to wreck one particular saloon in the neighborhood known as Skid Row, on Howard Street. When he saw what had happened, he was appalled. "I just didn't know my own stren'th," he muttered, and hurried back to St. Louis. There he killed Billy Lyons and was sent to the penitentiary at Jefferson City, Missouri. Some say that Stacker is still there; others think he died and went to Hell, where he's probably fightin' the Devil this very minute.

Down around Hot Springs, Arkansas, I heard the story of a strong man who bred fast horses. A stableboy somehow let one of the brag mares drown in a flooded stream. The boy fled, but the big man was so enraged that he picked up the sulky, whirled it round his head and threw it far out into the river. "If the Devil's got my mare, let him take the God damn' cart, too!" the big fellow cried.

My grandfather used to tell of a big man near Batesville, Arkansas, who was plowing in his field, when a traveler asked the direction to a neighbor's house. The big feller p'inted the way *with the plow*, lifting the whole business with one hand and jerking both horses plumb off their feet. This tale seems to be common all over the country. Sometimes it's a blacksmith coming down the road with a great anvil in his hand, who plays the part of the big feller; when asked the way to Cousin Elmer's place, he points with the anvil at arm's length and leaves the traveler open mouthed.

A nameless giant in Baxter County, Arkansas, was driving an ox team on a narrow mountain road. He met another traveler, and there was no room to pass. The big fellow unyoked his team, lifted 'em over the other outfit one at a time, and then set the wagon over behind them. They say that the strong man was breathing a little heavily now, but he hitched up again and went on his way.

E. A. Collins [6] reports a tall story about Boog Hargis' toothache, which had kept him awake for three solid weeks. Finally Boog, who was a big, strong man, tried to pull the tooth, but failed. He went to several dentists, and one after

[6] *Folk Tales of Missouri*, 1935, pp. 34–35.

another they exerted all their strength in vain. Then Boog asked a farmer, who was busy pulling stumps, to help him. The farmer hooked onto the tooth and started up the mules, while Boog sat down and locked his arms around a big stump. The farmer yelled, and the mules pulled their best, while Boog held fast to the stump. They ripped the big stump out of the ground, all right, but never did budge Boog Hargis' tooth.

A certain Missouri congressman became a legendary hero in his own lifetime, and many tales are still told of his exploits. In a political campaign it was said that this man could out-holler six bobcats a-courtin'. In fact, he made so much noise that the wind stopped a-blowin' whilst he was makin' a speech. One time he went up on Cooter Knob and hollered so loud that all the dead trees for miles around come a-crashin' down. "It was the vibration done it," a village loafer told me.

According to another story, this same congressman drank two five-gallon crocks of home-brewed ale, the stuff that used to be called "chock" in Oklahoma. Then he went to bed on the top floor of a hotel. When he awoke the building was full of smoke. The stairway was blocked, and there was no fire escape. But the weather was very cold, so our hero just kicked out a window-sash and urinated onto the crowd in the street below. The urine froze instantly into a thin yellow icicle seventy-five feet long. The congressman put on his gloves, and slid safely down the icicle into the street.

Arthur Aull, newspaperman of Lamar, Missouri, was one of the best story-tellers in the Ozarks. One of his finest tales concerned a local big fellow, who was always bragging of his athletic prowess and challenging people to duplicate his feats of strength. One day an undersized, elderly stranger called his hand. "I'll bet ten dollars," said the stranger, "that I can take a wheelbarrow and push a load of manure across the street, and you can't push the same load back." The big fellow looked at him contempuously, and put up the money. The little man rolled up his sleeves, and took hold of the handles of the wheelbarrow. "All right, get in!" said he.

There is an old tale of a man who came into Picher, Oklahoma, riding a wild bull, with a wildcat under each arm and a rattlesnake in his teeth. The rattlesnake was used as a whip, he said, being much superior to the ordinary synthetic "blacksnake" of braided leather. This fellow split big boulders by kicking them. He drank boiling coffee right out of the pot. Whenever he spit, the saliva set the prairie grass afire. Urinating carelessly one night, he washed several cabins into a creek. He shaved with a plumber's blowtorch and cut his hair with a brush hook. After a week or two somebody made bold to ask the big fellow where he came from. The man answered that he was borned an' raised in Bastard Valley, Arkansas. "The boys is kind of tough down there," he admitted. "A ordinary feller like me gets pushed around an' bullied till life ain't hardly worth livin'. So I just up an' left the God damn' place."

Old Gram Washburn, of Pittsburg, Kansas, who had lived in many parts of Missouri and Arkansas, used to tell about a hillbilly superman who fell off'n a high bluff. He struck the ground with such force that both eyes were jolted plumb out of his head. The man just picked them up, brushed the gravel and dirt off with his coat sleeve, and stuck 'em back in their sockets. The eyes worked as good as ever, except that one was p'inted just a little bit out of line.

Thomas Hart Benton [7] is a native of Neosho, Missouri, and he knows a lot of good stories. Among others, he recalls a tough riverman called "Wet Willie" Ahler, who has become a Mississippi River legend, a sort of modern Mike Fink. Flung into jail for wrecking two whore-houses, Wet

[7] *An Artist in America*, p. 127.

Willie slept soundly all night and bit off the jailor's thumb for breakfast.

Near White Rock, Missouri, I knew a farmer named Van Horn, whose corn always looked fine, although I never saw him working in the field. I mentioned this to another local character, who remarked that Van Horn hoed his corn at night in order to avoid the heat; the darkness didn't bother him at all, since he was a very fast worker. After thinking about this for awhile, I said mildly that being a fast worker couldn't help a man to see in the dark. Then the poker-faced loafer explained to me that Tom Van Horn worked so all-fired fast that the field was lighted by the sparks which always fly when a hoe hits the flint rocks.

Most mountaineers are riflemen rather than pistol shooters, but some boys in eastern Oklahoma still wear revolvers and practice with 'em in real Western fashion. It is said that one young farmer near Sallisaw, the old hangout of "Pretty Boy" Floyd and others, got so fast that he could stand in front of a mirror and beat himself to the draw.

There is a story in a guidebook published by the University of Oklahoma Press [8] about two men who practiced pistol shooting constantly. They rode along at a gallop, with their six-shooters in hand, and shot all the barbs off a long stretch of barbwire fence. Then they loaded their guns with glue, barbs, and powder; galloping over the course again, they shot all the barbs back into place. "An' if you don't believe that," the tale-teller says, "I'll take you out and show you the fence where it happened."

The character known as Ab Yancey really lived in southwest Missouri, and I was personally acquainted with several members of his clan. He was just a backwoods gambler and gunman, who wore his hair long in the fashion of Wild Bill Hickok. But in the stories told about him around the camp-

[8] *Oklahoma; a Guide to the Sooner State*, p. 114.

fires, his exploits have been exaggerated beyond recognition. Ab and another man are said to have eaten two big deer at a single meal, along with twenty pounds of fried catfish, a dozen heads of cabbage, and a barrel of apples by way of dessert. After dinner they lit their pipes and smoked twenty-five pounds of tobacco before nightfall. People used to say that Ab's breath smelled so strong of tobacco and sulphur matches that he could smoke out wolves and other varmints just by blowing into their burrows.

Along the Arkansas-Oklahoma border I have heard stories of "Loco Charlie" Coghill, who was distantly related to the Yancey family. He was supposed to be a hunter and Indian-fighter, and contemporary of Davy Crockett. Some say he fought in the Mexican War, then married a Cherokee squaw and lived for many years in what is now Oklahoma. A professor told me that Loco Charlie was perhaps identical with Pecos Bill, who was raised by the coyotes in Texas. Anyhow, Loco Charlie made a big reputation in eastern Oklahoma as a horse breaker. He could ride any horse that ever lived. They say he was never throwed but once, and that was the time he tried to ride a cyclone, being fuddled by popskull whiskey. He got his saddle and bridle on the critter, but only rode a little way. The cyclone didn't exactly throw him, at that. But when the damn thing seen that Loco Charlie had it licked, it just gradually turned into a snowstorm, an' poor Loco fell right through it onto a pile of rocks. He was still in the saddle when he lit, with his hat in one hand an' the bridle in the other'n. He wasn't hurt bad, but he was kind of shook up.

In some related tales, however, the man who rides a whirl-wind comes to a bad end. William Cunningham, professor at Commonwealth College, Mena, Arkansas, once published a story called "The Cloud Puncher," [9] about Tiny Fallon,

[9] *Mid Country*, pp. 361–365.

who saddled a female tornado. The blame thing would swoop down when he whistled, so as to let him mount. Tiny made big money out West by herding clouds over ranches that needed rain. Finally the cyclone got herself pregnant, foaled a premature litter of whirlwinds in mid-air, and dropped dead. Poor Tiny fell about 500 feet, and that was the end of the "Cloud Puncher." To have a horse die under the saddle is not necessarily fatal to the rider, but cyclones are different.

The loafers around Pineville, Missouri, always said that Si King was the best runner in the whole country. He ran so fast on one historic occasion, they said, that it took his own shadow ten minutes to catch up with him. King was pretty old when I knew him, and his running days were obviously over. I never heard him do any bragging. But there was a persistent story that he had once been the champion night-hunter of McDonald County, a man so fast that he often passed the dogs in full cry and treed the coon himself. On one big hunt back in the 1880's, it was said, Squire King outran his own foxhounds and jogged along beside the fox for several hundred yards.

The only other man I ever heard of who outran foxes was A. T. Still, of Kirksville, Missouri, remembered as the inventor of osteopathy. In his *Autobiography* [10] Dr. Still says that his frontier life had made him "very fleet on foot," adding that in the fall of 1839 he and his brother Jim "ran down and caught sixteen foxes." Doc Still must have been quite a fellow, in more ways than one.

Leonard Jones, a foxhunter of Brower Springs, Missouri, is said to be pretty light on his feet. "He can run as long as any dog, and he keeps right up with them on a hunt," according to an interview with Earl Greenwade in the Springfield, Missouri, *Leader and Press*.[11] But nobody ever claimed

[10] Page 20. [11] Oct. 8, 1938.

that Jones could actually outrun foxes, like Si King and Dr. A. T. Still.

One Jim Henderson, who lived in a mythical village called Durgenville, Arkansas, was a mighty fast runner until he shot himself in the rump, an experience which slowed him down considerably. The way it happened, according to my informants, was that he fired at a groundhog and then dashed forward to catch the animal before it could reach its burrow, in case the critter was not killed outright. Just as he reached for the groundhog, *slap* came something across his buttocks. "My Gosh," Jim gasped as the doctor was probing for the bullet, "it looks like I run a little *too* fast, that time!"

There is an ancient tale of a boy in Fort Smith, Arkansas, who was called as a witness in a murder trial. The prosecutor asked how many shots were fired and what was the interval between them. The boy answered that there were two shots, about twenty seconds apart. "When I heerd the first shot," said he, "I was standin' about ten feet from the man that done the shootin'. An' when I heard the second shot," he added, "I was three mile down the big road."

In another version of this old courtroom wheeze the lawyer asked the witness if he heard a bullet whistle past him as he ran. The boy replied that he certainly had; in fact, he had heard it twice. "You heard the same bullet twice?" demanded the attorney. "Yes, sir," was the answer. "I heerd it first when it passed me. Then I heerd it again when I passed *it*, after I got to runnin' good."

An old fellow at Noel, Missouri, told me a long story about some boys who had stolen a farmer's sweet potatoes and were cooking them at a campfire in the woods. Suddenly the farmer appeared, yelling with rage and firing his pistol at random. Everybody ran, of course, and one fellow ran all the way to the Big Rock schoolhouse, nearly twenty miles away. He must have run mighty fast, too. Because when he got there, his yaller-yam was still hot. So damn' hot, in fact, that it burnt all the hair off'n his tongue the minute he stuck it in his mouth.

A related windy concerns the alleged agility of a hunter named Fenton, who hadn't et for three days, because he'd been lost in the big timber somewhere south of Ava, Missouri. When he finally got back to camp he was pretty hungry, so he built a fire and started to bake him some biscuit-bread. A sudden gust of wind scattered the embers and set the woods afire. As the fire moved back Fenton kept shoving his dutch-oven forward, so as to keep it hot. He scooted the oven after that forest fire for miles, at top speed, before the baking was done. Then he sat down in the ashes and ate his biscuits. But by that time the camp was far behind, and the fire had changed the looks of the whole country, so that poor Fenton was lost again. It took him *four* days to find his way back, that time.

When Ray Wood was running his "That Ain't the Way I Heard It" column in the *Southwest Times-Record* at Fort Smith, Arkansas, in 1943–1944, he collected several tales and rhymes about a new folk character. "It was there," he wrote me (April 9, 1946) "that I discovered Peter Simon Suckegg, of whose existence I was entirely ignorant heretofore." Up to that time I had never heard of Suckegg, either, but I made some inquiries among my friends, and it now appears that he was known in eastern Oklahoma as a very fast runner. One story has it that Peter Simon Suckegg lived mostly upon jackrabbits, which he could overtake and capture on the open prairie. It was his custom to run alongside a jack for some little distance and feel its ribs. If the critter didn't seem fat enough for the pot, Suckegg would pass it up and run on ahead in search of a better eatin' rabbit.

A girl named Helen Stephens, raised on a farm near
Fulton, Missouri, was perhaps, the best runner in the whole
state. Quentin Reynolds [12] says that Helen fired at a rabbit
with a shotgun, but missed. Throwing down her gun, she
ran after the rabbit, grabbed him, and took him home to
show the folks. Nobody believed the story at first, says
Reynolds, but Helen went out and caught more rabbits in
the same way, until the skeptics were convinced.

My old friend Clarence Sharp, from Dutch Mills, Arkansas, told me about a man in his neighborhood who could
outrun deer and had actually caught many of them alive.
Once this man was chasing a big buck, and finally got close
enough to insert his forefinger into the animal's rectum.
It was a mighty close race, however, and the deer's top
speed was almost the same as that of its pursuer. Thus it
was that the hunter had to run another mile or so before
he could gain sufficient ground to crook his finger and hold
the animal.

A gentleman at Hot Springs, Arkansas, was asked if there
were any celebrated runners in that vicinity. He answered
that he had never heard of any such foot-racers as flourished
in the level lands, but that many of the country boys were
"right brisk an' nimble." One in particular, he recalled, had
got himself a good job in the powder-works, but on the
very first day he unthoughtedly threw a lighted cigaret
down in a big room full of powder. Nearly three bushels
of the stuff burnt up, before he could get the fire tromped
out.

In many villages one still hears about an early settler who
was noted as a great jumper. One of these tales relates the
adventures of a hunter pursued by a wounded bear, and the
only tree available was a tall pine. The lowest limb on this
tree was about forty feet from the ground, and the hard-
[12] *Collier's,* July 25, 1936, p. 22.

pressed hunter leaped straight for that limb. He missed it goin' up, they say, but he sure did ketch it on the way down.

The radio comedian known as Jim West, of Springfield, Missouri, says that his father was the best jumper in Missouri. The elder West could stand flat-footed and jump clear across the Niangua River. On a really long jump he always carried a lunch with him, to eat on the way back. And when he started to do a high jump he always put on his overcoat, even in the summer time, because it gets pretty cold in them high altitudes.

At Clarksville, Arkansas, a college boy mentioned a giant lumberman who could jump across the Arkansas River and back without touching the opposite bank at all. This somehow reminds me of Hal Norwood's tale [13] of a moonshiner who tried to swim a wide river while wearing rubber boots and carrying a crosscut saw. "He made it all right until he got within two hundred yards of the opposite bank," writes Norwood. "Then he saw that he was giving out and could not make it across, so he had to turn back and swim to where he had started."

Since most of the Ozark people use wood for both cooking and heating fuel, wood-chopping is an essential occupation. The hillman is incredibly clumsy in some things that city dwellers take for granted, but he's an artist with the choppin'-axe. Even small boys can cut down a tree and convert it into firewood with a celerity that makes a city feller's eyes bug out.

Jim Mitchell, who used to live at Crane, Missouri, was a large, powerful man. I have seen him many times, although I was never personally acquainted with him. It is generally agreed that he is the best wood cutter in the whole country. They say that when he wants to split wood already sawed

[13] *Just a Book,* p. 15.

into short lengths, he just drives the dull blade of his double-bitted axe into the ground, so that the sharp edge sticks straight up. Then he grabs up wood with either hand, and slams each chunk down on the axe with such force that it splits right open. By this method he can split three or four times as much cook-wood as any ordinary wood-chopper. Several responsible witnesses have told me that they actually saw Jim split wood in this fashion, and I have no reason to doubt the story.

Some other accounts of extraordinary wood-cutting are obviously tall tales. In Barry County, Missouri, they tell of a certain pioneer who was a mighty fast worker. By ten o'clock one morning he had cut and stacked up thirty ricks of stove-wood, and his axe was so hot that he stuck it in the creek to cool. Whereupon a dense cloud of steam arose, which reduced visibility for miles around, and chickens went to roost thinking it was night. When the steam cleared up a bit, the chips which had been cut early in the morning began to fall. This rain of chips made it impossible to do any more chopping, so everybody had to knock off work for the rest of the day.

The corn crops in the Ozarks cannot compare with those of Iowa and Illinois, but when it comes to yarns about shucking corn, the hillman rates right along with the best of them. A champion husker really does throw corn mighty fast; the air seems full of it sometimes, and the sound of the ears falling into the wagon rolls like a drum, or the tattoo of a woodpecker on the schoolhouse door. There is an old story of a certain super-shucker who was especially good at the "down row"—that's the row under the wagon, mostly trampled by the horses. One day he attacked the down row so fast that he shucked the shoes off both his feet and threw himself into the wagon. An instant later several ears of corn that had been in the air fell on him and knocked his head right up against the bangboard.

There are other tales of special skills, in a similar vein. A man at Willow Springs, Missouri, says that he once bet seven dollars that he could shear five hundred sheep before breakfast, and somebody called his hand. He just bent two brush-hook blades and whetted 'em to a barber's fancy. Then he fastened the blades to the gate of the corral, and drove the sheep through the gate. Some of them had to be driven through twice, and several were cut up a little, and the Willow Springs man was two hours late for breakfast. But he won his bet.

It was not too far from Willow Springs that the boys told me about old man Slocum who had been a big feller in his day. But for the last fifty or sixty years of his life old man Slocum's outstanding characteristic was his punctuality. He got up every morning just before daybreak, winter and summer. He was so regular about it that the neighbors used to set their watches when they heard him cussin' the critters out in the barnlot. Finally the old man got sick in the night and went out doors at four o'clock instead of five. A few minutes later it was broad daylight, with the birds a-singin' an' all like that. It was not just that he fooled the neighbors. Old man Slocum had fooled the sun.

This reminded somebody of another old codger, whose name I have forgotten. Anyhow, he died away back in the 1880's and was greatly missed. This fellow's chief claim to distinction was that he had set on the courthouse steps every sunshiny day for more than fifty years. Even the sun had got used to his being there. The story-tellers say that his shadow still showed on the wall for two or three weeks, after the old feller's body was buried in the Injun graveyard on the hill.

Many popular and widely known stories of the superman type deal with sexual exploits of the most fantastic sort. A shining example is a long involved windy about the Missouri politician who undertook to rape four women at once, and "come mighty close to gittin' the job done," as the great man's associates assured me. Davy Crockett, Mike Fink, Ab Yancey, Blinky Bluejohn and Kemp Morgan figure in similar yarns, none of which has ever been printed so far as I know. These bawdy absurdities are tall tales, right enough, and some of them are probably valuable from the folklorist's point of view. But their proper telling requires such explicit language that it is not practicable to record them in this book.

8 High wind and funny weather

THE HOTEL-KEEPERS and Chamber-of-Commerce people tell the tourists that there is no really bad weather in the Ozarks. But the truth is that it gets pretty hot sometimes. John Gould Fletcher, a native of Little Rock, the only distinguished literary figure that Arkansas has yet produced, gives you the real low-down [1] when he writes:

The Ozarks, though having six peaks of over two thousand feet, will never be a successful summer resort. . . . Summer, as any native son or daughter can testify, often starts in May, and does not end till the middle of November. Its first part is usually humid, with tremendous thunder-storms; its last part is usually intensely scorching and dry. . . . In summer, all is an overpowering blaze of humid torpor under an eternal scorching sun.

But it isn't necessary to read our Pulitzer-prize poet to get the truth about the Ozark summers. Just drive down in August and see for yourself, and talk with the people who live along the highways. A roadside merchant just west of Little Rock never cracked a smile when he told me that the gravel roads were almost redhot all through the summer of 1936. "Even the rabbits was pickin' up their feet, an' blowin' on 'em," he said. I laughed politely and bought another drink. "You know these big lizards we have down here?" he asked. "Well, every one of them lizards was carryin' a white-oak chip in his mouth." I pondered this awhile. "Why should a lizard carry a chip?" I inquired. "To put

[1] *Arkansas,* pp. 6–7.

under his tail, in case he wanted to set down," the fellow told me.

The old corn-popping-horse-freezing yarn is known throughout the Ozark country. "It got so hot down here one time," said an old gentleman in Mena, Arkansas, "that the corn took to poppin' right in the field. Pretty soon the damn' stuff was all over the ground, two foot deep on the level an' drifted ag'in the fences. The horses figgered it must be snow, an' began to shiver an' chill so bad I thought they'd freeze before I could git 'em to the barn." James Macon, of Poplar Bluff, Missouri, was quoted in the newspapers as saying that most of his corn popped on the cob during the scorching summer of 1935. He told reporters that "the old story of the mules that froze to death, thinking the popcorn which covered the ground was snow, might be true after all!" In Ripley's "Believe It or Not" column (Feb. 29, 1948) there is a picture of corn popping in a field, with a note that the crop was "owned by W. P. Miles, Springfield, Missouri, Aug., 1947."

Around Hot Springs, Arkansas, one hears an ancient wheeze to the effect that when a wicked man dies they bury him in his overcoat, meaning that hell will seem pretty chilly to one who has lived through a summer in Garland County. It was in this vicinity, I think, that the sun got so hot that tourists were advised to park their cars in the shade and carry water to pour on the tires. If you leave your car in direct sunlight, I was told, the intense heat will melt the rubber right off'n the wheels.

In some places it is said that a hot, dry summer causes the earth to warp plumb out of shape. Isabel France, of Mountainburg, Arkansas [2] quotes an ancient saying about this dreadful heat. "It shrunk up my well," says an old man

[2] *Arkansas Gazette*, Sept. 7, 1947.

in her newspaper story, "till the woman couldn't sink a bucket!"

There are many tales and wisecracks about drouths. Since most of the yarns in this collection were gathered in Missouri and Arkansas, they generally refer the worst conditions to the hill country of eastern Oklahoma. Along the western edge of Arkansas, when a wind blows dirt and sand into the houses, the old folks don't call it a dust storm. They call it an Oklahoma rain. The truth is, of course, that it gets just as dry on one side of the border as on the other, and political boundaries are unimportant in dry weather.

John Betsy Whittaker, of McDonald County, Missouri, used to say that you can always tell where a man comes from, by watching him when he first steps out of the house in the morning. If he's from Oklahoma he always looks up, kind of hopeful, to see if there's any sign of rain.

Not far from the Oklahoma line my wife asked an old hunter if the weather would be clear next morning, the first day of the deer season. "When God was a-runnin' the country, I used to be a pretty good weather prophet," he answered. "But now that the Government has took over, it's mighty hard to tell what's a-goin' to happen."

I spent several weeks at a village in the Cookson Hill country of eastern Oklahoma. We tried to buy some fryin' chickens, but none were to be had. An unsmiling old man told me that they hadn't raised any chickens for the last two years, on account of the dust storms. Settin' hens would leave their nests to get a drink of water, he said, and it was so dusty they couldn't find their way back to the eggs.

"Down around Tahlequah," I was told, "the air was full of dust for weeks at a time, an' no water to wet it down with. Pete Goodeagle always swore he had seen moles a-diggin' twenty feet above the ground! It got so God damn' dusty that you couldn't see your hand before your face. The chicken-hawks had to wear goggles an' fly backwards to keep from chokin' to death." The neighbors declared that when a raindrop fell on old Tom Burnside he fainted dead away, and they had to throw three buckets of dust in his face to revive him. And up in the Spavinaw country it got so dry in 1928 that the trees was a-follerin' the dogs around, and they had to prime the mourners at funerals before they could git 'em to cry.

There is also the story of the Oklahoman who was determined to have a little vegetable garden, even if the weather *was* a bit on the dry side. He built a big platform on a wagon, filled it up with rich dirt, and planted his garden there. When the sun seemed too hot he hitched up and hauled the wagon under a shade tree. When a little shower came up he drove out where it was, and followed the cloud at top speed until his garden was sufficiently watered. The scheme worked pretty well, everything considered. But it sure was hell on horses.

A backwoods preacher not far from Wauhillau, Oklahoma, was praying for rain. It was the bad summer of 1936, and everybody's corn was burning up. "Oh, Lord, send us fence-lifters an' gully-washers an' goose-drownders!" he cried. "The crops is too far gone, Lord, an' no use tryin' to save 'em, but we need rain for our souls' sake. It's the little children I'm a-thinkin' of, Lord. I've saw rain, myself."

A business man in Mena, Arkansas, told me that it got so dry there one summer that his office girl had to fasten stamps on envelopes with a stapler. "It's so dry here right now," he said earnestly, "that the cottonmouths carry little vials of water, to prime themselves before they can spit cotton." This gentleman and I belong to the same lodge, so I gave him a drink out of the bottle in my briefcase.

Another fellow in Polk County, Arkansas, declared that

during one severe drouth he had seen catfish three miles from the river, trying to swim in a dusty road. "We've got bullfrogs here ten or twelve years old, an' nary one of 'em has ever learned to swim." There is also a long story about the Arkansawyer who put some Oklahoma turtles into his watering trough, but they all drowned in a few minutes; they were not used to water, and couldn't swim a stroke.

"It got so dry here last summer," a farmer told me, "that our old sow went all to staves, and wouldn't hold slop unless we soaked her in water over night. The hell of it was," he added, "that we didn't have no water to soak her in."

"All this country needs," said a newcomer near Fort Smith, Arkansas, "is a little more water, an' a better class of people to move in." A cowpoke from Oklahoma grinned. "Yeah," he murmured, "they say that's all Hell needs."

There have been a few real tornadoes in the Ozark country; I remember one bad storm at Green Forest, Arkansas, and another that killed several people in the nearby town of Berryville. But the wildest cyclone stories are usually credited to eastern Oklahoma. The wind in the Cookson Hill country, according to my informants, is so all-fired strong it blows the squirrels right out of their holes in the hardwood timber. It blows the feathers off the chickens, too. On one occasion it blew so hard that it turned wells inside out, and throwed well-water all over Haskell County.

Nearly every farmer recalls some story about the so-called freaks perpetrated by cyclones, such as pine-needles and feathers blown into seasoned timber, fence rails driven through trees, and so forth. One man told me he found a chicken-hawk blown into a five-gallon jug so that its head stuck out at the top. When he smashed the jug with a hammer, the hawk flew away, apparently unhurt.

An elderly gentleman named Carlisle, who lived near Farmington, Arkansas, declared that after the big wind struck town he kept hearing one of his game roosters crowing somewhere in the wreckage. Finally the bird was located in a gallon jug, with only its head sticking out. Mr. Carlisle's relatives say that this didn't really happen at all; the old man just got tired of hearing the endless tales his neighbors were telling about the twister, and decided to go 'em one better.

Here's what the official Oklahoma guidebook [3] has to say on the subject:

The tall tale is not merely a highly improbable piece of fiction, but a method of "codding" a naïve youngster or a newcomer. The story starts innocently enough, and if the victim remains credulous it explodes into utter absurdity. The cyclone is a common subject for such stories. The "codder" begins with a series of events, credible enough, which he claims to have witnessed; his house was blown away, but the cookstove was left undisturbed with the fire going and the teakettle steaming. All of his listeners who are aware of what is going on pretend to be not at all interested. The conclusion of the story may be that a sack of meal had been hanging on a neighbor's porch and the wind blew the sack away, leaving the meal hanging there!

Near Fayetteville, Arkansas, they say that after a farmhouse was wrecked by a tornado, somebody found a five-gallon kerosene can standing upright in the pasture. The stopper was gone, and the vessel had been turned inside out, so that the bright inner metal was now on the outside. Not only that, but the can was still full of kerosene.

L. W. Shelton, of Reeds Spring, Missouri, used to tell a story about a fellow whose barn was blown away in the night, but the horses were left standing in the stalls. The funny thing about this was, that the harness was on the horses. Mr. Shelton says thoughtfully that he "don't believe

[3] *Oklahoma*, p. 114.

this one much," but adds that it might be the owner somehow forgot to take the harness off the night before.

A lady remarked that when she lived at Green Forest, Arkansas, the folks there all fed their turkeys buckshot, to keep 'em from bein' blowed plumb away. I made a note of this and showed no sign of disbelief, so she told me several other stories of the same type. Finally she said that one big cyclone blew a turkey-egg right through her Pappy's grindstone!

Casper Kilroy [4] tells of a big storm near his home in southwest Missouri. He and his father walked out to survey the damage.

On the way back to the barn [he writes] we found our hens, blown half a mile away from home, and not a feather on them. The wind had blown those feathers so hard that they had hit our hogs, and one side of each hog was sticking full of feathers. It didn't seem to hurt them a bit. I showed those hogs at the American Royal last fall in a class of their own, walked off with six blue ribbons, $500 prize money, and an offer to sell hatching eggs at a good premium.

"Just before the wind hit our place," an old tie-hacker told me, "I was a-settin' out by the corncrib. The smokehouse just fetched one big jump, an' then flopped its wings an' sailed off like a ragged-tailed buzzard. When I come to myself I was down the well, a-straddle of a churn, an' I warn't hurt a bit. The house an' all our buildin's was plumb gone, an' it rained shingles all evenin'."

A sudden tornado blew away the little still which a farmer had set up beside his spring, and smashed it all to pieces in the treetops. A few minutes later "the damn' cyclone come a-roarin' back" and picked up four barrels of mash from under a ledge; the mash barrels had not been touched the first time the storm came through the holler.

[4] *Missouri College Farmer*, Jan., 1947, p. 22.

"I reckon God Almighty never intended for me to make whiskey," said the farmer.

Oscar Ward's hired man used to tell about the big twister that caught him near Sallisaw, Oklahoma. "It tore the cover off'n my wagon," said he, "an' blowed it into the river. Me an' the old woman finally found it, way down by the mouth of the Canadian. The damn' thing was so heavy we had to hitch up the team afore we could git it drug out on a gravel-bar. That there tarpoleon was plumb full of yaller catfish, an' one of 'em weighed sixty-eight pound."

It appears that human beings are sometimes lifted into the air by wind storms, and returned to the ground unhurt. Allsopp [5] quotes a newspaper account of the tornado which wrecked Brinkley, Arkansas, in 1909. "Several citizens were picked up and carried several blocks from their homes, only to be let down as easily as they had been lifted. A gentleman who had a baby in his arms was lifted high in the air, without any serious injury to either."

Elbert Short, of Crane, Missouri, told me a very fine cyclone story of this type. When the great storm known as the Marshfield tornado struck near Hurley, Missouri, in 1880, Alec Hood and Joey Jones were lifted clear over the treetops and blowed around somethin' turrible, with horses, barns, and haystacks flying all about them. Once they passed so close to each other that they shook hands, saying "Goodbye, brother." They lit in a field three miles from home, unhurt. Mr. Short says that there's no doubt about these men being blown up in the air, but he thinks that the handshaking part of the story was probably added years later. It seems that Alec Hood told the story and that Joey just grinned and did not deny it.

Rufe Scott, of Galena, Missouri, recalled one about a backwoods family in Stone County. They had never seen

[5] *Folklore of Romantic Arkansas,* II, 310.

a cyclone, but had heard stories of the great Marshfield tornado. One day a little twister came along and unroofed an old stable. It scared the boys pretty bad. Several weeks later one of them saw a black cloud in the west. "Run for the creek, fellers," he shouted. "That's the same cloud that blowed the roof off Pappy's barn!"

The old gag about the hanging chain seems to be known all over the Ozark region, and doubtless elsewhere. I fell for it myself once, in 1922. Near Hartford, Arkansas, I noticed a heavy logchain hanging from a limb near a cabin. I asked the man what purpose it served. "Well, stranger," he answered, "when I wake up in the mornin' I knock out a piece of chinkin' an' take a look at that chain. If it's a-hangin' down, everything is all right. But if the chain is a-stickin' straight out from that there limb, I figger it's too windy for me to work."

Over in Oklahoma they use a crowbar instead of the chain. Almost every farmhouse has some opening that can be pointed out as a crowbar hole.[6]

The town innocent, inquiring into the purpose of the opening, will learn that it is to test the wind velocity. If the crowbar merely bends when thrust out through the hole, it is safe to go out. However, if the bar is broken off, it is better to stay in the house.

Out west of Tahlequah, Oklahoma, the wind blowed all the time, according to an old story, so hard that the boys used to ride into town on it. They'd just stand out in the road and hold their big hats up like sails, and in less'n a minute they'd light down right in front of the courthouse. A "furriner" tried it with a derby hat once, but it is said that he only rid as far as the river.

The folks in Sequoyah County, Oklahoma, say that the wind is pretty steady out that way, too. Farmers plow and

[6] *Oklahoma*, p. 115.

prepare the ground for wheat. Then they get on their ponies, ride five miles to the southwest, and throw the seed wheat into the air. The wind carries it back to the field. A man who tried to plant wheat directly on his own ground would never do any good; he'd have to harvest it several miles northeast, or maybe clear over in Arkansas.

At some other points along the Arkansas-Oklahoma border it is said that the velocity and direction of the wind remain constant for weeks on end. Buzzards, eagles, and other large birds have been blown up against cliffs, high above the ground, and held there by the wind until they starved to death. One old man told me that a war-party of Chickasaws had perished in this manner, in full view of five or six hundred fraternity brothers. But it happened so long ago, he said in answer to my question, that it was impossible to find any beads at the foot of the cliff.

There are many stories of vast quantities of sand and earth moved by windstorms. It is said that in eastern Oklahoma a discouraged nester came into town and was trying to sell his farm. It was a big tract of land, but pretty dry, and had only one small building on it. The farmer and his prospective buyer were preparing to drive out to the place, when a minor tornado struck the town. Taking shelter in the doorway of the stone courthouse, they saw a great cloud of dust, with some hay and an occasional bit of wreckage, whirling through the streets. Suddenly a wooden privy, torn from its mooring by the wind, came bounding and crashing across the courthouse lawn. The farmer eyed it morosely. "Stranger, it ain't no use drivin' out there now," said he. "That's my house, an' it looks like the farm has done follered me into town."

One hears also of a hillman who tied his horse to a tree and lay down to sleep through a severe windstorm. Next morning the wind had died down, but the horse was nowhere to be seen. The man finally located it high up in a tree. The wind had blown away twenty feet of sand and gravel, leaving the horse a-hanging by the halter.

An Oklahoma rancher once told me that back in 1898 a strong west wind slowed up the sun, so that it was still broad daylight at eleven o'clock in the night. That was a pretty good story, I thought, but a man from Fort Smith, Arkansas, went him one better. According to the Arkansas tale, a big wind came up out of the west about 2 P.M., an' blowed the sun clear back across the sky till it disappeared behind the hills east of town. There it was black as midnight, but everybody's watches showed it was only three o'clock in the afternoon, an' the kids not home from school yet. About eight o'clock that evenin' the wind died down, an' the sun come sneakin' up again. Now it was early mornin', with the birds a-singin' an' all, at 8.30 P.M. "We just had to set our clocks different," the man explained, "an' start another day's work without no sleep at all."

The same thing happened in southwest Missouri, and not so very long ago, either. "We just sat there in the barn waiting for milking time," writes Casper Kilroy.[7]

We sat there about four hours and the sun didn't seem to be a bit lower. We got out and looked around, and there the sun was, still way up in the sky, and trying its best to set against that wind. The wind didn't slacken until quite a while after dark, and by that time the sun was so puny and worn out from battling that west wind, that it took it until after midnight to set.

Weldon Stone[8] records the fact that once in the Arkansas backwoods the moon shone all night and all next day, "outdoing the sun." People didn't rightly know if it was day or night. They didn't know what the hell to do about it, but most of them stayed in bed. One would naturally

[7] *Missouri College Farmer*, Jan., 1947, p. 22.
[8] *Devil Take a Whittler*, pp. 93–97.

suppose that the wind was responsible for this, but the hillfolk in Stone's story didn't think so. They believed that the phenomenon was caused by Old Scratch himself, to stop a wedding that didn't fit in with his plans.

Down in the Cookson Hill country the wind is so all-fired strong it blowed the moon plumb away once, so the folks in Sallisaw never laid eyes on it for more'n four months. The old-fashioned farmers who "plant in the moon" were completely at a loss, and just set around fingerin' the almanac kind of wistful-like.

Akin perhaps to these tales of wind-born astronomical disturbance is the old story about the wind which blew so hard that it busted up the week, and brought in Easter on a Wednesday. I heard this yarn in Paris, Arkansas. The man who told it was not an unlettered hillbilly, but an educated fellow who had attended the Benedictine college at Subiaco.

In Franklin County, Arkansas, the old-timers spoke half-seriously of dead bodies being revived or resurrected by the wind, "the cool clean breeze off'n the Ouachitas." One bewhiskered veteran told me that just as they opened the coffin at a graveside ceremony, a little twister came roaring up the hill, scattering the mourners and rolling the dead man out of his casket. When the storm had passed a few minutes later, the corpse was walking about as briskly as anybody, demanding to know what the hell was going on and complaining that somebody had stolen his wallet.

Another story tells of an Ozarker who lay dying in California, but was miraculously restored to health by the air out of an automobile tire. The tube had been inflated, of course, at his home village in Newton County, Arkansas.

Several tales reflect the hillman's apathetic dependence on the weather, for good as well as for evil. A Missourian sat in the shade, according to one of these yarns, while a city fellow asked how the farm work was progressing. "Purty good," answered the farmer. "I figgered on fellin' them trees out in the pasture, but that big wind blowed 'em all down last week. Then I was aimin' to burn the brush, but the lightnin' set it afire yesterday, an' saved me the trouble." The city fellow remarked that there wasn't much more work to be done. "Yeah, I'm purty well caught up with my work now," said the hillman. "I'm just a-waitin' for a earthquake to come along, an' shake the 'taters out of the ground."

People who live on the river banks do not talk so much about cyclones and dust storms, but they tell some remarkable fog stories. Down at Pine Bluff, Arkansas, the fog gets so thick that people can't see what they're doing for hours at a time. Some of them wear masks of mosquito netting to keep the tadpoles out of their eyes. A man named Collier Lee was patching his roof, according to one of the local tales, when a dense fog suddenly appeared. Collier couldn't see very well, but he kept right on shingling. When the fog lifted, Collier felt himself slipping. He had nailed his shingles to the fog itself, and was not over his house at all.

One hears also the tale of a gentleman who rode his horse across the famous pontoon bridge at Dardenelle, Arkansas, in a heavy fog. People on the other side were astounded to see him come a-ridin' in, because part of the bridge had been washed away two days previously. This man swore, when telling the story years later, that the fog was so thick that it seemed just like water, and he could see big fish swimming about in it, high above his head.

A duck hunter in Taney County, Missouri, declared that he had seen a school of buffalo fish crossing a meadow in a fog, at an altitude of about one hundred feet. They were swimming in a V-shaped formation, like wild geese. He fired into the flock with his shotgun and brought down a fish weighing about four pounds. This man actually showed me the fish, which is more than most story-tellers ever do. It had been riddled with shot, all right. But perhaps he might have seen the fish in shallow water and shot it there, instead of high in the air as he claimed.

It must have been pretty foggy in Reeds Spring, Missouri, about 1945. According to a story credited to L. W. Shelton, some people there heard a kind of knocking or bumping at the door of their cabin. It was a school of suckers, and when the door was opened a lot of these fish swam right into the room. At Cape Fair, Missouri, only a few miles from Reeds Spring, a man said it used to get so all-fired foggy that everybody was ketchin' catfish in their rabbit-gums.

A village constable once told me about the time there come a turrible thick fog over Tumblebug Barrens, and one of the Pinkney boys was cutting hay with a scythe. The blade seemed to be very dull, or else the hay was getting mighty tough all of a sudden. When the fog finally blowed away young Pinkney seen he'd got out of the hayfield unbeknownst, and cut down more'n two acres of cedar saplin's.

The boys in an Arkansas lumber camp used to talk of a fog so dense, that when you cut a tree it didn't fall down. The fog was so damn' thick, that it just naturally held the trunk upright. The choppers cut about sixty pines in foggy weather once, and nary one of 'em touched the ground that day, nor that night. But early the next mornin', when the sun come out an' the fog lifted, you could hear them trees a-crashin' down all over the place.

There is very little snowfall in the Ozark country, but the old folks like to talk about the heavy snows of pioneer days, when the air was full of snowflakes as big as bed-quilts. I have heard lumbermen at Gurdon, Arkansas, refer to the cold spell of 1883, "when we had two winters in one

year, and it got so God damn' cold the snow turned blue."
It was pretty deep, too. "They had to let us down on ropes,"
I was told, "before we could reach the tops of the trees.'

Bob Burns used to tell of the big storm in Crawford
County, Arkansas, when all the houses were buried under
drifted snow. About dark a neighbor rapped feebly on the
door of a cabin. He lived half a mile away, and had tunneled
through the snow, and was so exhausted that he fainted as
soon as they got him inside. The family revived him with
whiskey and asked what was his errand. They thought some
of his people must be deathly sick or in dire need of help.
But the fellow just said, very faintly, that he had come
over to borry some nutmeg.

In Texas County, Missouri, an old man remembered that
back in 1892 the snow was so all-fired deep that folks had
to stand up to defecate—only he used a shorter word than
defecate. There are many other items with the same theme.
"Snow!" cried an old man at Siloam Springs, Arkansas.
"Jesus Christ, boy! When I was young the snow was so
God damn' deep we dug forty foot a-huntin' for the privy!"

Back in the 1880's there was a deep snow in Howell
County, Missouri, with a hard crust on it. The story goes
that a farmer rode into West Plains, tied his horse to what
seemed to be a hitchin' rack, and then set to work helpin'
the boys dig a hole so they could get to the saloon. Finally
they got down to the street level, and while they were all
drinkin' there came a sudden thaw. When the farmer came
out next day the snow was all melted, and there was his
horse, on a little platform at the very top of the courthouse,
tied to the railing around the flagstaff. They had a hell of
a time getting that there horse down.

An old story, heard in many parts of Missouri, relates
that the ground was covered with snow to a depth of fifteen
feet. Despite this, an ambitious newcomer insisted on clear-

ing land and forced his wife and children to help him. They worked hard all winter, cutting down pines and white oak trees. When the snow melted in the spring, the whole clearing was thickly studded with stumps fifteen feet high.

At Lamar, Missouri, an old joker told me that deep snow was a turrible thing for the farmer when he was a boy. "We had a hell of a time gittin' water for the cattle in them days," said he. "The snow an' ice got so thick that when we finally chopped holes through, the critters couldn't reach the water on account their necks wasn't long enough. The boys had to pull water up with buckets on well ropes, an' pour it out into tubs. One feller trained his stock to suck water through wheat-straws, like them dudes do at the sodyfountain. He figgered if the wheat crop failed, the cows would all die of thirst. But when the wheat did fail, the boys just cut the fire-hose up into sections, an' learned the critters to drink through that."

A few years ago we had some mighty cold weather at Neosho, Missouri, and a lot of tall stories came into being; perhaps they were only revivals, but I wouldn't know about that. "It's a common thing here lately," a local man said, "to see farmers buildin' fires under a cow of a mornin', to git her thawed out so's the milk will flow." And there was one fellow who got his Jersey thawed out and began to milk, but the stuff froze immediately and busted the bucket. So then he just milked right out onto the ground, and the milk froze as fast as it fell. When the cow wouldn't give down any more, he took an axe and chopped the frozen milk into chunks. "It's easy to split," he said, "long as you don't chop ag'in the grain." Then he gathered the milk up and carried it into the house, like an armful of cordwood.

A physician at Pineville, Missouri, told me about a big yellow tomcat belonging to Mrs. Marie Wilbur of that community. The cat upset a pan of milk and then froze fast to the ground while trying to drink the stuff. Mrs. Wilbur had to thaw out the milk around the animals feet with warm water, before the cat could walk. It was this same man who declared that in January, 1892, his horse's shadow froze fast to the ground at ten o'clock in the morning. He always mentioned this business of ten o'clock, and somehow made it appear that nobody would be surprised if a horse's shadow had frozen earlier in the day.

Near Caddo Gap, Arkansas, a bunch of old-timers were talking about severe winters. "The timber all froze in '62," said an old soldier. "I rode through the woods in the moonlight, with green trees a-bustin' wide open all around me. You could hear 'em poppin' like six-shooters." This tale may be true, for all I know. Woodsmen say that the sap in a tree does freeze under certain conditions, and might split the trunk with a loud report.

"This weather ain't really bad at all," a loafer remarked during a blizzard at Sulphur Springs, Arkansas. "When I was a youngster it got so God damn' cold we had to put wood on the fire all night with one hand, an' sleep with the other! The blaze froze right in the big fireplace, an' we had to chop the fire out of the chimney with a axe. It got so cold I couldn't blow out the candle, because the flame was froze stiff; just had to leave it a-burnin' till the sun rose in the mornin' an' thawed it out. If you'd happen to leave the door open a second or two, the coffee on the stove would freeze so quick the ice was still hot!" Another hillman nodded his head. "Purty near every mornin', in them days," said he, there was a skim of ice on top of the coffee, an' it a-boilin' all the while. We had to bust the ice before we could pour the coffee out of the pot." Floyd A. Yates, of Springfield, Missouri,[9] recalls a terribly cold winter at Hot Springs, Arkansas, when the whole place froze up solid. A

[9] *Chimney Corner Chats*, p. 3.

man was walkin' along the street when suddenly the ice broke, so he fell through into one of them boilin' springs an' was scalded plumb to death.

The boys claim that in Oklahoma one winter the oil froze as soon as it came out of the ground. The oil field workers just busted it up into chunks, so it could be loaded onto trucks and flatcars. "They can melt it easy enough," one young man said soberly, "when we git it to the refinery."

C. C. Williford, government weather-man at Springfield, Missouri, has a letter from a farmer who complains that "a cold wave came in on the radio wire and knocked the radio off the table. All the dishes in the cabinet froze and busted." At Granby, Missouri, they still talk of a winter away back yonder when the intense cold "froze the fence-posts off in the ground." But I am not sure just what is meant by this.

It is said that the boys near Cassville, Missouri, learned to catch rabbits in extremely cold weather by setting a lantern out in the field at night. The rabbits look at the light, which makes their eyes water. The water forms icicles, and the icicles freeze fast to the ground, so that the rabbits can't get away. All the boys have to do is go out in the morning and chop 'em loose.

Nearly every winter, in the Ozarks, one hears of dogs, sheep, and even cattle being frozen to death standing upright in the snow. When this happens the animal just stands there, stiff and stark as a marble statue, until the following spring. "Many's the time," an old joker told me, "I've set right here in my shanty eatin' beefsteak. An' I could look out the winder an' see the critter them steaks was cut off of, a-standin' there in the pasture, head throwed back an' mouth open just like it was fixin' to let out a beller."

Ed Thomas, of Camdenton, Missouri, in the winter of 1936, reported the case of two tomcats that were frozen stiff just as they were about to leap at each other's throats.

It was said that pilgrims flocked into Camdenton all winter to see the sight and that the tourist business fell off in the spring, when the cats thawed out and resumed their ordinary activities.

After hearing several old-timers speak of "cold thunder" in connection with the terrible winters of long ago, I finally broke down and asked what the phrase meant. "Well," said a bewhiskered old ruffian, "the water froze plumb to the bottom of the river, in them days. Then the banks was pushed back, of course, to make room for the expandin' ice. It was kind of like a earthquake, only it didn't do any real damage, just turned over a few houses down by the river bank. But it always made a big noise, an' that's what we called cold thunder."

Frank Hembree, of Stone County, Missouri, dug a pond in the pasture, to provide water for his cattle. One winter morning he saw a big flock of mallards on the pond and went out to take a shot at them. But a sudden freeze had caught the whole flock, and their feet were held fast in the ice. When Frank appeared they all flapped their wings and busted the ice loose from its moorings. "Them ducks flew away with my pond," Frank said later. "The last I seen of 'em, they was goin' south with a chunk of ice seventy-five foot long and fifty foot wide. Next time I dig a pond I'm goin' to put it under some big trees, so they cain't make off with it thataway."

In another version of this tale, the farmer sees that the birds are frozen fast to the ice and walks out there himself to wring their necks. It is then that the ducks all begin to flap their wings, and they carry away the pond with the farmer on it, holding to the birds for dear life. Sometimes the poor fellow rides so far south that the ice melts, and he falls to his death in some tropical jungle. In other forms of the story, the man kills a few ducks at a time, proceeding cautiously with the slaughter. Finally the birds still alive are unable to support the weight of ice, and the whole thing settles slowly to a safe landing.

A man from Fairfield, Iowa, visited the Arkansas frontier in the 1840's and heard some strange stories even then. Writing under the pen name "Skyscraper" [10] he tells of a cow whose calf was due in midwinter. But the weather turned so unreasonable cold that the cow "concluded to hold it over, and not have a calf. But she made up for it afterwards, for the next Spring she gave birth to a calf and a yearling."

It was a game-warden near Mincy, Missouri, who remarked that the difference between a poor man and a rich man was that the former had ice in the winter, while the latter had his in the summer time. This same man told me of an Arkansawyer who went up to Forsyth, Missouri, and returned with such a wild story that he was known thereafter as the biggest liar on the creek. He said the folks in Forsyth was makin' ice a foot thick, in August. But everybody in Arkansas knows that God Almighty cain't make it more'n five or six inches thick, even in the dead of winter.

It is said that several hillmen came down into the White River valley, where farms are prosperous and boast many improvements unknown in the mountains. Lost in a blinding spring snowstorm, they took refuge in a little shed, with straw and sawdust on the floor. It kept getting colder and colder. "My God, fellers," cried a shivering mountaineer, "if it's this cold inside, it must be turrible outdoors!" Finally one brave fellow started out into the storm to find help. A moment later he returned, shouting that it was warm outside. The others thought he was crazy at first, but discovered that it really was warmer in the open. When

[10] *Spirit of the Times,* March 17, 1849.

morning came they found ice under the straw, and realized that they had spent most of the night in an icehouse.

Some hillfolk express mighty strange notions about meteorological phenomena, but perhaps the wildest of these are superstitions rather than tall tales. I remember a farmer near Galena, Missouri, who declared that "the weather begins on the crest of the ridge, out back of my lick-log." One often hears men say that "the weather begins" at a particular spot, usually a high ridge or a mountain top. And if you try to argue with one of these fellows, he says: "Well, it has to start *some* place, don't it?"

A man who lives on a mountain in Madison County, Arkansas, told me that he has studied the weather for more than sixty years. It is his firm conviction, he says, that all heat waves have their origin in Madison County, and then spread to other parts of the United States.

An old friend of mine in McDonald County, Missouri, did not take in quite so much territory, but he said that high winds "for a hundred miles around" started in Bear Hollow. "I can tell you ten or fifteen hours ahead when bad weather is goin' to hit Joplin, or Fayetteville, or Monett," he said, "because every storm that hits them towns has got to pass my house."

It may be that some of the hillmen quoted above were in dead earnest with their theories about the origin of the weather. At any rate, I am not prepared to say that they were not serious. But the old-timers agree that Charles Dickey went 'em all one better, with the light-hearted thesis that the whole drainage system of the Ozark country began in Webster County, Missouri. God sent 'em one good rain to start with, said he, and water pouring off the courthouse roof at Marshfield formed the Pomme de Terre, Little Niangua, Osage, and Finley rivers.

I don't know who Charles Dickey was, or where he lived,

and it may be that he never lived at all. But I have heard hilarious references to his theory in at least a dozen places in the Ozark country. And, as a professor at the University of Missouri pointed out, the Dickey hypothesis is no more ridiculous than some of those seriously defended by geographers two or three centuries ago.

9 Fish stories

MANY BACKWOODS COMMUNITIES harbor vague and ancient tales of a big fish, which is often glimpsed but seldom clearly seen. There is a definite impression that this fish is somehow supernatural and that a fellow who sees it is a changed man from that day forward. Some go so far as to identify the big fish with the Devil, or at least with one of the Devil's agents. "That there fish," said an old deacon with a wry grin, "has made liars an' sabbath-breakers an' blasphemers out of half the men in our settlement." Sermons have been preached against the fish, much to the amusement of the ungodly, by visiting clergymen who did not realize that the monster was only a humorous legend.

Probably these old stories have a grain of truth somewhere in their depths, for there really are some mighty big fish in the Ozark streams. Alligator gars weighing 100 pounds are not uncommon, and much bigger ones have been reported occasionally. Elton Daniel caught a gar 7 ½ feet long, weighing 204 pounds, in the Ouachita River near Camden, Arkansas.[1] According to *Ozark Life*[2] a 300-pound gar was taken in Green's Lake, Bradley County, Arkansas. Avantus Green[3] says "it is the gospel truth that alligator gar in White River go as heavy as 300 pounds and as long as twelve feet." But these are real flesh-and-blood fishes, not to be compared with the monsters celebrated in the fireside legends.

Guides on the lower White River used to tell stories about a giant gar known as Big Al. There was a general notion that Big Al was immortal and had other supernatural character-

[1] *Arkansas Gazette*, July 11, 1947.   [2] Sept.–Oct., 1926, p. 17.
[3] *With This We Challenge*, p. 54.

istics. One man told me that he had seen this fish three times in the Arkansas River, and that it was not a "natural" gar at all, but some kind of a demon in disguise. It was about thirty feet long, he said, and was known to have killed many swimmers, being especially fond of Negro children. In some sections, when a young woman mysteriously disappeared the neighbors used to say "Big Al must have got her," meaning that she had run off with a stranger. Old rivermen say that this monster has been known as Big Al for more than a century, and is believed to have preyed upon Indians before the white man came. Big Al sometimes ascends the Arkansas River as far as Little Rock. When I was at Camp Pike, Arkansas, in 1917, there were men in Argenta who said that they had seen Big Al in the river there only a few months before. But the great gar's real home is in the Mississippi, somewhere above Natchez.

What we call a redhorse in the Ozarks is a variety of sucker. The hillfolk think very highly of the redhorse as a pan fish, and prefer it to bass or trout. I have seen literally thousands of redhorse in my time, but I do not think any of them weighed more than ten pounds. The old-timers all insist, however, that these fish grow to a much larger size. Men in Taney County, Missouri, told me that back in the 1870's they saw fifty-pound redhorse "wallerin' in the river like hogs," leaving a trail of mud for a hundred yards downstream.

In the Black River country one may still hear tall tales of a monstrous redhorse called Jube, captured after a struggle which involved more than one hundred men and boys, and almost assumed the proportions of a little war. The flesh of this great fish, pickled and dried and salted down, fed whole villages for several years. The natives saved the scales and used 'em for shingles, so that there was a new roof on every house in the valley. They even say that a blacksmith near

Newport gathered up some of the smaller scales, riveted wooden handles on them, and sold 'em for shovels. Some of these shovels are still used, it is said, in Jackson and Independence counties, Arkansas.

My friend Jim Haley, at Hot Springs, Arkansas, told me another yarn about a big redhorse. Two giggers sighted the monster in White River near Batesville, Arkansas, and chased it all the way through northern Arkansas, finally making the kill in the James River below Cape Fair, Missouri. That is a hell of a long way by water, and it took most of the summer to make the trip. When the boys were asked how they knew it was the same fish, they answered that there could be no doubt of its identity, because it was still sweating from the long journey when they stuck the gig into it at Cape Fair.

The Ozark streams afford the finest bass fishing in America, and there really are some big bass here. Smallmouth or black bass have been recorded up to 8 pounds, perhaps a little heavier. C. M. Shepherd [4] is credited with a smallmouth that weighed 7 pounds and 15 ounces. Bigmouth or lineside bass of 8½ and 9 pounds are taken occasionally. S. I. Smith caught one in Greene County, Missouri, that weighed 9 pounds, 5 ounces, according to the *Missouri Conservationist* (May, 1947, p. 10). Cobb Gaskins, of Eureka Springs, Arkansas, caught a 9¾ pound bigmouth in White River, August 19, 7947, which won the All-Arkansas Fishing Contest for that year. Dr. J. H. Young saw a lineside that some boys gigged near Ozark, Missouri, which weighed 10 pounds after it had been dead for several hours. Uncle Jack Short, of Galena, Missouri, told me that in 1900 he weighed a lineside bass that tipped the scales at 10 pounds, 9 ounces—a record for this vicinity, so far as I can learn. These are regarded as semi-official figures, but the bass described

[4] Kansas City *Star*, April 11, 1936.

around the campfires on the gravel bars run a good deal heavier.

Will Rice [5] quotes a guide to the effect that Sam Treece, of Leslie, Arkansas, caught "the biggest bass ever taken from the Buffalo River. It weighed 11 pounds and 4 ounces, and dragged Sam twice across the river before he landed it."

As recently as 1940 there were men near Bristow, Oklahoma, who babbled of a great lineside which they thought weighed at least 25 pounds. It lived upon redwing blackbirds and was never known to eat anything else. Several anglers declared they had seen this big fish leap out of the water and catch blackbirds, as often as three times in a single day. A gentleman told me that he once saw "Old Puddly" spring six feet out of the riffle to knock a blackbird off a willow. The bird was apparently stunned. It fluttered feebly and fell into the river, whereupon the monster rose and grabbed the bird just as an ordinary bass takes a cricket or a mayfly.

I have heard also of a monstrous bass known as Old King Solomon, which lived near the forks of the Buffalo River, in Newton County, Arkansas. The story of this fish was written up by Eldon Stone and published in *Field and Stream* magazine back in 1938. It was reprinted in a book, the *Field and Stream Reader*.[6]

Tales of a tremendous lineside, said to be nearly 12 feet long, were circulated a few years ago by the owner of a certain Ozark resort. When the newspaper boys arrived they were shown a slim oak tree, perhaps 30 feet high, from which the limbs and bark had been carefully removed. This tree stood near the water, and a short piece of log-chain dangled from the top of it. "The big fish busted all our tackle," said the resort-owner, "so we bought a new log-chain for a line, an' fastened it to the top of that there tree.

[5] *Arkansas Democrat*, April 11, 1948.   [6] Pages 106–116.

We bent the tree down, an' tied the top of it with a rope. Soon as the big bass grabbed the bait, I cut the rope with an axe. We figgered when the tree sprung back, it would yank him right out on the bank." The reporters gathered around, and one said impatiently "Well, where's the fish?" The innkeeper shook his head. "That's what we're a-tryin' to find out," he answered. "When that there tree flipped back it throwed the bass out, all right. But the chain busted, an' the damn' thing went a-sailin' off over the treetops. We've had men out a-scourin' the whole country for three days now, but they ain't never found our big fish yet!"

In the North Fork of White River, near Mountain Home, Arkansas, there once lived a big bass known to the rivermen as Sadie. This fish had been hooked many times, but she always smashed the fisherman's tackle and escaped. She was seen by almost every fisherman who visited the region. Some people used to take guests down to the river for a look at Sadie, regarding the big fish as one of the "tourist attractions" of the neighborhood. There were many fishermen who claimed to have known Sadie for 15 or even 20 years, and her weight was usually estimated at something like 13 or 14 pounds. Her demise was recorded in a Springfield, Missouri, newspaper, Dec. 31, 1936. Because of its comparatively small size, many fishermen did not believe that the bass killed was really Sadie, but it is generally admitted now that Sadie has never been seen since 1936.

Near Harrison, Arkansas, a man told me privately that he had seen the biggest bass in the world. It was in the Buffalo River, he said, and appeared to be about ten feet long, and maybe two and one-half feet across the back. He had set an illegal fish-trap, and when he came to inspect it at dawn, the big fish lay with its head thrust into the trap. As he approached, the bass made a great effort, busted the trap "all to flinders" and escaped. The trap was built of seasoned white-oak poles, each one nearly a foot thick. And four of these poles were snapped in two, just like this—and the man showed me what he meant by breaking a kitchen match between his fingers! It must have been a pretty big fish, to bust them poles thataway.

One hears many yarns about the abundance of game fish. A man at Waco, Missouri, told me seriously that the bass in Spring River are so numerous and ravenous that nobody dares open a minnow bucket or a bait box near the bank. A fisherman is forced to hide behind a bush while he baits his hook, or else to walk back about fifty feet from the shore.

Marguerite Lyon [7] went down to Mountain Home, Arkansas, and saw many large bass brought into the hotel. At Norfolk Lake, she was told, "the fish reach up and grab the hook before one can throw it into the water." Marge was apparently a little doubtful about this story, even if she did come from Chicago. "I have seen fish that were allegedly so caught," she writes. "I kept any private skepticism to myself, for the fisherman was permitting the fish to be served at a hotel supper, and I was one of the guests."

Frank Payne once found a pool near Galena, Missouri, where the James River bass were "swarmin' like bees." A big fellow jumped from the water and snatched a worm out of his hand, before he could put it on the hook. Frank reached in his pocket for another worm, but dozens of big bass chased him up the bank and out into the road. "If I hadn't jumped on my horse an' galloped off," Frank told me later, "them big fish would have tore me limb from limb!"

There are still plenty of bass in the Cowskin River, but in former years they were much more numerous. One afternoon in 1912 a group of city sportsmen were sitting on the hotel porch at Noel, Missouri, waiting for the season to open

[7] *Hurrah for Arkansas*, p. 49.

next morning. Several distant explosions were heard, probably a farmer blasting out stumps, or somebody working on the new highway. "What's all the shooting about?" asked a city man. "Oh, I reckon the fish-warden is a-bustin' up a bass-jam," a hillman answered carelessly. "Bass-jam," cried the tourist, "what's a bass-jam?" The hillbilly yawned. "There's so damn' many fish in the river," he explained, "that they jam up sometimes, just like logs do in the lumber country. The warden has to go out every once in a while, an' blast 'em loose with dynamite."

At a certain resort on the Gasconade River, a few years ago, the bass were so voracious that the boys used wooden minnows without any hooks on them. Dozens of fish would leap at the bait the moment it touched the water, and run together so hard they'd be knocked plumb unconscious. A few minutes of this tumult, and there were lots of nice bass floating on the surface, just as if they were dead. All the boys had to do was scoop 'em up in landing nets.

Perry Motley, veteran rod-maker of Kansas City, Missouri, used to tell of a man who caught twenty-six bass in one cast, using only one line and one wooden minnow. All the boys shouted their incredulity. Mr. Motley explained, after a while, that the bass were all strung together, having been lost by another angler. The plug cast by Mr. Motley's hero happened to snag the patent stringer to which the fish were attached.

Will Rice [8] had a fine tale of a doctor from Marshall, Arkansas, who went fishing in the Buffalo River.

He fished all night [the story goes] and was so lucky that the ten-foot rope on which he strung his fish was filled by morning. A man came along with a kodak and the doctor wanted a picture of his string, so he got another man to stand with him on a rock and help him lift. Well, when they got the string all out of the

[8] *Arkansas Democrat*, April 11, 1948.

water, but before the kodaker could snap, the stick on the end of the rope broke and the fish all slid back into the river.

In an earlier version of this tale the string of fish was forty feet long, and five men stood on top of the bluff to lift it clear of the water. Jon Kennedy illustrated Rice's story with a very fine drawing, which was clipped and pasted up in fish-camps all over the country.

Catfish weighing up to 50 pounds are not uncommon in the Ozark streams, and I have seen many such fish myself. In pioneer days it is said that they came much bigger. Back in the 1860's Joe McGill of Branson, Missouri,[9] helped eat a White River catfish that weighed 125 pounds. "They had a rail run through its gills," he said, "and the men carried the ends of the rail on their shoulders, and the fish's tail dragged on the ground." The *Missouri Conservationist* [10] tells of a blue cat weighing 315 pounds, taken from the Missouri River near Morrison, Missouri, about 1870. This great fish was caught by a man named Struttman, who used "a special hook hammered out by the local blacksmith and baited with half a spoiled ham." It is alleged also that Captain John Brown, of Becker, Missouri, caught a catfish estimated at 200 pounds, using "a sixteen-pound drumfish" for bait. Brown had no scales to weigh his fish, but he cut off its head and carried it back to town. The head alone weighed 38 pounds.

Clink O'Neill, who lived on Bear Creek in Taney County, Missouri, told me of a neighbor who swore he had caught a flathead cat that weighed 298 pounds. "Why don't you make it 300?" asked Clink. The man turned on him indignantly. "Do you think I'd tell a *lie*, just for two pounds of catfish?"

Marion Hughes [11] spins a long windy about a gigantic

[9] Hoenshel, *Stories of the Pioneers*, p. 49.   [10] June, 1947, p. 12.
[11] *Three Years in Arkansaw*, pp. 33–34.

fish that lived in the Arkansas River below Little Rock. Finally the boys got a blacksmith to make a hook out of a crowbar, tied it to a steamboat cable and for bait used "a muley cow that had died with the holler horn." When the fish was caught, they cut it open; in the stomach they found a small 200-pound catfish, three fat hogs, a yoke of oxen and an acre of burnt woods. This great fish was so big they couldn't get it on a wagon; they had to cut the carcass up and haul it to town in sections.

A fat man at Bella Vista, Arkansas, used to hold the tourists spellbound with his story of a huge catfish in a nearby stream. This fish had been seen many times, and our best local fishermen had tried to catch him. He had broken countless hooks, lines, rods, and trotline stagings. Spears and bullets made no impression upon his broad back, and many a gigger's john-boat had been capsized by a contemptuous swing of his mighty tail. And once, it is said, the big cat drowned a poor drunken noodler who was so foolish as to strap the noodle-hook to his wrist. In the summer of 1928 the fat man resolved to catch this catfish or perish in the attempt. He got the blacksmith to forge a hook three feet long, and used the well-rope for a line, with two sash-weights by way of sinkers. Baiting with a full-grown groundhog, he tied the rope to the top of a stout elm and lowered the hook into the depths of Sugar Creek. "I was down to the creek afore sunup next mornin'," he told me. "That big ellum-tree was tore plumb out of the ground, with roots ten foot long a-stickin' up in the air." I waited a moment. "Well, did you catch the fish?" I asked. "I clumb out on the tree an' got hold of the rope," the fat man went on calmly. "Then I pulled on the line, slow an' careful. There was a heavy weight on the other end, but seemed like it was a dead weight. There wasn't no fightin' like I expected. So I just figgered—" I couldn't stand the suspense any longer. "Did you get the fish?" I shouted. "Naw," he answered deliberately, "I didn't git the fish. But I did git about seventy-five pounds of his upper lip."

They still tell the tale of the Sugar Creek catfish in Benton County, Arkansas, but the details have been built up a little. Such stories generally get bigger, as they pass from one crossroads audience to another. When I last heard this one, near the statue of the flat-bottomed angel on the old Pea Ridge battlefield, the fisherman was using a hand-forged hook that weighed twenty-seven pounds, with a forty-pound live wildcat for bait.

A country doctor told me a related yarn of a gigger near Cotter, Arkansas, who located a gigantic catfish and made a special spear for its undoing. After a long series of hair-raising adventures, involving the wreck of several boats and the loss of expensive jack-lights and other equipment, the big fish escaped. But when the battle was over, there was a 60-pound strip of fish-skin sticking on one tine of the fisherman's gig.

Another big catfish in the Cotter neighborhood is said to have one red eye and one green eye. This fish, according to the local wise men, is so large and heavy that it cannot move about in search of food. Some say that there is no place in White River wide enough for it to turn around in. For more than fifty years it has lain concealed in a certain channel, directing the minnow traffic into its mouth simply by flashing the green light at appropriate intervals.

Will Rice, of St. Joe, Arkansas, always told the tourists that the Buffalo River used to be full of big alligators, but that none have been seen there in recent years. When some-body wondered about the cause of the reptiles' disappearance, Rice declared that it ain't safe for alligators in Searcy County waters nowadays. The catfish would eat 'em up, he said.

A druggist named Macdonnell, who used to live at Galena, Missouri, told me of a flathead cat the boys caught in James River, near the mouth of Mill Creek. "They didn't have any scales big enough to weigh it," said he. "But Frank Fox made a picture of the fish, and the photograph alone weighed three pounds and seven ounces." This somehow reminds me of Hawk Gentry, another James River fisherman, who swore that he had once caught a three-pound catfish with seven pounds of eggs in it.

G. T. Cazort, a poet who had a big plantation at Lamar, in Johnson County, Arkansas, must have been quite a story-teller on the side. Masterson [12] quotes the rhymer's tale of a catfish so big that no scales could weigh it. The only way to estimate its size, says Cazort, was to measure how far the water-level fell when they dragged the fish out of the river.

William L. Heckman, of Hermann, Missouri, is credited with the story [13] of a big catfish nicknamed Turntable Jack. This fish was the subject of many river legends around St. Joseph, Missouri, in the 1880's and 1890's. It was finally hooked by Frank Ashmore in 1899. The fish got away, but was badly wounded by a gaff. "Five months later," according to the tale, "they found the skeleton of Turntable Jack on a sand bar ten miles below St. Joe. The bones measured fourteen feet from head to tail."

"The biggest catfish in the world," according to *Time*,[14] "is Old Blue who inhabits the Missouri River, and is so big that he once got stuck trying to go through a canal lock. But Old Blue exists only in the imagination of Missouri River boatmen." Nearly all the rivermen I have interviewed say that Old Blue's home, for at least fifty years, was the Osage River, not the Missouri. Old Blue's adventures have been chronicled in the Kansas City *Star* and other local papers,

[12] *Tall Tales of Arkansaw*, p. 75.
[13] *Missouri Conservationist*, June, 1947, p. 12.   [14] Aug. 17, 1931.

and have been discussed around campfires and fish-camps throughout the Ozark country. A big book could be written about the attempts of Jerry English, well-known Osage River boatman, to catch Old Blue. Since the big dam was built at Bagnell, in 1930, Old Blue spends most of his time in the Lake of the Ozarks, where his doings are reported by "Skunk Hide" Turner and M. N. White, of Warsaw, Missouri. Old Blue has been known to help a trapper by retrieving his lost rabbit-gums and by killing a prime black mink in an unprintable fashion. Once he jumped over the Bagnell Dam and traveled all the way to Louisville on an errand for one of his friends. Another time, knowing that a big flood was on the way, he put his great tail under a boatman's shanty and moved it up on higher ground. "He done it so gentle like," said the riverman, "that my greasin'-skillet didn't even fall off its peg." Only a few years ago, according to the weekly Kansas City *Star* [15] Old Blue stuck his head out of the water and winked his left eye, a movement which caused such a rush of wind that a big elm tree was torn loose from its roots and blown into the river.

Old Blue has been hooked many times, but landed only once—and perhaps it wasn't really Old Blue that time. The story is that a fellow named Reeves caught a catfish so God-awful big that the lake fell fourteen feet when he dragged it out. Hundreds of launches and sailboats were stranded high and dry, and lakeside cottagers awoke to find half-a-mile of mud between their cabins and the water. Seeing the whole future of the summer-resort business in danger, local business men finally prevailed upon Reeves to return his prize to the water, whereupon the lake became normal. "I shore did hate to throw that there fish back," sighed the fisherman.

A man sometimes known as "Baldy" Huntoon caught the

[15] Jan. 8, 1941.

biggest catfish ever taken in the Ozarks; he admitted as much to me, in the jail-house at Joplin, Missouri. It seems that Baldy, when he first sighted the fish, perceived that it was too long to turn around in the channel. So he straddled the stream at a narrow point, and threw some stones into the water ahead of the fish. There was nothing for the monster to do but back slowly upstream, and as it passed under Baldy he mounted it just as one would a pony. Before the big fish could get away, Huntoon stuck his thumbs into its gill-slits and throwed it right out on the bank.

Baldy Huntoon's story, in many versions and variants, is known all over the country, usually as the exploit of some local character. In the village of Crane, Missouri, I found an old friend who told it hot off the griddle. One Jim Mitchell, while fording the White River on horseback, saw an enormous catfish swimming just beneath the surface. Leaping from his pony, he mounted the great fish, threw his arms around its neck, and socked his big spurs into its flanks. Upstream and down they went, but Jim finally beached it on a gravel bar, where the "critter bucked an' bellered like a young mule." When Jim told of his adventure in Crane, it appears that the sober citizens proved a bit incredulous. Some of them even laughed and utterly refused to credit the story. Thereupon Jim Mitchell took umbrage. Some say he took more umbrage than was good for him. He deplored the skeptical tendency of modern youth, and denounced all unbelievers in no uncertain language. The whole village roared with raucous laughter, and some of the boys became so noisy about it that four of them were arrested for disturbing the peace.

Something about this anecdote pleased me inordinately, but I regarded it as no more than a happy invention, told as a sort of joke on Jim Mitchell. I was astonished when Don Wright, editor of the Crane *Chronicle*, assured me that it was all true. Much more authentic than most of the stories printed about the Ozarks, he said. Ignoring this crack at my own writings, I asked for further light. Turning to his files, he showed me an account of the episode in the *Chronicle*. The four boys, according to this article, were tried in Justice John L. Bone's court and acquitted on June 7, 1934.

"But, Mr. Wright," I persisted, "do you mean to say that Mitchell actually caught that catfish in the manner described?"

"Oh," the editor sighed, "I wouldn't know about that."

When I last visited Crane, in the spring of 1947, Mitchell was still living there. He's a big, raw-boned, red-headed man, the best woodchopper in the whole region. People still laugh over the catfish story, and some of the boys refer to Mr. Mitchell as "Catfish Jim." But always behind his back, and well out of his hearing.

Tourists often refuse to believe that the boys in the Ozarks dive down under rocks and catch big catfish with their hands. But it's true enough. This method of taking fish is called noodling or rock-fishing, and is against the law nowadays. But it is still widely practiced. "Believe-It-Or-Not" Ripley [16] says that Alden Weaver, of Okmulgee, Oklahoma, caught a 75-pound catfish with his bare hands; it is not difficult for me to believe this, for I have seen many smaller fish taken in this fashion. Mrs. Dorn Higgins, who used to run a chicken ranch near Sulphur Springs, Arkansas, told me about a fellow named Eb Loveless, who was accustomed to noodle catfish with his feet. This I haven't seen, but I am not prepared to say that it can't be done. The *Ford Times* for April, 1948, carried an article by Brady Gibbs about noodlers on White River, with photographs showing two noodlers in action. Close-up photos are bad enough, but Gibbs actually printed the men's names and addresses. Their

[16] Dec. 28, 1937.

biggest catfish, he said, was nearly six feet long and weighed 100 pounds. I never heard the upshot of this case, but certainly the culprits must have been run down by the fish wardens and heavily fined.

Another item which few tourists can swallow is the story of jumping or "goosing" bass. In many Ozark streams, when the water is a bit murky, the fisherman catches bass without any tackle at all. He just paddles along near a weedy shore, and stirs the weeds a bit with a pole. The bass caught between the boat and the shore leap high out of the water, and often land in the boat. This method of taking bass is even more deadly at night, when a lighted lantern is carried by the boatman. The practice of jumping bass is illegal, and the wardens do everything they can to check it. When I first came to the Ozarks my neighbors told me about this, but I didn't believe a word of it. Why, any fool knows that fish don't jump into one's boat! But since that time I have seen it for myself; I saw two men catch at least twenty large bass in an hour or so; I have seen bass leap clear over boats, even over a boatman standing erect, and six feet tall at that. In 1928 I wrote an article about jumping bass for *Forest and Stream*, and was denounced as a liar from one end of the nation to the other. In 1939 I published another article on the subject in *Esquire*, and again the smart alecs in the cities regarded the story as a ridiculous falsehood. And yet every old riverman in the Ozark country knows that it is true.

Of course, some exaggerations have grown up about the bass-jumping story. They say that Ern Long, one of the best poker players who ever wet a line in the Cowskin, once came to the clubhouse soaking wet and in a very bad humor. He went to bed without a word, but everybody noticed that his fishing tackle was gone and that his new boat was missing. Next day he said that he had caught the limit early in the morning and started home through the reedy channel, when big bass began to jump into his boat. Ern had lost a hand in an accident several years before, and those bass jumped in faster than any one-armed man could possably pitch them out. Finally the boat sank from the sheer weight of fish. Ern managed to swim ashore, but lost his rod, reel, tackle box, and other items to which he was greatly attached. The only thing saved out of the wreck was a bottle of whiskey that somebody had put in his pocket as a joke. The boys thought that was very funny, because Ern Long was a total abstainer.

The fish that I have seen jump into boats were all bass, but I have been told that trotline fishermen, who use a light in their skiffs at night, are often annoyed by hickory shad leaping into the boats. Redhorse and other suckers, at shoaling time, sometimes jump into boats and even out upon the bank. There are some tall tales about this, too. A storyteller at Rockaway Beach, Missouri, said that big suckers and redhorse, coming up the meandering Ozark streams to spawn, sometimes take a short cut by jumping over hills and woodlands. And another honest Missourian assured me that perch and sunfish, in moving from one lake to another, often leap over mountains covered with tall trees. Thus it is, he said, that newly made artificial ponds become stocked with fish in an incredibly short time.

Jim West, radio entertainer of Springfield, Missouri, once remarked that in the early days fish were very large, and everybody knows that the Ozark streams are very crooked. The boys used to throw sacks of starch into the water, says West, and the big fish gobbled it up. Then the fishermen waited at the first bend of the river. When the big starched fish came along, their bodies were so stiffened that they couldn't make the turn, and were easily harpooned and dragged out on the bank.

Current in Jim West's territory, although not attributed to him, is the tale of a tourist who was so badly sunburned that he jumped into the creek to cool off. The water became so hot that it not only killed the fish, but cooked 'em. All the boys had to do was rake them out of the water, and the whole party enjoyed a big b'iled-fish dinner on a gravel bar.

Everybody knows that the North Fork is a mighty lively little stream, and one hears some strange stories about it. One fisherman who made a float trip there said that the water was actually heated by its friction against the rocks. The farther he floated, the warmer the water became, until the river was fairly steaming, and the bottom of the boat so hot that it blistered his feet, right through his horse-hide moccasins. When he finally left the river at Norfolk, Arkansas, the fish on his stringer, which had been trailing in the water, were cooked to a turn. Another version of this tale has it that the john-boat came through a certain riffle so fast and got so hot that the tar in the cracks melted. Then the boat began to leak, and they had to beach it on a gravel bar and give up the whole trip.

Bob Worthington was an engineer from Kansas, but he had fished in the Ozarks for many years and knew a lot of fish stories. One of his tales concerned a hillman down on War Eagle Creek, in Madison County, Arkansas, who was a clever wood-carver. When this man wanted a mess of fish he just waded along the creek, carving life-sized minnows in the wood of partially submerged stumps and tree trunks. The bass leap at these solid wooden minnows and are stunned, whereupon the wood-carver strings a few of the biggest ones and goes his way.

On Kings River, near Eureka Springs, Arkansas, they tell of a fisherman who went out at night and pasted up the entrance in a big hornets' nest. He fastened the nest to a heavy weight and sank it in a deep pool where there were many big bass. Then he took a long pole and punched a hole in the nest. The hornets buzzed out into the water, the bass grabbed 'em and were stung. Some bass were stung to death, others just "stung silly." In any case the fish came helpless to the surface, and the fisherman just gathered them up by the tubful.

A boy at Pineville, Missouri, heard that I had been a teacher of psychology at the university, and asked my advice about taking a correspondence course in hypnotism. Assuming that he contemplated the seduction of the local virgins, or some other dubious enterprise, I told him bluntly that hypnosis was of small value in such projects. I was astounded when the boy said that he "figgered on hypnotizin' bass" so as to direct them into his fish traps.

I have heard several tales about dogs which are of great assistance to fishermen. It is said that Cleo Bilberry, of Smithville, Arkansas, used to have a pair of shepherd dogs trained to catch bass. The Springfield, Missouri, *Leader and Press* [17] tells of one occasion when he heard the dogs bark treed down by the creek. They had cornered a whole school of bass in a narrow pool, and Bilberry had no trouble in catching a nice string while the dogs prevented the fish from escaping.

A boatman at Oceola, Missouri, swears that he used to own a trained fish-dog which could catch more bass than any two fishermen in the state. The animal wore a specially designed harness, to which a number of lines and trolling-spoons were attached. Sent into the water, he swam about until several fish had hooked themselves, and then returned to his master who stood waiting on the dock. Several times

[17] May 25, 1935.

the dog was pulled under by the sheer weight of bass, and once the owner had to dive under a raft to rescue him from a twenty-pound jacksalmon.

Guy W. von Schriltz, well-known sports writer, used to tell the story of a little mongrel dog near Cassville, Missouri, which was trained to catch trout. Von Schriltz saw this dog land a two-pound rainbow. The fish was hooked by a fisherman from Monett, Missouri, and the dog plunged into the water at his master's command. "After some swimming and some struggling," writes Von Schriltz, "the little dog grasped the trout by a fin and dragged it ashore, much to the enjoyment of the usual Sunday crowd."

W. S. Wickham, a game warden in Howell County, Missouri, reports that he saw a fish-catching dog in action.[18] "The dog, of unknown ancestry, would enter the water, thresh around the area, and soon come out carrying a carp in its mouth." Wickham says that he "watched the process several times."

The fish warden on duty at Roaring River State Park, in Barry County, Missouri, used a dog in his business, but the animal didn't catch fish. It was against the law to use any lures except flies, but the trout were hatchery-bred and had been raised on liver. Some fishermen discovered that by putting a tiny bit of liver on the fly they could catch big rainbows, while others who used unbaited flies caught nothing. The dog was trained to circulate through the crowd and "point" any man who was carrying liver on his person. Then the wardens would close in and arrest the fellow, who paid a heavy fine. It was quite some time, they tell me, before the fishermen found out that the dog had anything to do with the matter.

I have heard several tales about dogs which help the fisherman, not by catching fish, but by digging worms or finding

[18] *Missouri Conservationist*, July, 1947, p. 11.

some other sort of bait. One such story is credited to Dr. W. B. Lucas, of Mendon, Missouri, and concerns a man who lives on Yellow Creek, about a mile from Mendon. This man fishes with short bank-lines, using frogs for bait. "While I was talking to this fellow," says Dr. Lucas, "his dog began to whine. Curious, I asked why the dog was whining. He told me the dog was impatient to go to work. He said the dog would go up and down the creek to catch the bait, just jumping on the frogs with his front feet, then grabbing them and bringing them to his master!"

"If you want to catch bass in this country," said a loafer in Douglas County, Missouri, "you got to use a cork for bait, with a blue revenue stamp on it." He meant that it is well to give the guide a bottle of good whiskey. There are many stories on this theme. Governor Lloyd S. Stark, according to an old newspaper yarn, was fishing with very poor success, when he met a native angler. The Governor admitted that he hadn't caught any bass worth saving, and the native, desiring to be of help, poured a pint of whiskey into Stark's minnow bucket. This made the shiners much livelier than usual. Using one of these inebriated minnows as bait, the Governor caught a lineside nearly two feet long. "And you know," concluded the narrator, "the minnow had grabbed that bass right by the back of the neck!"

Another variant relates the experience of a Missouri angler who accidentally busted his jug and spilled a whole gallon of Stone county whiskey on the ground. Next day he dug some fishworms at the scene of the accident, and noticed that they were unusually active. They were so vigorous, in fact, that it required all his strength to hold one long enough to put it on his hook. Finally he got the bait into the water, and had a strike almost immediately. After a hard struggle he dragged out a four-pound bass. The big lineside wasn't hooked at all; the worm had just wrapped itself around the fish's tail.

Bruce R. Trimble, of Kansas City, Missouri, repeats a tale [19] that he got from Jake Vining, who lives on Roark Creek in Taney County, Missouri. It seems that Jake and Clarence Fawcett caught a nice string of bass in Lake Taneycomo, at a time when nobody else was catchin' 'em. Jake explains that he took the first fish away from a big water snake and gave the serpent a drink of moonshine by way of compensation. The snake soon returned with another bass, and so it went until the two of 'em strung twenty-four fish without ever wettin' a line.

One hears also of the fisherman who had used minnows all day with no success, when he suddenly spied a big snake with a frog in its mouth. The snake dropped the frog, which the fisherman used as bait and caught a fine bass at once. Taking a drink from his flask, he noticed that the snake was still there with its mouth open, so he poured a big snort down the reptile's throat, too. A few minutes later he heard a rustling in the grass. Looking down, he saw that the snake had brought him another frog, evidently hoping to trade it for another drink of whiskey. Sometimes this story ends with the solemn statement that the next time the fisherman visited that place at least fifty snakes appeared, every one of them with a frog in its mouth.

Another version of this yarn concerns a fisherman who had caught nothing all day, and whose flask contained only two drinks of whiskey. Finally he pulled out a miserable little sunfish, not big enough to be worth carrying home. "Poor little devil," said the fisherman, "you look unhappy too. Well, I'll split it with you." So he poured one drink of whiskey into the sunfish's mouth, and turned the little fellow loose in the river. Then he tossed the other drink

[19] *Fiddlin' Jake,* p. 15.

down his own throat and began to wind up his lines prepara-
tory to going home. Just as he was leaving, he heard a great
splashing and commotion in the water. Suddenly the little
sunfish surfaced with a five-pound bass in its mouth, shaking
it as a terrier does a rat, and threw it out on the bank at
the fisherman's feet.

Related to this tale of the grateful sunfish, though without the reference to liquor, is the story of the country boy
who had only one fishhook. When he lost this hook in a
deep pool, the boy burst into tears, because he had no money
to buy another and was dependent upon fish for food. In
a few minutes a big trout—the smallmouth bass is called a
trout in some parts of Arkansas—appeared near the bank
with the lost hook held carefully between its jaws. A moment
later the fish broke water and flipped the hook out on the
gravel, almost within reach of the boy's hand.

A big lineside bass that lived in Bull Creek, not far from
Rockaway Beach, Missouri, was called Jingle-Bells because
he carried so many hooks and spinners in his massive jaws
that they jingled like sleighbells whenever he broke water.
Scores of fishermen had hooked the huge bass, but it always
got away somehow. Finally a tourist who watched with
binoculars from a high tree solved the problem. An old
crawpappy always rode on Jingle-Bells' back, and whenever
the fish was hooked the crawpappy cut the line with his
sharp pincers. My friend George Hall heard about this, and
sent back to New York for a wire leader. When Jingle-
Bells struck George's lure the veteran crawpappy did his
best, but finally had to give up and drop off, leaving Jingle-
Bells to his fate. The great bass went to the kitchen at last,
and his collection of hooks and lures is still on exhibition in
Captain Bill's Hotel at Rockaway.

Several Missouri fishermen have told me of another bass,
a female, who made it her business to carry tin cans and old

shoes to all parts of a certain lake. Then, when a fisherman's hook came along, she just stuck on a boot or a can. Usually she gave a hearty tug on the line, and leaped out of the water to laugh at the angler's discomfiture. Sometimes, caught in an isolated spot, the fish couldn't find a tin can or an old shoe. All that she could do, in such cases, was to tie the line fast to a rock or a sunken log. It was poor sport, perhaps, but better than just sitting around twiddling her fins.

According to an Associated Press dispatch of March 11, 1936, Floyd Bevins, of Clinton, Oklahoma, caught a bass in Clinton Lake which had no left eye. "The fish in that lake are *all* one-eyed," he told a reporter. "That's why we haven't been catching 'em lately. We've been throwing our plugs on the blind side!" Other Clinton sportsmen seemed considerably impressed by the Bevins theory, but refused to comment for publication.

Old tales about fish humming or singing so loud that campers are unable to sleep on the gravel bars have often been repeated in newspapers and elsewhere. Will Rice [20] claimed that there was a big gar in the Buffalo River that scraped its bill in time with the jukebox in a nearby honky-tonk. Old rivermen tell me that these tales were started by a party of float-trippers from Kansas City, in the early 1900's.

Not so many years ago there were people in the Ozarks who believed that catfish sometimes speak to human beings. I remember a schoolteacher from St. Louis who declared that he heard a dying catfish cry "Oh Lord Jesus!" in the German language. It is true that certain species of catfish produce a squeaking noise when taken from the water. These fish are usually small, and the rivermen call them squealer-cats. I have seen and heard squealers myself, on the James and White rivers. But the sounds they made were

[20] *Ozark Guide*, May–June, 1944, p. 46.

not very loud, and they did not sound like words to me. The superstitious natives have many tales of birds and animals which cried out "Oh Lord!" or "Lord help me!" with their last breath. Cora Pinkley Call [21] says that the old hunters in Carroll County, Arkansas, could tell when a bear was fatally wounded, as the animal made a noise which sounded like "Oh Lord."

There is a persistent notion in the Ozarks that catfish are fond of milk and that they obtain milk by sucking the teats of cows. Many hillfolk really believe this, despite the fact that one has only to examine the fish's mouth, full of back-curving teeth, to see the difficulties involved. Marion Hughes [22] tells how one of his cows waded into the river, and a big catfish swam up to her and began to suck. He shot the fish and dragged it ashore. "It was an old suckle that had young ones," Hughes writes, "and tits an inch long!" Otto Ernest Rayburn [23] reports the experience of a farmer in western Missouri whose cows generally came home dry; he decided that the animals were wading in the river where they were milked by fish. So he fastened a fish-hook to each cow's teats, and turned 'em loose. Next night the cattle didn't come in, so the farmer hurried down to the river. There were the cows, standing out in the water. Wading into the stream, the man found that each cow had hooked four big catfish, the combined weight and pull being so great that the animals could not reach dry land.

Many persons in Crawford County, Arkansas, remember the case of Tubb Rawlings, who caught a big catfish and trained it to get along with very little water. He just put the fish in the rain barrel and then gradually lowered the level of the water. In about three weeks the barrel was

[21] *Pioneer Tales,* p. 25. [22] *Three Years in Arkansaw,* p. 31.
[23] *Ozark Guide,* Spring, 1947, p. 33.

practically dry, and the catfish seemed perfectly happy without any water at all. It became very tame and followed Tubb around the farm all day, mewing and wriggling along on the ground like a trained seal. Finally Tubb took it with him on a fishing trip. The boat capsized somewhere south of Van Buren, and the dry-land catfish was drowned.

Several Ozark story-tellers have mentioned a Sac River fisherman who dropped his gold watch into the water near Stockton, Missouri. A year later he caught a large bass near this place and found the watch in the fish's belly. The strange thing is that the watch was still running and had lost only four minutes in twelve months. A newspaperman named Oliver tried to sell this story, with appropriate photographs, to the company that manufactured the watch. But the unimaginative officeboy who answered his letter said they didn't want any part of it.

Another angler, in Barry County, Missouri, dropped his pocket pistol out of a boat. The water was very deep, and all efforts to recover the weapon were in vain. The next summer, fishing in the same vicinity, he hooked a large bass. Just as the fish was netted, it fired a shot which narrowly missed the guide. The long-lost pistol was found in the throat of the big bass, still in good working condition.

Everybody in the Ozark country has heard about the fellow who dropped a lantern into a deep hole on White River. Forty years later, while fishing in the same pool, he pulled out his old lantern, and it was still lighted. The lighted-lantern story has been printed many times. One of the best variants is that reported by Isabel France (*Arkansas Gazette*, Aug. 3, 1947) about a hillman who declared that he had caught a yellow cat that weighed 103 pounds. Another fisherman then came up with the old wheeze about pulling a lighted lantern from the waters of Possum Creek, in

Madison County, Arkansas. "I'll tell you what let's do," said the first angler. "You blow out that lantern, and I'll knock 100 pounds off my catfish."

There used to be a whole cycle of tales about the fisherman who started out with a minnow as bait. A small fish was hooked, and almost immediately it was pounced upon by a larger fish. Before the second fish could be landed, it was swallowed by a still larger one, and so on until the tackle and the listener's patience reached the breaking point. One frequently sees these stories in the country newspapers. Clyde Smith of Springfield, Missouri, according to the Springfield *Leader and Press* [24] was fishing in the Gasconade near Hazelgreen, Missouri. The story is that Clyde fell asleep, and a three-pound channel cat swallowed his bait. It swam around awhile, and then was gulped down by a flathead catfish weighing 43 pounds. Clyde woke up and landed the flathead, and when it was cut open the channel cat was found inside, with Clyde's hook firmly fastened in its throat.

Even today there are men and women in the Ozarks who believe some very odd stories about eels, as I have indicated in a previous book.[25] Collins [26] repeats the tale of a "witch fish" that lives "in a certain lake in eastern Missouri." The witch fish is simply a large eel, so far as outward appearance goes, but the story is that it contains the spirit of an Indian girl who committed suicide when her Spanish lover deserted her. The girl's father cursed her memory in some heathen ceremony, so now she must remain an eel forever. The witch fish roams the shallow waters near the shore and listens to lovers' talk; when a man proves faithless the witch fish follows him, and sometimes drags him into deep water to his death. Professor Collins does not tell us where he got this

[24] July 18, 1933.   [25] *Ozark Superstitions*, pp. 250–251.
[26] *Folk Tales of Missouri*, pp. 113–114.

story, and it may be that the business of the Indian maiden and her Spaniard are recent additions to the tale. However, related stories about giant eels which have supernatural powers and sometimes kill human beings are still circulated among the old-timers.

Angleworms are good bait for many pan-fish, but these worms are difficult to obtain in August and September. There used to be a guide named Brown who had a great reputation as a procurer of fishin'-worms. He spent most of his time at one of the Lake Taneycomo resorts, and people came from miles around to buy bait from "Fisher" Brown. It was said that he got his worms by beating on a sapling with a club; the concussion made them come to the surface, and all Brown had to do with pick 'em up. Some fishermen believed that the tapping must be done in a certain tempo, to make the worms think it was raining.

The boys in Springfield, Missouri, tell me that Dave McGregor once bought an electrical device guaranteed to shock fishworms right out of the ground. It appears that Dave had no success with this appliance, and explained his failure by saying that the moon wasn't in the proper zodiacal sign. Another theory is that he turned on too much juice and electrocuted the worms before they could get to the surface.

A gentleman from Hot Springs, Arkansas, who does not want his name mentioned here, had an unhappy experience with one of these galvanic worm-catchers. He plugged the thing into the light circuit at a tourist camp, but no sooner had he stuck the point into the ground than he began to "turn flipflops an' holler," according to reliable witnesses. The lady who was traveling with him rushed out of the cabin and grabbed his arm, whereupon she also went into the flipflop routine. This spirited performance continued until a tourist camp attendant disconnected the machine. "It damn' near killed the both of us," the gentleman told me later. "From now on out, I'll bait my hook with chicken-guts."

One could fill a book with tales of men who have caught birds, bats, minks, squirrels, bears, and even women on fish-hooks. Some of these anecdotes are probably true. I heard one at Noel, Missouri, about a fly-fisherman who arrived at dusk. Wishing to limber up his new flyrod with a few practice casts, he walked out onto the lawn next the O-Joe clubhouse, which is called Shadow Lake nowadays. He tied on a White Miller and was electrified to get a strike in mid air. Shaking like a leaf, he nevertheless played the thing as best he could, and finally got it reeled in to the tip of his rod. Walking into the light which streamed out from the clubhouse door, he held up his catch for the crowd to see. It was a bat, which had taken the Miller in full flight, high above the fisherman's head. This tale is often credited to Joe Waskey, a well-known sportsman from Kansas. I asked Joe about it once, but he volunteered to buy a drink, refusing to confirm or deny the bat story.

My grandfather used to tell of a man who was still-fishing in the Arkansas River, and caught a large yellow catfish. Just as the fish was landed the hook came out of its mouth, and flew into the top of a nearby tree. While stringing the catfish, the fisherman noticed his long cane pole swinging in the air. Snatching it instantly, he found that a wild turkey, which had been hidden in the foliage, was firmly impaled on the hook. One sees this tale printed in the country newspapers every year or so, with a squirrel or some other animal substituted for the turkey. Very often it is related as the truth, usually as the experience of some prominent citizen.

Harold L. Fulton, an insurance salesman from Kansas City, caught a mudhen on a flyrod at Bennett Springs Park, according to the Kansas City *Journal-Post*.[27] Fulton was

[27] May 3, 1936.

fishing for trout, and the mudhen swam nearby. Suddenly Fulton's fly struck the bird, and the hook was firmly embedded in its breast. The mudhen took off and flew wildly about, with Fulton playing it like a trout in an effort to save his light tackle and prevent it from fouling the line in the treetops. Finally the bird became exhausted, and Fulton brought it down to the tip of his flyrod. Then, after taking the names and addresses of several witnesses, Fulton unhooked the mudhen, which flew away and doubtless lived happily ever after.

Then there was Jim Garvin, of Talihina, Oklahoma, who cast his baited hook into the Kiamichi River and pulled out a big hoot owl, acording to the Associated Press.[28] The bait settled at the surface of the water near some overhanging willows, and the owl snatched it.

At Lake Hamilton, near Hot Springs, Arkansas, W. A. Akers was casting for bream, using a live minnow as bait. Suddenly a stray pelican grabbed the minnow in mid-air, and was so firmly hooked that Akers and another man dragged it into their boat, removed the hook, and tied its bill shut with twine. The *Arkansas Gazette* [29] tells the whole story, adding that the pelican was presented to an ostrich farm.

Such items as the above furnish the basic material from which elaborate windies are evolved. The boys at Hot Springs, Arkansas, used to tell one about a bait-caster who inadvertently hooked a diving grebe, known locally as a di-dapper. The bird swam wildly through the shallow water, and an enormous bass grabbed it by the neck, actually trying to take it away from the angler. The man cut a cedar sprout for use as a club, and beat the big fish until it became unconscious, when he was able to land it. During the struggle he struck a hollow stump with his club, and a large coon fell

[28] June 8, 1939.   [29] May 3, 1949.

out, cracking its skull on a rock and killing a rabbit in its death agony. A passing game warden arrested the fisherman for catching a protected bird, having more than twenty pounds of game fish in his possession, killing fur-bearing animals out of season, and cutting cedar on a Government reservation without permission. The rabbit was disregarded, since there's no law on rabbits in Arkansas.

10 Miscellaneous tales

THE ITEMS THROWN TOGETHER under this heading have little in common, beyond the fact that they do not easily fit into any of the previous chapters. How should one classify, for example, the strange places so often mentioned by the storytellers, which cannot be found on any official map?

Several Ozark blanket-stretchers have chosen a mythical community called Rumpus Ridge as a setting for their wildest stories. The late Tom P. Morgan, of Rogers, Arkansas, who published many humorous tales in the 1890's and early 1900's, made frequent reference to Rumpus Ridge, and the name was applied to a disorderly neighborhood in Benton County, Arkansas, as recently as 1932. A dry, windy hogback just north of Galena, Missouri, is still known as Rumpus Ridge; T. A. McQuary, the postmaster at Galena, tells me that people who live there frequently get letters addressed to Rumpus Ridge, although most of them resent the name nowadays.

Possum Trot is not so turbulent and rowdy a place as Rumpus Ridge, but it is recognized as a small, backward, hillbilly settlement. It is said that the name was once given to a village in Greene County, Missouri, and there used to be another Possum Trot not far from Neosho, Missouri. Wayman Hogue [1] refers to a place called Possum Trot in Van Buren County, Arkansas. A little group of buildings three miles west of Pea Ridge, Arkansas, bears the name Walnut Grove, but when I was there in 1931 most people

[1] *Back Yonder*, pp. 50, 101.

called it Possum Trot. The *Arkansas Gazette* [2] mentions Possum Trot as "a mythical community in Representative Trimble's district in northwest Arkansas." Speaking to a House Public Works Committee in Washington, in June, 1947, Congressman Trimble referred several times to Possum Trot, saying "The folks up in Possum Trot will want to know this," or "How can I explain this to the boys in Possum Trot?" Jim Trimble lives in Berryville, Arkansas, and his neighbors say that a small community near Berryville is generally known as Possum Trot, although it has another name. I drove out to see about this, but the villagers replied indignantly that no such name has ever been applied to their town. "I've heerd of Possum Trot," one old gentleman told me. He cocked an eye at the Missouri license plates on my Ford. "I reckon it must be up in Missouri somewheres," he added gently.

In many parts of the Ozarks one hears the word Hookrum used to mean a colony of thieves and small-time criminals. Any gang of backwoods ruffians is referred to as "them Hookrum boys." Governor Charles Hillman Brough once told me that "Hookrum is the Arkansas equivalent of Podunk," but it is really a much stronger term, with implications of larceny as well as ignorance. Hookrum originally designated the Evening Shade community, in Sharp County, Arkansas. When an honest farmer ventured into town, it is said, the villagers were accustomed to ply him with rum and hook his valuables. According to the official guidebook [3] "Hookrum struck some peculiar chord in Arkansas folk humorists, who used the word until it had become identified all over the State with backwoods rusticity. The name has been disavowed by the citizens of Evening Shade." A few years ago I visited Evening Shade, and inquired about Hook-

[2] July 6, 1947.　　　　　[3] *Arkansas*, p. 258.

rum. To say that "the name has been disavowed by the citizens" is a triumph of understatement.

There was a time when Pine Ridge was applied derisively to any backwoods settlement and was almost as offensive as Possum Trot or Hookrum. But the radio comedians known as Lum and Abner have changed all that. These fellows are Chet Lauck and Norris Goff, native Arkansawyers who grew up at Mena, in Polk County. Their hillbilly heaven was really the village of Waters, in Montgomery County, Arkansas, but they called it Pine Ridge on the air. The people of Waters recognized their local characters in the Lum and Abner program and had sense enough to take advantage of this free publicity. Realizing that their backwardness was a commercial asset, the villagers put up DRIVE KEERFUL signs and others calculated to catch the eye of the "furrin" motorist. Almost immediately tourists were swarming all over the place, and the residents made good money by being picturesque and selling souvenirs. Finally it was decided to change the name of the town to Pine Ridge, and this legal formality was completed at the Capital in Little Rock, with the Governor of Arkansas and other dignitaries participating. It was a good show, and the radio and newsreel men made the most of it. This performance really put the villagers on the map, and it now appears that Pine Ridge attracts almost as many out-of-state visitors as the Hot Springs National Park.

When I lived in McDonald County, Missouri, it seemed to me that a native who wanted a definite location for some outlandish story chose either Bear Holler or Gotham. Bear Holler is well known as a wild, rugged, almost inaccessible region near the Arkansas line, headquarters for moonshiners during the Volstead Era. But Gotham does not appear on any map, and the tourist who inquired about it would get no information from the Ozarks Playgrounds Association. The roadmap shows the tiny village of Jane, but the people who lived there in the 1920's always spoke of their community as White Rock. "Jane's just the postoffice name," a woman told me, "an' we don't never use it only when we go to back a letter." When local humorists referred disparagingly to the settlement, they didn't call it either Jane or White Rock. They called it Gotham, meaning a parcel of fools, or sometimes Gottem, which means lousy. When a fellow who lived in a big town like Pineville (population 422) told a hillbilly story, he nearly always set the scene somewhere "up around Gotham, which ain't far from Bear Holler."

Near the Arkansas-Oklahoma line, between the border towns of Southwest City and Fort Smith, there is a community known as Bug Tussel, or Bug Scuffle, celebrated for the alleged abundance of the scavenger beetles known as tumblebugs. The name Bug Tussel has no official standing, but it has been used freely by politicians and newspapermen. The reader who knows about the habits of tumblebugs will understand the indignation of the citizens at having their home town called Bug Tussel. I spent several weeks in a village to which this name has been applied, but I do not intend to identify it here. It is a nice little town, full of pleasant people, and I might want to go back there sometime.

People who live in the northern foothills of the Missouri Ozarks sometimes speak of Poosey, meaning a backward, unenlightened region. E. A. Collins [4] discusses this at some length.

Poosey is a mythical county [he writes] lying somewhere within the triangle formed by drawing a straight line from Chillicothe to Trenton, then west to Jamesport and back again to Chillicothe. No one knows exactly where the boundary line really is.

[4] *Folk Tales of Missouri*, pp. 23–30.

BUG TUSSEL
1 MILE →

There is no agreement about this, for I have known Missourians who placed Poosey much farther south than Professor Collins does, and some of them locate it south of the Missouri River. It is said that the name originated with some early settlers from Posey County, Indiana; these people did not mix well with the Southerners, who called them Poseyites, later corrupted to Pooseyites. Today the name is used derisively, like hillbilly or hayseed or ridge-runner. Isolation, poverty, ignorance—all these are implied. When one wants to tell a rube story, he just says that it happened somewhere down in Poosey.

The old residents tell of several other odd places, but even the names of some of them are unprintable, and to describe the goings-on there is out of the question. I have heard wild tales about Hockey Center, Duckbutter Knob, Ingern City, Jingleberry Junction, and Shankerville. Many amusing stories refer to a mythical mining town called Chippy's Delight, somewhere in Jasper County, Missouri. It is said that the mayor of this camp stood twelve feet four inches in his stocking feet, without getting out of bed.

Fabulous things are said to happen in the Windy Mountains of eastern Oklahoma, but I have never found anybody who could exactly locate these mountains. My neighbors at Pineville, Missouri, used to say that a certain noisy cattleman was borned an' raised in the Windy Mountains, but he and I were not friendly, and I never had the courage to ask him about it.

Ticklegrass Canyon is another liars' colony to which the pioneers consigned their story-tellers. Some say that blanket-stretchers who go too far are driven into the canyon by indignant neighbors and forced to remain there. Another view is that Ticklegrass Canyon does not exist on earth at all, but is just a place where liars are supposed to congregate after they die.

My neighbors in the Ozarks don't believe in Purgatory and they never heard of Limbo, but many of them refer occasionally to Fiddlers' Green, which is seven miles the other side of Hell. This place was originally set aside for fiddlers only, but later regulations admit banjo-pickers and story-tellers and ballad singers and other fellows with colorful accomplishments, even if they can't scrape the fiddle. There are sailors and peddlers and tinkers in Fiddlers' Green, and a few cowpokes, and maybe a thin scatterin' of old soldiers. Some people say that the dance-hall girls from West Hell are allowed to come over on Saturday nights, but there is a divergence of opinion about this.

The village jokers often speak of an isolated holler called Paradise Valley. It's only a tale, because nobody has any first-hand information about the place. Tourists go into the holler sometimes, but they are never seen again by anybody on the outside. The story is that if a man wants to leave, the authorities figure he must be crazy, and lock him up in the Paradise Valley pokey until he comes to his senses. I have known men and women in several whistle-stop towns who share this attitude, in a measure. There is just enough truth in the Paradise Valley story to make it seem very funny to those of us who live in the Ozarks.

One sometimes hears guarded references to Jaybird Heaven, but most of the stories about it are pretty vague. Jaybird is a nickname for an inept timber worker, and there is an old saying that jaybirds carry firewood to Hell every Friday. A man in Scott County, Arkansas, told me that Jaybird Heaven is a place where wicked lumberjacks go when they die. It's a vast forest of virgin pine, he said, but the law of gravity is not in force there, and everything runs arsey-varsey. When you cut a tree down, it falls uphill, and so on. An experienced woodsman would be very unhappy in Jaybird Heaven, because it's hell for a skilled craftsman to be compelled to do everything backward, and spend all eternity with a gang of bungling amateurs besides. Several persons have told me that Jaybird Heaven is just an old and libelous name for Waldron, Arkansas, but I have small confidence in their testimony.

It's true, however, that some very strange stories have come out of Waldron. Even now there are men near the town who pretend to find something praiseworthy in the fact that they have lived thereabouts for a long time without losing their minds. People who live in a small town love to recall the days when the place was even smaller, and sometimes these reminiscences expand into windies of the first water. "When I first come to this country," cried a retired lumberman, "the moon wasn't no bigger'n a dime! There was only seventeen stars in the sky, an' the Dipper didn't have no handle! Magazine Mountain looked like a ant-hill, an' the Arkansas River was no more'n a spring branch, you could jump acrost it anywheres!" I once met a man near Mena, Arkansas, who said that when he was a boy, full-grown bears were no bigger than chipmunks.

One hears these small-then-big-now yarns all over the country, of course. Near Pineville, Missouri, I sat with a deputy sheriff at the entrance of a rock-shelter known as Saltpeter Cave. He looked up at the stone ceiling above our heads, then into the black depths of the cavern. "They tell me this here cave is twenty mile deep," said the officer. "It beats all how things have changed. Back in 1898, when we first moved to McDonald County, Saltpeter Cave warn't nothin' but a groundhog hole."

Like all limestone regions, the Ozark country is full of caves, and there are many wild stories about these places. In various parts of Missouri and Arkansas country folk tell of a great pit, surrounded by rugged cliffs, where hunters have heard strange sounds and smelled unusual odors. Some say that the Devil lives in a big cave, imprisoned under a fall of rock. There are stories of old men who claim to have visited the place as children. Some of these fellows swear that they heard the Devil's groans and smelled burning flesh and brimstone. But stories of this type deal with the supernatural and are not tall tales in the ordinary sense.

A man in Galena, Missouri, repeated an old story about a very large cave somewhere in his neighborhood. It had a wide entrance, according to the tale, and the cattle used to enter it on hot days because of the lower temperature inside. Sometimes they would wander so far into the great cavern that a man standing at the entrance couldn't hear the cowbells. This may seem unimpressive to a city feller, but every country boy knows that the sound of a cowbell carries a long distance.

In a country full of big caves and rugged cliffs, it is natural that there are many stories about echoes. Otto Ernest Rayburn told me of a farmer who used an echo as an alarm clock for many years. Just about dark this man would go out behind the house and holler at a flint-rock bluff across the valley. "Time to git up!" he yelled at the top of his voice. Then he would read his paper awhile and go to bed, knowing that the echo would wake him promptly at five the next morning.

A big cave on Roark Mountain, near Notch, Missouri, is widely known for the remarkable echo heard at the entrance. Whenever a tourist mentions this, some hillman is moved to saw off a whopper. "Talkin' about echoes," one farmer said, "that there Devil's Den echo ain't nothin'. You holler down one of them cave-holes on my place, an' you got to wait forty-eight hours for the echo to git back to the gate!"

Fiddlers who play for the outdoor dances complain a good deal about the distracting echoes, and so do the auctioneers and congressmen and hog-callers. Ed Marley learned to call hogs in the hills of Christian County, Missouri, and he says that callers who rate mighty high in Illinois or Iowa are not much good in the Ozarks.

Callin' hogs in the hills is different from callin' 'em in a prairie country [he told a reporter] [5] on account of the echo. You don't get any echo in the flat country, but in the hills hogs have been known to worry themselves down to nothing trying to keep up with the hog-caller, then chasing back where they hear the echo from. It drives a lot of hogs plumb crazy.

There are several other tales about the Ozark hog-callers. Howard Dunn [6] says that he lived in Taney County, Missouri, for fifteen years, and during that period all the farmers for miles around had to build extra high fences. His call was so irresistible that hogs came for miles around when he got to hollerin' good. And W. L. Crosby, according to the same newspaper story, said that he once entered a hog-calling contest at a picnic, and a hog which he had sold four years previously heard his call three-quarters of a mile off and came running to him as fast as it could.

In many sections of the Ozarks one finds the story of a farmer whose hollerin' voice didn't amount to much, so he called his pigs by beating with a stick on the rail fence. This man's swine had enormous appetites, but they didn't gain much weight. Finally it was discovered that the poor critters spent the whole day running after woodpeckers, and kept it up till they were trained down as thin as foxhounds. The habit was so firmly established that it couldn't be broken, and all these peckerwood-follerin' hogs had to be sold at a loss.

I don't mean to imply that yelling at livestock renders a man untruthful, although there are those who defend this thesis. But it was a professional hog-caller who told me about

[5] Springfield, Mo., *Leader and Press*, Feb. 24, 1934.
[6] Springfield, Mo., *Leader and Press*, Feb. 26, 1934.

the time a fat woman fell off the bridge into Swan Creek, at a place called Shadow Rock, near Forsyth, Missouri. "The old gal lit belly-buster," said he. "She splashed the swimmin'-hole plumb dry, an' wet the bluff clear to the top!" It is true that a lady fell off the bridge that day, just as he says. Probably she did make quite a splash, but since Shadow Rock appears to be about 150 feet high at this point, I believe the hog-caller was exaggerating a bit.

And it was another master hog-caller, Kinney Tennyson by name, who first introduced me to the flyin' beehive yarn. We were sitting on a windy hilltop in McDonald County, Missouri, with a little stone jug between us, and Kinney was talking of his pioneer experiences. "I was settin' right over there under that tree, back in the 80's," said he, "when I seen somethin' mighty peculiar a-flyin' through the air. It was about four foot long, an' maybe a foot an' a half thick. Looked like a holler log, with a board nailed on one end. What do you reckon it was?" I answered that I had no idea what the strange object could have been. "Well, I didn't have no idy myself, at first. But come to find out, it warn't nothin' but a swarm of bees, a-leavin' Gabe Durbin's bee-yard." I pondered this for a moment. I used to be a beekeeper myself, and I have seen hundreds of swarms in the air. But they all looked like swarms of bees, not like wooden cylinders, and I said as much to Kinney. "It was a swarm of bees, all right," he answered. "But you see, they was takin' their gum with 'em," he added. This story of bees carrying a beehive seems to be widely known. Hal Norwood [7] tells an almost identical tale, which he credits to George Nall, of Lockesburg, Arkansas.

A related yarn is attributed to Frank Payne and Deacon Hembree, of Stone County, Missouri. They went up into the woods east of Galena and were baiting the bees with

[7] *Just a Book*, p. 14.

honey in a tin pan set up on a stump. Bees came to the bait all right, more bees than either of the bee-hunters had ever seen before. No trouble about linin' 'em this time, and no need to strain the eyes, either. These bees flew away with the honey, pan and all. Payne and Hembree watched the pan as it was carried off over the treetops, and thus located the biggest bee tree ever cut on Horse Creek.

Since the pioneers had no sugar and depended almost entirely upon honey for sweetenin', the location of bee trees was an important matter to every backwoods family. Some woodsmen made a regular profession of bee hunting, and they really did find some enormous stores of wild honey. Colonel Noland of Batesville, Arkansas [8] repeats the following story, which he heard in 1852.

A fellow was boasting that he had a bee-tree on his place, so large that he had a door and several windows in it, and a few days before had taken out fifteen barrels of honey to send to St. Louis. The person to whom he told this admitted that it was a tolerable fair bee-tree, but nothing to one he had. "Why," says he, "I took two of my best Negro men and my large wagon, and went to one I had on the Merrimack River. We all three chopped steady ahead from Monday morning until Saturday night, when we found that three men on the other side had commenced the same time we did; so we compromised, and each filled our wagon chuck full with fine honeycomb, when a puff of wind blew the tree down, and ke-whop it went into the Merrimack River. And if there is any truth in me, that river was pure metheglin for six weeks and three days."

Metheglin is a fermented drink made by mixing honey and water, and maybe a little yeast. The old-timers claim that metheglin is better than hard cider, but I don't agree with them. The stuff packs a considerable wallop, though. And it doesn't taste too bad if you lace it with whiskey and serve it hot.

[8] *Spirit of the Times,* Jan. 29, 1853.

The character known as Ab Yancey is credited with perhaps the most extravagant bee-hunting yarn of all time. Ab's grandpap was a famous bee hunter. One fall he followed some bees into an unexplored hollow. The farther he went, the thicker the bees, and finally he came to a place where so many bees were flying that the sky was darkened, and the insects buzzed so loud that he was almost deafened. The old man knowed in reason there wasn't a tree in the world big enough to hive such a swarm as that. After a-while he saw a big limestone cliff. It was just plumb black with bees, and they was a-hangin' down in clusters forty foot long. There was beemartins from all over creation a-ketchin' the stragglers, and dead bees four foot deep in the creek bottom. Grandpap looked the situation over, and he figgered there must be two hundred million pound of honey in that bluff, and maybe more. The whole mountain was just made of comb honey and bee-bread, with a few rocks in it. But there was no way in the world to get the honey. Nobody could smoke a beegum four hundred foot long and a hundred and fifty foot high. And it would be certain death for a man to go a-messin' around there if the bees weren't smoked.

Grandpap went home and told the family, and the next day they all came over and examined the honey mountain. All winter long they studied how to get the honey, and finally the old man figured it out. Early next spring they built a new cabin right on top of the bluff. They filed on the land, so's to get a good title from the Government, and the whole family moved into the new house. As soon as they got the fences up and the corn patch planted, they went to work diggin' a well. Most people thought the Yanceys had all gone crazy, because there was a good spring right back of the house, but the folks just kept on a-digging. They built windlasses and piled up rocks higher than fodder stacks.

Them Yancey boys growed calluses on their hands big as
walnuts. About sixty foot down a little trickle of yaller
stuff come out under a rock. "We've struck honey, boys,
an' the job's done," says Grandpap. "Bail her out good,
an' let her clear up. Put a lid on top, to keep the bugs out'n
the well. An' when you-uns git that done, just go up an'
set on the gallery like a gentleman. Ye won't have to do ary
'nother lick of work as long as you live."

The Yanceys did no farming at all for two whole generations. Strained honey sold for four cents a pound, and the
Yancey honey was strained through fifty foot of rocks an'
gravel. They put it up in barrels, and hauled it to Springfield and Fayetteville. The Yanceys was the richest family
in Arkansas in them days, and they just about run the whole
country. They'd probably be a-runnin' it yet, if they hadn't
got to fightin' with the Hammonses. After two or three was
killed on both sides, the Hammons boys sneaked over one
night and dropped more'n two hundred pound of gunpowder down the honey-well. They say that the whole
Hammons clan mortgaged their farms to buy that powder.

When they touched fire to the fuse it just blowed the
whole cliff plumb off. It scattered comb honey and bee-
bread all over Snake County. It ruined the Yancey's forever,
because the honey was gone for good. They say that a
million tons of honey fell into the creek. For ten years after
that the people used the creek water for long sweetenin',
and a millpond six miles down the valley tasted kind of
sweet up till three or four years ago. The big cliff is still
known as Bee Bluff, and the old millpond is called Honey
Lake to this day.

Rivers flowing with sweetened water and metheglin are
common in backwoods folklore, and many an isolated valley
is described as a place "where the flitter-tree stands close
to the honey-pond." Some Ozark people have always been

a little crazy on the subject of streams and springs and magic water. Hillmen who live near an unusually cold spring go around boasting of its coldness. If their drinking water is tepid, the villagers gabble about the therapeutic value of warm springs. Go to a settlement where the spring smells like rotten eggs, and you'll find the people declaring that sulphur-water will cure any ailment, up to and including cancer. If a spring flows clear and sparkling in the sunlight, the local wise men cry up the merits of clarity; if it looks muddy, they all agree that clear water is tasteless and "ain't got no body to it." The Chamber of Commerce people have an analysis made, and then gather to sing the praises of whatever mineral the chemist may report. If the analysis shows nothing significant, the citizens shout louder than ever, boasting that their water is "free from mineral impurities."

The folly of this water-mania was recognized in some quarters as early as 1880. One of Mark Twain's characters [9] declared that Mississippi River water, being muddy, was much better to drink than water from the Ohio River, which is comparatively clear. Muddy water is full of rich earth and fertilizer. "Look at the graveyards; that tells the tale," said a raftsman who called himself the Child of Calamity. "Trees won't grow worth shucks in a Cincinnati graveyard, but in a Saint Louis graveyard they grow upwards of eight hundred foot high. It's all on account of the water the people drunk before they laid up. A Cincinnati corpse don't richen the soil any."

There are people today in Missouri and Arkansas who talk just as wildly about magic water as their grandparents did, and a lot of tall stories have grown out of their ravings. The old-timers in Garland County, Arkansas, used to tell of a man who died in St. Louis, but was brought back to

[9] *Life on the Mississippi*, p. 50.

Hot Springs for burial. A drunken comrade, at the wake, somehow spilled a bucket of water on the body. Next day the coffin lay beside the open grave, in the warm sunlight, while the preacher prayed. Suddenly the cover of the casket was pushed aside, and the corpse sat up, blinking. The spring water and the balmy Arkansas sunlight had revived him, and a few minutes later he was able to take a few swallows of good Garland County whiskey. Next day he was sitting on a bench in the park, swapping lies with the other old codgers.

Even the notorious Thomas W. Jackson [10] who visited Hot Springs at the turn of the century, was impressed by stories about the curative properties of the water. "In the hotel I stopped at," he writes, "they told me they hadn't bought any firewood for ten years. The cripples that had come there and been cured had left crutches enough to keep them in wood."

According to Bob Burns [11] the healing baths at Hot Springs are nothing out of the ordinary, because there is magic water all over Arkansas. It was somewhere near Van Buren that the train cut his dog's tail off, but Bob just threw the dog into a big spring, and the animal swam out with a new tail. Then he threw the severed tail into the water, and it came out with a new body. So it was that Bob went home that night with two dogs instead of one.

Otto Ernest Rayburn used to tell of a tourist who met a resident of Eureka Springs, Arkansas. Both were drinking from a spring near Hatchet Hall, the old home of Carry Nation. "When I started drinkin' this water," said the resident, "I didn't have a hair on my head or a tooth in my mouth. And now. . ." he showed a great shock of black hair and a set of perfect natural teeth. The city fellow made

[10] *On a Slow Train through Arkansaw*, 1903, p. 41.
[11] *Ford Times*, April, 1948, p. 19.

no comment, though he obviously thought the resident's tale was a lie. But it wasn't. The man who told the story was born nearby, and the water from that spring was the first he ever tasted.

A party of my old friends camped on a gravel bar in the James River, somewhere below Galena, Missouri. It is said that they drank ten gallons of whiskey in one night, and then broke up the keg for cookwood, in case anybody wanted breakfast. Just before dawn Hawk Gentry awoke with a mighty craving for water, and took a big drink out of a nearby spring. A moment later he staggered back to the tents and raised such an uproar as to wake the whole camp. It was such incredibly *good* water, he shouted, that everybody must get right up and drink some.

This recalls the tale of a drunken farmer near Pineville, Missouri, who came running into the settlement at 3 A.M. yelling "Fire! Fire!" After he had awakened about half the people in town and had them milling around the streets in their night clothes, it was learned that he wanted everybody to come out to the old Bosserman Mill, about two miles up the creek, and help drag the millpond. The moon had fell into it, he said.

There is plenty of water in the Ozark country, but not too much soil, so that we don't worry much about mud. Our roads may be steep and rocky, but they aren't muddy. There are local exceptions to this rule, of course, and the main thoroughfare of Eureka Springs, Arkansas, was formerly known as Mud Street. Tall stories about mud are still common in this vicinity. One of the old tales concerns the traveler who saw a man's hat in a puddle, picked it up, and found a bewhiskered head underneath. Shocked and surprised, he grabbed the man by the collar and tried to help him out of the mud. "Let me alone, stranger," cried the hillman, "you're a-pullin' me right out of the saddle."

A variant of this yarn is about the city fellow who found a fine Stetson in a quagmire near Rolla, Missouri. He got a long pole to drag the hat within reach, but soon discovered that there was a man's head under it. "Good God, you're in a bad fix!" he cried. The man in the mudhole shook the water out of his eyes. "Yeah, I *shore* am," he admitted. "It's lucky I've got a good horse under me, or I might have got kind of damp."

Lowell Thomas [12] tells of a man who came to Missouri in the rainy season. Standing on the sidewalk, he saw a farmer moving slowly along down the middle of the street, up to his knees in mud. "It seems to be kind of muddy out there," shouted the man on the sidewalk. "Sure is," answered the fellow in the street. "It's a good thing I'm standin' on top of this load of hay."

The mention of impassible roads was a conventional excuse for tardiness in the 1870's, just as car trouble and traffic jams are today. The old settlers tell of a backwoods couple who came into a Missouri town and asked for a marriage license, while their ten children waited outside the clerk's office. Asked why he had not attended to this formality sooner, the old man said: "Well, you see, the roads has been so turrible bad . . ."

The best stories about cattle come from the short-grass country west of the Ozarks, but even Oklahoma has nothing to compare with Paul Bunyan's famous blue ox Babe. However, one recalls the farmer in Benton County, Arkansas, who was always bragging about his dairy herd. "The milk from them cows was so God damn' rich it was all thick cream, plumb to the bottom of the crock," he said. "It couldn't be skimmed nohow, an' my woman had to pour in three-four buckets of water before she could churn the damn' stuff. We had to thin it down some more, for the

[12] *Tall Stories,* pp. 160–162.

kids to drink. None of my children ever even *seen* bluejohn till they growed up an' went to college down in Fayetteville."

Many Ozark humorists used to talk of the fabulous breachy cow owned by Shanklin Gilkeson, of Warrensburg, Missouri. The breachiest cow in the world, everybody said, and no wooden fence could hold her. She had ruined truck gardens over half of Missouri, and the Mississippi River was all that saved Illinois. When they built the big new water tower in 1894 there was an ornamental iron filligree round the top, perhaps sixty feet above the ground. The townspeople solemnly assured strangers that the railing was necessary to keep Shank Gilkeson's cow out of the water tank.

Along the western border of Arkansas there is an old tale about the two brothers who wanted a horsehide to make themselves vests, like those fancied by cowpunchers in Oklahoma. They sneaked up behind their father's bay filly, whooping and hollering till they scared her so bad she jumped right out of her skin. For this trick the boys were severely whipped and turned out of the cabin. Their father told them not to come back until they had fixed up the filly some way. The boys killed two sheep, and used the fresh pelts to replace the horsehide. The skin grew on the filly all right, but she always looked kind of peculiar after that. "The filly didn't grow much wool the first season," one of the boys said later, "but the second year she had wool four foot long an' p'inted three ways. The whole family worked seven days a-shearin' her. Just as we was gettin' the job done she kicked Pap into the pile of wool, so deep it took us half the night to find him an' dig him out. He like to a sultered under that there wool, too, an' he suffered with asthmy all the rest of his life."

In several Ozark towns I have heard the story of a nameless pioneer who made a fine harness out of rawhide. He lived on a hilltop, and when he hauled his first load of pumpkins up from the field it was raining a little, and the rawhide began to stretch. The man walked beside the horses, and when he got up to the house the load of pumpkins was nowhere in sight. The wagon was still down in the corn patch, and the rawhide tugs were stretched out more than six hundred feet long, no bigger than fiddle-strings. The hillman hooked the harness to a big stump, and turned the horses out to graze. It wasn't long till the skies cleared, the sun came out, and the rawhide began to shrink. Pretty soon he could hear the wagon squeakin', and here it come up that there hill. It didn' foller the road, though, and most of the pumpkins was throwed out and busted when the wagon climbed the bluff. The wagon was considerable tore up, too, when it run ag'in the stump where the harness was tied.

Wild turkeys were mighty important to the early settlers, and some strange old stories about turkeys have come down to us. Sam A. Leath, secretary of the Chamber of Commerce at Eureka Springs, Arkansas, told me that the pioneers used to drive great herds of wild turkeys all the way from Carroll County, Arkansas, to the market at Springfield, Missouri. They corralled the birds in a narrow hollow just below Hog Scald. A man rode ahead on horseback, dropping shelled corn in the road. If one old gobbler could be induced to follow the trail of corn, the rest would come along like a flock of sheep. The best turkey-drivers sent a boy on ahead, to tell the farmers that the turkeys were on the road, and ask them to tie up their dogs. Just about sundown the turkeys would all go to roost in the trees, and at dawn the drive would start again. Mr. Leath does not claim that he ever *saw* anything like this, but he said that the old-timers had told him about it, and that he knew of no reason to doubt the story.

Leath got one eye-witness account of the turkey drive from an old lady named Hammer, who lived in a place called the Wilderness, just north of Blue Eye, Missouri. The Hammers settled in the Wilderness about 1830, and many of their descendants still live in the neighborhood. One fall in the late 1840's, according to the old lady's tale, five men came up from Arkansas driving three thousand wild turkeys and about five hundred tame geese. At dusk, right in front of the Hammer cabin, the turkeys went to roost in the trees. But the geese wouldn't stop, since there was no water. Mrs. Hammer told the drivers to go ahead with the geese and camp on White River; the Hammer boys would bring the turkeys up in the morning. So that's what they done. When the Hammers drove the turkeys up to the crossing next day, they found the Arkansawyers having a hell of a time getting the geese out of the river. They all agreed that it was easy enough to drive wild turkeys, but these here tame geese were pretty hard to handle.

I have known Sam Leath for many years, and have often heard him tell these turkey-driving stories. He tells them seriously, and there is no doubt in my mind that he believes them to be true. There used to be plenty of old-timers in Missouri and Arkansas who backed him up absolutely; I have met old men who declared that they *saw* flocks of wild turkeys driven along the roads as late as 1870. But for a man who has hunted turkeys as I have, and spent hours in the attempt to get within gunshot of a single gobbler, it's mighty hard to imagine three thousand of these wild birds being driven along the road by men on horseback.

It must be admitted, however, that some recent turkey stories are as difficult to swallow as anything the pioneers ever told. Only a few years ago Walter Siegmund, of the Western Cartridge Company, went down to a place called McCaw Lodge, in Texas County, Missouri. And there, according to *Field and Stream* [13] a wild turkey gobbler attacked him and chased him into a house.

When a big flock of wild geese was struck by lightning near Galena, Missouri, in 1943, the villagers picked up more than two hundred of the birds, and most everybody had roast goose next day. This much is true, for I was there at the time and saw these lightnin'-struck geese, and helped eat one of them. But a lot of tall tales grew out of the incident. One man told a reporter that the goose he picked up in a pasture was cooked plumb through an' still smokin' when he got home with it; he and the old woman just put the bird on the table and ate it without any further cooking.

The typical hillman is always interested in wild turkeys and waterfowl, but pays little attention to other birds. An exception is made in the case of crows, since these marauders interfere with his business at corn-planting time. Several counties along the Oklahoma border used to pay a five-cent bounty on crows. Farmer boys and sportsmen shot a good many and brought their heads to the courthouse, but the bounty hardly paid for their ammunition. Crows are wild birds and hard to kill. It was not often that a hunter brought in more than a dozen heads at a time.

There is an old story, current in northeastern Oklahoma, that two young fellows in Nowata County busted up the crow-bounty business overnight. The tale goes that these boys located a crow roost, where countless thousands of crows spent the night in a little grove. The boys borrowed money and invested it in gunpowder. They dug shallow trenches between the trees, planted the powder, and covered it with gravel. Late at night they fired the gunpowder with

[13] Oct., 1938, p. 6.

a battery. They killed more than ten thousand crows at one discharge, since the gravel worked just like birdshot. They strung the heads on baling-wire, one hundred heads to a bunch, and loaded them into a pick-up truck. When they began to carry crow heads into the courthouse next morning, the county treasurer was horrified. It was his duty to count the heads and pay the bounty. There was blood all over the office floor, dirt and feathers and bad smell everywhere. He said it would bust the county to pay for all them crow heads. Asked how they had killed so many, the boys allowed that was a professional secret; one of them told the sheriff that they had done give up farmin', and aimed to devote their whole time to crow-killin' from now on. Finally the county commissioners paid $100 for two thousand heads and persuaded the boys to take the rest over into adjoining counties. That night the County Commission held a meeting, and repealed the crow-bounty provision. A dirty trick, but there was nothing that the crow-killers could do about it.

Farmers have tried many tricks to discourage crows. Wholesale shooting, and dynamite, and various kinds of traps, and poisoned grain, and all sorts of mechanical devices to frighten birds out of the cornfields. A man near Southwest City, Missouri, used to spin a long windy about his invention of a marvelous life-like scarecrow. It was made of tin, he said, and not only waved its arms at irregular intervals, but emitted a loud yell every few minutes. "Did it scare the crows?" I asked. "Skeer the crows!" he cried, "I should say it did. Why, gentlemen, that contraption skeerd the crows so bad that some of 'em fetched back corn they had stole two years before!"

Somebody told Frank Payne, of Galena, Missouri, that by soaking beans in whiskey and mixing them with his seed-corn, he could protect the crop from marauding crows. He tried it, but the scheme didn't work worth a damn. A few hours after the planting began, it seemed that all the crows in Missouri had gathered in Frank's little corn patch. The whole field was torn up, with wide excavations everywhere, and hundreds of crows digging feverishly. One old crow seemed to be directing activities from a large sycamore stump. Frank told me himself that this old bird was trading one whiskey-soaked bean for seven grains of corn, and doing a land-office business.

A curious old story about a crow or a buzzard with a bell attached to it crops up in the Ozark country at intervals. The Springfield, Missouri, *Leader and Press* [14] printed the following:

John H. McDaniel, of Arditta, Missouri, and his son were plowing corn when they heard a soft tinkle in the air. Looking up, they observed a buzzard flapping lazily overhead with a bell around its neck. The bird has been seen before, and Mr. McDaniel is curious to find the person who belled the buzzard, and how.

In early October, 1938, the newspapers reported that Floyd Easley, near Eagle Rock, Missouri, saw a buzzard with a bell fastened to its left wing. This bird was followed by "more than two thousand" other buzzards, according to the press. That's a lot of buzzards.

Ira W. Ford, who used to live in Branson, Missouri, refers [15] to the belled buzzard yarn as "a tradition which had its origin in the Ozark mountains." During an epidemic of hog cholera, he says, farmers became convinced that buzzards were spreading the disease. Because there was an "unwritten law" against killing these birds, they trapped one and tied a small sheep bell to it. When the belled buzzard was released, the buzzards all disappeared for a season, and the hillfolk thought that the bell had driven them away. At

[14] June 10, 1935.   [15] *Traditional Music of America*, pp. 187–188.

the end of that summer, however, the belled buzzard was heard again, and soon afterward came the typhoid which killed a lot of people in the neighborhood. Ever since that time the belled buzzard appears at intervals, always bringing trouble and calamity in his wake. Some people think that this buzzard still lives, possessed by an evil spirit, although the original belling took place more than a hundred years ago. There are still people in the Ozarks who are alarmed by a report that a belled buzzard has been heard. The supernatural element in the story as told by Ford was mentioned by various newspaper writers, but I have never known a real old-timer who took any stock in it.

A farmer in Taney County, Missouri, once told me that all the crows for miles around roosted in a grove behind his barn. One of these birds, he said, was twice the size of an ordinary crow and wore a little bell round its neck. I went out to this fellow's place and saw a great many crows at the place he indicated, but the big one with the bell was not in sight. A neighbor told me that he had seen one crow in the flock much bigger than the others, almost as big as a buzzard. "There was somethin' hangin' to it," he said, "that looked like a piece of fish-line, maybe. But I didn't hear no bell." Another man in the neighborhood said that he had heard talk about big crows with bells on 'em for years, but had never seen such a bird, or heard any bells a-ringin'. I offered a cash reward to anybody who would bring me the outsize crow with the bell on its neck, but nobody ever came to claim it.

When somebody told me, years ago, that woodpeckers were destroying public buildings in the Ozarks, I supposed it was just another Yankee libel. But it now appears that the tale originated right here at home. Some old-timers think that it's a great joke to say that the courthouse in Izard County, Arkansas, was literally "et up by the peckerwoods." There is a kind of pun involved in this. Peckerwood means woodpecker right enough, but it also means a low-class backwoodsman, the sort of man who would be called "white trash" in the deep South. "The peckerwoods built the courthouse," said an old fellow in Calico Rock, Arkansas, "an' I reckon the peckerwoods tore it down."

Several Arkansas writers have discussed the peckerwood-courthouse story. Allsopp [16] mentions "a hazy tradition" that Izard County was once so wild and woolly that "the woodpeckers ate up the courthouse." The tale was that the log building became so rotten and worm-eaten that the birds just pecked right through the walls, and finally the whole thing collapsed. There is some doubt whether it was the old Wolf cabin at the lost village of Liberty, used as a courthouse in 1827, or the one built at Athens, on Piney Creek, in 1830. These were both log buildings, of course. "Whether strictly true or not," says Allsopp, "the story has caused many laughs." Karr Shannon [17] thinks the tale refers to the courthouse at Athens. "Legend has it," he writes, "that the woodpeckers were so bad in the vicinity they almost ate up the court-house during the first two years, until a bounty of five cents a head was offered by a public-spirited levying court."

Most hillfolk prefer fat pork to any other meat; they don't care much for beef, and few of them will eat mutton at all. When times are hard people are obliged to eat rabbits, and there are many humorous tales about this. Near Bentonville, Arkansas, an old woodsman said: "I et so many rabbits when Hoover was president, that every time a dog barked I run for a holler log!" There are places in Missouri and Arkansas where rabbit meat is called "Hoover pork" to this day.

[16] *Folklore of Romantic Arkansas,* II, 269.
[17] *History of Izard County, Arkansas,* p. 12.

A young "furriner" named Rankin bought a farm in southwest Missouri. His neighbors were astounded to see him jump off'n his horse and begin chasing a cottontail on foot, running wildly through the brambles and trying to catch the rabbit with his hands. The hillfolk thought the man was crazy, of course, and nicknamed him "Rabbit." Years later he told me that he was reared in Maine and had never seen any rabbits except the big snowshoe hares of the North Woods. When he noticed the Ozark cottontails, he thought they must be very young and easy to catch. I tried to tell the home folks about this, but they had never heard of snowshoe rabbits and took no stock in my explanation. They still thought the "furriner" was a little crazy, and continued to call him "Rabbit" Rankin the rest of his life.

There have always been brush rabbits and cottontails in the Ozarks, but the old folks say that jackrabbits were almost unknown until about 1900, when they began to drift in from Kansas and Oklahoma. When the jackrabbits first appeared in McDonald County, Missouri, the boys figgered they would have a jackrabbit drive, like those famous on the Kansas prairies. The first drive was not a conspicuous success. Most of the hunters brought their jugs, and some had never seen a jackrabbit. There was a good deal of wild shooting and confusion, and several men were injured. They tell me that four of old man Lauderdale's mules were killed by mistake.

I have heard that one of the Baker boys, who lived in Barry County, Missouri, hired out to a sheepherder south of Tahlequah, Oklahoma. Told to put the sheep in the corral, he was gone a long time and finally returned utterly exhausted. "Didn't have no trouble with the sheep," he gasped, "but I sure had a hell of a time gettin' them lambs in." The sheepman's jaw dropped. "Hell, Baker," he cried, "we ain't got no lambs! There *ain't* no lambs, at this time

of the year!" He hurried out to the corral, and found fourteen big jackrabbits tearing around among the woollies.

Many hillfolk who don't like rabbit meat are very fond
of a young groundhog or whistle-pig. This always seems
strange to city people, who know about rabbits but are
not familiar with groundhogs. Mistaking me for a tourist,
an old windbag at Protem, Missouri, spun a long tale about
the time he planted corn on an island in White River. The
crop was badly damaged, apparently by groundhogs, though
none of these animals could be found on the island. There
were no ledges for groundhogs to hide under, and no
groundhog burrows. "I couldn't figger out where the varmints was at," the fellow said. So he hid himself in the corn
one moonlight night. About ten o'clock he saw groundhogs
coming from the mainland. There were dozens of 'em. Each
one floated on a stick of cordwood, paddling with all four
feet and steering with his tail.

Down in Scott County, Arkansas, the old-timers had an
ancient windy about a man who caught young groundhogs
and trained them to dig post holes, but I have never been
able to track this one down. I did find a related yarn about
beavers, which was told around Southwest City, Missouri, in
the 1920's. According to this tale, some Indian boys were
using tame beavers to cut stovewood. All the boys had to
do was fish the wood out of the water and rick it up for
sale. Once they made a trip into Arkansas after cane fish-
poles, taking four of their best beavers along to do the cutting. In less than no time they had a whole truckload of
poles, which they sold along the highways of Missouri. There
is always a demand for these poles, because the cane in Missouri doesn't grow big enough to make a decent fishing
rod.

That crack about the inferiority of Missouri cane in-
dicates that the tale of the trained beavers came from Arkan-

sas or Oklahoma. The story-teller never misses a chance to ring in one of these endemic insults or local allusions. Many old-timers base their windies upon the rivalry between two towns, usually separated by some political frontier, such as the Missouri-Arkansas line. According to one story, the citizens of Thayer, Missouri, had installed some fine new street lights, while the village of Mammoth Springs, just across the line in Arkansas, had no lights worth mentioning. The Missourians let their new lamps burn all night, and a Thayer newspaperman said that his fellow citizens were so full of civic pride that they couldn't sleep much anyhow. An Arkansas humorist spread the news that it was not pride that kept these fine-haired folks up nights, but chinches— which means bedbugs. There were hard feelings about that crack for a long time, and probably there are old folks in Oregon County, Missouri, who remember it to this day.

As recently as 1945 I heard an illiterate backwoodsman near Branson, Missouri, state positively that very few Arkansawyers can count up to twenty, an' they got to be barefoot or they can't even do that. If a boy learns to count as high as fifty, without takin' his boots off, they set him to teachin' school. I thought about this for awhile, and then asked the fellow what happened to an Arkansawyer who could count up to a hundred, or even more. "I never heerd of such a case," he answered solemnly. "You see, if a feller is that smart, he ain't goin' to *be* in Arkansas!"

In the Cookson Hill country of eastern Oklahoma they used to tell of a half-witted bravo who regarded himself as the mayor of a town. There were only four houses in his settlement, and they were just little shanties on the bank of a creek. But this fellow said he had been duly elected mayor, and he was ready to fight anybody who did not address him by his proper title. Finally, when the mayor got into serious difficulties with the authorities in what was then the Indian Territory, he decided to move his town over into Arkansas. He hitched up two teams of horses and dragged the buildings off through the woods, just as the Indians used to move their teepees in the old days.

A few years ago a man told me that his home town really had been moved. Linn Creek was the name of the settlement, in Camden County, Missouri. When they built Bagnell Dam in 1930 they set the new Linn Creek on higher ground, several miles away from the original site which is now covered with water. This part of the story is true, I think. And when the man said that they moved the old Linn Creek cemetery, I could believe that, too. But his statement that the citizens moved all the best wells and springs, along with their other property, seemed to be carrying things a little too far.

For the benefit of a gaping tourist, a farmer in Baxter County, Arkansas, said that he planned to move his artesian well from one farm to another. He thought he could do it easily enough, as soon as the water froze solid. The neighbors "ketched his meanin' " instantly. Without even a glance at the city fellow, they advised the farmer to give up the whole idea. "If it was an old-fashioned *dug* well, that's a horse of another color," one old man said earnestly. "A dug well can be moved, if the moon's right. But these new-fangled *bored* wells ain't hardy, an' they won't stand transplantin'."

Will Rice [18] repeats an old yarn about some backwoods people who discovered that their house and farm buildings were on another man's land. They prayed over this, and in the night they felt "a small tremor like an earthquake." In the morning they found that "their whole building spot had slipped down the side of the mountain for a distance of one hundred feet. This put them over the section line, and onto

[18] *Arkansas Democrat*, April 4, 1948.

what was beyond question their own land. The well had been moved with the buildings, without even muddying the water." Rice goes on to say that such landslides are common in the hills.

In a Missouri village I heard some talk of a similar land-slide story, credited to a certain "Lyin' Jim Basswood." I made it a point to get acquainted with this character, only to find that he wasn't a windy-spinner at all. When I wondered how-come him to have such a monicker, it was explained to me that the town harbored two men of the same name. Second cousins, I think they were. One was called "Lyin' Jim Basswood" and the other "Stealin' Jim Basswood." The nicknames identified them all right, but the terms were not mutually exclusive. I asked a local attorney if it was true that "Lyin' Jim" wouldn't steal, and that "Stealin' Jim" wouldn't lie. The lawyer gazed at me open-mouthed for a moment, then he laughed. "If you want my opinion," said he, "both of them boys is ambidextrous."

Some backwoods comedians have a whole cycle of rambling tales without any climax, the point being some glaring inconsistency which the story-teller tries to slip over without attracting the listener's attention. It is something like the "What's wrong with this picture?" gag, except that the narrator tries to make it appear that there isn't anything wrong.

One of these fellows may begin his tale by saying, "I was a-shuckin' pawpaws for old man Hobbs that winter," and the guileless tourist may see nothing wrong with this gambit, but it is very funny to anybody who knows paw-paws and old man Hobbs. If this first sentence gets across all right, the story-teller goes on to further absurdities. "I didn't have no gun," he says distinctly, but when a monstrous bobcat appeared he "just took an' shot the varmint's head right off!" At this point he steals a glance at the "furriner," and if the chump still looks innocent, the narrative proceeds with "I carried him home on my back, an' that bobcat was so big his head drug on the ground all the way," and so forth. It is surprising how much of this stuff a city fellow will take sometimes.

Another old story of this type throws further light on the singular mentality of men from the city. A native, talking at random with a summer boarder, remarked that he had once hooked a 400-pound catfish, but was unable to drag it out of the water. "Yes," answered the tourist, "I imagine it's difficult to land those big ones." Then the native went on to explain how he scratched the fish's head for awhile, after which it leaped out of the water and followed him about like a dog. The city fellow nodded, saying that he had heard that catfish were easily tamed. "I just throwed a bridle on her, an' rid her plumb into town," added the hillman. The tourist apparently believed that, too. "I tied her to my strawstack, an' bedded her down with the cattle all winter," cried the farmer. Still the city fellow showed no sign of disbelief. In desperation the hillman declared that he bred the big catfish to a mule, and foaled two horse colts! "I do not believe that part of it," said the tourist coldly. "Everybody knows that mules are not fertile."

Down in McDonald County, Missouri, an old hunter spun me a long windy about the time he was picking blackberries on Little Sugar Creek. Suddenly he was attacked by a she-bear with cubs. The bear chased him for miles, up hills and down hollers and through berry patches. She surely would have caught him, except that she slipped on the ice and fell over a precipice. At this point some outsider is expected to intimate that the story can't be true, because there isn't any ice in blackberry season. "Well," says the story-teller composedly, "the b'ar first took after me in blackberry time, 'bout the middle of July. But it was late November when she fell off'n the bluff. She run me purty nigh five months, altogether."

There are many of these tales. Not long ago I heard another one from Ralph Bates, veteran fiddler who lives on Elbow Creek, near Kissee Mills, Missouri. The hero of Bates' story was bragging about his wheat, the finest crop ever raised in that vicinity. "When it was ripe, the stuff was so thick you could throw your hat out into the field anywhere, an' it never touched ground at all. No, sir, it just stood right there on top of the wheat, like it was floatin' on water," he said. One day, when the prize wheat was just ready for harvesting, some wild turkeys came along, and the man shot an enormous gobbler in full flight. The bird just set its wings and sailed down into the wheat field. Even its great weight, estimated at near seventy-five pounds, didn't make a dent in that wheat. No, sir, that gobbler layed right there on top of the wheat, in full view! So the farmer forced his way through the standing grain, retrieved the turkey, and started home with it. The story up to this point is ostensibly about the wheat crop, and the big gobbler is only incidental. But now the fellow begins to talk about the great weight of the turkey, and the difficulty involved in getting the monster up to the house. Finally it is revealed that he just took the bird by the neck and drug it all the way, through snowdrifts that were five feet deep in some places. Theoretically, the audience has accepted the tale as true, but now some chump begins to wonder about such a deep snow at the same time that the wheat was ripe for harvest. Some fellers are so dumb takes 'em quite a while to see how bad they've been sold.

Most of the best stories are group compositions, told many times and painstakingly revised in rehearsal. But occasionally one appears full-blown, to meet some particular exigency. The boys were sitting in front of a crossroads store in Mc-

Donald County, Missouri, when a local whacker rode up on a mule. "Howdy, Emmett," shouted the postmaster. "Light down, an' tell us one of them big windies." Emmett paused only for a moment, looking very serious. "No time for foolishness today, Bill," he said. "Old man Slinkard has fell off'n the barn, an' it looks like his back's broke. I'm goin' after Doc Holton." When Emmett rode away the loafers got on their horses and galloped over to the Slinkard place, anxious to help the injured man's family in this emergency. And when they got there, they all saw old man Slinkard out in the field, placidly plowing his corn.

There are several versions of the tale about the hillman who made a trip to St. Louis in 1904 and came back with lurid accounts of what he had seen at the World's Fair. The folks at home enjoyed his talk at first, but when he kept insisting that it was "all true as God's own gospel" they got pretty indignant. Sawin' off whoppers is one thing, but this was just plain lyin'. So they put him out of the church, and the best people ignored his existence thereafter. Several months later another fellow from the same settlement went to St. Louis, where he visited the Fair and saw the same sights that the first man had reported. Those wild stories were all true. But this second hillman was smart. When he returned home, he told his neighbors that St. Louis was just like Rocky Comfort, except that there was a little more of it. The people lived in log cabins, he said, and they had two saloons, and three churches, and a stake-an'-rider fence round the courthouse. The first traveler was an outcast all the rest of his life, while the second was honored by everybody, and for several years served his district in the Missouri Legislature.

As I look back through this book in manuscript, it strikes me that nearly all the stories are pretty old. That is as it should be. But the reader must not assume, because of the antiquity of the material, that the art of spinning windies is obsolescent. Story-tellers are thicker than seedticks all over the Ozark country, and a tourist can find plenty of them, even in these degenerate days. Go into any little town in southwest Missouri, or northwest Arkansas, or northeast Oklahoma. If you are a Northerner the villagers will know it instantly, and you'll hear plenty of windy talk. But if you come from the South or the Southwest, the local humorists often seem a bit reluctant at first. In that case you may have to disguise yourself, but don't try any hayseed makeup, or the boys will take you for a revenuer or some kind of Government snooper. Just buy some cheap, loud sports clothes, hang a little camera round your neck, and tell 'em you're from Chicago.

Bibliography

CONSIDERING THE WEALTH OF MATERIAL in oral circulation, it is surprising that I have found so few Ozark windies in print. Doubtless many more are buried in old newspaper files and in obscure publications to which I have no access. Several important collections are still in manuscript. A considerable amount of folklore material was assembled by the Federal Writers' Project in the 1930's and delivered to the Folklore Archives, Library of Congress. These WPA manuscripts include many tall tales from rural Missouri, Arkansas, and Oklahoma. Mrs. Isabel France, of Mountainburg, Arkansas, is preparing a book of Ozark lore, with some windy stories collected in northwest Arkansas. Mr. Fred Starr, of Fayetteville, Arkansas, collected many tales which have not appeared in his books and newspaper articles to date. Mr. Otto Ernest Rayburn, of Eureka Springs, Arkansas, has much unpublished material. The following list of titles is of necessity incomplete, but it's a beginning, and I set it down here for the record.

Abernathy, John R. In Camp with Theodore Roosevelt; or, The Life of Jack Abernathy. Times-Journal Pub. Co., Oklahoma City, Okla., 1933.

The story of a preacher who claims (p. 65) to have caught more than 1,000 wolves alive with his hands. Theodore Roosevelt saw him catch wolves in this manner near Frederick, Okla., in 1905 (pp. 103–143). For other tallish tales see pp. 34, 148–151, 193, 200,242, 251–252, and 254–255.

Allsopp, Fred W. Folklore of Romantic Arkansas. 2 vols. New York, Grolier Society, 1931.

Allsopp was managing editor of the *Arkansas Gazette* for many years, and his work is a hodgepodge of old clippings and newspaper anecdotes, badly indexed and without documentation. But it contains some valuable material. In Vol. I, see chap. v, pp. 108–200, and chap. vii, pp. 232–280. In Vol. II, the best stuff is in chap. iii, pp. 46–140, chap. viii, pp. 237–251, and chap. x, pp. 262–325.

Appleby, John T. "Cross-Country: the Ozarks," *Partisan Review,* VII (Nov.–Dec., 1940), 449–452.

Writing from Yellville, Arkansas, Appleby gives a very fair picture of life in this region. "The Ozark people," he tells us (p. 452) "have a sense of humor compounded of ludicrous under-statement and the wildest exaggeration."

Arkansas, a Guide to the State. New York, Hastings House, 1941.

Compiled by the Federal Writers' Project, sponsored and copyrighted by the Secretary of State at Little Rock, this contains a vast amount of information, but it's pretty dull going, and some sections are not much better than Chamber-of-Commerce propaganda. Sprinkled through the book, however, almost as if they had been inserted surreptitiously into the manuscript, are dozens of brief items which give the reader a glimpse of the real folk-life of Arkansas. See pp. 4–5, 59, 76–78, 97–102, 120–121, 125, 204–205, 207, 209, 215, 217–219, 222–223, 234, 248, 254–259, 271–272, 297–298, 305, 316, 319, 335, 339, 346–347, 372–373, 375, and 386. I am told that most of these colorful passages were written by Walter E. Rowland, of Little Rock.

Benton, Thomas Hart. An Artist in America. New York, Robert McBride & Co., 1937.

There are several tall tales from Missouri and Arkansas in this book. Note especially the ancient story (pp. 210–211) about the rattlesnake which lost its fangs in a pair of boots.

Botkin, B. A. A Treasury of American Folklore. New York, Crown Publishers, 1944.

A vast collection of heterogenous material from all parts of the United States, mostly quotations from old books and magazines. Only four items are listed under "Ozarks" in the index, but many scraps and fragments are associated with this region. See pp. 54–56, 66, 183, 227, 285–286, 312–313, 318, 386–388, 392, 435–436, 571, 598, 599, 602, 609–610, and 613–615.

—— A Treasury of Southern Folklore. New York, Crown Publishers, 1949.

Similar to A Treasury of American Folklore, but all the stories are from the southern states. For tall talk from Missouri and Arkansas, see pp. 34, 49, 51, 112, 116, 129–130, 173–174, 465–466, 474–475, 551, 565, and 615–616.

Brashear, Minnie M. "The Missouri Short Story as It Has Grown Out of the Tall Tale of the Frontier," *Missouri Historical Review*, XLIII (April, 1949), 199–219.

The first part of this paper carries a brief mention of Alphonso Wetmore, Joseph M. Field, Sol Smith, John S. Robb, and other early St. Louis story-tellers.

Broadhead, Garland Carr. "Notes on the Jones Family in Missouri," *Missouri Historical Review*, III (October, 1908), 2.

An anecdote about Lewis Jones, who was stripped of his clothes by Indians. He killed a panther and put on its skin. The panther's pelt stuck to Jones's body, and he had some difficulty in getting rid of it.

Burns, Bob. "Bob Burns and His Bazooka," *Arkansas Gazette*, July 5, 1936, pp. 7, 14.

—— "Durned If I Didn't Do It," Kansas City *Star*, Feb. 14, 1937, pp. 1–3.

—— "How to Tell a Funny Story," *Liberty*, New York, April 11, 1942, p. 21.

—— "Tall Tales of Arkansas," *Ford Times*, April, 1948, pp. 14–19.

Bob Burns of Van Buren, Arkansas, is probably the most popular story-teller who ever came out of the Ozarks. He told plenty of windies on the air, and some of them have been repeated in newspapers and magazine stories like those listed above. In the 1930's he conducted a syndicated column of Arkansas humor in about 100 newspapers. Burns's best yarns, I think, are genuine backwoods folktales; I heard some of them in the Ozarks myself, told by men who could not read and had never listened to the radio. But Bob ran out of real

Arkansas stuff eventually, and some of his later programs were probably cooked up by the professional gagmen of Hollywood and New York.

Call, Cora Pinkley. Pioneer Tales of Eureka Springs, Arkansas. Eureka Springs, Ark., 1930.

This book is concerned with genealogy and family history, of interest chiefly to descendants of the Eureka Springs pioneers. But the chapter entitled "Hunting Stories" (pp. 23–28) contains a fine account of the author's grandfather, who attacked a full-grown bear and killed it with his knife.

Clark, Thomas D. The Rampaging Frontier. New York, Bobbs-Merrill Co., 1939.

There are a few Missouri and Arkansas references in this book, mostly quoted from the *Spirit of the Times*. See pp. 49–51, 88–89, 98–101, 207, and 288.

—— "Manners and Humors of the American Frontier," *Missouri Historical Review*, XXXV (October, 1940), 3–24.

Mostly commentary, but contains some scattered tall tale material.

Clemens, Nancy. "Ozark Laughter," *University Review* (Kansas City, Mo.), Summer, 1936, pp. 246–248.

Several splendid windy stories from southern Missouri and northwestern Arkansas.

Clugston, W. G., and others. Facts You Should Know about Arkansas. Girard, Kan., Haldeman-Julius Pub. Co., 1928. Little Blue Book No. 1297.

There are some tall tales in the chapter "Clay Fulks and the Culture of the Ozarks," by Fred Blair, pp. 24–57. Note especially the bear story on pp. 47–48.

Collins, Earl A. Folk Tales of Missouri. Boston, Christopher Publishing House. 1935.

One chapter (pp. 33–43) is devoted to "whoppers" as such, but there is much interesting material elsewhere. Note the items from the mythical county of Poosey (pp. 23–30); also the Missouri story of Johnny Appleseed (pp. 47–51), according to which Johnny married an Indian girl and lived on Turkey Creek in Ralls County, Missouri. See other tall-tale material on pp. 56–58, 83–88, 91–94, 99–101, and 121–123.

Cravens, John Park. Tall Tales of the Arkansaw Ozarks. Magazine, Ark., 1944.

This is a rare book, and I am not certain that it was ever offered for sale. Otto Ernest Rayburn showed me sixteen sheets of printer's proof, 8 by 11 inches, and 10 cuts from photographs, bound in heavy paper, with the title and the author's name in large letters. On the fourth sheet, under the date-line Magazine, Ark., Oct. 1, 1944, Cravens writes: "About twenty-five years ago I wrote and published many of my own original tall tales of Arkansas in my weekly newspaper, the *Magazine Gazette* of Magazine, Ark." Under the photograph of an old man with his mouth open is the inscription: "Ben Ashworth, commonly known as the prevaricator of the Arkansaw Ozarks, in the act of telling a whopper." A picture of another man is labeled "Tom Beason." Citizens of Logan County, Arkansas, tell me that Ben Ashworth and Tom Beason are well known in that vicinity.

Cunningham, William. "The Codder," in *Folk-Say IV, the Land Is Ours*, Norman, Okla., University of Oklahoma Press 1932, pp. 210–214.

Note the tales of swayback horses (p. 210) and freak cyclones (p. 211). Cunningham was a professor of English at Commonwealth College, near Mena, Arkansas.

—— "The Cloud Puncher," in *Mid Country*, Lincoln, Neb., University of Nebraska Press, 1945, pp. 361–365.

A fine story about Tiny Fallon, who saddled a female tornado and rode it all over Oklahoma.

Davis, Clyde Brion. The Arkansas. New York, Farrar & Rinehart, 1940.

This is one of the "Rivers of America" series, edited by

Stephen Vincent Benét and Carl Carmer. It contains some good stuff about the Ozark region, but not many tall tales. However, Davis does tell us (p. 268) about Albert Pike's goose-gun, which he loaded with a bucketful of shot and killed a hundred geese with one discharge. For other items see pp. 277–279, 310.

Dunckel, John F. The Mollyjoggers. Springfield, Mo., H. S. Jewell Pub. Co., n.d.

Described on the title-page as "A Brief History of the Origin and Experiences of an Old James River Fishing and Hunting Club, and a Collection of Stories, Poems, etc. as Told and Recited around the Campfire." It is said that the club was organized about 1895, but the book was published after 1905, as that date is mentioned in the preface. Most of the tall stories in the Mollyjogger repertory were credited to Wid Crumpley, a farmer who lived near the old campground at the mouth of Finley Creek.

Featherstonhaugh, George William. Excursion through the Slave States. New York, Harper, 1844.

Featherstonhaugh was employed by the War Department to report on the geological possibilities of several frontier states. He visited Arkansas in 1834 and 1835. Note pp. 42, 81–82, 99. Masterson (*Tall Tales of Arkansaw*, 1943, pp. 306–307) says that "the *Excursion*, though an ill-natured book, contributes substantially to the history of American humor." See the index of Masterson's book for quotations from Featherstonhaugh. Thomas D. Clark (*The Rampaging Frontier*, 1939, pp. 350) quotes several good Arkansas stories from the *Excursion*.

Field, Joseph M. The Drama in Pokerville and Other Stories. Philadelphia, Peterson Pub. Co., 1847.

Field was a resident of St. Louis in the middle 1840's and wrote stories of the Missouri frontier for the eastern newspapers. Many of the yarns in this book were reprinted from newspaper files. The collection includes a whopper about two men who outran sixteen elk and covered seventy-five miles in eleven hours (pp. 108–112). See also "The Death of Mike Fink" (pp. 177–184).

Fletcher, John Gould. Arkansas. Chapel Hill, N.C., University of North Carolina Press, 1947.

The best short history of Arkansas that has yet appeared, with an adequate discussion of the hill country. Of the Ozark hill-folk Fletcher says (p. 317) "their mode of living is in many respects wilder than that of the dweller in the Appalachians and the Cumberlands." For references of interest to the student of tall stories see pp. 6, 226, 319, 323, 377–382.

Ford, Ira W. Traditional Music of America. New York, Dutton, 1940.

Despite the comprehensive title, this is just a collection of fiddle tunes. But the author lived for some time near Branson, Missouri, and he tells one tall tale about the belled buzzard (pp. 187–188), described as "a tradition which had its origin in the Ozark mountains."

France, Isabel. "The Hills of Home," a weekly column in the *Southwest Times-Record*, Fort Smith, Ark., April, 1936—. Since April, 1944, this column has appeared also in the Sunday issue of the *Arkansas Gazette*, Little Rock, Ark.

"The Hills of Home" is addressed primarily to bird watchers and other nature lovers, but there are occasional anecdotes and tall tales.

Gerstäcker, Friedrich. Wild Sports in the Far West. Boston, Crosby, Nichols & Co., 1859.

This is a translation of lurid selections from his *Streif- und Jagdzüge durch die Vereinigten Staaten Nordamerikas* (Dresden, 1844).

—— Western Lands and Western Waters. London, S. O. Beeton, 1864.

Sensational extracts from Gerstäcker's travel journals. He spent the years 1838–1842 in Arkansas. Having little money, he went out among the pioneers and earned his living by farm labor, hunting and trapping. Gerstäcker had more first-hand information about the Arkansas frontier than most American writers of the time. In the main, he told the truth about his own experiences and recorded the tall tales as he heard them.

Gibbs, Brady. "A-Noodlin' and A-Giggin'," *Ford Times* (Dearborn, Mich., Ford Motor Co.) April, 1948, pp. 38–42.

A feature story about noodling catfish in White River, north of the Missouri-Arkansas line. Fine photographs of noodlers in action. One of the catfish taken "weighed 100 pounds, and was nearly six feet long."

Graham, Jean. Tales of the Osage River Country. Clinton, Mo. Martin Printing Co., 1929.

See pp. 18–22 for a tale about the steamboat whistle that frightened the pioneers; they thought it must be some kind of superpanther.

Green, Avantus. With This We Challenge; an Epitome of Arkansas. Little Rock, Ark., 1945.

—— Look Who's Laughing; a Joyful Compendium on Arkansas. Little Rock, Ark., 1947.

These books are bound in yellow paper and profusely illustrated in the *Slow Train through Arkansaw* tradition. Full of splendid tall-tale material. Instead of exaggerating the ignorance of the hillbilly, as Hughes did in *Three Years in Arkansaw*, Green exaggerates the boasting of the Chamber-of-Commerce crowd to a degree which reduces the whole thing to absurdity. The stories are not original with Green, of course, but he tells them in a vivid, mock-naïve fashion which lays the tourists in the aisles.

Harlan, Amos R. For Here Is My Fortune. New York, Whittlesey House, 1946.

A fine book about the early 1900's in Howell County, Missouri. The author was there, and he knows his stuff. This book contains (pp. 61, 93–106) a good account of the "Post," a secret organization of story-tellers and practical jokers.

Hoenshel, E. J., and L. S. Hoenshel. Stories of the Pioneers. Branson, Mo., White River Leader, 1915.

Reminiscent interviews with some of the old settlers in Taney County, Missouri. The Hoenshels owned a weekly newspaper, the *White River Leader*, and these tales were printed in the paper before being published in this book. A lot of valuable first-hand information about pioneer life is included. The tall tales are mostly stories of hunting and fishing. Note especially pp. 12, 38, 77.

Hogue, Wayman. Back Yonder; an Ozark Chronicle. New York, Minton, Balch & Co., 1932.

Back Yonder is the finest piece of nonfiction ever written about the Arkansas Ozarks. It contains some good stories about panthers eating babies (pp. 171–181), hunters pursued by packs of wolves (pp. 188–189), and men killing bears with knives (pp. 192–193). Hogue has also (pp. 278–285) a series of splendid ghost stories and witch tales.

Hughes, Marion. Three Years in Arkansaw. Chicago, Donohue & Co., 1905.

Hughes lived in Polk and Sevier counties, Arkansas, in the late 1890's, and his book is full of fantastic tales about the ignorance and depravity of his hillbilly neighbors. These are exactly the sort of stories that the backwoodsman loves to tell. But the respectable townspeople do not care for them, and Hughes's book never sold as well as the innocuous *On a Slow Train through Arkansaw*. Wayman Hogue (*Arkansas Gazette*, May 10, 1942, p. 8) says that *Three Years in Arkansaw* "was suppressed by the state legislature." Masterson (*Tall Tales of Arkansaw*, 1943, pp. 96–106) devotes a whole chapter to Marion Hughes, and it is a chapter well worth reading.

Jackson, Thomas W. On a Slow Train through Arkansaw. Chicago, Jackson Pub. Co., 1903.

This is a paper-bound volume, full of old minstrel jokes, conundrums, puns, and med-show wisecracks. Some items which might be called tall tales are found on pp. 40, 41, 43, 66, 75, and 84. Many of the stories have no connection with Arkansas. It is hard to see why the citizens got so indignant about this harmless jokebook. Jackson lived in Springfield, Missouri, in the 1890's, according to Val Mason of Springfield and Bob Kite of Hollister. He was a brakeman with a crippled hand, and was known as Three-Finger Jackson. "He could hardly write his own name," says the Springfield *Leader and Press* (June 9, 1934) "but he could tell a story well and his wife would write it in readable form." Mrs. Jackson's name was Prater, and she came from Polk County, Missouri. The book sold millions of copies, and is still selling today. It made Jackson rich, so that he "blazed with diamonds" when he visited his old friends in Springfield.

Kilroy, Casper. "Tall Corn," column in the *Missouri College Farmer*, Oct., 1946–May, 1947.

The *College Farmer* is a monthly magazine published by students of agriculture at the University of Missouri. The "Tall Corn" feature was originated by Melvin E. West of Golden City, Missouri, who wrote under the pseudonym "Casper Kilroy." Tall tales about phenomenal fertilizer, giant vegetables, and so forth.

Masterson, James R. Tall Tales of Arkansaw. Boston, Chapman & Grimes, 1943.

This book is not, as one might think from the title, merely a collection of tall tales, but a fully documented survey of the whole field of Arkansas humor. Dr. Masterson did not gather his material in the Arkansas backwoods, but in the great libraries at Harvard University, and at Washington, D.C., and in New York City. He read all the funny songs and stories about Arkansas that have been published, and set down the best of them here, with brief biographies of their long-forgotten authors. He devotes more than 70 pages to the old fiddle-tune and dialogue "The Arkansas Traveler," the first adequate study of this masterpiece that has ever been printed. Fine tall-tale material is scattered throughout the book, from the writings of Pete Whetstone, Friedrich Gerstäcker, Thomas Bangs Thorpe, and other early humorists, down to Marion Hughes and Thomas W. Jackson. *Tall Tales of Arkansaw* is required reading for every serious student of these matters.

McCord, May Kennedy. "Hillbilly Heartbeats," weekly column in the Springfield, Mo., *Leader-News*, 1932–1938; appeared thrice weekly in the Springfield, Mo., *News*, 1938–1942.

This column was made up of old songs, pioneer reminiscence, folk remedies, ghost stories, and the like, sent in by Mrs. McCord's fans in southern Missouri and northern Arkansas. The files contain a lot of interesting material, including some windy stories.

McCullough, Florence Woodlock. Living Authors of the Ozarks and Their Literature. Joplin, Mo., F. W. McCullough, 1941.

On pp. 82–83 the editor reprints several tall tales about rifle shooting, credited to Thomas Daniel, of Pea Ridge, Arkansas.

Missouri; a Guide to the "Show Me" State. New York, Duell, Sloan, and Pearce, 1941.

Compiled by the Missouri Writers' Project, and sponsored and copyrighted by the Missouri State Highway Department. See pp. 127, 137, 141, and 436.

Missouri Conservationist, April, 1943—

This is an illustrated monthly magazine, published by the Missouri Conservation Commission, Jefferson City, Mo., with fine articles about the protection of forests and wildlife in Missouri. The "Notes from the Field" department, made up of reports from fish- and game-wardens, carries occasional tall tales about hunting and fishing.

Missouri Historical Review. Columbia, Mo., State Historical Society of Missouri, October, 1906—

A quarterly review, now in its forty-fourth volume. The files contain much valuable material. See "Folk Tale of Johnny Appleseed," XIX (July, 1925), 622–629; "Ozark Hunting Story," XXVII (April, 1933), 295–296; "Owls on the Osage," XXVIII (April, 1934), 215–216; "Tall Tales from St. Charles," XXVIII (July, 1934), 296–297; "Tall Tales from Callaway," XXIX (Oct., 1934), 45–46.

Montigny, Jean François Dumont de. Mémoires Historiques sur la Louisiane. 2 vols. Paris, J. B. Bauche, 1753.

Captain Dumont's story of the giant frogs (II, 266–268) is quoted in Masterson (*Tall Tales of Arkansaw*, p. 15).

Norwood, Hal L. Just a Book. Mena, Ark., Starco Print, 1938.

Norwood served several terms as Attorney General of Arkansas and practiced law at Mena. His book is full of reminiscences of his boyhood, anecdotes about his experiences as a young lawyer, and a number of old-time jokes which are still funny. For tall tales see pp. 5–6, 12–15, 24–26, 46–47, 56, 60.

Oklahoma, a Guide to the Sooner State. Norman, Okla., University of Oklahoma Press, 1941.

Compiled by the Writers' Program of the WPA, sponsored by the University of Oklahoma. Not much tall-tale material in this book, but there are some six-gun and cyclone stories on p. 114. See also pp. 115–116, 126, 150, 333–334.

Pipes, Gerald Harrison. Strange Customs of the Ozark Hillbilly. New York, Hobson Book Press, 1947.

Tall tales about hoop snakes and caves and big mosquitoes, pp. 29–31, 36–38, and 45.

Porter, William T., ed. The Big Bear of Arkansas, and Other Sketches. Philadelphia, Carey & Hart, 1845.

—— Colonel Thorpe's Scenes in Arkansas. 2 vols. Philadelphia, T. B. Peterson, 1858.

Most of the material in these books is reprinted from the *Spirit of the Times*, a humorous weekly edited by Porter.

Randolph, Vance. Ozark Mountain Folks. New York, Vanguard Press, 1932.

Chapter IX, entitled "Windy Hilltops," is a selection of tall tales. Several items from this book are reprinted in B. A. Botkin's *Treasury of American Folklore* (New York, Crown Publishers, 1944, pp. 692–696) and B. C. Clough's *The American Imagination at Work* (New York, Knopf, 1947, pp. 198–199, 632–633.

—— "Jumping Bass in the Ozark Country," *Forest and Stream*, April, 1928, pp. 219, 244–246.

An account of a strange method of taking bass. I used much

of the same material in another article "They Jump Right into the Boat," Esquire, August, 1939, pp. 67, 149.

—— The Camp on Wildcat Creek. New York, Alfred A. Knopf, 1934.
This is a story for boys, but it makes use of several authentic Ozark windies. See pp. 67–73, 98–104, 139–143, 154–161, and 194–195.

—— Funny Stories from Arkansas. Girard, Kan., Haldeman-Julius Pub. Co., 1943.

—— Funny Stories about Hillbillies. Girard, Kan., Haldeman-Julius Pub. Co., 1944.
There are numerous tall tales from the Ozarks in these two pamphlets. Much of the material is reprinted in the present book.

—— Ozark Superstitions. New York, Columbia University Press, 1947.
Sometimes it is difficult to distinguish between genuine superstitions and folktales of the windy variety. This book contains a considerable amount of borderline material.

Rayburn, Otto Ernest. Many short articles in *Ozark Life* (Kingston, Ark., 1925–1930), *Arcadian Magazine* (Eminence, Mo., 1931–1932), *Arcadian Life* (Caddo Gap, Ark., 1933–1942), and *Ozark Guide* (Eureka Springs, Ark., 1943—).
Rayburn has lived in the Ozarks since the end of the First World War. His writings deal with folksong, dialect, pioneer dances, play-parties, superstitions, old customs, and backwoods history of a sort not often found in textbooks. Rayburn has done a great deal to arouse popular interest in folk material, and the files of the little magazines noted above, all of which he edited and published himself, are full of fascinating stuff. Tall-tale material is sprinkled throughout all the magazines and is found also in the features Rayburn writes for the *Arkansas Democrat* and the *Arkansas Gazette*.

—— Ozark Country. New York, Duell, Sloan & Pearce, 1941.
This is the fourth volume of the "American Folkways" series,

edited by Erskine Caldwell. It is Rayburn's best work. There are many references to tall tales, especially pp. 136, 181–185, 189–190, 193, 262–264, 266–268, 302–303, 313, and 315–316.

Read, Opie. *The Arkansas Traveler,* a weekly newspaper published in Little Rock, Ark., June, 1882—Oct., 1887. In 1887 Read moved the *Traveler* to Chicago, and from then on there was little Ozark stuff in the paper. The files of the Little Rock period contain some tall-tale material.

—— Up Terrapin River. Chicago, Laird & Lee, 1888.

—— Len Gansett. Chicago, Laird & Lee, 1888.

—— Opie Read in Arkansaw, and What He Saw There. New York, J. S. Ogilvie Pub. Co., 1891.

—— The Fiddle and the Fawn, and Other Stories. New York, Rand, McNally & Co., 1903.

—— Opie Read in the Ozarks, Including Many of the Rich, Rare, Quaint, Eccentric and Superstitious Sayings of the Natives of Missouri and Arkansas. Chicago, McKnight Pub. Co., 1905.

—— My Friends in Arkansaw. Chicago and New York, M. A. Donahue & Co., 1906.

—— I Remember. New York, Robert R. Smith, 1930.

All Read's works listed above are more or less concerned with Arkansas and the Ozark country, and they all contain bits of tall-tale material. Read told me that he once considered editing a collection of Arkansas whoppers, but gave up the idea because the best of these tales were "too vulgar" for publication in the United States. According to a file card in the library at the University of Arkansas, Read disclaims responsibility for the publication of *Opie Read in Arkansaw,* but it contains many of his anecdotes. Maurice Elfer's biography (*Opie Read,* Detroit, Mich., Boyten Miller Press, 1940, pp. 282–283) makes Read declare that he saw Indians in the Ozarks killing each other with tomahawks and that a man in "one of the hilly districts of Arkansas" fed him rattlesnake meat for dinner.

Reynolds, Quentin. "Galloping Gal," *Collier's*, July 25, 1936, p. 22.

News story about Helen Stephens, of Fulton, Missouri, who ran down rabbits and caught them barehanded.

Rice, Will. "Fish Stories Are Stranger Than Fiction," *Arkansas Democrat* (Little Rock, Ark.), April 11, 1948, pp. 3, 11.

Rice has lived on a farm in Searcy County, Arkansas, since 1918. About 1920 he began writing news items and brief anecdotes for the Kansas City *Star*, the St. Louis *Post-Dispatch*, and other midwest newspapers. Since 1923 the *Arkansas Democrat* of Little Rock has used Rice's stuff regularly, and the Harrison, Arkansas, *Times* carried one of his stories every day from 1939 to 1945. These items have been reprinted in all parts of the country, often unsigned but always with the date-line St. Joe, Arkansas. Some of the tall tales from St. Joe are genuine backwoods whacks that Rice got from his neighbors, while others are fantastic inventions of his own. Marquis James (*The Cherokee Strip*, New York, Viking Press, 1945, pp. 245–246) has some illuminating comments on "the journalistic adaptation of the tall tale" which apply to much of Rice's work. For further information about Rice see an article by Diana Sherwood, "The Beloved Sage of St. Joe," (*Arkansas Democrat Sunday Magazine* (Little Rock, Ark.), July 18, 1948.

Russell, Jesse Lewis. Behind These Ozark Hills. New York, Hobson Book Press, 1947.

The author was born in Carroll County, Arkansas, in 1870, and has lived in this vicinity nearly all his life, working as a printer and editing country newspapers. "Ninety percent of the people here during the 70's would be classed as wholly illiterate," he tells us (pp. 61, 162). "It is safe to say that not more than one in a dozen could read and write. Practically all of the veterans of the Civil War signed their pension vouchers by mark." Russell tells some fine stories about tomatoes (p.

26), wild pigeons (pp. 61–64), and rocky farms (p. 69). There is a lot of good stuff in this book.

Schoolcraft, Henry Rowe. A View of the Lead Mines of Missouri. New York, Charles Wiley & Co., 1819.

—— Journal of a Tour into the Interior of Missouri and Arkansas . . . in the Years 1818 and 1819. London, Richard Philips & Co., 1821.

—— Scenes and Adventures in the Semi-Alpine Regions of the Ozark Mountains of Missouri and Arkansas. Philadelphia, Lippincott, Grambo & Co., 1853.

Schoolcraft traveled through Missouri and Arkansas in 1817–1819, and set down detailed information about the people he encountered. There are occasional references to the pioneer's extravagant tales. Masterson (*Tall Tales of Arkansaw*, 1943, p. 2) quotes one of these items, which he says "is probably the earliest specimen of backwoods humor ever recorded in Arkansas."

Shannon, Karr. History of Izard County, Arkansas. Little Rock, Ark., Democrat Printing Co., 1947.

This is a revised and enlarged version of another book of the same title, published at Melbourne, Arkansas, in 1927. It is written as straight history, but Shannon repeats one tallish tale (p. 3) about the abundance of wild strawberries, and he mentions (p. 12) the old story of the woodpeckers that "almost ate up the courthouse."

—— On a Fast Train through Arkansas. Little Rock, Ark., Democrat Printing Co., 1948.

The yellow-paper cover has a familiar look, and Shannon uses the subtitle "A Rebuke to Jackson's *Slow Train*." He begins by denouncing Henry Rowe Schoolcraft, Sandford C. Faulkner, Mark Twain, Opie Read, and other writers. I think he means to denounce John A. Lomax too, mistakenly regarding him as the author of a song "The State of Arkansaw," but since he spells it John A. Lenox, one can't be sure. Every student of backwoods humor should read this book. The reader who fully comprehends the Shannon point of view will understand why so many humorists have "picked on Arkansas."

Sheehan, Murray. Half-Gods. New York, E. P. Dutton & Co., 1927.
A fantastic novel about centaurs at Fayetteville, where Sheehan was a professor of journalism in the University of Arkansas.

Simonson, S. E. "The St. Francis Levee," *Arkansas Historical Quarterly* (Arkansas Historical Association, Fayetteville, Ark.), VI (Winter, 1947), 420.
Stories of men who catch wolves and kill panthers with their bare hands.

Spotts, Carle Brooks. "Mike Fink in Missouri," *Missouri Historical Review*, XXVIII (Oct., 1933), 3–8.
Many quotations and references to the literature.

—— "The Development of Fiction on the Missouri Frontier, 1830–1860," *Missouri Historical Review*, XXIX (Oct., 1934–April, 1935), 19–26, 104–108, 188–192.
Some excerpts from pioneer windies.

Spurlock, Pearl. Over the Old Ozark Trails. Branson, Mo., White River Leader Printers, 1936.
Pearl Spurlock was a woman taxi driver who took tourists out to see the "Shepherd of the Hills" country, so named from a novel by Harold Bell Wright. She worked up a "spiel" to be delivered along the road, with many anecdotes and tall tales. After several years, Mrs. Spurlock was persuaded to publish the material in this book. See pp. 18, 28–30, 41–44, 46–48, and 85.

Starr, Fred. "Hillside Adventures," a weekly column in the *Northwest Arkansas Times* (Fayetteville, Ark.), May 6, 1937–.
Humorous anecdotes, superstitions, folk remedies, hunting stories, and occasional tall tales. Starr's copy is always worth

reading. The author is a schoolteacher who lives on a farm near Fayetteville, and writes about the Ozarks in his spare time.

—— From an Ozark Hillside. Siloam Springs, Ark., Bar D Press, 1938.

A selection of Starr's newspaper stories, with a preface by Lessie Stringfellow Read. Note especially the items on pp. 57 and 62.

—— "When It's Possum Time in the Ouachitas," *Arcadian Life* (Caddo Gap, Ark.), March–April, 1939, pp. 20–24.

A fine article about the Polk County Possum Club, with photographs.

—— Pebbles from the Ozarks. Siloam Springs, Ark., Bar D Press, 1942.

A second book of extracts from Starr's newspaper columns. There are some good squirrel-hunting yarns on pp. 12, 20–21.

Still, Andrew Taylor. Autobiography of Andrew T. Still, with a History of the Discovery and Development of the Science of Osteopathy. Kirksville, Mo., The Author, 1897.

The story of the inventor of osteopathy, who could run so fast that he caught sixteen foxes in one month (p. 20). Compare Ruth Ann Musick's "Miracle Man Steele" (*Prairie Schooner*, Lincoln, Neb., University of Nebraska Press, Fall, 1946, pp. 202–209) which is fiction based upon the A. T. Still legends remembered by the old-timers around Kirksville.

Stockard, Sallie Walker. History of Lawrence, Jackson, Independence and Stone Counties, Arkansas. Little Rock, Ark., Arkansas Democrat Co., 1904.

A fascinating book, long out of print and difficult to obtain. On p. 190 Stockard tells a fine story about sweet potatoes talking underground in Jackson County.

Stone, Weldon. "That Big Buffalo Bass," *Field and Stream Reader*, New York, Doubleday & Co., 1946, pp. 106–116.

The tale of a monstrous bass called Old King Solomon, in the

Buffalo River, Newton County, Arkansas. The story was first published in *Field and Stream* magazine in 1938.

—— Devil Take a Whittler. New York, Rinehart & Co., 1948.

Fantastic story of a whittler in the Arkansas backwoods, member of a wild clan, who had dealings with the Devil. No ordinary witchcraft novel, but a strange tale of how the whittler and the Devil combined to carve a female figure which came to life. Next they tried an elephant, but it was too small and the family cat ate it, thinking it was a mouse. The backwoods dialect is good; the jacket blurb says that Stone spent eleven summers in the Arkansas Ozarks collecting his material.

Sturges, J. A. History of McDonald County, Missouri. Pineville, Mo., The Author, 1897.

This book is intended as a straight historical record. I knew Sturges, and he was a serious-minded old chap, not given to windy stories. But the boys up the creek put one over on him. See pp. 195–196 for a fine tall tale about wolves and turkeys.

Thomas, Lowell. Tall Stories, the Rise and Triumph of the Great American Whopper. New York, Harvest House, 1945.

Reprinted from an earlier work (*Tall Stories*, Blue Ribbon Books, Inc., New York, 1931, p. 244). The stories in this collection were sent to Thomas from all over America, by people who heard him tell similar yarns on his news broadcast. With each item Thomas prints the name and address of the person from whom he obtained the tale, and the Ozark region is represented on pp. 17, 25, 36, 39, 50, 79, 102, 105, 119–120, 128, 162, and 166–167.

Thorpe, Thomas Bangs. "The Big Bear of Arkansas," *Spirit of the Times* (New York), March 27, 1841, pp. 43–44.

The *Spirit of the Times* was a "sporting and humorous" weekly published by W. T. Porter, 1831–1856. It carried a great number of stories about the backwoods of Arkansas, by various writers. This "Big Bear" yarn is said to be "the most celebrated anecdote ever published about Arkansas" (Masterson, *Tall Tales of Arkansaw*, p. 56). Thorpe had many similar tales in the *Spirit of the Times* from 1839 to 1847. The best of these were reprinted in his two books *Mysteries of the Backwoods* (Philadelphia, Carey & Hart, 1846) and *The Hive of the Bee Hunter* (New York, D. Appleton & Co., 1854).

Trimble, Bruce R. Fiddlin' Jake, Son of the Ozarks. Kansas City, Mo., Soto Pub. Co., 1947.

This pamphlet tells the story of Jake Vining, old-time fiddler of Taney County, Missouri. Jake is a guide who entertains tourists by telling them about the characters in Harold Bell Wright's novel "The Shepherd of the Hills." See p. 15 for a familiar snake-and-fish tale.

Vestal, Stanley. Short Grass Country. New York, Duell, Sloan & Pearce, 1941.

Some good yarns about Oklahoma weather, particularly dust storms, which Vestal calls "Oklahoma rain" (pp. 188, 202–206). Several of these items are reprinted in B. C. Clough's *The American Imagination at Work* (New York, Alfred A. Knopf, 1947, pp. 141–143).

Wade, Leila A. "On the Trail of the Snawfus," *Arcadian Life* (Caddo Gap, Ark.), Oct., 1936–March, 1938.

Serial story of a walking trip from Republic, Missouri, to Eureka Springs, Arkansas. Interesting because of the references to the legendary snawfus.

Weeks, Raymond. The Hound-Tuner of Callaway. New York, Columbia University Press, 1927.

Weeks was a professor at the University of Missouri (1895–1898) and this book is a collection of stories about early days in the Missouri Valley. They are literary pieces rather than folktales, but contain much traditional stuff. Note especially the razorback yarn "Arkansas" (pp. 139–155), the story entitled "Woodpeckers" (pp. 156–174), and "The Snakes of Boone" (pp. 257–265). See some other amusing tall-tale references on pp. 2–3, 237.

West, Don. Broadside to the Sun. New York, W. W. Norton & Co., 1946.

This is the story of a mare named Ribbon, who lived in the

hills near Winslow, Arkansas. The book carries a lot of realistic information about life in the Ozark backwoods. Some pretty tall tales on pp. 32, 85–86, 89, 131–144, 153, and 178.

Whetstone, Pete. Some forty-five letters published in the New York *Spirit of the Times: a Chronicle of the Turf, Agriculture, Field Sports, Literature and the Stage*, at irregular intervals from 1836 to 1853.

"Pete Whetstone" was the pen name of Colonel Charles Fenton Mercer Noland, of Batesville, Arkansas. He was a lawyer, a politician, and editor of the Batesville *Eagle*. The *Spirit of the Times* was the outstanding sporting and humorous weekly of the United States. The Whetstone letters are in dialect, and include many yarns about the Arkansas frontier. Masterson (*Tall Tales of Arkansaw*, 1943, pp. 29–54) discusses Colonel Noland at length and reprints many extracts from the famous letters.

Wilson, Charles Morrow. "Folk Beliefs in the Ozark Hills," in *Folk-Say; a Regional Miscellany* (Norman, Okla., University of Oklahoma Press), 1930, pp. 157–172.

This paper deals primarily with superstition, but there are several fantastic hunting stories on pp. 167–168.

——— Backwoods America. Chapel Hill, N.C., University of North Carolina Press, 1935.

A fine book about the Ozark way of life, with some penetrating observations about rural humor. Note the tall-tale references on pp. 17, 19–20, 70, and 111.

Wister, Owen. The Virginian. New York, Macmillan Co., 1902.

One section of this novel (pp. 174–200) is devoted to whoppers. Most of these are Western tales, but one fellow declares that Arkansas is full of little brown skunks and that all of them have rabies. He knew a man at Bald Knob, Arkansas, who died from a skunk bite. But the skunks aren't sick. "No, sir! They're well skunks. You'll not meet skunks in any state in the Union more robust than them in Arkansaw. And thick." This tale is reprinted in Ben C. Clough's *The American Imagination at Work* (New York, Knopf, 1947, p. 476).

Yates, Floyd A. (The Duke of Dead End). Chimney Corner
     Chats. Springfield, Mo., 1944.

     This pamphlet is poorly written and badly printed on cheap
     paper, and the price is only ten cents, postpaid. But it contains
     more genuine Ozark stories than many pretentious books. I
     believe that Yates must have collected some of this material
     directly from the old settlers. Certainly he did not get it
     from any printed source with which I am familiar, nor from
     the fake hillbillies of radio-land.

Zevely, W. J. "A Paul Bunyan Story from Missouri," *Missouri
     Historical Review*, XXXVIII (April, 1944), 367.

     An account of the hinge-tailed bingbuffer, reprinted from
     the Jefferson City, Missouri, *Daily Tribune* of July 23, 1891.

Index

Missouri, magic water, 251; stories told by Arkansawyers about, 22; those featuring their traditional antagonism, 24

Missouri, University of, Department of Agriculture, 80

Missouri Conservation Commission, 54

Missouri Conservationist, 29, 103, 208, 213

Missouri Foxhunters' Association, 7

Missouri Historical Review, 51

Missouri River, 59, 213, 216

Mitchell, Clyde, 166

Mitchell, Jim, 179, 218

Mollyjoggers, 9

Monsters, fabulous, 41-74; birds, 62-68; fish and other aquatic creatures, 61, 69-74; panthers (painters) and other cats, 53-59; reptiles, 41-49; stories still in circulation: the local and the published, 41

Montigny, Jean F. Dumont de, 70

Moogies, 60

Moon, blowed away, 194; fell into millpond, 253; powder horn a-hangin' on, 161; shone all day, 193

Moore, Ike, 108

Moorehouse, 64

Moore's Ferry, Mo., 108

Morgan, Gid or Gib, 162

Morgan, Kemp, 39, 162

Morgan, Tom P., 237

Morrison, Mo., 213

Mosquitoes, 146 ff.

Mother-in-law in the bedroom, 3

Motley, Perry, 212

Mountainburg, Ark., 184

Mountain Home, Ark., 32, 165, 210, 211

Mouth in foxhunters' parlance, 124

Mud, stories about, 253

Mudpuppy, giant, 48

Murray, "Alfalfa Bill," 11

Nall, George, 101, 247

Nation, Carry, 252

Nelson, Rome, 34, 35

Neosho, Mo., 172, 198

Newbill, John G., 52

Newport, Ark., 37, 72, 73

News and Leader, Springfield, Mo., 140

Newton County, Ark., 14, 104, 194, 209

Niangua River, 179; guides, 166

Noah's Ark, 149

Noel, Mo., 87, 103, 162, 176, 211, 234

Noland, Colonel, 248

Noodling or rock-fishing, 219

Noon-bird, 68

Norfolk Lake, 211

North American Review, 47

North Fork of White River, 210, 222

Norwood, Hal L., 101, 179, 247; quoted, 105

Norwood family, 23

Nowata County, Okla., 258

Nude waitresses, 6

Ohio River water, 251

Oil fields, 162

Oil Trough, Ark., 38

O-Joe clubhouse, Noel, Mo., 98, 234

Oklahoma, cyclone stories, 187-93 *passim*; guidebook, excerpts, 188, 191

Oklahoma, University of, Press, 173

"Oklahoma rain," 185

Old Blue, catfish, 216

Old Blue, coon-hound, 166

Old King Solomon, fish, 209

O'Neill, Clink, 213

"On the Trail of the Snawfus" (Wade), 49

Orance, 52

Oregon County, Mo., 29, 265

Organizations and contests of windy-spinners, 7 ff.

Osage County, Mo., 51

Osage River, 53, 54, 204, 216

Osceola, Mo., 223

Oto, Mo., 10

Ouachita Forest, Ark., 103

Ouachita River, 104, 206

Owen, Jim, 70